D1711545

LARAMIE
HOLDS THE RANGE

**Center Point
Large Print**

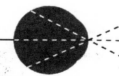

**This Large Print Book carries the
Seal of Approval of N.A.V.H.**

LARAMIE
HOLDS THE RANGE

FRANK H. SPEARMAN

CENTER POINT LARGE PRINT
THORNDIKE, MAINE

0 0022 0392567 8

This Center Point Large Print edition
is published in the year 2011.

Originally published in the U.S. in 1921
by C. Scribner's Sons.

The text of this Large Print edition is unabridged.
In other aspects, this book may vary
from the original edition.
Printed in the United States of America
on permanent paper.
Set in 16-point Times New Roman type.

ISBN: 978-1-61173-131-6

Library of Congress Cataloging-in-Publication Data

Spearman, Frank H. (Frank Hamilton), 1859–1937.
Laramie holds the range / Frank Spearman.
p. cm.
ISBN 978-1-61173-131-6 (library binding : alk. paper)
1. Large type books. I. Title.
PS3537.P347L37 2011
813'.52—dc22
2011007618

TO MY SON
FRANK HAMILTON SPEARMAN, JR.

CONTENTS

CHAPTER 1

Sleepy Cat

All day the heavy train of sleepers had been climbing the long rise from the river—a monotonous stretch of treeless, short-grass plains reaching from the Missouri to the mountains. And now the train stopped again, almost noiselessly.

Kate, with the impatience of girlish spirits tried by a long and tedious car journey, left her Pullman window and its continuous, one-tone picture, and walking forward was glad to find the vestibule open. The porter, meditating alone, stood below, at the car step, looking ahead; Kate joined him.

The stop had been made at a lonely tank, for water. No human habitation was anywhere in sight. The sun had set. For miles in every direction the seemingly level and open country spread around her. She looked back to the darkening east that she was leaving behind. It suggested nothing of interest beyond the vanishing perspective of a long track tangent. Then to the north, whence blew a cool and gentle wind, but the landscape offered nothing attractive to her eyes; its receding horizon told no new story. Then she looked into the west.

They had told her she should not see the Rockies until morning. But the dying light in the west brought a moving surprise. In the dreamy afterglow of the evening sky there rose, far beyond the dusky plain, the faint but certain outline of distant mountain peaks.

Bathed in a soft unearthly light, like the purple of another world; touched here and there by a fairy gold; silent as dreams, majestic as visions, overwhelming as reality itself, Kate gazed on them with beating heart.

Something clutched at her breath: "Are those the Rocky Mountains?" she suddenly asked, appealing to the stolid porter. She told Belle long afterward, she knew her voice must have quivered.

"Ah'm sure, Ah c'dn't say, Miss. Ah s'pecs dey ah. Dis my first trip out here."

"So it is mine!"

"Mah reg'lar run," continued the porter, insensible to the glories of the distant sky, "is f'm Chicago to Council Bluffs."

A flagman hurried past. Kate courageously pointed: "Are those the Rocky Mountains, please?" He halted only to look at her in astonishment. "Yes'm." But she was bound he should not escape: "How far are they?" she shot after him. He looked back startled: " 'Bout a hundred miles," he snapped. Plainly there was no enthusiasm among the train crew over mountains.

When she was forced, reluctant, back into the sleeper, she announced joyfully to her berth neighbors that the Rocky Mountains were in sight.

One regarded her stupidly, another coldly. Across the aisle the old lady playing solitaire did not even look up. Kate subsided; but dull apathy could not rob her of that first wonderful vision of the strange, far-off region, perhaps to be her home.

Next day, from the car window it was all mountains—at least, everywhere on the horizon. But the train seemed to thread an illimitable desert—a poor exchange for the boundless plains, Kate thought. But she grew to love the very dust of the desert.

The train was due at Sleepy Cat in the late afternoon. It met with delays and night had fallen when Kate, after giving the porter too much money, left her car, and suitcase in hand struggled, American fashion, up the long, dark platform toward the dimly lighted station. Men and women hastened here and there about her. The changing crews moved briskly to and from the train. There was abundance of activity, but none of it concerned Kate and her comfort. And there was no one, she feared, to meet her.

Reaching the station, she set down her suitcase without a tremor, and though she had never been more alone, she never felt less lonely. The eating-house gong beat violently for supper. A woman dragging a little boy almost fell over Kate's suitcase but did not pause to receive or tender apology. Men looking almost solemn under broad, straight-brimmed hats moved in and out of the station, but none of these saw Kate. Only one man striding past looked at her. He glared. And as he had but one eye, Kate deemed him, from his expression, a woman-hater.

Then a fat man under an immense hat, and wearing a very large ring on one hand, walked with a dapper step out of the telegraph office. He did see Kate. He checked his pace, coughed slightly and changed his course, as if to hold himself open to inquiry. Kate without hesitation turned to him and explained she was for Doubleday's ranch. She asked whether he knew the men from there and whether anyone was down.

John Lefever, for it was he whom she addressed, knew the men but he had seen no one; could he do anything?

"I want very much to get out there tonight," said Kate.

"Jingo," exclaimed Lefever, "not tonight!"

"Tonight," returned Kate, looking out of dark eyes in pink and white appeal, "if I can possibly make it."

Lefever caught up her suitcase and set it down beside the waiting-room door: "Stay right here a minute," he said.

He walked toward the baggage-room and before he reached it, stopped a second large, heavy man, Henry Sawdy. Him he held in confab; Sawdy looking meantime quite unabashed toward the distant Kate. In the light streaming from the station windows her slender and slightly shrinking figure suggested young womanhood and her delicately fashioned features, half-hidden under her hat, pleasingly confirmed his impression of it. Kate, conscious of inspection, could only pretend not to see him. And the sole impression she could snatch in the light and shadow of the redoubtable Sawdy, was narrowed to a pair of sweeping mustaches and a stern-looking hat. Lefever returned, his companion sauntering along after. Kate explained that she had telegraphed.

At that moment an odd-looking man, with a rapid, rolling, right and left gait, ambled by and caught Kate's eye. Instead of the formidable Stetson hat mostly in evidence, this man wore a baseball cap—of the sort usually given away with popular brands of flour—its peak cocked to its own apparent surprise over one ear. The man had sharp eyes and a long nose for news and proved it by halting within earshot of the conversation carried on between Kate and the two men. He looked so queer, Kate wanted to laugh, but she was too far from home to dare. He presently put his head conveniently in between Sawdy and Lefever and offered some news of his own: "There's been a big electric storm in the up country, Sawdy; the telephones are on the bum."

"How's she going to get to Doubleday's tonight, McAlpin?" asked Sawdy abruptly of the newcomer. McAlpin never, under any pressure,

13

answered a question directly. Hence everything had to be explained to him all over again, he looking meantime more or less furtively at Kate. But he found out, despite his seeming stupidity, a lot that it would have taken the big men hours to learn.

"If you don't want to take a rig and driver," announced McAlpin, after all had been canvassed, "there's the stage for the fort; they had to wait for the mail. Bill Bradley is on tonight. I'm thinkin' he'll set y' over from the ford—it's only a matter o' two or three miles."

"Are there any other passengers?" asked Kate doubtfully.

"Belle Shockley for the Reservation," answered McAlpin, promptly, "if—she ain't changed her mind, it bein' so late."

Sawdy put a brusque end to this uncertainty: "She's down there at the Mountain House waitin'— seen her myself not ten minutes ago."

Scurrying away, McAlpin came back in a jiffy with the driver, Bradley. Thin, bent and grizzled though he was, Kate thought she saw under the broad but shabby hat and behind the curtain of scraggly beard and deep wrinkles dependable eyes and felt reassured.

"How far is it to the ranch?" she asked of the queer-looking Bradley.

"Long ways, the way you go, ain't it, Bill?" McAlpin turned to the old driver for confirmation.

" 'Bout fourteen mile," answered Bradley, "to the ford."

"What time should I get there?" asked Kate again.

Bradley stood pat.

"What time'll she get there, Bill?" demanded Lefever.

"Twelve o'clock," hazarded Bradley tersely. "Or," he added, "I'll stop when I pass the ranch 'n' tell 'em to send a rig down in the mornin'."

"That would take you out of your way," Kate objected.

"Not a great ways."

A man that would go to this trouble in the middle of the night for someone he had never seen before, Kate deemed safe to trust. "No," she said, "I'll go with you, if I may."

The way in which she spoke, the sweetness and simplicity of her words, moved Sawdy and Lefever, the first a widower and the second a bachelor, and even stirred McAlpin, a married man. But they had no particular effect on Bradley. The blandish-ments of young womanhood were past his time of day.

With Lefever carrying the suitcase and nearly everybody talking at once, the party walked around to the rear door of the baggage-room.

The stage had been backed up, a hostler in the driver's seat, and the mail and express were being loaded. Sawdy volunteered to save time by fetching

Belle Shockley from the hotel, and while McAlpin and Lefever inspected and discussed the horses— for the condition of which McAlpin, as foreman of Kitchen's barn, was responsible—Kate stood, listener and onlooker. Everything was new and interesting. Four horses champed impatiently under the arc-light swinging in the street, and looked quite fit. But the stage itself was a shock to her idea of a Western stage. Instead of the old-fashioned swinging coach body, such as she had wondered at in circus spectacles, she saw a very substantial, shabby-looking democrat wagon with a top, and with side curtains. The curtains were rolled up. But the oddest thing to Kate was that wherever a particle could lodge, the whole stage was covered with a ghostly, grayish-white dust. While the loading went on, Sawdy arrived with the second passenger, Belle Shockley. She had, fortunately for Kate's apprehensions, *not* changed her mind.

Belle herself was something of an added shock. She wore a long rubber coat, in which the rubber was not in the least disguised. Her hair was frizzed about her face, and a small, brimless hat perched high, almost startled, on her head. She was tall and angular, her features were large and her eyes questioning. Had she had Bradley's beard, she would have passed with Kate for the stage driver. She was formidable, but yet a woman; and she scrutinized the slender whip of a girl before her with feminine suspicion. Nor did she give Kate a chance to break the ice of acquaintance before starting.

Under Lefever's chaperonage and with his gallant help, Kate took her seat where directed, just behind the driver, and her new companion presently got up beside her.

The mail bags disposed of, Bradley climbed into place, gathered his lines, the hostler let go the leads and the stage was off. The horses, restive after their long wait, dashed down the main street of the town, whirling Kate, all eyes and ears, past the glaring saloons and darkened stores to the extreme west end of Sleepy Cat. There, striking northward, the stage headed smartly for the divide.

The night was clear, with the stars burning in the sky. From the rigid silence of the driver and his two passengers, it might have been thought that no one of them ever spoke. To Kate, who as an Eastern girl had never, it might be said, breathed pure air, the clear, high atmosphere of the mountain night was like sparkling wine. Her senses tingled with the strange stimulant.

To Belle, there was no novelty in any of this, and the strain of silence was correspondingly greater. It was she who gave in first:

"You from Medicine Bend?" she asked, as the four horses walked up a long hill.

"Pittsburgh," answered Kate.

"Pittsburgh!" echoed Belle, startled. "Gee! some trip you've had."

Belle, encouraged, then confessed that a cyclone had given her her own first start West. She had been blown two blocks in one and had all of her hair pulled out of her head.

"They said I'd have no chance to get married without any hair," she continued, "so I got a wig— never *could* find my own hair—and come West for a chance. And they're here; if you're looking for a husband you've come to the right place."

"I haven't the least idea of getting married," protested Kate.

"They'll be after you," declared Belle sententiously.

"Are you married?" ventured Kate.

"Not yet. But they're coming. I'm in no hurry."

She talked freely about her own affairs. She had worked for Doubleday, for whose ranch Kate was bound. Doubleday had had a chain of eating houses on the line, as Belle termed the transcontinental railroad. They had all been taken over except the one where she worked—at Sleepy Cat Junction— and this would be taken soon, Belle thought.

"That's the trouble with Barb Doubleday," she went on. "He's got too many irons in the fire— head over heels in debt. There's no money now-a-days in cattle, anyway. What are you going up to Doubleday's for?"

"He's my father."

"Your father? Well! I never open my mouth without I put my foot in it, anyway."

"I've never seen him," continued Kate.

Belle was all interest. She confided to Kate that she was now on her way, for a visit, to the Reservation where her cousin was teaching in an Indian school, and divided her time for the next hour between getting all she could of Kate's story and telling all of her own.

On Kate's part there was no end of questions to ask, about country and customs and people. When Belle could not answer, she appealed to Bradley, who, if taciturn, was at least patient. Every time the conversation lulled and Kate looked out into the night, it seemed as if they were drawing closer and closer to the stars, the dark desert still spreading in every direction and the black mountain ridges continually receding.

CHAPTER 2

THE CRAZY WOMAN

They had traveled a long time it seemed to Kate, and having climbed all the hills in the country, were going down a moderate grade with the hind wheels sputtering unamiably at the brakes, when Belle broke a long silence: "Where are we, Bill?" she demanded, familiarly.

"The Crazy Woman," Bradley answered briefly. Kate did not understand, but by this time she had learned in such circumstances to hold her tongue.

"He means the creek," explained Belle. "It's way down there ahead of us."

Strain her eyes as she would, Kate could see only the blackness of the darkness ahead.

" 'N' b' jing!" muttered Bradley, as Kate peered into nothingness, "she's whinin' t'night f'r fair."

Again for an instant Kate did not comprehend. Then the leads were swung sharply by Bradley to the left. The stage rounded what Kate afterward frequently recognized as an overhanging shoulder of rock on the road down to the creek, and a vague, dull roar swept up from below.

Bradley halted the horses, climbed down, and taking the lantern went forward on foot to investigate.

"Must have been a cloudburst in the mountains," remarked Belle, listening; and Kate was to learn that a cloudless sky gives no assurance whatever for the passage of a mountain stream.

The lantern disappeared, to come into sight again farther down the trail, and while both women talked, the faint light swung at intervals in and out of their vision as Bradley reconnoitered. Kate was a little worried, but her companion sat quite unmoved, even when Bradley returned and reported the creek "roarin'."

"That bein' the case," he muttered, "I'm thinkin' the Double-draw bridge has took up its timbers and walked likewise."

The Double-draw bridge! How well Kate was to know that name; but that night it seemed, like everything else, only very queer.

"Bradley," protested Belle, now very much disturbed, "that can't be."

"We'll see," retorted Bradley, gathering his reins and releasing his brake as he spoke to the horses. "I don't guess myself there's much left o' that bridge." Only the expletive he placed before the last word revealed his own genuine annoy- ance and Kate prudently asked no further questions. Some instinct convinced her she was already a nuisance on the silent Bradley's hands. The ford—off the main road—was where he had purposed setting Kate over, as he expressed it, to the ranch. Double-draw bridge—on the road to the fort and Reservation—was two miles above.

The horses climbed the long hill again and started on the road for the bridge.

"If the Double-draw is out," sighed Belle resignedly, "I reckon we're trapped."

For the first time now they could hear the hoofs of the two teams sinking into and pulling out of mud. It grew deeper as they descended the long grade toward the bridge and clouds obscured the light of the stars.

With the horses stumbling on, the women watched for something to meet either sight or hearing, but there was nothing until they again neared the creek. Then the same vague roar rose on the night and as they rimmed the bench above the creek a faint, ghastly light on the eastern horizon betokened a rising moon. Down the trail they stopped in darkness and Bradley again clambered down from his box with the lantern to investigate.

" 'Z fur 'z I c'n see," he reported when he came back, "th' bridge is all right, but mos'ly under water."

"Can we get across?" Belle Shockley asked querulously.

Bradley answered with hesitation: "Why— yes—"

"Oh, good!"

"And no."

"What does that mean?" snapped Belle.

"We can't get across tonight—we might in the mornin'."

Kate kept silence, but Belle was persistent. "What are we going to do?" she demanded; "go 'way back to Sleepy Cat?"

"Not in a milyun years," returned Bradley, calmly. "We're goin' to pull out t' one side 'n' camp right here till daylight. Ef I didn't have you wimmen on my hands, I might take a chanst with the mail," he went on, drawing his horses carefully around to where he meant to camp. "Me and the horses could make it, even 'f we lost the wagon. But I w'dn't like the job of huntin' for you folks in the Crazy Woman with a lantern—not tonight. She's surely a-rip-roarin'. Well; t'hell with her 'n' all creeks like her, say I," he wound up, chirruping kindly to his uncomplaining beasts.

"You don't like creeks," suggested Belle.

"Dry creeks—yes. Wouldn't care if I never seen another wet creek from now till kingdom come —Whoa, Nellie!" he called to the off lead mare who was feeling the way for her companions back to a safe spot for a halt. "This is good, right here."

Belle showed her fellow-traveler how to lie down with some comfort on the leather seat, and as they had one for each she gave Kate her choice. Kate, to put Belle between her and any man in front, took the back seat. The side curtains were let down and with a mail sack supplied by Bradley for a pillow, Kate, drawing her big coat over her, curled up for a rest.

The excitement of the journey had worn away. The delay she was disposed to accept philosophically. It took some time for Bradley to unhitch and dispose of the horses to his satisfaction, and theirs, and his mumblings and the sound of their moving about and champing their bits fell a long time on Kate's drowsy ears. Belle went to sleep at once, and though sleep was the last thing Kate expected to achieve, she did fall asleep— with the Crazy Woman singing wildly in her ears.

She had hardly lost herself, it seemed, when Bradley roused his passengers. The storm waters were creeping up over the bench where they had camped and with much impatient sputtering,

Bradley hitched the pole team to the stage and, in his pet, retreated into the hills for assured safety. Even the noise of the flood failed to follow them there and they disposed themselves once more to rest.

How long she slept this time, Kate did not know, but she was awakened by voices.

The night had grown very cold and death itself could not have been more silent. Yet at intervals Kate heard the low converse of two voices; they were not far away and both were men's.

A panic seized her. Her heart beat like the roll of a drum and then nearly stopped. What might happen now? she asked herself. And what could she fear but the worst? In the dead of night—marooned in a wild country, with only a queer woman and two strange men. Could it be a plot? she asked herself. In the fear that gripped her she could hardly breathe, and to think was only to invite added agonies of apprehension. She sat quickly up, breathing hurriedly now and her heart racing. Then she heard the even breathing of her companion on the seat ahead. To make sure it was she, Kate put her hand over and touched Belle's shoulder. Reassured a little, but ready to push aside the curtain and spring from the stage at the least alarm, Kate listened painfully; the voices reached her ears again.

One was Bradley's—of that she felt sure; the other, deeper, more full, and with a curiously even carrying quality through the silent night, she knew she had never heard before; but the darkness, the solitude, the shock of strange surroundings, if nothing else, made it terrifying to her. Kate had never been reckoned a timid girl, but she listened dumb with fear. Bradley did most of the talking. He was recounting, with occasional profanity, the mishaps of his trip, beginning with the late train.

"Any passengers?" Kate heard the stranger ask.

"Two women—c'n y' beat it? One of 'em a girl for Doubleday's."

"What can a girl be wanting at Doubleday's?"

"D'no. Came off the train tonight."

"The Double-draw is out."

"Jing!" exclaimed Bradley, "it was there an hour ago."

"The ford is your only chance to get her over."

"Can I make it?"

"You've got good horses; you ought to make it by daylight."

"Hear they got a new foreman over at Doubleday's," Bradley said.

There was no comment, unless the silence could be so construed.

"Tom Stone," added Bradley, as if bound to finish.

There was an instant and angry exclamation, none the less ferocious because of the restrained feeling in its sudden utterance.

"Doubleday sets a good deal by what Van Horn says; I reckon he put him in there," suggested Bradley.

There was a further silence. Then she heard the stranger dryly say: "I expect so." It seemed as if behind everything he did say there was so much left unsaid.

"I never got rightly, Jim," Bradley went on, "how you 'n' Van Horn's related."

"I hope you never will," returned the man saluted as "Jim," in the same low, cold tone. "We're not related. He was my partner—once."

"Stone will change things at the ranch."

"He can't hurt them much."

"I guess they're full bad," said Bradley, and then, lowering his voice: "The gal's asleep there in the stage. How'd the land contest they made on y' at Medicine Bend come off?"

"The cattlemen own that Land Office. I'll beat the bunch at Washington."

"Doubleday wanted me to go down to swear. I wouldn't do it—wasn't even at the trial—"

"No honest man was, from Doubleday's."

"Was it Stone cut your wire, Jim?"

"You know as much about it as I do."

"Got it up again?"

"All I could find."

"Meaner 'n' hell over there, ain't they?"

There was no comment.

"How long you goin' to stand it, Jim?" persisted

Bradley. And after the odd pause, the slow answer: "Till I get tired."

"That'll be about the time they rip it off again."

"About that time, Bill."

"Well," hazarded the old driver, meditatively, "the boys are waitin'. They say you're slow to start anything, Jim; but they look f'r hell t' pay when y' do."

To the stranger—it seemed to Kate—words must be worth their weight in gold, he parted with them so sparingly.

"What's this talk 'bout Farrell Kennedy makin' y' a depity marshal, Jim?"

"Mostly talk, Bill. Good night."

"Farrel offered it to y', didn't he?"'

"So Lefever says."

"Where y' headin' f'r now?" persisted Bradley, as Kate heard the shuffle of a horse's feet.

"Home."

"They ain't burned your shack?" Bradley asked with a half chuckle.

Kate just heard the man's reply: "Not yet."

The hoofbeats drew away. Kate cautiously pushed back her curtain.

The late moon was shining in an old and ghostly light. Distant heights rose like black walls against the sky. At intervals a peak broke sharply above the battlements, or a rift in a closer sierra opened to show the stars.

Kate could hear but could not for some time

see the galloping horseman. Then of a sudden he reached the brow of a low hill and rode swiftly out into the spectral light. There he halted. Horse and rider stood for a moment silhouetted against the sky. The horse chafed at his bit. He stretched his head restively into the north, his rider sitting motionless, a somber flat hat crowning his spare figure. For barely a moment the man sat thus immovable. Then he turned slightly in the saddle and the horse struck off into the night.

Drowsiness had deserted the tired girl that watched him. While her companions slept she sat in the solitude waiting for day. Bradley, as good as an alarm clock, was stirring with the first streak and feeding his horses. He told his passengers that the bridges were all out and he was going back to the ford.

Belle, incredulous, when first told by Kate of a visitor in the night, had no scruples in asking questions:

"Who was here last night, Bill?"

"Wha'd' y' mean?" he countered, gathering up his lines.

"What man was it, you were talking to?" she demanded.

"I guess if I was talkin' to any man," he grumbled, "I was talkin' in my sleep. You must 'a' been 'a' dreamin'."

"Oh, come now, 'fess up, Bill." Belle nodded toward Kate. "She was awake."

28

Bradley started the horses, shifted on the box and looked not too well pleased: "I wasn't talkin' to nobody last night—"

"Bill, what a whopper."

"If you mean this mornin'—" he went on, doggedly.

"Well—who was here?"

"Jim Laramie."

"Jim Laramie!" echoed Belle, catching her breath and poking Kate with her elbow. "Wonder he didn't hold us up."

Bradley scowled but said nothing.

"Bradley doesn't like that," murmured Belle to Kate, as soon as the creaking of the wheels gave her a chance to speak without his hearing. "He's a friend of Jim's."

"Where did he come from?" continued Belle, raising her voice toward Bradley.

Bradley took his time to answer: "Claimed he was goin' home," he said laconically.

"How could he get across the creek with the bridges out?" persisted Belle.

Bradley's eyes were on his horses. He was weary of question: "High water wouldn't bother him much."

"Well, I want to know! I should think it would bother anybody the way it was sweeping down last night."

"Hell!" ejaculated Bradley, parting with his manners and his patience together: "Jim could swim the Crazy Woman with his horse's feet tied."

"Who *is* 'Jim'?" Kate demanded of her companion in an undertone.

"Jim Laramie? He lives in the Falling Wall."

CHAPTER 3

DOUBLEDAY'S

When they got back to the ford it was daylight and the Crazy Woman was hurrying on as peacefully as if a frown had never ruffled its repose. Gnarled trees springing out of gashes along its tortuous channel showed, in the débris lodged against their flood-bared roots and mud-swept branches, the fury of the night, and the creek banks, scoured by many floods, revealed new and savage gaps in the morning sun; but Bradley made his crossing with the stage almost as uneventfully as if a cloud-burst had never ruffled the mountains.

Kate was eager to meet her father, eager to see what might be her new home. The moment the horses got up out of the bottom, Bradley pointed with his whip to the ranch-house. Kate saw ahead of her a long, one-story log house crowning, with its group of out-buildings, a level bench that stretched toward the foothills. The landscape was bare of trees and, to Kate, brown and barren-looking, save for a patch of green near the creek where an alfalfa field lay vividly pretty in the sun. The ranch-house, built of substantial logs, was ample in its proportions and not uninviting, even to her Eastern eyes.

Bradley, with a flourish, swept past the stable, around the corral and drew up before the door with a clatter. In front of the bunk-house on the right, a cowboy rolling a cigarette, was watching the arrival, and just as Bradley plumped Kate, on his arms, to the ground, her father, Barb Doubleday himself, opened the ranch-house door.

Kate had never seen her father. And until Bradley spoke, she had not the slightest idea that this could be he. She saw only a rough-looking man of great stature, slightly stooped, and with large features burnt to a deep brown.

"Hello, Barb," said Bradley, without much enthusiasm.

His salutation met with as little: "What's up?" demanded Doubleday. Kate noticed the huskiness in the strong, cold tone.

"Brought y' a passenger."

From the talk of the night she recognized her father's nickname. It was a little shock to realize that this must, indeed, be he. And the unmoved expression of his face as he surveyed her without a smile or greeting, was not reassuring.

But she hastened forward: "Father?" there was a note of girlish appeal in her greeting: "I'm Kate—your daughter. You don't remember me, of course," she added with an effort to extort a welcome. "You got my letter, did you?"

He looked at her uncertainly for a moment and nodded slowly. "Was it all right," she asked, now almost panic-stricken, "to come to see you?"

Confused or preoccupied, he stumbled out some words of welcome, spoke to Belle on the stage, took the suitcase out of Bradley's hand and led Kate into the house. In the large room that she entered stood a long table and a big fireplace opened at the back. On the left, two bedrooms opened off the big room, and on the right, the kitchen.

The chill of the strange greeting embarrassed Kate the more because she felt Belle could hardly fail to notice it, and her own resentment of it did not easily wear off. But hoping for better things she freshened up a little, in her father's bedroom, and by that time a man-cook was bringing break-fast into the big room, which served as living-room and dining-room. Bradley, Belle, Kate and her father sat down—the men had already breakfasted.

Kate, her head in a whirl with novelty and excitement, was overcome with interest in every-thing, but especially in her father. Sitting at the head of the table—at one end of which fresh places had been set—he maintained her first impression of his stature. His spreading frame was covered with loose corduroy clothes—which could hardly be said to fit—and his whole appearance conveyed the impression of unusual physical strength. It had been said of Barb Doubleday, as a railroad builder, that he could handle an iron rail alone. His powerful jaw and large mouth—now fitted, or rather, supplied—with artificial teeth of proportionate size—all supported Kate's awe of his bigness. His long nose, once smashed in a railroad fight, was not seriously scarred; and originally well-shaped, it was still the best feature of a terrifically weather-beaten face that had evidently seen milder days. The good looks were gone, but not the strength. His mouth was almost shapeless but unmistakably hard, and his grayish-blue eyes were cold—very cold; try as she would, Kate could discern little love or sympathy in them. This was the man who almost twenty years earlier had deserted her mother and wee Kate, the baby, and long disappeared from Eastern view—until by accident the fact that he was alive and in the far West had become known to his wife and daughter. Kate thought she understood something of the tragedy in her mother's life when the first sight of her father's eyes struck a chill into her own heart.

But he was her father—and her mother had tried, in spite of all, to hide or condone his faults; and more than once before she died, had made Kate promise to hunt him up and go to him. What the timid girl dreaded most was finding another woman installed in his household—in which case she meant to make her stay in the West very short.

But every hour lessened these fears and as he himself gradually thawed a little, Kate took courage.

The breakfast went fast. Platters were passed without ceremony or delay. Her father and Bradley ate as Kate had never seen men eat; only her amazement could keep pace with their quiet but unremitting efforts to clean up everything in sight. There was little mastication but much knife and fork work, with free libation of coffee; and Belle, Kate noticed, while somewhat left behind by the men, paid strict attention to the business in hand.

Conversation naturally lagged; but what took place had its surprise for Kate. Doubleday asked a few questions of Belle—everybody seemed to know everybody else—and learning she was headed for the Reservation, possibly to teach school, hired her on the spot away from the job, to go back to his eating-house at Sleepy Cat Junction. No sooner was this arranged, and Bradley told to take her luggage off the stage, than a diversion occurred.

A horseman dashed up outside and presently strode into the room. He was tall and well put together; not quite as straight as an arrow, but straight, and not ungraceful in his height. This was Harry Van Horn, a neighboring cattleman, and he wore the ranchman's rig, including the broad hat and the revolver slung at his hip. But everything about the rig was fresh and natty, in the sunshine. He looked alert. His step was clean and springy as he crossed the room, and his voice not unpleasant as he briskly greeted Doubleday and looked keenly at his guests—last and longest at Kate sitting at her father's right hand.

Doubleday introduced him to his daughter. Van Horn nodded, without much deference, to Belle and to Bradley, neither of whom responded more warmly. He sat down near Kate and with a look of raillery scrutinized the remnant of meat left on the general platter: "How is it, Barb?" he asked.

"What?"

"The antelope."

"All right, I guess."

Van Horn with a laugh turned to Kate: "Excited over it, isn't he? I got an antelope yesterday, so I sent half of it over to your father." Then he lowered his voice in pretended disgust. "*He* doesn't know what he's eating—it might as well be salt pork. And you're a stranger here? I never knew your father had a daughter. He's very communicative. How do you like antelope?"

Without paying attention to anyone else, he set out for a moment to entertain Kate. When he talked his face lighted with energy. Every expression of his brown eyes snapped with life, and his big Roman nose, though not making for beauty, one soon got used to.

Barb broke abruptly in on the conversation: "What did Stone find out?" he asked.

Van Horn answered a question of Kate's and

turned then, and not until then, to her father: "That's what I came over to tell you. Dutch Henry and another fellow—described like Stormy Gorman—sold ten head of steers to the railroad camp last week—that's where our cattle are going right along now. And Abe Hawk," he exclaimed, pointing his finger at Doubleday and poking it forward to emphasize each point, "sold ten head of your long yearlings to a contracting outfit north of the Falling Wall and never changed the brands!"

Doubleday stared at the speaker. Van Horn, speaking to Kate, went right on: "There's a bunch of rustlers over in the Falling Wall, snitching steers on us right and left," he explained in a lower and very deferential tone, but a warm one.

While Van Horn talked and Doubleday muttered husky and bitter questions, Bradley and Belle paid continuous attention to their coffee and griddle cakes.

Doubleday by this time had forgotten all about Kate. Completely absorbed by the reports brought in he rose from the table and followed Van Horn to the open door where Van Horn turned and paused as he kept on talking so that with his eyes he could still take in Kate at the table. The two men were now joined at the door by a third. This man looked in to see who was at the table. Bradley glanced up at him only long enough to recognize Tom Stone, the new foreman; no greeting passed. Kate looked longer, though when she saw the eyes of the new-comer were on her she gave her attention to Belle.

Belle had told her that a woman at the ranch would be a great curiosity and Kate every day resigned herself to inspection. When she got better acquainted with the men, and while there were good and bad among them, she liked them all, except Stone. His face did not seem kindly. At times agreeable enough, he was only tolerable at best and when even slightly in liquor he was irritable. His low forehead, over which he plastered his hair, and his straight yellow eye-brows and hard blue eyes were not confidence inspiring; even his big mustache was harsh and lacked a generous curve—his normal outlook seemed one of reticence and suspicion. Kate refused to like him; his smile was not good.

On this morning he showed the signs of a hard journey. He had brought the news from the Falling Wall and was just in after a troublesome ride. Bradley and Belle left the table together and Kate followed to the door. Bradley tried to edge past the three men without speaking, but Stone not only stopped him with a cold grin but followed the driver toward the stage: "Wouldn't that kill you"—Kate heard him say to Bradley, and she saw his attempt at an ingratiating grin: "Abe Hawk rustling?"

Bradley gave him scant sympathy: "What did Doubleday discharge him for?" he demanded.

"What did the cattlemen blacklist him for? He's the best foreman this ranch ever had—or ever will have," added Bradley, summoning his scant courage to rub it in. "He fired him because he took up a little piece of land agin the Falling Wall and got together a few cows of his own. That's a crime, ain't it? Like —. These cattlemen will learn a thing or two when they get old."

Stone flared back at him: "What are you over here eating their bacon for?"

"Not f'r any likin' I've got f'r 'em," retorted Bradley, "n'r f'r any o' their pets."

The old driver got away without a fight, but he had little to spare. Van Horn rode off presently with Stone, and Doubleday returned to the house, where Kate was sitting with Belle. He told Belle he would send her over to the Junction in the afternoon, and after dinner told Kate she had better go over and stay at the Junction with Belle till they could get a room "fixed up" at the ranch.

There were really no accommodations at the ranch-house for Kate until some could be prepared. A room had to be made ready and there was no bed or furniture. And Belle told her that her father spent most of his time at the Junction, anyway, where he had a cottage. She explained about the railroad branching off the main line at the Junction. Her father had built this to coal mines on the Falling Wall river. He was supposed to own this branch line and the mines, but she hinted strongly that his creditors had got everything there was of the railroad but the rust, and would sometime get that.

Kate wished her new acquaintance had been less candid.

CHAPTER 4

AT THE EATING HOUSE

Doubleday drove the two women down from the ranch. At the Junction there were, besides the railroad eating house, a few houses and a few stores, and almost as many saloons as at Sleepy Cat itself—the place being, Belle said, a shipping point both for cattle and for miners.

Kate was relieved to find her father's cottage, on a hill across the railroad track, quite livable-looking. It was, like all the other houses, one story and square, being divided into kitchen, dining-room and two bedrooms. The interior, its shiny furniture covered with dust, was dreary enough, but Kate knew she could make the place presentable, and after the first few days in her new surroundings, began to recover her high spirits. Her father had not yet said she was to stay; but she thought he liked her—Belle told her as much—and she set about making her woman's hand felt. Her father took his meals at the eating-house, and the cottage had been indifferently cared for by old Henry, the eating-house porter. Kate, as a housekeeper, was a marked improvement, one that even so absorbed a man as her father could not but notice.

She naturally spent much time at the eating-house herself, because Belle, her sole acquaintance at the Junction, was there.

"How you going to like it out here?" demanded Belle, scrutinizing Kate critically, after she had known her a few months.

"I love it," was the prompt answer.

Belle seemed dismayed: "How about the alkali?" she asked, as if to convict Kate of deceit.

Kate only nodded: "It's all right."

"And the sagebrush?"

"I like it."

"And the greasewood?"

"Why not?"

Belle had begun to like Kate's laugh: "Not going to get lonesome out in this country?" Belle flung at her, as a gloomy clincher.

"Lonesome!" At this idea Kate laughed outright. "Do I look it?" she cried.

"Guess you like to horseback pretty well," muttered Belle, casting about for a solution of so surprising an attitude and unable to find any other fault with her protégée.

"I'd rather ride than eat," declared Kate, youthfully exuberant.

"What about swimming?" inquired Belle, determined to fasten discontent on her.

"I hate swimming."

"Well," grumbled her companion, defeated at every point, "Barb's got plenty of horses." Kate did not like to hear her father called Barb, but Belle would not call him anything else.

Back of the cottage, Doubleday had a small barn, where Henry—an ex-cowboy—looked after Doubleday's driving horses. And the very first pledge from her father that she was to be tolerated in the strange household she had invaded in this far-away country, came to Kate when he sent down for her use two saddle ponies. The fleeting suspicion of loneliness that she would not confess even to herself, all vanished when the ponies came: She could then ride to and from the ranch. And when Henry failed to appear, Kate took care of her pets herself. After her father told her they were really hers, she would hardly let Henry himself lay a hand on them.

When the evenings grew tedious she would go down for supper with Belle and sit with her in the small alcove off the office, where the two could see and hear without being seen; and Belle's stories had no end.

The only feature of her situation that would not improve was her father's aloofness. He seemed to try at times to thaw out but he persistently congealed again. One evening he got in late from the ranch, cold and wet, complaining of rheumatism. The driver went on with the team to Sleepy Cat and

Doubleday told Kate he would stay all night. She had a good fire in the grate and made her father a toddy.

He sat with her before the fire late and talked for the first time about his affairs, which seemed mostly money troubles.

Next morning he could hardly get out of bed, but he was set on going to the ranch and Kate helped him to dress and got him a good breakfast, with a cup of strong coffee. He softened enough to let her go up to the ranch with him. She had already coaxed from him the furniture for the spare room so she might spend the night there occasionally. Van Horn had promised to teach her sometime how to use a rifle and to take her out after antelope and Kate was keen for going. The next day her father brought her the rifle from Sleepy Cat.

They drove out in the evening, but the minute they reached the ranch-house, Kate perceived something was up. Van Horn greeted her with a good deal of freedom, Kate thought—but apologized for hurrying away after she had shown him her new rifle—with the hint that they had bigger game in sight just then, and after a long talk with her father and much preparation he and Stone rode off, two of the men from the bunk-house with them. Her father plainly let Kate see that he himself had no intention of entertaining her. He was outside most of the time and

Kelly, the cook, being the only man to talk to, Kate in self-defense went to bed.

During the night she was awakened by voices. Van Horn and Stone were back and they were talking to her father in the living-room. Kate thought at first some accident had happened. Van Horn, eager, pleased and rapid in utterance, did much of the talking, Stone breaking in now and again with a few words in harsh nasal tones—harsher tonight than usual. Her father seemed only to ask a question once in a while. Kate tried not to eavesdrop, but she could not occasionally help hearing words about wire, which Van Horn was sure somebody would never find. The men had apparently been somewhere and done something. The clink of glasses indicated drinking, and there was much cursing of something or somebody. Then the talk got loud and her father hushed it up and the party went to bed.

There seemed something furtive and secret about the incident that Kate could not fathom. Why should honest men get together in the dead of night to exult and curse and drink? She composed herself to sleep again; these were simply things she did not understand. She thought she did not want to understand them, but even after she got back to the Junction she wondered why her father should be mixed up in them.

Meantime she spent a week of delight at the ranch, mostly on horseback, learning the

Western horse and Western riding.

After her outing, Doubleday took Kate down to the Junction. He went on to Sleepy Cat, but that night he came back ill. In the morning he was not able to get up.

Kate telephoned, as he directed, to Sleepy Cat, for Doctor Carpy.

The doctor, when he came, looked Kate over with interest. He was a smooth-faced, powerfully-built man, rough-looking and rough in speech, but he knew his business. It was an acute attack of rheumatism, he said, and he told Kate to keep her father in bed and to keep him quiet and nurse him.

"He's so active," said Kate regretfully. "He seems to be on the go all the time."

"Damn him!" exclaimed Carpy with blunt emphasis. "He's nervous all the time—that's what's the matter. He's got too many irons in the fire."

Kate swallowed her astonishment at so extraordinary a medical outburst. She reminded herself she was really out West.

Belle, when Kate saw her the following morning at the eating-house, said much the same thing and added in her coldly philosophic way, "I reckon the banks have got him. And say, Kate, here's a telegram just come for your father."

Kate took the despatch up to the cottage. It was from Van Horn at Medicine Bend, and it so upset her father that she was sorry she had had to

44

deliver it. After an interval, unpleasant both for the disabled man and his nurse, Kate ventured to ask whether there was not something she could do. There was not. Litigation against him, long dormant—he explained between twinges—had been revived, papers issued and a United States deputy marshal was on the way to serve him. "I thought," he growled, "the thing was dead. But nothing against me ever dies. If it'd gone past today it would 'a' been outlawed. You'll have to send some telegrams for me."

He gave her the substance of them and of a letter he wanted written—all of which she carefully took down. Then putting on her hat, she hastened to the eating-house to send the telegrams.

It was well past noon. At the lunch-counter desk Kate copied the messages on telegraph blanks, took them up to the operator and came downstairs to write the letter for her father.

While she was doing this, the two o'clock Medicine Bend train pulled in. It was the big through train of the day, the train that Belle had said must bring the dreaded summons server from Medicine Bend, if he came that day at all. But Kate, absorbed in her letter writing, had forgotten all about this unpleasantness when something— she was never able to say just what—recalled her to herself. She became all at once conscious that she was writing a letter, and at the same time conscious that she *was* no longer alone in the little room.

CHAPTER 5

CROSS PURPOSES

The only thing Kate could have noticed was a slight darkening of the room; something momentarily obscured the sunlight streaming through the platform doorway; someone sauntered into the room itself, but Kate was signing the letter and gave the entrance no thought. Still she could not shake off the consciousness of somebody walking up close to the desk where she stood and sitting down on one of the counter stools. She refused to look up, even though she felt that eyes were on her.

A natural impulse of defiance at the uninvited scrutiny possessed her. And being resolved she would not admit she was conscious of it, she turned from the desk and looking straight toward the glass door connecting with the dining-room, and behind the end of the counter, she walked briskly past the intruding presence.

As she did so, Kate somehow felt with every step that she could not get out of the room unchallenged. But even then she was riding to a rude surprise for she had reached the door without incident when she heard two words: "Slow, Kate." She had already laid her hand on the knob and she turned it with indignation. The wretched door refused to open! It was Belle's afternoon off and she had locked the door.

Even then a collected girl would not have surrendered to the situation. But Kate never could be collected at just the right time. She was usually quite collected when it made no difference whether she was collected or not. All she now did was to look blankly around. A man sat at the counter, a man she had never seen before. He was deliberately lifting a broad horseman's hat from a rather round, high forehead and disclosing a head of inoffensive-looking sandy hair, very much sun-and-wind bleached. His smooth face, his ears and neck and open throat, were colored by a strictly uniform pigment—tinctured by many mountain winds into a reddish brown and burnt by many mountain suns into a seemingly immutable bronze. The face was long with an ample nose, a peaceful-looking mouth and unruffled gray eyes. The man was very like and yet unlike many of the mountain men she had seen. She remembered afterward that this was her first impression: at that moment she was not analyzing it: "Where are you going?" he asked, as she stood looking at him.

Her resentment at the rudeness rose. Could a prophetic spirit have warned Kate that this was to be only the first of more than one serious encounter with the eyes steadily regarding her, her astonishment and indignation might have been restrained. As it was, forgetting her own position and descending to Western brusqueness, she retorted icily: "I can't see how that can possibly interest you."

If she hoped that a frigid tone and utterance might abash her intruding questioner, they failed. He spoke again with surprisingly even impertinence—quite as if she were as friendly as he. "You're wrong," he said. "I'm mightily interested. I want some coffee and you don't act to me as if you meant to come back."

It was undignified and improper for her to bandy words with a heckler, but Kate had already breathed too much of the freedom of the mountains to resist a second retort, and said, almost without thinking—and certainly in a very positive manner: "I am not coming back."

"Give me a cup of coffee before you go."

"There is no service here this afternoon."

"Beg your pardon. There will be one service here this afternoon. You will serve me." His emphasis was slight, but unmistakable. She was so fussed she turned to the door and grasped the knob the second time. Her persecutor raised his left hand firmly. "You can't get out there," he said.

"Why can't I?" demanded Kate indignantly.

"Because you can't open the door." She stood mute at his assurance. "Come," he continued, "give me some coffee, like a good girl."

What should she do? She did not speak the

question, but weighed it pretty rapidly in her mind. What manner of man had she to deal with? If not actually threatening he was extremely domineering. While she hesitated he regarded her calmly.

But there was one way to do as he demanded and to punish him as well. Of the two coffee urns kept filled in readiness for the rush in serving a trainload of passengers, only one was now heated. Kate stepped to the urns, murmuring as if to herself: "I know nothing about these."

"I don't either," he said. From the nearer urn Kate drew a cup of coffee; it was very cold—but she pushed it with a jug of cream and a bowl of sugar, toward him.

"A teaspoon, please?" Kate's excitement had already heightened her color. She looked very much alive as she added, impatiently, a spoon to the equipment—expecting then to be able to get out of the room. It seemed as if this ought to be easy; it was not. Her tormentor professed to have had no dinner and wanted a sandwich. The sandwiches were rebelliously hunted up—a plateful was supplied. If he was surprised at the prodigality he made no comment, but at intervals some tantalizing word from him entangled her in another exchange; and at each encounter of wits, just enough fear tempered her resentment to make her irresolute.

She was malicious enough to observe in silence

the unobtrusive pantomime by which the enemy tried to coax a semblance of warmth into his cold coffee. He had begun by pouring cream into it, but the cream refused to assimilate and only made the mixture look less inviting.

"I'm glad I met you today," he said, while she was getting her breath. "Looks lonesome around here. Not much doing at the mines, is there?"

"Not a great deal," she answered coldly.

"How about Barb Doubleday—is he up at the mines, or here?"

He was indifferently lifting matches from the stand at his hand, striking them and burning them patiently against the side of his cup of coffee. Like a flash came to Kate with his question, the thought that this disagreeable person must be the court officer. He looked up at her now as if waiting for an answer: "Why do you ask?" she countered.

"Mostly because I'd like to hear you say something."

"Anything, I suppose," she suggested ironically.

"That's not far from it," was the reply. "Also, I want to see Barb."

"What about?" she asked, borrowing his own assurance. It was time, she thought, for defensive strategy.

"Just a little business matter." It was long, very long afterward that Kate learned, and fully realized, the significance of the indifferently spoken words; when she did, she wondered that a man's manner could so completely mask all that lay behind them.

"He isn't hiring any men," she ventured, adapting a set phrase she had often heard Belle use.

"And in spite of my looks," he returned, "I'm not hunting a job—for a wonder."

But now that Kate wanted to hear more he took his turn at reticence. "Where are you from?" she asked as unconcernedly as she could.

"Medicine Bend."

"From the marshal's office?" It was foolish of her to ask. She fairly blurted out the words. He looked at her for the first time keenly—and just the change in his expression, undefinable but unmistakable, almost frightened her to death.

"I was in the marshal's office yesterday," he answered, picking up a sandwich evasively. Kate was no longer doubtful. This was the man to serve the dreaded summons. An instant of panic seized her. Fortunately her persecutor was regarding his stubborn coffee as he stirred it. Her heart, which had stopped, started with a thump. Her thoughts cleared. Instinct, self-preservation, asserted itself. She thought hard and fast. The first step was to temporize.

He looked up in time to see the blood sweeping back into her cheeks; and almost spoiled the first really good breath she was drawing. In his lean, bronzed hands he clasped his cup of coffee as if trying to put a degree of heat into it: "What would be the extra charge for a shot at that hot tank?"

he asked, directing his glance first at the other tank, then at Kate's burning face.

With all his confidence, he must have been surprised at the revulsion of manner that greeted him. Kate recovered her poise—her coldness vanished, a smile broke through her reserve and her confused regret was promptly expressed: "Did I give you coffee out of the *cold* tank? How stupid!"

"And never in my life," said her queer customer, as if continuing her words, "did I do anything mean to you."

"Oh, yes, you did," objected Kate, coupling nervous haste with the declaration as she tried to take the cold cup from between his hands. The ease with which she assumed the role of a lunch-counter waitress astonished her.

"What did I do?" he drawled, resisting her attempt to make amends.

"You said I couldn't go out that door," she answered, refusing to be denied the cup.

"I was hoping if you stayed a few minutes, you wouldn't want to." A moment earlier she would have been indignant. Now she reconciled herself to necessity. She was, indeed, wildly hoping she might be able to coax him not to serve any paper. And she had to repress an absurd laugh at the thought as she set a fresh and steaming cup before him.

While he made ready to drink it she leaned with assured indifference against the buffet shelf behind her. She spread her left arm and hand innocently along its edge as she had seen waitresses do—and with her right hand, toyed with the loose collar of her crepe blouse—chatting the while like a perfectly good waitress with her suspect. The funny part seemed to her that he took it all with entire seriousness, hardly laughing; only a suspicion of a smile, playing at times around his eyes, relieved the somberness of his lean face. His parted lips showed regular teeth when he spoke, and gave a not unpleasant expression to his mouth. His eyes were as inoffensive as a mountain lake.

But there remained something stubborn in his dry manner and at times her heart misgave her as to the hope of dissuading him from his purpose. Trying to form some idea of how to act, she studied him with anxiety. All she could actually reach as a conclusion was that he might be troublesome to dissuade.

Yet with every moment she was the more determined to keep him from carrying out his mission and the more resolved to make him pay for his Western manners. All this was running through her head while the coffee was being sipped. Unhappily, her father was where she could not possibly reach him with a warning until Belle should reappear on the scene. She tendered her now tractable guest a second cup of coffee. It was accepted; he talked on, asking many questions, which were answered more or less to his satisfaction. Not that his inquiries were impertinent; they were chiefly silly, Kate thought. He seemed most intent on establishing a friendly footing with a lunch-counter attendant.

When his third cup had been drunk and payment tendered for it, and for five or six sandwiches, Kate decided her time to escape had arrived. She refused to accept his money: "No," she persisted, "I will not take a thing for your lunch. Positively not. Oh, you may leave your dollar on the counter, if you like—it will never go into the register."

"Why not?"

"I've told you."

"Say it again."

"You were very patient over my blunder in giving you cold coffee."

"To tell you the truth," he remarked with candor, "it didn't look to me altogether like a blunder."

"Oh, it was," she insisted shamelessly; but she did not feel at all sure he believed her. "And I won't take your money. I want you—" her eyes fell the least bit with her repentant words—"to have a better impression of this counter than cold coffee would give you. We're trying so hard to build up a business."

"Golly!" observed her calm guest. "I thought a few minutes ago you were trying to wreck one."

"You Medicine Bend men always make fun of this valley," Kate complained.

"I don't really belong in Medicine Bend," was his return.

"Where do you belong?"

"In the Falling Wall."

"Oh! that awful place?"

"Why knock the Falling Wall?"

"I never heard any good of it. No matter anyway; you may put up your money. And some time when I am up in your country," she added jestingly, "you can give *me* a cup of cold coffee."

"We'll say nothing more about the coffee," he declared in blunt fashion. "Just you come!" He yielded so honestly to deceit that Kate was half ashamed at imposing on him.

"Tell me," he went on, spinning his silver dollar in leisurely fashion on the smooth counter, "how am I going to get up to the mines today after I look around here for Barb—where can I get a horse?"

Kate reflected a moment. "I can get you *some* kind of a horse," she said slowly. "But it would take you forever to get there on horseback—the trail runs around by the river. The train will get you there first. It goes up at four o'clock."

She knew she said it all blandly, though conscious of her duplicity. It was not exactly falsehood that she spoke—but it was meant to mislead. The man was regarding her steadily with eyes that seemed to Kate not in the least double-dealing.

"What am I going to do till four o'clock?" he asked, making without discussion her subtle suggestion his own.

She lifted her eyebrows disclaimingly—even

shrugged her shoulders: "What are you going to do?" he persisted. She was ready. She looked longingly out of the window. The sun blazed over the desert in a riot of gold.

"It's my day off," she observed, adding just a suspicion of discontent and uncertainty to her words. She fingered her tie, too; then dropped her eyes; and added, "I thought I might take a ride."

He started: "Couldn't get two horses, could you?"

"Two?" echoed Kate, looking surprised.

He rose: "I'll turn up two if I have to steal 'em," he declared, reaching for his hat.

"That would be too much trouble for one little ride," Kate said ironically. "I'll see what I can do, first. But," she added, basely, "if you want to be sure of catching the train, I should advise you to stay right here. It backs down and doesn't stay but a minute—just long enough to hook on to the empties."

Her warning had no effect. It was not meant to have any. She knew if he got to the mines and learned that her father was at the Junction he would return in no time to serve him. He was decently restrained now, but he swallowed her bait, hook and all: "Where do you think you can find horses?" he asked.

"Where I work."

"Where do you work?"

"Sometimes here and sometimes up at Mr.

Doubleday's cottage. The barn-boy gets up a horse for me any time."

He raised an unexpected difficulty: "I wouldn't feel just right, today, riding a horse of Barb Doubleday's," he said doubtfully.

The words only confirmed her suspicions. Her fears rose but her wits did not desert her: "Ride mine," she suggested. "I've got my own horse, of course."

He drew a breath: "All I can say is, if you ever come over my way, I'll show you as good a time as I know how to."

She put up her hand: "Wait till you see how you like *my* good time."

He was quick to come back. "I'll agree right now to like anything you offer—and I don't care a hang what it is, either."

Looking straight at him she asked a question. Its emphasis lay in her quiet tone: "Will you stand to that?" He looked at her until she felt his eyes were going right through her: "I've got enemies," he said slowly, and there was now more than a touch of hardness in his voice; "most men have. But the worst of 'em never claimed my word isn't good."

"Then," exclaimed Kate, hastening to escape the serious tone, "you tend counter while I go and see about the horses."

"No," he objected, "that's a man's job. You tell me where to go and *I'll* get the horses."

Kate was most firm: "If you're going to ride

with *me*," she said, "you must do my way. Take a woman's job for a few minutes and see how you like it."

He regarded her with the simplicity of a child, but replied like a case-hardened cowboy: "I don't like a woman's job, of course. But I'm ready to do any blamed thing you say."

"Do you suppose," Kate demanded with an air, "they would turn two horses over to *you* up at Doubleday's?"

She had put her foot in it: "I tell you," he protested, "I don't want to ride a horse of Doubleday's. I'm up here to talk to Barb Doubleday. And nobody can say just how it's coming out. At the ranch they swore he was at Sleepy Cat. I rode down there and they told me he was at the Junction, so I took the train over here. Now you tell me he's at the mines—that's where I'll say what I've got to say. But I don't want to take any advantage. And I don't want to impose on his property rights so much as a single hair. That's exactly what's between us."

Kate, established in treacherous ambush, felt qualms at his stern, clear code.

She tried to shut him off, but he was wrought up: "Barb swore to me once he had nothing to do with it," he persisted obstinately. "All I can say is, if a man fools me once it's his fault; if he fools me twice, it's mine."

"What about a woman?" asked Kate, trying hard to say one thing and think another.

He opened his eyes: "I never thought much about that. A man can't fight a woman," he returned reflectively. "And I've yet to see one I could fool."

"What should you do," she asked, turning her back while she straightened her hat in the buffet mirror, "if you ever met one that fooled you?"

"No woman would ever take the trouble."

She laughed a little: "You never can tell."

"If a woman ever fooled me, she'd have to fool herself first—so she'd be the loser."

"What a philosopher!"

"First and last, I've been called a good many names—some full hard—but never a philosopher before."

Kate started for the front door: "Hold on a minute," he objected, "what's to do here while you're gone?"

"Serve coffee and sandwiches if anybody comes in. This time of day there's never anybody comes in."

He turned on his stool: "How soon'll you be back?"

"In a few minutes."

"Get a good horse for yourself."

Kate gave him a parting shot: "Of course you think I can't ride."

It did not take her long to get up the hill. Breathless, she encountered old Henry in the garden, asked him for the ponies and almost ran into the house. Her father was asleep. There was no reason to stir him up over a situation that she was resolved to handle and felt she could handle. She got into her riding clothes in a trice, all the time wondering whether she could hold her wild man in leash long enough to defeat him. Had he been more like anybody she had ever met and known, the problem would have been less confusing. But she determined to shut her eyes and win the fight if she could, and to this end draft every resource. So she thought, at least, as she caught up her little revolver and, dropping it into the scabbard she had belted about her waist, set forth.

She rode back one of her own ponies and led the other. Her enemy had good ears for when she was half way to the eating-house he walked out on the platform and silently surveyed her approach. Kate watched him narrowly and drew up before him to estimate the effect. She was disappointed, she had to confess, at his cool indifference, for she thought her riding rig unusually pretty. It had seemingly failed to impress her queer Westerner. His eyes were all for the horses. "Clean ponies," he observed, taking the bridle rein from her hand as he looked the two over.

"I forgot to ask what kind of a saddle you like," she observed indifferently. He was scanning the horses and his eyes not being on her she got her first real good look at her antagonist—whether he was to be her victim she was in somewhat anxious doubt.

CHAPTER 6

WHICH WINS?

He was long of limb, rather loose-jointed; but not ungraceful, except as his simple manner and unassuming rig—neither soiled nor fresh—made him seem so; at all events what he might look like was apparently of slight moment to him. He had a good walk—Kate noticed that when he crossed the platform; not the choppy, high-heeled gait of a man that never does anything but ride, but an easy step that matched the expressions of his eyes. His quick movements seemed, as usual with bronzed Western men, younger than his face; and his twenty-eight years would, as a first impression, have passed for well above thirty, with Kate. She had struggled too long with charcoal and lead pencils not to perceive that his frame was clean and his shoulders good; and his head was well set on them, if the man would carry it where it belonged. But he was plainly not vain; and since we usually accept at sight whatever draft men and women themselves draw on our impressions, Kate would have regarded him ordinarily with no more than he demanded—indifference.

"Any kind of saddle will do me," he answered in response to an inquiry; and he repeated his compliment to the horses. He looked well at his own: "This is a good pony." Kate assumed a little: "All our ponies are good."

"I wish you'd show them to me sometime," was his unassuming request. The remark should have been enough to warn Kate that her deception rested on very thin ice; that it was more than probable he had already penetrated much of it. But, a beginner in deception, she was intent only on her own part and took his good-natured acquiescence at its face value. The moment he saw her ponies he knew they were Doubleday's: yet he seemed willing to forego his scruple rather than to lose the ride.

Kate, too, was disposed to be amiable: "I will show them to you sometime," she said promptly.

But whenever she thawed for an instant she felt directly the necessity of freezing up again. Her remarks were divided as evenly as a mountain April day—one moment spring, the next winter. Happily for her purposes, the day itself *was* spring. She had mounted her horse but as she spoke, she slipped from her saddle, threw her lines and, walking hurriedly into the dining room, returned with a handful of wrapped sandwiches. She looked at him as she held the package out: "How can we carry them?"

He disposed of the store in a capacious pocket and then hesitated: "I wonder if you'd mind waiting five minutes while I go up to Doubleday's house."

"What for?" she asked, professing surprise.

"To see what I can find out about where he is."

"I've told you all you can find out by going to the house," she returned deprecatingly. He looked at her as if undecided. "When you ask to go riding with me and I get the horses—I come first, don't I?" she asked cavalierly; and before he could help her she was back again in the saddle.

He hesitated no longer: "You come first any time," he said, "and anywhere," he added, swinging up on his own pony.

She looked sidewise at him as they trotted up the street: "You don't mind rather rough riding?"

"Anything the ponies can stand," was all he said.

Kate had given him her dun pony. Spirit-free all the time the trim beast either through instinct knew his rider or meant to cast off care in a long fling. He took the stage the moment his rider touched the saddle. Kate rode Dick, her lighter but faster gray pony. He danced attendance for a time, but the dun kept the spotlight and gave Kate a chance to regard the man just from Medicine Bend critically. She had meant to put him on exhibition—perhaps cherished a hope he might ride only indifferently well—yet in a country where everybody rode, this was much to hope for. At all events, the result, with an added surprise, was a disappointment.

If there be a latent awkwardness in a man, the saddle mirrors it; and if there lie in him anywhere dormant an unsuspected alertness, it wakes in the saddle to action. Her companion had hardly found his stirrups before Kate perceived a change. His body sprung molded from the cantle, his careless shoulders came to attention, and as the pony curvetted riotously, the rider's head, rising like a monitor straight from his slender neck, invited his horse to show its paces.

"You take the trail," said Kate's guest tersely, as they swung out on the desert.

"No," she returned, "you."

"We'll take it together," was his reply.

But despite her disclaiming, Kate did the guiding and her object was to get a good way from town. Her companion's frequently repeated effort was to slow down for a talk; hers was to tantalize him by speeding away from one. But she couldn't speed all of the time, and he eyed either her riding, or her habit, pretty closely for a good while without comment. Then a chance offered itself and he put a question: "Where did you learn to ride?"

"All mountain girls ride, don't they?" she suggested.

"You're not a mountain girl."

"It was a mountain girl that taught me to ride, —away back in the Alleghanies—long before I ever saw this country."

"Your mountain girl's pupils don't all ride like that, I'll gamble."

"I wasn't very bright." Kate spurred ahead. The dun pony kept after her.

"Compliments don't set very well on you,

do they?" was the shot from her left a moment later.

She turned a full face on her companion: "I hate them," she declared with energy.

In luring this man away from his errand, she had yielded to a really wild impulse and now the spirit of recklessness that ruled her mood seemed to revenge itself by counseling added dangers. She invited riding-hazards, that her victim disdained to comment on, until they must have appeared silly to him. A long way from home they were crossing a high bench above the Falling Wall river, a bench cut by frequent lateral washes—some wide and all very deep. These breaks they jumped one after another without taking serious trouble to head them, though Kate's companion, riding on the river side, gave her every chance to do so.

"I suppose," he suggested at length, "you're pushing into rough country because you like it."

She looked at him: "Yes," she said, icily, "I do like it. But," she added, "if it's too rough for you, we'll go back." In that much of a challenge she felt safe.

"I'm riding with you," he returned, a little dryly. "I like anything you like."

And at this juncture Kate's luck deserted her; it always seemed to when she most needed it. Ahead, there lay a stretch of smooth bench and she took a run to cross it. But below a slight rise on the near side an ugly break suddenly faced her.

Decision was forced. Recklessness said: "Take it." She spurred. The gray hesitated—almost as if to give his wanton mistress a chance to reconsider; but he got the quirt for his pains.

The wiry beast was almost on the brink—he had hardly a moment to coil, but he shot across the gulf with a convulsive leap that carried his rider over, with nothing—absolutely nothing—to spare. He made the farther side with three feet—the left hind foot slumped on the edge of the bank and down went the leg!

Kate never forgot that moment. It was thirty feet, sheer, to the rocks below. And it would have been poor Dick on top of his foolish mistress. Kate really expected nothing better until with a terrific snort the pony scrambled to safety. What a horse will do for thankless man!

The frightened girl hardly dared look around even after she recovered her breath—which she thought would never come back. On the sudden spurt, her companion had been a little behind her. She presumed that the dun with commendable sense had refused the jump for when she glanced half way around—she was afraid her white face would betray her little panic—his rider was galloping him back in an easy circle and heading him the second time for the formidable break. This time, too, the rider was letting his reluctant beast understand who was master; and with enough of authority to force him and enough consideration to give him confidence, he jumped him over the gap as Kate *should* have jumped Dick—with room and to spare.

Her cheeks were burning again: "You did it much better," she said coolly, as he joined her. "Dick is getting slow."

"That wasn't Dick's fault," he remarked, for he appeared a trifle upset himself by the misadventure. "It was yours," he added bluntly.

Her only answer was to push ahead. She could at least keep the man busy—though she felt somewhat diffident about offering him further lessons in horsemanship.

The trail led up a commanding ridge and her companion scanned the valley lying to the north beyond. Through it they could trace a slender water course. "This should be not far from Falling Wall Canyon," he suggested. "And that creek must be a branch of the Sinking Water."

"Oh, I've heard about that wonderful canyon," she exclaimed. "Tell me about it."

"It breaks through that near range," he said, pointing. "There are elk in the park across the next divide. There isn't a great deal to tell about the canyon—it's just there, that's about all."

"How deep is it?"

"Three to six hundred feet."

"Straight up and down, they say."

"As near as the Lord could make it."

"Is there any way of getting to the bottom of it?"

67

"The easiest way would be to jump from the rim."

"Oh, could we see it?"

"Not tonight unless you want to camp out; and we're not exactly fixed for that. Up close to the old mine bridge there's a trail into the canyon. It's pretty stiff. A sailor would warp his way down with a rope."

The horses had halted by consent and their riders were contemplating the mountains and valleys surrounding them. Her companion took advantage of the pause to dismount and inspect the legs of the ponies—and while he examined those of his own horse for politeness' sake—he looked more closely at Dick's.

"He must have got a wrench in that jump," confessed Kate, watching. "We were riding pretty fast, weren't we?"

"For that kind of country, yes. I thought for a while," added her companion, in a dry way, "you must be showing me how to ride. Then I figured out you must be showing me how *you* could ride."

Kate stared straight ahead: "How absurd!" she exclaimed with cold contempt for his conclusions, yet feeble in her sarcasm against his penetration.

"All I want to say is," he continued, remounting, "that I see you can ride. You don't have to cover much country to prove that. You ride like a Western girl—and talk like an Eastern girl. Which are you?"

She unfeelingly closed all inquiries: "Both," she answered indifferently. "Let's head for the bottoms; about two miles from here there's a spring—good water."

He looked skeptical: "If you can show me good water near here, I'll be learning something. I didn't know there was a water hole within ten miles—but I don't know this lower country as well as my own."

"What is your own?"

He pointed to the Northeast to where a range of snow-capped peaks rose above from the desert: "Those are the Lodge Pole mountains. That's where the Falling Wall river begins—where you see that snow. It circles clear around the range, crosses the Reservation to the West and opens South into a high basin—that's my country— the Falling Wall. Then the river cuts out of there through the canyon we're talking about and gets away to the West again." Coming a step nearer to her he pointed again: "Now look close to the left of that strip of timber. You can just see a break above it—that's the high point of the canyon. A long time ago there was a mining camp in those mountains—Horsehead—they started to build a railroad up there—did a lot of grading and put in the abutments for a bridge across the canyon. Before they got the road built the camp played out; they never finished it. All that country below there is the Falling Wall."

"Are they all thieves and outlaws over there?"

He started a little in spite of himself and took his time to reply: "It must have been a thief or an outlaw that put that idea in your head," he observed finally.

"Oh, no, it was Tom Stone."

His expression changed into contempt: "I didn't need but one guess."

Kate asked him to explain, but he did not and she was not in a position to object. She found the trail to the spring. Van Horn had taken her there once. Dismounting at a little distance, the two made their way down to it. "Score one for the rough rider," said her companion after he had drunk. "And I thought I knew every drop of water in this country."

He produced the sandwiches and they sat down. Kate could judge the hour of the day only from the sun and dared not mention "time." Her companion asked as many questions as he could think of, and she managed her answers with a minimum of information. And she asked herself one question that did not occur to him: "Why was she not frightened to death?" It must have been the duel she felt she was fighting with this man to keep him away from her father that banished her fears. In the saddle, events moved too rapidly to admit of extended misgivings, and she had purposely assigned to him the slower horse.

It was only when they were taking the almost enforced moment of rest together at the water hole—which might as well have been a thousand miles from help as ten—that little chills did run up and down her back. As for her companion, it was useless to try to read him from his face or manner; if she were playing one game, he might well be playing another as far as anything she could gather from his features was concerned. But she had to confess there was never a look in his eyes— when she did look into them—that frightened her.

And as she cautiously regarded him munching a sandwich and keeping his own eyes rather away from than on her own, she asked herself whether she had undertaken too much, and whether this sphinx-like face might hide danger for her. She at least knew it was far from being possible to tell by looking at the outside of a man's head what might be going on inside. Only the plight of her father's affairs had seemed to justify her; even this did not seem to now, but it was too late to wish herself out of it. Besides—for most extraordinary notions will come into foolish girls' minds—was she not in the company of a great Federal court; and shouldn't she feel safe on that score?

He certainly ate slowly. His appetite was astonishing. He invited Kate more than once to continue eating with him, but her first hasty sandwich and her latent uneasiness had more than satisfied her.

"It must be very exciting, to be a deputy marshal," she remarked once, when she could think of no other earthly thing to say, and was still afraid they might get back in time for the train.

"It must be sometimes."

"How does it feel to be chasing men all the time?"

"I've had more experience myself in getting chased."

She attempted to laugh: "Do they ever chase deputy marshals?"

He took up, gravely, the last sandwich: "I expect they do once in a while."

"You ought to know, I should think."

He offered her the sandwich and on her refusal bit into it: "No," he returned simply, "for I'm not a deputy marshal."

Kate was stunned: "Why, you said you were! What do you mean?" she demanded when she could speak. He ate so deliberately! She thought he never would finish his mouthful and answer: "I mean—not regularly. Once or twice I've been deputized to serve papers—when the job went begging. Farrell Kennedy, the marshal at Medicine Bend, is a friend of mine—that's the nearest I come to working for him."

"But if you're not a deputy marshal, what are you?" demanded Kate, uneasily.

His face reflected the suspicion of a smile: "I guess the answer to that would depend a good deal on who told the story."

"I could hardly imagine anyone chasing you," she continued, not knowing in her confusion what to say.

"You ought to see me run sometime," he returned.

"Oh, there's a prairie dog!" she exclaimed. She was looking to the farther side of the water hole. "See? Over there by that bush! I wonder if I could hit it?" She put her hand to her scabbard: "I've lost my revolver!" She looked at him blankly. "Had it when you started, didn't you?" inquired her companion, undisturbed. Her hand rested on the empty scabbard in dismay: "I must have lost it on the way."

He plunged his left hand into a capacious side pocket and drew out her revolver. But instead of handing it to her he began to examine it as if he might return it or might not. She was on pins in an instant. Now she *was* at his mercy. "Is that mine?" she asked, frightened.

"It is."

"Where did you get it?" she demanded. Was she to get it back? He made no move to let her know; just fingered the toy curiously. "Where you dropped it—before you made your leap for life." And looking up at her, he added: "We ought to've eaten our sandwiches first and drank afterward."

"I don't understand—what did I do?" Kate knew her voice quivered a bit though she was bound she would not show fear. "And while we are talking"—she pointed—"the prairie dog is gone."

"He'll be back," predicted her companion with

slow confidence. "The gun bounced from your scabbard when you were running your horse along the bench. So I picked it up for you." He presented it on the palm of his hand.

"How odd!" she exclaimed, trying to take it without appearing in a hurry. "How stupid of me!" She knew her face, in spite of herself, flushed under his gaze.

"You were going a pretty good clip," he continued.

"But a man would never do such a thing as to drop a revolver—you never would."

"It might be a whole lot worse for me to do it than it would for you—though if I carried a nice little gun like that it maybe wouldn't make so very much difference. There's your prairie dog again," he added, looking across the hole.

"Of course a man would have to make fun of a pistol like this," she answered, the revolver lying in her hand. "Let me see yours." Thus far she had seen no sign of any scabbard or holster. "And shoot that prairie dog for me," she added.

"Mine would be pretty heavy for a prairie dog. You try him."

"Oh, my poor little pistol is in disgrace," she returned, putting it up. "See what you can do."

He slipped his left hand under the right lapel of his coat and drew from a breast harness a Colt's revolver. Had she realized it was carried that day in this very unobtrusive manner in anticipation of an unpleasant interview with her father, Kate would have been speechless with fear. As it was, no gun, though she had seen many since coming to the mountains, ever looked so big or formidable. The setting of the scene and her situation may have magnified its impressiveness.

"Why smash the prairie dog?" he asked quietly. "Look at his whiskers—he may be the father of a family."

"You might miss him."

"If I should it would be time for me to quit this country."

"Shoot at something else."

"Why shoot at all?"

"I want to see you."

"We might get a shot at something on the way home."

"You're not obliging." She held out her hand for his revolver. "Let me see."

"It makes me feel kind of foolish," he said defensively, "kind of like an old-fashioned cowboy, to be shooting right and left." On his right hand he held the heavy gun toward Kate.

"How do you get practise?" she asked.

He lifted his eyebrows the least bit: "To tell the truth I haven't had much lately."

"How can you tell then whether you could hit anything if you did shoot at it?"

"That wouldn't be hard. If I didn't hit it, it would most likely hit me."

"How could I practise to learn to shoot the way you do?"

He looked at her inquiringly; "What do you know about the way I shoot?"

"Nothing, of course. I mean the way that men who carry guns like this shoot."

He thought a moment. "Get down into a dark cellar with just one window. Block out all the light from that window except one small circle. Shoot, off-hand, till you can put five bullets through the circle without mussing up the general surroundings."

"That sounds like hard work."

"It's certainly—" He just hesitated and then continued: "hard on the ammunition."

She found by this time she could tolerate the dry smile that lighted his face now and again, and the drawl of words that went with the expression. At times he seemed simple, yet there was shrewdness behind his humor.

"I didn't see you stop back there on the bench to pick anything up," she remarked abruptly, thinking of her own pistol again.

"I circled back to get it."

"Without dismounting?"'

"You wouldn't hardly want to get off to pick up anything as light as that."

"I wish I'd seen you do it."

"If you'd been looking I might've been trying to get hold of it yet."

She examined the Colt's gun curiously. She

asked him how to handle it. He obligingly broke it, emptied the cylinders and explained how it was fired. But she was not equal to handling the big thing, and told him so.

"Though if I should want to kill you now it would be easy, wouldn't it?" she reflected, after he had reloaded the gun and laid it in her hand, the muzzle pointing toward himself and her finger resting on the trigger.

"Not without cocking the gun."

"No, but I mean suppose I really *should* want to kill you—"

"I'll show you." He cocked the revolver and placed it again in her hand and it lay once more with her finger on the trigger.

"Now," he explained, "I'm covered."

"And to kill you all I have to do is to pull the trigger."

"Pulling the trigger, the way things are now, would certainly be a big start in that direction. But"—the dry suspicion of a laugh crossed his eyes—"to point a gun at a man and pull the trigger doesn't always kill him—not, anyways, in this country. If it did, the population would fall off pretty strong in some of these northern counties. And you might be surprised if I told you you couldn't pull the trigger right now, anyway."

"How do you know that?"

"Try it."

"But I might kill you!"

"That's the point."

"Nevertheless," she persisted, "I could if I *wanted* to."

"No matter how you put it, it's all the same—you can't want to."

"No, but suppose I were bound to keep you from doing something—like serving papers, for instance."

His legs were crossed under him and he was tossing bits of the gravel under his hand: "You'd have a better show to do that if you went at it in another way."

"What way?"

"Well—by asking me not to serve them, for instance."

"Do you mean to say if I asked you not to serve papers you wouldn't do it?" She eyed him with simulated indignation.

He returned her gaze unafraid: "Try it," was his answer.

She took a deep breath. Then she tossed her head: "I probably shouldn't care enough about it for that. Why don't you carry two revolvers?"

"Too much like baggage."

"Wouldn't it be a lot safer?"

He smiled: "If one gun refused to go off promptly, two wouldn't help a lot."

Her eyes and her thoughts returned to the gun in her hand. For a moment she had forgotten it. Suppose her finger, while she was talking, had mechanically closed on the trigger. She blanched. "Take it," she said, holding the gun out in both hands and looking away.

"Shall we let the dog go this time?" she heard him ask as he lowered the hammer.

CHAPTER 7

THE CLOSE OF THE DAY

They rode straight home. On the way Dick went lame and both dismounted to examine him. "This will make you miss your train," she suggested, hypocritically.

He had Dick's foot up. His comment on the remark was very like the rest of his comments. "Not this," he said—and without looking up.

"Do you mean to say you've missed it anyway?" asked Kate.

"What does the sun say?"

She bit her lip: "Too bad," she exclaimed, looking across the distance that still lay between them and the Junction.

"I don't see anything wrong with his foot," he announced, completing his inspection. "I think he wrenched himself."

He said no more till they started again. And then resumed in his odd way just where they had left off talking: "I've been trying to figure out why you wanted me to miss the train." She looked at him in surprise. "I think you did want me to," he continued. "But I can't figure out why."

She protested, but not with too many words. She felt sure he was not easily to be deceived. In any case, however, he was unflinchingly amiable.

After they got back to the Junction the totally unexpected happened. They dismounted and she went into the lunch-room. Her victim pursued an examination of Dick's leg. An early supper was being served in the dining-room to a freight train crew. Two of the Doubleday cowboys from the ranch came into the lunch-room from the front door. Kate, at the desk, was making ready to manage her own escape from the scene. The smaller cowboy, walking in last, looked back curiously at her riding companion as he stood with Dick's hoof on his knee. The man slouched up to the counter: "Wouldn't that kill you?" muttered the smaller man to his partner.

"What do you mean?" demanded the other.

The first speaker hitched his thumb guardedly over his shoulder: "Know who that is out there?"

"No, I don't—who is he?"

Kate's ears were wide open: "None other," continued the man, pulling a face, "than the well-known Jim Laramie himself." His partner checked him and the two, talking in low tones, walked into the dining-room.

Kate could not at first believe her ears; then

she felt that the cowboy must know what he was talking about.

Worst of all, Laramie, at that moment—before she could think of collecting herself—walked in through the open door. He came directly to the counter. She hardly attempted to hide her consternation: "Are you Jim Laramie?" she burst out in her excitement.

It must have been the manner of her words rather than the words themselves that startled him. For just an instant the curtain lifted; a flash of anger shot from his eyes; it was drawn again at once: "Is my reputation over here as bad as that?" he asked.

Kate was dumb. Try as she would, she could not think of a thing to say; the recollection of her reckless ride overwhelmed her. "What's happened?" he continued with a little irritation. "If you weren't afraid of me when you didn't know my name, why be afraid now?"

She stammered something, some apology, which he received, she afterward thought, coldly: "I'm running up to the house now to change," she went on hurriedly, "but I must thank you for—"

What on earth was she to thank him for? He helped her out: "Before you go," he interrupted, sitting up on the counter stool nearest her and looking at her without paying the slightest attention to her meaningless words, "before you go, tell me your name."

Oddly enough, by just speaking he restored order to her faculties. She looked straight at him: "You guessed that this morning," she said frankly.

"Kate?"

She nodded.

"That's queer," he mused. "It must've been pure accident. I heard that the man I came to round up today had a girl named Kate, so I suppose that was the first name came into my head. Kate, what else?"

"Suppose," she suggested gravely, "we keep the rest for the next time."

"For our next ride?"

She looked just away from his persistent eyes: "Perhaps."

"Will your name," he went on, "surprise me as much as my name surprised you?"

"Who knows?" she retorted, and speaking she started for the front door.

"Stop." He stepped in front of her just enough to bar her way. There was a tinge of command in his voice and manner quite new. Halted, but not pleased, she waited for him to go on: "You'll come back, won't you?"

"I'll try to."

"I want to listen," he added coolly, "to the worst story you ever heard about Jim Laramie."

"I don't pay much attention to cowboy stories."

He certainly paid no attention to her words: "Will you come back?" he persisted.

"I will if I can," she said, confusedly.

He was just enough in front of her to detain her: "Say you will."

It was somewhat between command and entreaty. Old Henry at the side of the platform was just mounting the dun horse. Kate was getting panicky: "Very well," she answered, "I'll come back."

The moment she got to the cottage she locked the front door and drew all the shades. And every mouthful of the cold supper she ate with her father lodged in her throat. To him she dared not say a word. Once in the evening the door bell rang and some man asked for Barb Doubleday. He made a few inquiries when Henry answered that Doubleday was not in town, but he did not ask for Kate. She felt curious tremors, listening to the low voice. But Laramie—for it was he—presently turned from the door and she heard his footsteps crunching down the gravel path to the street.

In the morning Henry told her a man had lingered around the lunch-room until the lights were put out at ten o'clock. By that time he must have known every pine knot in the varnished ceiling. When peaceably put out of the room by the night man he had walked out on the platform to the post where the horses had stood and looked long across the tracks toward Doubleday's cottage on the hill. No lights were burning in the cottage. He turned to walk toward it. But as he stepped into the street the whistle of the eastbound Overland train sounded in the hills to the west. Evidently this changed his mind, for he retraced his steps and entered the waiting-room, walked to the ticket window and bought a ticket for Sleepy Cat. He waited until the train pulled in and loitered on the platform till it was ready to pull out, speaking to no one. When the conductor finally gave the starting signal the man looked for the last time around toward the lunch-room door. Everything was dark.

He caught the hand rail of the last open sleeper and swung up on the step. There he stood looking down the platform and across the street while the train drew slowly out. Then turning to go into the car he uttered only one word to himself—and that a mild one: "Gypped!"

But, even then, had Kate heard it she would have been frightened.

CHAPTER 8

THE HOME OF LARAMIE

Almost due north of Sleepy Cat the Lodge Pole Mountains, tumbling over one another in an upheaval southward, are flung suddenly to the west and spread in a declining ridge to the Superstition range. South of the Lodge Poles the country is very rough, but at the point where the range is so sharply deflected there spreads fanlike to the east an open basin with good soil and water. It is known locally as the Falling Wall country, and, as the names of the region indicate, it was once famous as a hunting ground, and so, as a fighting ground, for the powerful tribes of early days. And an ample Reservation in this basin—ending just where the good lands begin—is the stamping ground of the last of the mountain red men.

But the struggle for possession of the Falling Wall country did not end with the red men. White men, too, have coveted the lands of the Falling Wall and fought for them. Among the blind the one-eyed are kings, and the Falling Wall basin lies amid inhospitable deserts, barren hills and landscapes slashed to rags and ribbons by mountain storms—regions that have failed to tempt even a white man's cupidity. The Indians fought for the basin with arrows, bullets, tomahawks and scalping knives; the whites have fought chiefly in the land offices and courts, but, exasperated by delays and inflamed by defeat, they have at times boiled over and appealed to the rifle and the hip holster for decrees to quiet title.

It is for these reasons, and others, that the Falling Wall country has borne a hard and somewhat sinister name, even in a region where men have been habitually indifferent to restraint and tolerant of violent appeals to frontier justice. In the very early days of the white man the Indian clung to the

Falling Wall country as his last stand; for the bad lands along the canyon of the Falling Wall river made, as they yet make, an almost impenetrable fastness for sally and retreat.

But even before the Indians were driven into their barren cage to the north, white adventurers had penetrated the basin and it became, with the shifting of possession, a region for men of hard repute. Its traditions have been bad and few in the Falling Wall country have felt concern over the fact.

Yet, from the earliest days, despite the many difficulties of living in the widely known but not large park, a few hardy settlers managed from the beginning, in secluded portions of the region, to keep their scalps and their horses and to live through Indian days and outlaw days—though not often in peace, and never in quiet.

Among these early adventurers was one known as "Texas" Laramie, because he had the extraordinary courage, or hardihood, to bring into the Falling Wall the first cattle ever driven into the mountains from the Panhandle. In a country where the sobriquet is usually the only name by which it is courteous or safe to address a man, and where it is invariably apt, few men are accorded two. But Laramie had also been known as "Pump" Laramie because he brought into that country the first Winchester rifle; and the instinctive significance the mind attaches to the combination of cows and a repeating rifle was, in this instance, justified—there was between the two a direct, even dynamic, connection. Laramie thus figured prominently in the older Falling Wall feuds. It would have been difficult for him to figure obscurely, and do it more than once.

Enemies said that he stole the bunch of cattle he first drove into the Falling Wall. It was not true but it made a good story. And in any event, Texas Laramie defended his steers vigorously against all men advancing claim to them between darkness and daylight—as enterprising neighbors not infrequently undertook to do. With the cattle, Laramie had brought into the mountains a wife from Texas. She was a young mother with a little boy, Jim; a good mother, never happy in the country so far away from the Staked Plain—and not very long to live there. But she lived long enough to send Jim year after year to the Sisters' School on the Reservation.

To obtain for a boy any sort of an education in a region so wild and so inhospitable would have seemed impossible. Yet devoted Sisters—refined and aristocratic American women—were already in this mountain country devoting their lives to the Indian Missions. Under such women little Jim learned his Catechism and his reading and from them and their example a few of the amenities of life—so far removed from him in every other direction. Under their care he grew up, after he had lost his mother, among the Indian boys. With these he learned to fish and hunt, to trap for pocket money, to use a bow and arrow and a knife, to trail and stalk patiently, to lie uncomplainingly in cold and wet, to ride without saddle or bridle or spur, to face a grizzly without excitement, to use a rifle where the price of every cartridge was reckoned and a poor aim sometimes cost life itself.

And every summer at home his father added extension courses in the saddle and bridle, spur, hackamore and lariat to his education. He taught him to rope, throw and mark, to use a coffee pot and frying pan, and at last on the great day—the Commencement day, so to say of the boy's frontier education—he presented him with his degree—a Colt's revolver and a box of cartridges—and died. As he lay on his deathbed, Texas Laramie left a parting advice to his young son: "You've learned to shoot, Jim—you don't shoot bad for a youngster. A man's got to shoot. But the less shooting you do, after you've learned—without you're forced to it, mind you—the more comfortable you'll feel when you get where I am now. All I can say is: I never killed an honest man that I knowed of. In fact," his breath came very slowly, "I never yet seen an honest man in the Falling Wall to kill."

And Jim began life with the ranch, youth, a little bunch of cattle, no money and much health in the

Falling Wall. His first year alone he never forgot, for in the spring he drove all his steers—not a great many—into the new railroad town, south—Sleepy Cat—and sold them for more money than he had ever seen at one time in his life. He wandered from the bank into Harry Tenison's gambling rooms—Harry having sold out his livery stable to Joe Kitchen shortly before that—just to look on for a little while before starting home. When Laramie did start home, Tenison had all his steer money and Laramie owed the sober-faced gambler, besides, one hundred dollars. Laramie then went to work on the range for twenty-five dollars a month. He worked four months, and it was hard work, took his pay check in and handed it to Tenison. That was strangely enough the beginning of a friendship that was never broken. Tenison tried to give the check back to Laramie. He could not. But Laramie never again tried to clean out the bank at Tenison's.

The Laramie cabin on Turkey Creek—the son built afterward on the same spot—stood on a slight conical rise some distance back from the little stream that watered the ranch. From his windows Jim Laramie could look on gently falling ground in all directions. Toward the creek lay an alfalfa field which, with a crude irrigating ditch and water from the creek, he had brought to a prosperous stand. Below the alfalfa stood the barn and the corral.

• • •

The day after Kate Doubleday's adventure with him at the Junction, Laramie was riding up the creek to his cabin when a man standing at the corral gate hailed him. It was Ben Simeral. Ben, old and ragged, met every man with a smile—a bearded, seamed and shabby smile, but an honest smile. Ben was a derelict of the range, a stray whose appeal could be only to patient men. Whenever he wandered into the Falling Wall country, where he had a claim, he made Laramie's cabin a sort of headquarters and spent weeks at a time there, looking after the stock in return for what John Lefever termed the "court'sies" of the ranch.

Laramie, greeting Ben, made casual inquiry about the stock. Ben looked at him as if expectant; but Ben was not aggressive for news or anything else. He grinned as he looked Laramie over: "Well, you're back again, Jim."

Laramie responded in kindly fashion: "Anybody been here?"

"Nary critter," declared the custodian, " 'cept Abe Hawk—he came over to borry your Marlin rifle."

"What did he want with that?"

"Said he was going up into the mountains but he's comin' over again before he starts. I knowed he helped you track them wire scouts over to Barb's. The blame critters tore off all the wire t'other side the creek, too. Get any track of 'em?"

he asked, sympathetically alive to what had been most on Laramie's mind when he had started from home.

Laramie barely hesitated but he looked squarely at Ben and answered in even tones: "No track, Ben."

Ben looked at him, still smiling with a kindly hope: "Hear from the contest on the creek quarter?"

"They told me at Medicine Bend it had gone against me."

"Psho! Never! You've got another 'go' to Washington, hain't y'?"

Laramie nodded and got down from his horse. Ben, removing the saddle, asked more questions—none of them important—and after putting up the horse the two men started for the house. Its rude walls were well laid up in good logs on which rested a timbered roof, shingled.

A living-room with a fireplace roughly fashioned in stone made up the larger interior of the cabin. To the right of the fireplace a kitchen opened off the living-room and adjoining this, to the right as one entered the front door, was a bedroom. To the left stood a small table, on which were scattered a few old books, a metal lamp and well-thumbed copies of old magazines. Beside the table stood a heavy oak Morris chair of the kind sold by mail-order houses. Two other chairs, heavily built in oak, were disposed about the room, and on the left of the entrance—there was but one door—stood a cot bed. On the floor between the door and the fireplace lay a huge silver tip bearskin, the head set up by an Indian taxidermist. It was some time afterward when Kate saw the cabin, but she remembered, even after it lay in ruins, just how the interior had looked.

The four walls were really more furnished than the rest of the room. To the right and left of the fireplace hung twin bighorn heads, and elk and stag antlers on the other walls supplied racks for an ample variety of rifles, polished by familiar use and kept, through love of trusty friends, in good order. Trophies of the hunt, disposed sometimes in effective and sometimes in mere man fashion, flanked the racks and showed the tastes of the owner of the isolated habitation; for few trails led within miles of Laramie's ranch on the Turkey.

"Breakfast?" Simeral looked at his companion, who stood vacantly musing at the door of the kitchen.

"Coffee," answered Laramie, taking off his jacket, laying his Colt's on the table and slipping off his breast harness.

"I got no bread," announced Ben, to forestall objection. "Flour's low 'n' I didn't bake."

"Crackers will do."

"Ain't no crackers, neither," returned Ben, raising his voice and his smile in self-defense.

"Give me coffee and bacon," suggested Laramie, impatiently.

" 'N' I'll fry some potatoes," muttered Ben, shuffling with a show of speed into the kitchen, and calling inquiries back in his unsteady voice to the living-room, patiently digging at Laramie for scraps of news from Sleepy Cat, volunteering, in return, scraps from the range and ranch. Laramie sat down in the nearest chair, tilted it slightly back, and resting one arm on the table gazed into the empty fireplace. He appeared as if much preoccupied—nor would, nor could, he talk of what was in his mind, nor think of anything else.

Some minutes later he began in the same absent-minded manner on a huge plateful of bacon, with a pot of coffee in keeping, and was eating in silence when the stillness of the sunshine was broken by the sound of a horse's hoofs. Laramie looked out and saw, through the open door, a horseman riding in leisurely fashion up from the creek.

The man was tall. He swung lightly out of his saddle near the door, and as he walked into the house it could be seen that he was proportioned in his frame to his height; strength and agility revealed themselves in every move. A rifle slung in a scabbard hung beside the shoulder of the horse, and the man's rig proclaimed the cowboy, though aside from a broad-brimmed Stetson hat his garb was simplicity itself.

It was the way in which he carried his height and shoulders that arrested attention, nor was his face one easily to be forgotten. He wore a jet-black beard that grew close and dropped compactly down. It was neither bushy nor scraggly and with his black brows it made a striking setting for strong and rather deep-set eyes which if not actually black were certainly very dark. His smile revealed white, regular teeth under his dark mustache, and his olive complexion, though tanned, seemed different from those of men that rode the range with him—perhaps it was owing to the glossy, black beard.

Abe Hawk was evidently at home in Laramie's cabin. He stepped through the door and pushing his hat back on his forehead took a chair and sat down. The two men, masters of taciturnity, looked at each other while this was taking place, and as Hawk seated himself Laramie called for a cup and pushed the coffee pot toward his visitor. Paying no attention to the unspoken invitation, Hawk's features assumed the quizzical lines they sometimes wore when he relaxed and poked questions at his friend.

"Well," he demanded, banteringly, "where's Jimmie been?"

"Medicine, Sleepy Cat—pretty near everywhere."

"I hear you got a job."

"I was offered one."

"Deputy marshal, eh?"

"Farrell Kennedy got me down to Medicine Bend to talk it over."

"What's the matter, couldn't you hold it?"

"I didn't want it."

"You're out of practise on this law-and-order stuff—you've lived up here too long among thieves, Jim. Find out who tore down your wire?"

Laramie replied in even tones but his voice was hard: "I trailed them across the Crazy Woman. It was somebody from Doubleday's ranch."

"They had a story at Stormy Gorman's you'd gone over there to blow Barb's head off."

"Barb wasn't home."

Hawk was conscious of the evasion. "Was Stormy's talk true?" he demanded curtly.

"I expected to ask Barb whether he wanted to put my wire back. I was going to give him a chance."

"It wouldn't be hard to guess how that would come out. Where was he?" asked Hawk, with evident disappointment.

"They said he was in Sleepy Cat. I rode in and missed him there. He'd gone to the mines. I took the train up to the Junction. There I accidentally got switched off my job and came home."

"How'd you get switched off?" asked Hawk, resenting the outcome.

Laramie's manner showed he disliked being bored into. He leaned forward with a touch of asperity and looked, straight at his visitor: "By not 'tending strictly to my own business, Abe."

Hawk knew from the expression of Laramie's

eyes he must drop the subject, and though he lost none of his bantering manner, he desisted: "They didn't have a warrant for me down at the marshal's office, did they?"

"They were short of blanks," retorted Laramie coolly.

"How you fixed for flour?"

"Plenty of it." Laramie spoke loudly for fear Simeral might protest. Then he called promptly to the kitchen: "Ben, get up some flour for Abe."

Ben quavered a protest.

"Get it up now before you forget it," insisted Laramie.

"Is Tom Stone still foreman over at Doubleday's?"

"I guess he is," returned Laramie.

"What does Doubleday aim to do with Stone?" asked Hawk, cynically, "steal his own cattle from himself?"

"A cattleman nowadays might as well steal his own cattle as to wait for somebody else to steal 'em." Laramie spoke with some annoyance. "There's going to be trouble for these Falling Wall rustlers."

"Meaning me?" asked Hawk, contemptuously.

"I never mean you without saying you, Abe—you ought to know that by this time. But this running off steers is getting too raw. From the under-talk in Sleepy Cat there's going to be something done."

"Who by?"

"By the cattlemen."

"I thought," Hawk spoke again contemptuously, "you meant by the sheriff."

"But I didn't," said Laramie. "I meant by the bunch at the range. And when they start they'll stir things up over this way."

Hawk hazarded a guess on another subject: "It looks like Van Horn—putting in Stone over at Doubleday's."

"It is Van Horn."

Hawk looked in silence out of the open door at the distant snow-capped mountains. "Why don't you kill him, Jim?" he asked after a moment, possibly in earnest, possibly in jest, for his iron tone sometimes meant everything, sometimes nothing.

Laramie, at all events, took the words lightly. He answered Hawk's question with another. But his retort and manner were as easy as Hawk's question and expression were hard. "Why don't you?"

The bearded man across the table did not hesitate nor did he cast about for words. On the contrary, he replied with embarrassing promptness: "I will, sometime."

"A man that didn't know you, Abe, might think you meant it," commented Laramie, filling his coffee cup.

Hawk's white teeth showed just for the instant that he smiled; then he talked of other things.

CHAPTER 9

At the Bar

The arrival of a baby at the home of Harry Tenison in Sleepy Cat had an immediate effect on Kate Doubleday's fortune in the mountains—and, indeed, on the fortunes of a number of other people in Sleepy Cat—wholly out of proportion to its importance as a family event. It was not, it is true, for the Tenisons a mere family event. Married fifteen years, they had been without children until the advent of this baby. And the birth of a boy to Harry Tenison excited not alone the parents, but the town, the railroad division and the hundred miles of range and desert, north and south, tributary to the town.

For a number of years Tenison had run his place in Sleepy Cat undisturbed by the swiftly changing fortunes of frontiersmen and railroad men. Tragedies, in their sudden sweep across the horizon of his activities, the poised gambler and hotel man had met unmoved. Men went to the heights of mining or range affluence and to the depths of crude passion, inevitable despair and tragic death, with Harry Tenison coldly unruffled. He was a man in so far detached from his surroundings, yet with his finger on the pulse of happenings in his unstable world. But the birth of one baby—and that a small one—upset him completely and very unexpectedly shocked others of his motley circle of acquaintance.

The complications followed on the announcement—on a Monday when the baby was three days old and the mother and boy were reported by the nurse to be coming along like kittens—that the following Saturday would be "open day" at the Mountain House—Tenison's new and almost palatial hotel; with the proprietor standing host for the town and the countryside.

Before the week was out this word had swept through the mountains, from the stretches of the Thief River on the South to the recesses of the Lodge Poles on the North. It was the one topic of interest for the week on the range. Few were the remote corners where the news did not penetrate and the unfortunates who missed the celebration long did penance in listening to long-winded accounts of Sleepy Cat's memorable day.

It dawned in a splendor of blue sky and golden sun, with the mountain reaches, snow-swept and still, brought incredibly near and clear through the sparkling air of the high plateau. The Sleepy Cat band were Tenison's very first guests for breakfast.

" 'N' you want to eat hearty, boys," declared Ben Simeral, who had reached town the night before in order that no round crossing the Tenison bar should escape him: "Harry expec's you to blow like hell all day."

Few men are more conscientious in the discharge of duty than the members of a small-town brass band. The Sleepy Cat musicians held back only until the arrival of the early local freight, Second Seventy-Seven, for their bass horn player, the fireman. When the train pulled up toward the station on a yard track, the band members in uniform on the platform awaited their melodic back-stop, and the fireman, in greeting, pulled the whistle cord for a blast. The switch engine promptly responded and one whistle after another joined in until every engine in the yard was blowing as Ben had declared Tenison expected the band itself to blow.

In this wholly impromptu and happy way the day was opened. The band, laboriously trained for years by the local jeweler—said to be able to blow a candle through an inch board with his South Bend B flat cornet—now formed in marching order, the grimed fireman gamely in place even after a night run, with his silver contrabass. At an energetic signal from their leader they struck up a march and started down street with the offering as a pledge of what they might be expected to do. They were not called on, however, to do all, for at noon the Bear Dance Band arrived from the West and an hour later came the crack thirty-two-piece military band from Medicine Bend, carrying more gold on their lacings and their horns than the local musicians carried in the savings bank.

By the time the noon whistle blew at the

roundhouse every trail and road into Sleepy Cat showed dust—some of them an abundance. The hotel was naturally the center of attraction, and Main Street looked like a Frontier Day crowd. The Reservation, too, sent a delegation for the occasion and mingling in the jostling but good-natured crowd were chiefs, bucks and squaws, who, in a riot of war bonnets, porcupine waistcoats, gay trappings and formal blankets, lent yellows and reds and blues to the scene. All entrances to the Mountain House were decorated and a stream of visitors poured in and out, with congratulations for Tenison, who received them at the bar in the big billiard hall opening on Main Street.

By evening the hall presented an extraordinary scene. Every element that went to make up the shifting life of the frontier could be picked from the crowd that filled the room. Most numerous and most aggressive in the spectacle, cattlemen and range riders in broad hats, leathern jackets and mottled waistcoats, booted and spurred and rolling in their choppy steps on pointed heels, moved everywhere—to and from the bar, around the pool tables and up and down the broad flight of stairs leading to the second floor gambling rooms. At the upper end of the long bar there was less crowding than nearer the street door and at this upper end three men, somewhat apart from others, while nominally drinking, stood in confab. First among them, Harry Van Horn was noticeable. His strong face, with its hunting nose, reflected his active mind, and as he spoke or listened to one or the other of his companions—standing between them—his lively eyes flashed in the overhead light. On his left stood Tom Stone, foreman of the Doubleday ranch. His head, carried habitually forward, gave him the appearance of always looking out from under his eyebrows; and the natural expression of his face, bordering on the morose, was never lighted by more than a strained smile—a smile that suggested a grin, that puckered the corners of his eyes and drew hard furrows down his cheeks, but evidenced nothing akin to even the skim-milk of human kindness.

On Van Horn's left stood an older man of massive features, the owner of the largest ranch in the north country, Barb Doubleday.

Miners from Thief River, with frank, fearless faces, broad-throated, belted and shirted, and with brawny arms for pick and sledge and doublejack, moved to and from the bar like desert travelers breathing in an oasis. Men from the short spill-way valleys of the Superstition Range—the coyotes and wolves of the Spanish Sinks—were easily to be identified by their shifty eyes and loud laughter and handy six-shooters. Moving in a little group rather apart from these than mingling with them, talking and drinking more among them-selves, were men from the Falling Wall—men professedly "ranching" on the upper waters of the Horse, the Turkey and Crazy Woman creeks, tributaries of the Falling Wall river—in point of fact, rustlers between whom and the big cattlemen of the range there always existed a deadly enmity and at times open warfare.

At two card tables placed together in the upper inner corner of the room sat a little party of these Falling Wall men smoking and drinking in leisurely, or, more correctly, in preliminary fashion, for the evening was still young; and inspecting the moving crowd at the bar. At the head of the table sat the ex-cowboy and ex-pugilist, Stormy German, his face usually, and now, reddened with liquor—square-shouldered, square-faced and squat; a man harsh-voiced and terse, of iron endurance and with the stubborn- ness of a mule; next him sat Yankee Robinson, thin-faced and wearing a weatherbeaten yellow beard. And Dutch Henry was there—bony, nervous, eager-eyed, with broken English stories of drought and hardship on the upper Turkey. These three men—brains and resource of several less able but not less unscrupulous companions who preyed on the cattle range north of Sleepy Cat—led the talk and were the most carefully listened to by the men that surrounded them.

It was later that two men entered the room from the hotel office together. The contained, defiant walk of the slightly heavier and taller of the two was characteristic, and without the black beard, deep eyes and the pallor of his face, would almost have identified him as Abe Hawk; while in the emotionless, sandy features of his companion and in his more frank, careless make-up, the widely known ranchman of the Falling Wall, Jim Laramie, was easily recognized.

Hawk, separating from his companion, walked to the right. Gorman hailed him and Hawk paused before the table at which the former prize fighter sat with his friends. Each of these in turn had something effusive to say to Hawk. Hawk listened to everything without a change of countenance—neither smile nor word moved him in the competition to arouse his interest. When all had had their fling of invitation and comment he refused an oft-repeated invitation to sit down: "I might injure your reputations," he said grimly, and moved unconcernedly on.

Van Horn's eyes had not missed the inconspicuous entrance of the two Falling Wall men: "There's the man himself, right now," he exclaimed, looking toward Laramie.

"No better time to talk to him, either, than right now," added Barb Doubleday hoarsely. "Take him back into the office, Harry. When you're through come up to the room."

Van Horn, leaving the bar, intercepted Laramie. Doubleday and Stone, pretending not to observe, saw Van Horn, on the plea of important talk, succeed, after some demur, in inducing Laramie to return with him to the hotel office. Once there and in a quiet corner with two chairs, Van Horn lost no time in opening his subject: "You know as well as I do, Jim, what shape things are in on the North range. It can't go on. Everybody is losing cattle right and left to these rustlers. They've been running Doubleday's steers right down to the railroad camp on the Spider Water—we traced the brands on 'em. You know as well as I do who took 'em."

Laramie listened perfunctorily, his eyes moving part of the time over the room. "Speak for yourself. Harry," he intervened at this juncture. "I know exactly nothing about who took anybody's steers, nor that any were taken."

Van Horn uttered a quick exclamation: "Well, you sure heard about it!"

"In this country a man can hear anything," observed Laramie, not greatly moved. "I've heard there isn't a crooked cattleman north of Sleepy Cat."

Van Horn stared.

"Go on," continued Laramie, looking at the passers-by, "I'm listening."

"Doubleday has sold the eating house and disposed of his property at the Junction—"

"You mean his creditors took it, don't you?"

"Put it any way you like. He's going in for more cattle and we're going to put this range on the map. But—we've got to clean out this Falling Wall bunch first. The big men can't stand it any longer and won't stand it."

"What then?"

"I want you to get in right, on the move, with us, Jim—this is your chance. You're in a tough neighborhood over there. Now I know you're not a rustler."

"No, you don't."

"Yes, I do," averred Van Horn. "But everybody doesn't know you as well as I do. And your name suffers because you don't get along with the cattlemen—Doubleday, Pettigrew and the rest."

"What then?"

"What then?" echoed Van Horn, feeling the up-hill pull. "Why, line up with us against these rustlers. We're going to have a big get-together barbecue this summer and when it's pulled we want you there. You'll have a friend in every man on the range—however some of 'em feel now. They know the stuff you're made of, Jim; they know if you put your hand to your gun with them, you'll stay; and if you do it, they know it's good-by to the rustlers."

Closely as Van Horn, while speaking, watched the effect of his words, it was impossible to gather from Laramie's face the slightest clue as to the impression they were making. Laramie sat quite relaxed, his back to the corner, his legs crossed, listening. He looked straight ahead without so much as blinking. Van Horn, nervous and impatient, scrutinized him: "That's my hand, Jim," he said flatly. "What have you got?"

Laramie paused. After a moment he turned his eyes on his questioner: "No hand. This is not my game."

"Make it your game and your game in this country is made. Doubleday and Dan Pettigrew want you. They're the men that run this country —what do you say?"

"The men that run this country can't run me."

Van Horn, in spite of his assurance, felt the blow. But he put on a front. "What makes you talk that way?" he flared.

"This is the same bunch," continued Laramie evenly, "that sent two different men to get me two years ago—and when I defended myself— had me indicted. That indictment is still hanging for all I know. This is the bunch that owns the district court."

Van Horn made a violent gesture. "What's the use raking up old sores? That's past and gone. That indictment's been quashed long ago."

"This is the bunch," and Laramie spoke even more deliberately; he looked directly, almost disconcertingly at Van Horn himself, "that sent the men to rip off my wire just a while ago. I tracked 'em to Doubleday's and if I'd found Doubleday or you or Stone there that day—if I'd got my eyes on Barb Doubleday that day— you'd've turned the men that pulled that wire over to me or I'd known the reason why.

"Now these same critters and you have the gall

107

to talk to me about joining hands. Hell, I'd quicker join hands with a bunch of rattlesnakes. When that crowd want me let them come and get me. I'm not hiding. They talk about cattle thieves! Why, your outfit would steal the spurs off a rustler's heels. And when men like Hawk and Yankee Robinson and Gorman set up a little ranch with a few head of cows for themselves your bunch blacklists them, refuses 'em work anywhere on the range. Where did Dutch Henry learn to steal? Working for Barb Doubleday; he branded mavericks for him, played dummy for his land entries, swore to false affidavits for him. Now when he turns around and steals the steers he stole for Barb, Barb has the nerve to ask me to round him up at my proper risk and run him out of the country!"

Van Horn rose: "That's the answer, is it?"

Laramie sat still. He looked dead ahead: "What did it sound like?" he asked, as Van Horn stood looking at him.

"Just the same, Jim," muttered Van Horn, "the rustlers have got to go."

Laramie looked across the office: "That all may be," he observed, rising. And he repeated as Van Horn started away: "That all may be. And the men that ripped off my wire have got to put it back. Tell 'em I said so."

Van Horn whirled in a flash of anger: "You talk as if you think I'd ripped it off myself."

"I do think so."

For one instant the two men, confronting, eyed each other, Van Horn's face aflame. Both carried Colt's revolvers in hip holsters; Van Horn's gun slung at his right hip, Laramie's slung at his left. Both were known capable of extremes. Then the critical moment passed. Van Horn broke into a laugh; without a yellow drop in his veins, as far as personal courage went, he had thought twice before attempting to draw where no man had yet drawn successfully. He put out his hand in frank fashion: "Jim, you wrong yourself as much as me when you talk that way."

He made his peace as well as it could be made in words. But when his protestations were ended Laramie only said: "That all may be, Harry. But whoever pulled my wire—and left it in the creek —will put it back—if it's ten years from now."

The two men, Van Horn still talking, made their way back to the billiard hall—Laramie refusing to drink, and halting for brief greetings when assailed by acquaintances. After they parted, Van Horn, as soon as he could escape notice, passed again through the door leading to the hotel office. He walked up the main stairway to the second floor, thence to the third floor and following a corridor stopped in front of the last room, slipped a pass key into the lock and, opening the door, entered and closed it behind him.

Two men sat in the room, Doubleday and Stone. Stone was just out of the barber's chair, his hair parted and faultlessly plastered on both sides across his forehead, and his face shaven and powdered. His forehead drawn in horizontal wrinkles rather than vertical ones, looked lower and flatter because of them. To add to the truculence of his natural expression, he was now somewhat under the influence of liquor and looked perplexed.

Van Horn did not wait to be questioned; he walked directly to the table between the two men and took a cigar from the open box: "Can't do a thing with that fellow," he reported brusquely.

Doubleday, by means of questions, got the story of the fruitless interview. Stone listened. The slow movement of his eyes showed an effort but none of the story escaped him.

Van Horn, answering with some impatience, had lighted one cigar, and bunching half a dozen more in his hand stowed them in an upper waistcoat pocket. Doubleday, between heavy jaws and large teeth, shifted slowly or chewed savagely at a half-burned cigar and bored into Van Horn. Van Horn was in no mood for speculative comment: "You might as well talk to a wildcat," he said. "Pulling that wire has left him sore all over."

Doubleday looked at Stone vindictively: "That was your scheme."

"No more than it was Van Horn's," retorted Stone.

"What's the use squabbling over that now?" demanded Van Horn impatiently. "I'm done, Barb. You've got to go ahead without him."

Doubleday chewed his cigar in silence. Van Horn, restless and humiliated, spoke angrily and thought fast. From time to time he looked quickly at Stone—the foreman was in condition to do anything.

"Look here, Tom," exclaimed Van Horn in low tones, "suppose you go downstairs and give him a talk yourself. What do you say, Barb?" He shot the words at Doubleday like bullets. Doubleday understood and his teeth clicked sharply. He said nothing—only stared at the foreman with his stony gray eyes. Stone drew his revolver from his hip and, breaking the gun, slipped out the cartridges and slipped the five mechanically back into place.

Laramie in the meantime had joined a group of men at the upper end of the bar in the billiard hall —McAlpin, Joe Kitchen's barn boss; Henry Sawdy, the big sporty stock buyer of the town, and the profane but always dependable druggist and rail-road surgeon, Doctor Carpy. With one of these, Sawdy, Harry Tenison from behind the bar was talking. He interrupted himself to hold his hand over toward Laramie: "Been looking for you, scout," he said, in balanced tones. "Been looking for you," he repeated, releasing Laramie's hand and holding up his own. "If you'd failed me today, Jim—"

"I wouldn't fail you, Harry."

"It's well you didn't—champagne, Luke," he added, calling to a solemn-faced bartender who wore a forehead shade.

"No champagne for me, Harry," protested Laramie.

"What are you going to have?" asked the mild-voiced bartender, perfunctorily.

Laramie tilted his hat brim: "Why," he answered, after everybody had contributed advice, "if I've got to take something on this little boy, a little whisky, I suppose, Luke."

"No poison served here tonight, Jim," growled Sawdy, throwing his bloodshot eyes on Laramie.

"I don't want any, anyway, Henry," was the unmoved retort.

Luke, wrapping the cork of the champagne bottle under his long fingers, hesitated. Tenison, looking with his heavily-lidded eyes, did not waver: "You'll drink what I tell you tonight," he maintained coldly. "Open it, Luke."

Laramie stood sidewise while talking, one foot on the rail, his elbow resting on the bar, and with his head turned he was looking back at Tenison, who stood directly opposite him behind the bar. Laramie submitted to the dictation without further protest: "A man will try anything once," was his only comment.

As he uttered the words he felt a point pressed tightly against his right side and what was of greater import, heard the familiar click of a gun hammer.

It was too late to look around; too late to make the slightest move. All that Laramie could get out of the situation, without moving, he read, motionless, in Tenison's eyes, for Tenison was now looking straight at the assailant and with a frozen expression that told Laramie of his peril. The next instant Laramie heard rough words:

"Turn around here, Jim."

They told him all he needed to know, for in them he recognized the voice. In the instant between hearing the words and obeying, a singular change took place in the Falling Wall ranchman's eyes. Looking over at Tenison his eyes had been keen and clear. Slowly and with a faint smile he turned his head. When his eyes met those of Tom Stone, who confronted him pressing the muzzle of a cocked Colt's forty-five gun against his stomach, they were soft and glazed. Laramie had changed in an instant from a man that had not tasted liquor to a man half tipsy.

It was a feint, but a feint made with an accurate understanding of a dangerous enemy.

CHAPTER 10

LARAMIE COUNTS FIVE

There was not a chance of escape. Laramie's left arm was resting on the bar. Under the overhang, Stone, as he faced Laramie, now pressed the gun with his right arm, into Laramie's stomach. For

Laramie to attempt to knock it away with his own right hand would be to take an almost certainly fatal chance; while for any friend of his to touch Stone or shoot him would mean certain death to Laramie. Feeling that he had his enemy dead to rights, Stone baited him:

"Laramie," he began, fixing his eyes on those of his victim, "there's some men's lived in this country too long."

The words carried the irritable nasal tone familiar to Stone's acquaintances. Laramie's eyes merely brightened a little with the effort to reply: "Tom," he declared, with just enough of hesitation to play the game, "that's the first thing my wife said yes'day morning."

Stone stared: "When," he demanded, "did you get married?"

"Put up your gun. I'll tell you about it."

Stone only grinned: "I can hear pretty well, right now."

"If you want to see her picture, Tom, uncock your gun."

"Not a little bit. I've got you right."

Laramie smiled: "Sure, Tom, but there's plenty of time; put down the hammer." Stone, without moving his gun, did silently lower the hammer. Laramie counted one. Then he began to describe his trick bride. Stone cut him off. He cocked his gun again: "Show me her picture," he snarled.

Tenison took the instant to lean impressively

across the bar. He pointed a long finger at Stone: "Tom," he said, with measured emphasis, "no man can pull a gun here tonight and get away with it. That'll be enough."

Stone scowled: "Harry, this scout is through; nobody wants him any longer in this country," he said.

"Take your quarrel somewhere else tonight—this is my celebration—do you get me, Tom?"

Under the implied threat of the determined gambler the hammer of Stone's gun came down: "I c'n get along with any man that'll do what's right," asserted Stone, trying to keep his head clear. "Laramie won't."

"Why, Tom!" expostulated Laramie, reproach-fully.

The revolver clicked; the hammer was up again.

"Y' won't do what's right, will y', Laramie?" demanded Stone thickly.

There were probably fifty men in the room. As if by instinct each of them already knew on what a slender thread one man's life hung. Hawk, the quickest and surest of Laramie's friends, stood ten paces away, up the bar, but the silence was such that he could hear every deliberate word. Glasses, half-emptied, had been set noiselessly down, discussions had ceased, every eye was centered on two men and every ear strained. A few spectators tiptoed out into the office. Others that tried to pass through the swinging front-door screen into the street found a crowd already peering intently in through the open baize.

"Tom," resumed Laramie, in measured serious-ness, "it's not you 'n' me can't get on—it's men here has made trouble 'tween you and me, Tom. You 'n' me rode this range when we didn't have but one blanket atween us—didn't we, Tom?" he demanded in loud tones.

Stone, in drunken irresolution, uncocked his gun but held it steady. "That's all right, Laramie," he growled.

"Did we quarrel then?" demanded Laramie, boisterously. "I'm asking you, Tom, did you 'n' me quarrel then?"

"When a man can't turn in with Harry Van Horn an' Barb Doubleday," grumbled Stone, "it's time for him to quit this country." His revolver clicked again; the hammer went up.

Laramie regarded him with sobering amaze-ment: "Who told you I wouldn't turn in with Barb Doubleday?" he exclaimed loudly. "Who told you that?"

"Harry Van Horn told me."

Tenison tried to interpose. "You shut up, Tenison," was the answering growl from Stone. But Tenison stuck to it till the hammer came down. It was only for a moment—the next instant a score of breathless men heard the click of the gun as it was cocked again.

"Why," demanded Laramie, more cool-headed

116

than his friends, drawn-faced and tense about him, cooler far than his maudlin words implied, and still fighting for a forlorn chance, "why didn't Harry Van Horn tell me to turn in with a friend— why didn't he tell me to turn in with you, Tom Stone—with a man I rode and bunked with? Why did they make you their scapegoat, Tom? You've got me all right; I know that. But what about you? You can't get ten feet. Abe Hawk's right back of you, waitin' for you now. They'd dump us into the same hole, Tom. You don't want to go into the same hole with me, do you? Let's talk it over."

The rambling plea sounded so reasonable it won a brief reprieve from Stone.

"Don't uncock your gun till I'm through, Tom," urged Laramie. "I don't want to take any advantage at all of an old pardner. Keep it cocked but listen.

"I don't want to talk with Van Horn," Laramie went on, "not even with Barb Doubleday, fine a man as he might be—I ain't 'a' sayin', Tom. But I don't want to talk to him. I want to talk to you. Just you and me, Tom—talkin' it over together. Don't be goat for nobody, Tom. What?"

The drunken foreman's brow contracted in irresolute perplexity: "What do you say?" urged Laramie. Vacillating, Stone let down the hammer to talk it over. It went up again almost instantly. There may in that last brief instant have flashed across his muddled consciousness a realization of his fatal mistake; perhaps he saw in the wicked flash of Laramie's glazed eyes a warning of blunder.

Knowing that mountain men carry only five cartridges in their revolvers, leaving the hammer for safety on an empty chamber, Laramie had parleyed with Stone only long enough to suit his own purpose.

His right arm shot out at Stone's jaw. As his fist reached it, the gun against his stomach snapped viciously. But the hammer, already raised six times, came down on the sixth and empty chamber. It was the chance Laramie had played for. Stone sank like an ox. As he went down his head struck the foot-rail. He lay stunned.

Men drew long breaths. McAlpin, stooping in a flash, wrenched Stone's revolver from his hand and with a grin, laid it on the bar. Laramie, watching Stone coldly, did not move. His left foot still rested on the rail, his left arm on the bar. But without taking his eyes off the prostrate man he in some way saw the white-faced bartender peering over in amazement at the fallen foreman:

"It seems to take you a good while, Luke," protested Laramie, mildly, "to open that bottle."

CHAPTER 11

A Duel with Kate

When the eating-house at the Junction was closed, Harry Tenison sent for Belle and offered her the position of housekeeper at the Mountain House. This Belle declined. She had long had in her head the idea of taking a place and serving meals on her own hook, as she expressed it. Her instinct for independence, always strong, had not only prevented her getting married but made her restive under orders. She was stubborn—her enemies called her abusive names and her best friends admitted that she was sometimes difficult. At Sleepy Cat she took a cottage in lower Main Street. She had some furniture, and having a little money saved and a little borrowed from McAlpin, Belle bought a few new pieces, including a folding bed secured at a bargain, and opened her doors for business. And whatever her faults of temperament, Belle could cook.

Kitchen's barn was headquarters for the small ranchers from the north and for the Falling Wall men, and McAlpin soon had a trade seeking Belle's place. The cottage itself faced the side street, but a little shop annex opened on Main. In this and in the cottage dining-room Belle served her meals. Very soon, however, she made trouble for McAlpin. It developed that she would not serve anybody she did not like and as her fancy was capricious she gave most of McAlpin's following the cold shoulder. He spent much time in the beginning, hot-footing it, as Belle termed it, between the barn and the cottage trying to straighten things out. In the end he gave over and told Belle she could starve if she wanted to. Whereupon she said tartly that she did want to; and McAlpin snatching off his baseball cap, as he did when greatly moved, and twirling it in his hand asked for his money—which he failed to get.

Yet one man among the hardy friends of the barn boss did find favor at the cottage and he the last whom McAlpin would have picked for a likely favorite. This was Jim Laramie. Laramie soon became a regular customer of Belle's and his friends naturally followed him.

The closing out of her father's interests at the Junction was without regret for Kate, since it sent her up to where she wanted to be—at the ranch. For some time after establishing herself there she rarely came into Sleepy Cat. Then as the novelty wore off and small wants made themselves felt, she rode oftener to town—mail and shopping and marketing soon established for her a regular round and when she did ride to Sleepy Cat she nearly always saw Belle; sometimes she lunched with her. Belle was a stickler in her home for neatness, even though the cyclone might have been supposed to harden her to dust.

More than this, Belle knew what was going on—she had the news. Little, in the daily round of the town and its wide territory, got by the modest scrim curtains of Belle's place; she became Kate's reporter. Men would say this was the principal attraction for Kate, and that the cooking came second—not so. The real reason Belle got the gossip of the country was because her customers were men. Kate was probably the only woman, certainly almost the only one, among her patrons. Belle explained this by saying that none of the rest of the ranchwomen would spend their money for lunch. The truth really was that Belle did not like women, anyway—Kate she tolerated because she did like her.

It was the day after Tenison's big celebration that Kate rode into town for the mail, and after some shopping walked down to Belle's for lunch. Belle was at the butcher shop across the street, telephoning. She came in after a moment.

"It seems to me you spend a good deal of time with that butcher," said Kate, significantly.

"Oh, no, he's got a club foot. Has Harry Van Horn been shining up to you?"

Kate was taken aback, but she had been to blame for giving Belle an opening and could only enter a confused denial.

"The first serious symptom," said Belle,

garrulously, "will be, he'll have a headache; he'll ask for cold cloths on his forehead. When that works pretty well he'll tell you your hair is like his sister's and some evening he'll ask you to take it down. He asked me one night to take mine down. I handed him my wig. Say! he was the most surprised man in Sleepy Cat. I've been trying for an hour to get that rascally milkman on the telephone—there's not a drop of cream in the house. Well, how are you? Was Tom Stone home when you left?"

One question followed another. Kate had not only not seen the ranch foreman—she had not heard of the excitement of the night before. From Belle she got the details of Stone's attempt to kill Laramie. The story lost nothing in Belle's hands. She had heard all versions and was pretty good at story telling herself.

"After McAlpin picked up Stone's gun Laramie told him to turn it over to Luke; and he told Luke not to give it back to Stone till this morning—I guess they hid Stone last night." She wound up with an abusive fling at Doubleday's foreman. "What do you keep such a beastly critter around for?" she asked, looking at Kate hard for an answer.

Humiliated at the recital, Kate thought it time to say something herself: "Why do you ask me a question like that?"'

Belle arched her eyebrows belligerently. "Why shouldn't I?" she demanded. And bridling with further criticism of Stone and by implication of those that employed him, she let fly again.

Kate tried to ignore her outburst: "You know perfectly well," she said firmly, "I have nothing to say about the ranch or how it is run, or who runs it. And I don't care to listen to any comments on that subject."

"If you don't like my comments you needn't come here to listen to them," retorted Belle, flaming.

The two were standing at the cook stove.

"While I am here," returned Kate with tart dignity, "please don't abuse me."

"I say what I please to anybody if it's right," exclaimed Belle rudely.

"You'll be ashamed of yourself when you cool off," Kate returned, pointing to the broiler: "You don't expect me to eat all that meat, do you?"

Belle answered with an offended dignity of her own: "I expect Jim Laramie to eat the biggest part of it. And there he comes now!"

The front door opened, in fact, while she was speaking; Kate stood with her back to it and though by turning she could have peeped through the curtained archway, she would not have looked for a million dollars. If Belle wanted her revenge she had it at that moment. Kate could not sink through the floor to escape, but how she wanted to! She did step quickly aside hoping she had not been seen, and retired to the farthest corner of the kitchen. Belle's mouth, before the stove, set grimly and with her left hand she gave her wig the vicious punch she used when wrought up. Kate motioned to her frantically. Belle regarded her coldly but did come closer and Kate caught at her sleeve: "For heaven's sake," she begged in a whisper, "don't let him know I'm here."

Kate eyed her anxiously. Belle's face was hard, and quick, firm steps were coming from the front door.

"Hello, Belle!" was the greeting. Had they been Kate's death message the words could not have frightened her more. She knew, too well, the voice.

"You didn't get my message," were the next words flung through the archway.

"I got it," answered Belle, going forward and providentially stopping Laramie before he reached the curtains.

"Sit down right there," she added, pointing to a table at the rear of the lunch-room. "I hurried all I could but that rascally milkman hasn't been here yet and there's no cream for your coffee. Your dinner's most ready though."

She started back to the kitchen.

"Not enough for two, is there?" asked Laramie.

"Who's coming?" demanded Belle, stopping in her tracks.

"Belle, you're suspicious as a cattleman. Nobody's coming, but I'm hungry."

While he continued his banter she served him

and attempted to serve Kate behind the curtains. By persistent, almost despairing pantomime, Kate dissuaded her from this. But at that moment the front door opened again, a brisk greeting was called out and a heavy tread crossed the uneven floor of the outer room.

"John Lefever!" Laramie got up to welcome the big deputy marshal. "Just in time. Take off your manners and sit down."

A bubbling laugh greeted the sally: "Jim, I just can't do it."

"Oh, yes, you'll eat with me. Where you from?"

"Bear Dance; and Medicine Bend on the next train. Heard you were in town and dropped off for just one hour. Say, this is more like life's fitful fever to set eyes on you. Heard you were threatened last night with appendicitis. How about it?" and John bubbled over again. In the next breath he greeted Belle as gaily. Laramie asked for another plate and Lefever promptly resumed: "You look kind of down in the mouth, Jim. What's the matter with you?"

"Nothing's the matter with me."

Lefever shrugged his shoulders: "You're a kind of low-spirited Indian, anyway. What you doing up in the Falling Wall?"

"Nothing."

"Always nothing," repeated Lefever.

"Better come up," suggested Laramie. "What are you doing?"

Lefever's eyes expanded with cheer, but his voice choked with emotion: "Doing? Rusting!"

"That doesn't sound much like 'life's fitful fever.'"

John glared at his companion: "Life's fitful *fever!* Why, this is only a passing flash! How about it when you can't raise even a normal temperature? Fever? I haven't felt so much as a gentle perspiration for months! The rust is eating into my finger tips," he declared with violence. "I'm a fat man. A fat man must have action,"—his voice fell—"else he gets fatter. I've got to do something. Once or twice I've come pretty near having to go to work."

Laramie's expression may have been skeptical; at all events John pointed a corroborating finger at him: "You don't believe it! Just the same," he added, moodily, "it's straight."

"What's de Spain doing, John?"

The tone of the answer bordered on the morose: "Running a nursery at Medicine Bend."

"Trees?"

"Trees!" John snortingly invoked the hottest place he could think of. "Trees? Babies! Jim," he exclaimed, "I'm no family man—are you?"

"You like Medicine Bend, don't you?"

"Too many people there." John settled gloomily back. Then with wide-open eyes he started suddenly forward: "Give me a gun, Jim," he said wildly, "a gun and a horse."

"And a north wind!" exclaimed Laramie.

"And a high country," cried Lefever with flashing eyes, "a country where you can't see a damned thing in any direction for a hundred and fifty miles!"

Though talking vigorously he was eating, without protest from Laramie, everything in sight. Kate could not help listening; Lefever's high spirits were contagious.

"Jim," came next between mouthfuls. "What was that story about you being up at the Junction the day I wanted you to serve those papers on old Barb Doubleday?"

"I went up there that day because I had business of a different kind with Barb."

"About the wire ripping, yes. But I heard you got sewed up by a skirt and didn't talk wire to Barb at all."

"No more of that, John."

"What was there to it?"

"I guess there was."

"A ride or something—what?"

"Something, John."

"Thunder! It must have been the ride. I had deputy marshalship all lined up for you if that hadn't happened. And believe me, boy, a deputy marshalship isn't lying around loose every day!"

Kate listened keenly for Laramie's comment:

"The ride was worth the price, John," was all he said.

"Some skirt, eh?"

Laramie squirmed and with an expletive protested: "Hang it, John—"

"No matter, no matter. I'll get it all from Belle some day. And after you get through with your wire thieves we'll tell the story of your brief romance—"

"Over my grave."

"Right, Jim—over your grave."

"John," Laramie ran on, "do you remember that song Tommie Meggeson used to sing on the round-up—a pretty little thing. It had one good line in it: 'Death comes but once, and then, sometimes—too late.' "

Belle appeared with a vegetable: "It won't keep you waiting an awful while if things go on the way they're going now," she put in grimly.

"That was a good song," mused Laramie, "a good old song." But he heard a slight sound in the kitchen and his eyes were turned toward the archway.

"Just the same that song won't keep you from getting killed," persisted Belle.

"Even that would beat appendicitis clean to death, Belle," maintained Laramie, still listening.

"You've got lots of time," he added, as Lefever looked at his watch.

"I haven't," exclaimed his companion. "I've got to send a message. Come over to the train."

"I've got to write a couple of letters."

"Come over to the station and write your letters."

Laramie shook his head: "I couldn't even get to the station by one o'clock. Every man in Main Street wants to talk about Tom Stone. You'd think I had a million friends among the cattlemen this morning."

"I heard old Barb Doubleday is grinning like a hangman today."

"If Belle's got some ink I'll write my letters right here."

Kate's spirits, which had risen at the hope of being so luckily rid of one who might prove troublesome, fell at his refusal to leave. John urged, but Laramie only asked Belle again for the ink. Lefever tried to coax Belle to go to the train with him. Belle would do almost any fool thing —as John bluntly averred—but this time she must have had pity on Kate and would not leave her unprotected. Lefever went his way. From a shelf near where Kate, with clasped hands, sat in silence Belle took paper and ink in to Laramie and began to clear the table.

At this unlucky moment the front door was opened swiftly and a boy from the butcher shop stuck his head inside.

"Miss Shockley," he called, "the milkman is on the 'phone now, if you want him." Closing the door he ran back across the street. With a sense of her wrongs keen upon her, Belle, forgetting her charge in the kitchen, hurried after him.

Even then, Kate hoped that by keeping deathly

still she might escape an unpleasant meeting. She never breathed more carefully in her life, yet she was doomed. She heard Laramie's chair pushed back and heard his footsteps. She could not be sure which way he was walking, but she thought only of flight. As stealthily and rapidly as possible, she started for the back door. Without looking around she felt as if he had come to the archway and was looking at her. With courage and resolve, she grasped the knob to open the door. It was locked. She fumbled with the key. Behind her, silence. She locked and unlocked the door more than once, and with a fast-dying hope, for the wretched door would *not* open. Flushed with annoyance, she turned around only to see Laramie standing precisely where she had imagined him.

They faced each other. Kate could not have found a word to say had her life depended on it. Laramie held in his left hand an ink bottle, in his right a pen. He, too, seemed surprised but he recovered himself: "You are certainly unlucky with doors," he said. "If you'll tell me where Belle keeps her ink, I'll tell you how to open that," he added calmly.

Kate stiffened and shrugged her shoulders the least bit: "I haven't any idea where Belle keeps the ink," she replied, clearing her throat of its huskiness.

He pointed to beyond where she stood: "I think the ink supply is on that shelf; she gave me an empty bottle. Should you mind handing me one with ink in it?"

Kate turned to the shelf: "There seem to be two kinds here," she said as coldly as possible.

"Any bottle with a hole in the top will do," he suggested. "This one," he held the bottle up in his hand and looked at it, "seems to have a hole top and bottom. Give me the blue ink, will you?"

"I am sure I don't know which is which. Perhaps you had better help yourself," Kate said icily.

"Thank you. But I'll show you how to open the door first."

"Don't trouble yourself."

"No trouble at all." He walked to the door, explaining as he took hold of the knob: "The door wasn't locked, but the catch held the latch. I could tell that from the way you handled it. You locked it, yourself—"

Kate could not hide her resentment: "It wouldn't open when I first took hold of it," she declared hastily. "I tried it before I touched the key."

"That's what I'm explaining. When you did take hold of the key you locked the door with the dead bolt and then you couldn't open it; so you unlocked it and tried it again. After that you worked so fast I lost track." He pointed to the back of the rim lock: "The catch was on." And pushing down the catch, he turned the knob and opened the door.

Kate was thoroughly incensed: "You are doubtless better acquainted here than I am."

"To tell the truth, I have to be acquainted with rooms I go into. If *I* ever tried to get through a door and failed, it might not be pleasant for me. And there's a board fence, six feet high, all around this yard, so unless you're a good climber you couldn't have got out anyway."

Kate felt she looked very silly, standing staring at him, and perhaps looking frightened—as she really was—for he went on as if he were explaining to a child: "I'm not permitted to tell you, but I'm going to—"

"Don't bother, please—"

"Yes, I'd rather: There is a way to get out without climbing the fence; a loose board I'll show you sometime—but you must handle yourself fast to make your get-away."

"I never expect," she said contemptuously, "to have to make a get-away."

"Then I was wrong," he returned frankly, "for I kind of thought you were trying to make one a minute ago."

His composure irritated Kate: "You are very much mistaken," she declared with spirit in her words, for she saw—indeed knew—how persistent he was. "I was only trying to leave for home quietly and quickly."

His eyes were a study in silent laughter: "That's all I've ever claimed to be doing, any time in my life."

"But I can just as well leave by the front door —which, perhaps," retorted Kate, "you haven't always been able to do."

"Before you go"—he was standing directly in the archway, so she had to listen—"tell me about things at the Junction; I hear the lunch-room was closed up a while ago."

"It was. But"—Kate thought the time for explanation had come—"I was not working at the eating-house when you came in there. I am Kate Doubleday and I wanted to save my father that day and I'm not a bit sorry for it."

"I suppose, then, I ought to speak out, too. I was sure you were Kate Doubleday soon after I got into the lunch-room that day and I'm not a bit sorry for it. And I knew pretty soon you were trying to save your father. And I helped you."

"Oh—" Kate suppressed an incredulous exclamation.

"Believe it or not as you like, I helped you. And I'm not a bit sorry for it. Though he is no friend of mine, you have been, from that day on; and if you ever give me a chance I'll prove it. The worst thing you did was to go back on your word—"

"My word was not freely given," Kate was speaking furiously.

"It shouldn't have been given at all, then. But it's all right. Will you be friends with me?"

"No man that speaks of my father as you spoke of him a moment ago can be my friend."

"It was Lefever spoke of your father. I couldn't shut him off. Of course he didn't know you were here. I did know after I'd been here awhile. I heard you whisper. That's why I asked for the ink—I had no letters to write. There's a lot of hard feeling in this country right now. Every man in it has his friends and enemies. You mustn't take it seriously when you hear hard words—I don't; and I hear plenty. Hadn't you and I better be friends to begin with, anyway?"

"No," she exclaimed angrily. "Please let me pass."

He stepped promptly aside: "I never dreamed of doing anything less."

Kate started rapidly for the front door. Whom should she run into just as she opened it but Belle coming back from her wretched telephoning and with a bottle of cream! Kate inwardly blamed her for all her trouble, and she was on edge, besides: "Where you going?" demanded Belle.

"Home," answered Kate, shortly.

"Home? You haven't had your lunch."

"I don't want any."

Belle caught Kate's arm: "Now you just hold on. What's the matter? Is it Laramie?" Belle must have read her face for she answered nothing, only tried to get away. "But, child!" she exclaimed. "Where's your coat—wait till I bring it—and your gloves!" Kate paused at the door. In a minute Belle came running back: "He's gone, absolutely. There isn't a soul anywhere about. Now you

134

shan't go till you take a cup of coffee. Here's the cream—he left it at the wrong door, the stupid!"

Kate could not get away. And Belle had told the truth: Laramie was gone.

CHAPTER 12

THE BARBECUE

Whatever the shortcomings of the American frontier code there never was a time in its history when a man could violate the principles of fair play and keep public opinion on his side. In this instance, Stone's conduct reacted unfavorably on the cattlemen. The townspeople that made money out of the trade of the big ranches always stood up for the cattlemen, but they were put most unpleasantly on the defensive by the incident. Even had Stone's attempt on Laramie's life succeeded it would have been easier, for the partisans, to handle than the failure it proved. As a *fait accompli* it would have been regretted, but forgotten; as a failure it settled nothing.

Among the few townspeople that sturdily retained independence of opinion on all matters, none stood higher than the surgeon, Doctor Carpy. And encountering Doubleday in the street shortly after the Stone incident, he took it on himself to talk to him.

The doctor had his office at his home, but back of the prescription case in his little drug store— no bigger than a minute—he had a small room for emergency consultations. To this he invited Doubleday, and, having ushered him in, seated him and closed the door, Carpy sat down: "There's few men, Barb, in this country," the doctor began, "that dare talk to you the way you ought to be talked to; of them few, I'm probably the only one that would take the trouble. Your enemies won't talk and everybody friendly with you is afraid of you. You've got so much property and stuff here they're plumb afraid of you. I'm a poor man, Barb—don't never expect to be anything else, and I don't give a hang for anybody," averred the erratic surgeon, "and nobody gives a hang for me."

Doubleday, chewing the stub of a cigar, eyed his medical adviser with an unsympathetic stare, but this in no way disturbed the self-appointed critic. "For a long time now, Barb," he continued, "you've been in the nastiest kind of a fight on Jim Laramie. You've tried to run him off the range and you tried to beat him out of his land and you've tried to break him. He's got the best land in the Falling Wall and he's in your way. One time his wire is all pulled off his fence. Another time your foreman pokes a gun into his stomach."

Doubleday flared up: "Am I the only man that Laramie's got differences with? When his fence is tore down, am I to blame? Am I to blame for every drink Tom Stone takes? What are you talking about?" demanded Doubleday with violence.

The doctor could not have been calmer had he been reaching at the critical moment of an operation for Doubleday's appendix. "Be patient a minute; be ca'm, Barb; I'll tell you what I'm talking about. I don't know who cut his wire. I don't know who done it and I won't undertake to say, but what I do say to you, Barb, and I say it hard, you're making a big mistake on this man, and if you don't slow up it'll cost you your life yet."

Doubleday was grimly silent. "I've known Jim Laramie," Carpy went on, "since he was a boy. He's stubborn as a broncho if you try to ride him. He's the easiest man in the world to get along with if you make a friend of him. No matter what's said of Jim Laramie there ain't a crooked hair in his head; but he's no angel and when his patience quits—look out. What I'm going to tell you now, Barb, is on the square. It can't go no further. I tell you because you ought to know. A while back, just after this wire pulling, Jim Laramie walked into this room, shut the door and locked it and sat down right where you're sittin' now. He told me the wire story; he told me he was through. He'd tracked the men to your ranch and was going to square accounts with you and Stone and Van Horn. He was on his way to the Junction and he told me he might not come back and wanted to tell me how to dispose of his property. He was after you and he meant, before he fell down, to get some or all of you. He asked me where you were, because he heard I knew. I did know but I didn't tell him. I lied, Barb. I told him the mines, but I knew you were at the Junction. He started for the mines. What happened to turn him off your trail I never yet learned. I never asked.

"Now you saw, or you heard anyway, what happened when Stone tried to kill him the other night. That man never can get Laramie. And don't depend on Stone and Van Horn to play you fair, for if they had to save their hides, Barb, they'd sell you. My advice is this: Put back Laramie's wire. Let the cattlemen, you and Pettigrew to lead 'em, do it to clear their own names. Say you know nothing about it, but it was a dirty trick, and tell this town that cattlemen fight but they fight fair. It'll do more to set you right and to set everything else right on the range than anything else you could possibly do. And don't make a mistake. Laramie'll follow that wire pulling for years but what he'll get the man that did it. I know him. He's got a memory like an Indian."

Like all well-meaning and candid friends, the doctor found himself at once in for a deal of angry abuse, but, as he explained, he had taken so much abuse from patients at various periods of his career—and abuse fully justified—that nothing Barb could add, deserved or undeserved, to the volume would move him: "As our old governor

138

back in Wisconsin said, Barb, 'I seen my duty and I done it,' " was the doctor's only retort to Doubleday's wrath. "Now if you're in a hurry, Barb, don't let me keep you, not a minute. I had my say and if there's anything pressing you down street go to it."

But angry as Doubleday appeared, Carpy had given him something to think about. Consultations were held—by precisely whom, no one could say, but in them there was dissension. Van Horn vehemently opposed any further overtures to Laramie and he was vastly put out at being overruled. While the discussions were going on, he talked in a veiled but emphatic way to Kate about the queer way her father was acting. Van Horn would shake his head with violent emphasis at the way things were going. But when Kate poured oil on the waters of his discontent, Van Horn was always responsive and stayed to supper or for the evening, if he were asked—and Kate was alone. On the gentler side, however, he could make no headway. When he tried headaches for sympathy, Kate was stony hearted. When he asked her one day at the spring to take down her hair, she told him she wore a wig. He looked at her amazed.

And in spite of his objections to placating Laramie a decision very unpalatable to him was reached. Pettigrew, as spokesman, approached Laramie and insisted, in order to allay bad feel-ing, on replacing the barb wire. When Laramie declared the wire must be put back by the men that had cut it, there was naturally an *impasse*, but Tenison and Carpy aided jointly by the representations of Lefever and Sawdy, induced Laramie to forego his punitive attitude and accept the amende as offered. This, as the doctor had predicted, put a pleasanter face on the tangled affairs of the range. And to strike while their iron was hot, and to keep it hot, the cattlemen announced a big Fourth of July celebration, at which old scores should be forgotten and friends and enemies meet in good-fellowship. The place for it, after much talk, was fixed at Doubleday's ranch. The saloon-keepers of Sleepy Cat, except Tenison, fought this, but they lost out.

Since her own home was to be the scene of the celebration, Kate took a particular interest in the undertaking. She made herself, in a way, hostess and her father gave her free rein. The eager crowd that responded to the public invitation found awaiting them, as they picturesquely rode in twos and threes and groups up the creek to the ranch house, all the "fixin's" for a rousing celebration. Men came for as much as fifty miles and some of them by trails and over passes Kate had never even heard of. There were cattlemen, cowboys, sheepmen, little ranchers—all the conflicting elements of the country, besides a crowd from Sleepy Cat with the band, and all the town loafers that could possibly secure conveyance.

There was for these latter worthies the attraction of a free feed—for they knew the prodigality of cattlemen; but there was also the underlying hope that where so discordant elements were assembled a fight *might* occur; and nobody wanted to miss a fight. The principals necessary for a serious affair were present. The fact that all were armed was not significant, merely prudent. Men careless on this point were no longer attending celebrations of any sort around Sleepy Cat.

From the Falling Wall came the rustlers, every one of them except Doubleday's old foreman, Abe Hawk, who scorned all pretense of compromise. He advised Laramie not to go near the celebration. When Laramie intimated he might go, Abe was greatly incensed. A master of bitter sarcasm, he trained his batteries on his sandy-haired friend and these failing he warned him he would be in serious danger. He intimated that the scheme was to get the rustlers all together and finish them in a bunch. In which event, one as hated as Laramie could hardly hope to escape unmolested. But Laramie persisted in his resolve to go, and he went.

Doctor Carpy made it a point to go. He was usually needed professionally at Fourth of July celebrations. But on this occasion he was, in matter of fact, a sort of sponsor for the whole affair and he brought Sawdy, Lefever and Tenison along. The four drove out in the smartest wagon and behind the best team in the Kitchen barn,

Kitchen with them and McAlpin driving.

By noon the big end of the crowd had arrived. The barbecue tables were set out under the trees along the creek. The roasting itself was in the skilled hand of John Frying Pan and before one o'clock he was ready to serve.

Doubleday had told Kate, when arranging for the tables, that his particular friends would sit at his table, and she was on her way down to the creek to ask him how many there would be in the party when whom should she find him talking with, of all men, but Laramie, who had just ridden over from the Falling Wall.

Before Kate could retreat, her father had seen her. He called her over. To her astonishment he insisted on introducing her to his friend, Jim Laramie, of whom he was making as much as it was possible to make of a wholly undemonstrative man.

The band not far away was playing full tilt. Kate wished they could have made even more noise to hide her confusion, but there was nothing except to face the situation, much as it surprised her. Laramie, fortunately, seemed indisposed to say anything. He spent most of his time listening. Kate, being far from animated, her father was left to do the honors. And on such rare occasions as Barb was communicative, he was quite capable of good-fellowship.

Laramie, however, seemingly under some restraint, soon made excuses and left to join the crowd.

Some of the little ranchmen had brought their wives along. A few of these women had their babies with them, and Kate returned to the house, where she made the mothers comfortable. There, her father afterwards ran across her. He stopped as he came up: "You remember that man I introduced you to—Laramie?"

"Very well," assented Kate, wondering.

"Treat him well at dinner."

"But I'm going to eat here at the house."

He shook his head: "You eat at the creek at my table."

She had no choice but to obey. When she returned to the pits the stones had been removed and John Frying Pan, with a pair of Sleepy Cat ice tongs, was lifting out the first big chunks of roasted meat. The crowd, being called, ran for the creek whooping and yelling, and while Kate watched John and his helpers dish up the meat, the guests—nearly all men—seated themselves pell mell at the long benches. It was a noisy assemblage, overflowing with good-nature, and when Kate, very trim in corduroy, appeared again at the tables the demonstrative ones rose and led in a burst of cheers. Kate enjoyed it but when they began calling for a speech, she ran to join her father. She found him and old man Pettigrew at the table, Laramie calmly seated with them and the fourth place waiting for her.

Van Horn, as host to other cattlemen and guests,

presided at the next table. Unluckily, where he sat, he could see Laramie opposite Kate. But if he was discomfited, the group at the next table below, where Doctor Carpy presided, flanked by Lefever, Sawdy, Kitchen and McAlpin, was correspondingly elated at the spectacle of the Falling Wall and the Crazy Woman sitting in harmony.

Despite the unpleasant stories Kate had heard about him she found nothing to complain of in Laramie's manners. But he was, she told herself, on his good behavior, and under the circumstances would naturally try to appear at his best. Little as she relished her assignment of making things pleasant for him, the friendly spirit of the occasion to some extent infected her, and soon she found it not difficult to help along with small talk and make the queer combination at the table go.

There was really no great need for her to work hard in this way—both her father and Pettigrew were very lively. Laramie seemed a bit dazed at being set up with such honors in the house of his enemies. But though he did not volunteer much, when Kate said anything that afforded a chance for comment, he improved it.

The talk went a good deal to cattle, and range matters, but Pettigrew, a crafty fellow, told good stories about men that everybody in and out of Sleepy Cat knew, and appealed frequently to Laramie for confirmation or a laugh. Some of the laughs he got were a little dry but they were not ill-natured, and Kate enjoyed the rough humor. The two cattlemen finished their dinner, and without ceremony got up to see how the crowd was being served, leaving Kate with Laramie. "How do you like old Pettigrew?" was the first thing Laramie asked as the bearded cattleman moved away with her father.

"The only thing I don't like about him," answered Kate candidly, "is his eyes."

She was looking at Laramie as she spoke.

"You're a good observer," he said.

"How so?"

"A man's eyes are all there is to him. You don't mind if I smoke?"

"Not a bit."

He drew a sack of tobacco from a breast pocket.

"Not going to run away, are you?" He was fishing for cigarette paper when he asked. He spoke as if he had no special interest in the matter, yet the question startled her. Kate had not made a move to go, but she *was* thinking, when the question came, of how she might manage to escape. She flushed a little at being anticipated in her intention —just enough perhaps to let him see he had caught her, not to say irritated her. As luck would have it, Van Horn, who had risen, sauntered towards them. Kate was glad just then to see him: "I hope you got enough to eat," she said as he approached.

He seemed stiff—Kate did not realize what he

was put out about. He made some answer and turned to Laramie. She felt at once the friction between the two men, not from anything she had reason to suspect or know—for she knew then nothing whatever of their personal relations. Nor was it from anything said; for an instant neither man spoke. Instinct must have made her conscious for as soon as Van Horn looked at Laramie she felt the tension: "Well, Jim, where'd you blow from?" demanded Van Horn after a pause.

Laramie was making ready to smoke. He was in no haste to answer, nor did he look at Van Horn, but continued, cowboy fashion, rolling his cigarette in the finger-tips of one hand, his other hand resting on his hip: "I didn't blow," he retorted.

"How'd you get here?" asked Van Horn.

"I was invited."

Van Horn laughed significantly. While Kate would rather have been out of it, she thought it proper, since she was in it, to say something herself: "I didn't suppose anybody needed a special invitation for a Fourth of July celebration," she interposed. "The town has been covered for two weeks with bills inviting everybody."

Van Horn laughed again. "It wasn't you invited him, eh?" he demanded of Kate. The thing was said so unpleasantly she would have retorted on impulse, but Laramie took any possible words out of her mouth.

"Why don't you ask me who invited me? Barb

Doubleday invited me. That's enough, isn't it? And Pettigrew invited me. And," he added, completing his cigarette in leisurely fashion, "while that wouldn't be any particular inducement—you invited me."

Van Horn stared: "How do you make that out?" he asked quickly.

"You asked me to take in this barbecue when you tried to get me to line up with you at the Mountain House."

Van Horn took alarm: "That was put up to you in confidence," he said angrily.

"So was the barbecue," responded Laramie. "I wouldn't take in the first proposition, so I'm enjoying the second." He turned from Van Horn, and, ignoring him, spoke to Kate: "You remember you said you were going to show me your ponies."

It was Kate's turn to stare: "You must be mistaken."

He did not press the subject: "Perhaps you've forgotten," was all he said.

"When or where did I ever say that?" Kate asked, resenting the intimation.

He looked down, then looking up his eyes rested on Kate's. He was not disturbed: "Is that a challenge?" he asked.

"If you wish to make it one," she returned coolly.

"The 'where' was one day at Sleepy Cat Junction, the 'when' was the day we rode up the Falling Wall river."

"Oh," she exclaimed, collecting herself, "I *had* forgotten."

"Do you remember now?" he asked; and she thought there was resentment in the question. "If you don't," he added, "we'll let it go."

"Why, I suppose I must have said something like that. Anyway," she added, "we'll go see them to make sure I've kept a promise. Come, Mr. Van Horn," she suggested, turning sweetly to him, "don't you want to see the ponies?" To include Van Horn, it was plain to be seen, would spoil the trip for Laramie, but she cared little for that. "Wait just a minute," she continued, "I must tell John Frying Pan before I go to give the Indians something to eat."

The feeling between the two men she left together flared up at once: "Does this mean you're going to hitch up with the cattlemen, after all?" demanded Van Horn.

Laramie, who had lighted his cigarette, stood looking after Kate: "I hitch up with nobody."

"Then don't spend your time hanging around Kate Doubleday."

"So that's where the shoe pinches?" Laramie threw away his cigarette as he spoke. "I've taken a good deal from you, Van Horn."

Van Horn egged him on unabashed: "You've got your nerve with you to show up here at all."

"A man needs his nerve, Van Horn, to do business with crooks like you."

Doubleday, passing near the two men at that

moment, heard the last exchange. He called out in his heavy, raspy voice to Van Horn: "Look here, Harry." Laramie walked away and Doubleday took Van Horn in hand: "You messed up things once with Laramie, didn't you? And you didn't get him, did you?" continued Doubleday, choking off Van Horn's words: "Now we've got him here, let me run this thing."

"I can tell you right now *you* won't line him up," blurted out Van Horn, very angry.

Doubleday had a way of raising his chin to override objection; and his voice grew huskier with stubbornness: "Just let me run this thing, will you?"

"Do as you please," retorted Van Horn, but with a stiff expletive that irritated Barb still further. Then swinging on his heel, Van Horn marched off. Barb was so incensed he could only keep his raised finger pointed after Van Horn; and as his eyes blazed he shouted through a very fog of throat-scraping: "I will."

CHAPTER 13

Against His Record

On the level stretch between the ranch-house and the creek the cowboys staged, after dinner, a Frontier Day show and a Fourth of July celebration combined. The fun began mildly with the three-legged races and the business of the greased pig. From these diversions it proceeded to foot races, in which Indians shone, and to keenly contested pony races between cowboys, Reservation bucks and sports from Sleepy Cat. Money was stacked with freedom and differences of opinion were intensified by victory and defeat.

While the spirit ran high, rodeo riding began with the master artists of the range and the pink of American horsemanship in the saddle. In each succeeding contest the Sleepy Cat visitors headed by Sawdy and Lefever with big loose bunches of currency backed their favorites freely, and men that counted nothing of caution in their make-up took the other end of every exciting event. Flushed faces and loud voices added to the rapidly shifting excitement as one event followed another, and the betting fever keenly roused called, after every possible wager had been laid, for fresh material to work on.

It was at this juncture that the shooting matches began. In a line and in a country in which many excelled in perhaps the most important regard, rivalry ran high and critics were naturally fastidious. The temptation to belittle even excellent work with rifle and revolver was, in Sawdy and especially in Carpy, partly due to temperament. Both men were bad gamesters because they bet on feeling rather than judgment. They would back a man, or the horse of a man they liked, against a man they did not like and sometimes thereby knew what it was to close the day with empty pockets.

On this Fourth of July at Doubleday's, both men, as well as Lefever, had been hit by hard luck. Their free criticism of the horse-racing and the shooting did not pass unresented and the fact that Tom Stone and his following had most of the Sleepy Cat money while the sun was still high did not tend to temper the acerbity of their remarks.

Nothing that the crack shots of the range could do would satisfy either Sawdy or Carpy. Van Horn, himself an expert with rifle and gun, was master of these ceremonies and the belittling by the Sleepy Cat sports of the best the cowboys could show, nettled him: "Before you knock this any more," he said, "put up some better shooting."

The taunt went far enough home to stir the fault-finders. Sawdy and Carpy took grumpy counsel together. Presently they hunted up Laramie, who in front of the ranch-house was talking horses with Kitchen and Doubleday. They told him the situation and asked for help: "Come over to the creek and show the bunch up, Jim," was Sawdy's appeal.

The response was cold. Laramie refused to take any part in the shooting. Sawdy could not move him. In revenge he borrowed what money Laramie had—not much in all—and went back in bad humor. With the peeve of defeated men, the Sleepy Cat sports called for more horse racing to retrieve their fortunes—only to lose what money they had left and suffer fresh jeering from Van Horn and his following.

But abating in defeat and with empty pockets, nothing of their confident swagger, Carpy and Sawdy reinforced this time by Lefever—McAlpin trailing along as a mourner—headed again for the ranch-house after Laramie.

They found him on a bench where he could command the front door, whittling and talking idly with Bill Bradley. Laramie was there intent on waylaying Kate, within. His friends descended on him for the second time in a body. They laid their discomfiture before him. They begged him to pull them out of the hole. It was too much in the circumstances to refuse men he counted on when he, himself, needed friends, but he yielded with an ill grace: "What do you want me to do?" he demanded finally.

They told him. He would not stand up before a target, nor would he shoot in competition with anybody else.

"I've only got a few cartridges, anyway," he objected. "Suppose when they're shot away these fellows get a fight going on me?"

It was argued that there were enough gunmen in the Sleepy Cat crowd for defensive purposes and that there was no end of available ammunition. A way was found to meet Laramie's objection on every point and it only remained to hatch up a scheme for lightening the cattlemen's pockets.

With Carpy, Lefever and Sawdy, Laramie sat down apart. An exchange of views took place. Sawdy had in mind something he had once seen Laramie achieve and on this—and the possibility of its success—the talk centered. The feat, it was conceded, would be a stiff one. It was put up to Laramie; he consented, after some wrangling and with misgivings, to try to save the day for his misguided Sleepy Cat friends. The moment consent was assured, his backers hurried away in a body—McAlpin as crier, Lefever and Sawdy to raise money, and Carpy to bully Van Horn and Stone and their following.

The news that Laramie would shoot caused a stir. Not everyone present had seen him shoot. His reputed mastery of rifle and gun was often in question; and no more grueling test before friends and enemies could ever be given than what he was to attempt now.

Not everyone got clearly as the talk went on just what the trial was to be. Sawdy having reinforced his resources, announced the event as Laramie against his record—to tie or to beat.

Laramie, himself, unmindful of the controversy, held to the bench. He was still sitting, head down, and still whittling, when Bradley came to say the crowd was waiting. He asked Bradley to bring up his horse.

Kate coming out of the house drew his attention. He threw away the stick in his hand and rose.

153

"I hear you are going to shoot," she said.

"Can't get out of it very well, I guess."

"You wouldn't shoot, the time I asked you to."

"I didn't actually refuse, did I?"

"Pretty near it."

"It's a harder case today. Your men have got all the money. My friends are broke. And they've asked me to help them out somehow. That's the only reason. If you really want to see me shoot, all you've got to do is to tell me the next time you see me."

"Oh, I'm going to see you shoot now." She looked at the gun holster slung at his left hip. "I hear you are left-handed."

"They've got work enough lined up today for two hands."

Bradley returned with the horse and climbed awkwardly down from the saddle. Laramie tried the cinches and turned to Kate.

"Are you all ready?" she asked.

"Just about."

"You try the cinches; I should think you'd want to try your gun."

"I tried that this morning before I left home. All I've got to do before I begin is to slip an extra cartridge into the cylinder."

Leading his pony, Laramie, clinging to the talk as long as he could, walked with Kate toward the creek. Leaving her on a slight rise, where he told her he thought she could see, he got into the saddle and rode down to where the crowd had assembled.

On a stretch of the trail extending along the creek, John Frying Pan, under the direction of Sawdy and Van Horn, was placing at intervals of from fifty to one hundred and fifty yards a series of targets. These were ordinary potatoes, left over from the barbecue, but selected with great care as to size and shape by the man whose money was up —Sawdy; Frying Pan's work was to impale them on low-growing scrub along the trail to serve as targets. Against these targets—six in number— Laramie was to undertake to ride and to split five out of the six as he galloped past them with six and no more bullets. The potatoes were up when Laramie joined Sawdy, and Lefever with leather lungs announced the terms of the test. Accompanied by Sawdy, Van Horn and Frying Pan, Laramie rode slowly down the course—a quarter of a mile long—examining the roadway and the targets. Here and there a loose stone was removed from the trail; one potato was moved from a dip in the course to a safer point; one was raised and one placed more clearly in sight.

Having ridden to the end, Laramie expressed himself as satisfied with the conditions. Alone, he went back over the course and starting down the creek made a trial heat at full speed past the targets. One of these at his request was shifted again. While he watched this change, Sawdy and Lefever, surrounded by their followers, were crowding him as race touts crowd a favorite jockey with final words of admonition and advice. When the one target was satisfactorily adjusted, Laramie breaking away from everybody returned alone to the starting point. Dismounting, and taking his time to everything, he again tested his cinches, drew his gun from its holster and breaking it slipped a sixth cartridge into the cylinder. Dropping the gun back into place, he pulled his hat a little lower, glanced down the course and up toward the little hill on which he had parted from Kate. She was standing where he left her but Van Horn had ridden up and, joining Kate, was talking to her. While she listened to him she watched the preparations below.

Laramie spoke to his pony, patted him on the neck and mounted. Wheeling, he swung out into a wide circle across the level bench and with gradually increasing speed into a measured gallop. Molded into one flesh with his mount, Laramie, impassive in the saddle as a statue, watched and nursed to his liking the pony's gait. When the rhythm suited, he urged the horse to a longer stride and circling back into the course, drew his gun, held it high in the air and, swinging it slowly as if like a lariat, bore down at full speed on the first target.

Markers for both sides in the betting stood to watch each potato. No signal would mean the potato had been missed; for each hit, a hat was to be thrown into the air. In a complete silence among the spectators every eye was fixed on Laramie. Those close at hand saw him, with his left arm still high in the air, sway slightly backward and slowly forward, while with the circling gun poised at arm's length he shrank closer and lower into the saddle. When he neared the first target, throwing his left arm toward it like a bolt, he fired, sped on and was again swinging his gun. He had hardly covered six more paces before a hat was tossed into the air behind him.

A yell went up from his friends. Horsemen wheeled into the course behind the flying marksman. With five potatoes still to negotiate they were afraid to cheer. But as one hat after another along the shooting line—the second, the third and the fourth—were tossed up from the target behind the speeding horseman, the Sleepy Cat men bellowed with joyful confidence. The fifth target was of unusual distance—a hundred and fifty yards— from the fourth. Leaving the fourth, Laramie's horse broke and the onlookers saw that his rider was in trouble. He kept the swing of his gun without breaking the rhythm, but his efforts were in his bridle arm to steady his horse.

The hopes of his backers fell as they saw how stubborn the pony had become. The hundred and fifty yards were barely enough to bring him under control. Laramie still circling his raised gun did bring him under. But he was already nearing the fifth target. And to the horror of his friends passed it without attempting to fire.

Of the two chances left him to tie—which meant to win—he had passed up one; the sixth and last meant life or death to the shaken hopes of his backers.

They saw him settled once more into the long, even stride he needed for the shot and their breaths hung on each flying leap that brought the rider nearer his last chance. The sixth target was separated by barely fifty yards from the fifth. Laramie had covered half the distance when he completely reversed his form. He stretched gradually up in the saddle and riding close in on the target itself, rose to his full height in the stirrups and smashed his fifth shot almost straight down on it; the potato split into a dozen fragments. Bill Bradley at the sixth was watching for Sawdy; his hat sailed twenty feet in the air. The yelling crowd rode Laramie down as he galloped in a long circle back, his lines swung on his forearm, while he slipped four fresh cartridges into the warm cylinder of his revolver.

He dismounted to ease his cinches. "I guess I overdid it," he explained to the friends that crowded closest. "I got the cinches a little tight. The pony didn't like it. I couldn't get the gait in time for the Number Five. But I knew I could make Number Six."

Remounting, he made his way through the crowd back over the course. Kate was still on the hill. "You won, didn't you?" she cried as he rode toward her.

"If I hadn't, I guess I'd have had to head straight across the creek for home. Could you see?"

"I watched you the whole way. What a long arm you have."

"While these tin horns are counting their money, would you like to show me the ponies?"

"You have a long memory, too."

"I was brought up a good deal with Indians. Shall I hunt up Van Horn to go with us?"

She darted a quick glance at him: "Why, yes, surely," she retorted, "if you want him."

Laramie was tearing out a cigarette paper: "I could look at them without him," he returned calmly.

"I don't see him, anyway," murmured Kate, professing to sweep the crowded course with her eyes.

"Don't look too hard," cautioned Laramie.

"I suppose we might save time," she suggested, ignoring his last remark, "by going without him."

CHAPTER 14

LEFEVER ASKS QUESTIONS

Those closest to headquarters sometimes know least of what is going on. That the big celebration at the ranch could have been anything more or less than what it professed to be, did not occur to

Kate; nor could anyone actually say that it was more or less. Hawk could contemptuously refuse its overtures; Laramie could for reasons of his own accept them; the Falling Wall rustlers were out for a good time or they would not have been rustling and they would celebrate any time at anybody's expense—except their own; Carpy could believe it was to usher in a better feeling—everyone to his taste.

But the suspicious, because they did not quite understand such a move, harbored their suspicions, and among the doubting was Belle Shockley—shrewd and very much alive to the drift of things since her struggle with a cyclone. Had Belle, instead of Kate, been out at the ranch, things now coming along that Kate failed to see, would have told volumes to her.

But Kate did not feel at liberty to make of Belle a confidant in everything—certainly not in what happened at home; so she neither said anything to Belle nor asked of her any explanation of things that she herself did not understand—such as guarded and more frequent consultations between her father and Van Horn, Pettigrew and Stone; and such as men riding up with a clatter to the ranch-house at night and calling Doubleday out and calling for Van Horn who often now spent the night at the ranch and left before daybreak.

Some of this, Kate saw. She could see how absent-minded her father was. He grew so taciturn she hardly knew him but the reason for it was beyond her. More than she saw, she picked up from Bradley, working then at the ranch. Bradley had taken a liking to Kate and often reminded her of the night he brought her into the Falling Wall country.

Whenever she was in Sleepy Cat, Belle was inquisitive. She always wanted to know what Van Horn was doing, what her father was doing, and then fell back on vaguely general questions about ranches and the range and rustlers. More than once she spoke of strangers in town, Texas men—cowboys and gunmen she called them—who bothered her for meals, and whom she scornfully sent packing.

And Henry Sawdy, too, one of her frequent visitors, was trying to court her, she complained; all this made her suspicious. Of whom? Of what? Kate asked. Belle could not tell exactly of whom, of what—she was just suspicious: "Why should that big fat man come courting me?" she demanded one day when Kate had come in for lunch.

"You don't think it possible he likes you?" suggested Kate, barely glancing Belle's way, and taking care to make her tone very skeptical. Belle only snorted contemptuously and turned to her cooking; but as she did so, she gave her wig a punch.

By the merest chance, John Lefever came in a few minutes later. Belle and Kate were at the table. John asked for something to eat. When Belle wanted to be rid of him he refused "no" for an answer:

"You wouldn't send me away without a cup of coffee, would you? No potatoes? Well, I never eat potatoes"—John coughed. "They are fattening." Then he looked up cheerfully as if a new idea had struck him: "What's the matter with a little soft-boiled ice cream?"

The upshot was that he had to be asked to share the lunch which he did with relish, paying his way with his usual foolery. When the plates were emptied and John had officiously asked leave to light a cigarette, he glanced toward the folding bed and asked Belle to play something.

"That's no piano," exclaimed Belle, with contempt. "That's a bed."

John seemed undisturbed: "Curious," he mused, "we used to have an upright piano at home with that same kind of wood, same pattern exactly; you could have that bed made over into a piano, Belle. Straighten out the springs and you wouldn't have to buy hardly any wire at all."

Belle stared at him: "Where would I sleep if I did?" she demanded.

John threw back his head, blew a delicate puff of smoke toward the ceiling and looked across at his unsympathetic hostess. Then he brought his fist down on the table: "Marry me, Belle, and sleep in a regular bed! What?"

Belle was justly indignant. Kate's laughing made her more indignant. For John had fairly bubbled his proposal through a laugh of his own.

"I used to sleep in a box like that myself," he went on. "But the year it was so dry the grasshoppers got into it." John coughed again unobtrusively. "I raffled that bed off," he continued, low and reminiscently. "A conductor won it. But it didn't fool him. He knew the bed as well as I did; he'd slept in it. So I bought it in again, cheap, and traded it to an old Indian buck—a one-eyed man —for a pony. Many a time I've laughed, thinking of that bed up on the Reservation. Those bucks, you know, are desperate gamblers. I understand they've been playing hearts with that blamed bed ever since and putting it on the high man."

At this, John laughed harder than ever, Belle sputtering as she watched him.

Then he turned his amiable face on Kate: "How are you all at the home?"

"Very well."

"What's the news up your way?"

"Not a thing since the Fourth of July."

"Father pretty well?"

"Quite."

"When did you see him last?"

It was an odd question: "Last night—why?" asked Kate in turn.

"He didn't come in town with you today?" countered John.

"He rarely does," said Kate.

John nodded soothing assent to her explanation: "How's Van Horn?" he asked casually. "And Stone?" he added, with undiminished interest. "All well," was his echo to her perfunctory answers. "Say, Belle, was Jim Laramie in town yesterday?"

Belle shook her head. "How about the day before?" he asked. Again she said, "no"; and went on with an impatient comment of her own: "You're always asking questions. What for? That's what I want to know."

John laid his cigarette on the rim of his plate and appealed to Kate: "Did you ever in your life see a more unreasonable woman than Belle? How am I to find things out without asking questions of my friends? And among them I number you both," he added.

Leaning forward, he spoke on: "Now I'll tell you why I asked those harmless little questions—for I wouldn't ask either of you any other kind. This news will get to each of you, about evening. By morning it will be all over Sleepy Cat and by tomorrow noon across the Spanish Sinks. This morning, early, Van Horn, Tom Stone, Pettigrew with Bradley, and a bunch of Texas men and cowboys rode over into the Falling Wall country and there's been hell to pay there every minute since daylight—that's the word I got about half an hour ago, by telephone, from a little ranch away up on the head-waters of the Crazy Woman."

He drew his handkerchief and wiped his brow. "The only man up there—Belle knows that—that I'm any ways interested in, is Jim Laramie. According to what I can hear, Jim is home. That's worrying me just a little.

"What will Jim do? That's what I'm thinking of. How will he stack up if that bunch goes to his ranch on the Turkey? He hates 'em like poison. They've gone up there, you understand," he added, speaking to Kate, as if some further explanation were due a comparative stranger, "to clean out the rustlers. You can imagine it'll be done—or at least attempted—without much talk. There won't be very much talk. I've known for some little time what's been going forward. They tried to get Jim to join them; offered him about anything he wanted; offered to see that the contests on his preemption and homestead be withdrawn; offered him quite a bunch of cattle, I heard; and some money."

Belle's face, her staring eyes and strained expression as she listened, showed how well she knew what the news meant. "What answer did Jim give?" she asked anxiously.

"From what I can pick up," declared John, dropping calmly into the inelegant expression, "he told 'em to go to hell.

"That's what I'm worrying about now. Not about their going, but about what Jim will do. What do you think, Belle?"

Belle shook her head; she offered no comment.

165

"And," John added, looking at Kate, "that was hatched mostly, right at your place. And they rode away from there about two o'clock this morning. That's why I was pumping you a little, till I see you didn't know a thing about it."

Why Kate had not asked before, she could not tell; but the possibility never crossed her mind—until Lefever told her of their starting from the ranch that morning—that her father might have gone. She recollected now she had not seen him, as she usually saw him, the first thing when she came from her room. Her heart leaped into her throat: "Was my father with them?" she asked.

She must have shown her excitement and fear in her manner, as well as in her words, for Lefever looked at her considerately: "According to my reports," he answered carefully, "your father was with them."

"Godfrey!" muttered Belle. Kate could say nothing.

CHAPTER 15

THE RAID OF THE FALLING WALL

Against the alert, the effective blow is a sudden blow. Secrecy, and a surprise, were the only hope of success in what the cattlemen were now attempting in the Falling Wall. Of the men on whom they could count to organize and carry through such a raid, they had just one capable of energizing every detail—Harry Van Horn. Laramie, the man Doubleday and Pettigrew would have chosen, they had failed to enlist, and what was more serious —though this, perhaps, Doubleday did not realize—they had likewise failed to rid themselves of; Tom Stone had bungled.

But Doubleday in especial was not a man to lose time over a failure. He knew that Van Horn had "go" enough in him to clean out a whole county if he were given the men and backing, and that he stood high in the councils of the range. When Van Horn spoke, men listened. His eye flashed with his words and his long, straight hair shook defiance at opposition. He swore with a staccato that really meant things and cut like a knife. When once started, mercy was not in him.

In the Falling Wall park there lived a mere handful of men, and these widely scattered; but Van Horn was the last man to underestimate the handful he was after. He knew them every one, and knew that no better men ever rode the range than Stormy Gorman, Dutch Henry, Yankee Robinson and Abe Hawk, and their associates—if, indeed, for a man that never mixed with other men, Hawk could be said to have associates.

But the four named were the men to whom the lesser rustlers of the park looked; the men whose exploits they imitated, and these were the men on whose heads a price had, in effect, been set.

Van Horn assembled his men, earlier than Lefever had been informed. An old trail from Doubleday's ranch to the Falling Wall crosses the road to the Fort some distance north of Sleepy Cat. The party from the ranch—Tom Stone with some of the most reckless cowboys and Doubleday— waited there for the Texans whom Van Horn was bringing from Pettigrew's. Both parties were at the rendezvous that night by twelve o'clock, and within thirty minutes were headed north by way of the Crazy Woman for Falling Wall park.

The night for the raid had been chosen. The sky was overcast, and when the party left the crossing between twelve and one o'clock their exact destination was still a secret to the greater number. Small ranchers along the creek might have wakened at the smart clatter of so many horses, but men to and from the Fort traveled late at times and made even more noise. This night there were riders abroad; but there was no singing.

Dawn was whitening the eastern sky when the raiding party halted near a clump of trees on the south fork of the Turkey. The valley into which they had ridden during the night was very broken, but offered good grazing. Along the tortuous water course, Stormy Gorman, the old prize-fighter, and Dutch Henry, the ex-soldier, had preempted two of the very few pieces of land that did not stand directly on edge and built for themselves cabins.

Gorman's cabin lay a mile above the fork where the raiders had halted; Henry's lay a few miles farther up the creek.

During the long night ride it had been decided to strike at Gorman's ranch first; thence to follow the creek trail up to Dutch Henry's, despatch him in turn, to cross rapidly a narrow rough divide beyond which they could reach Hawk's cabin on the east fork of the Turkey and thence sweep into the northwest to clean out the smaller fry—the "chicken feed" rustlers—as Van Horn called them. But toward morning, following much ill-natured dispute between Stone and Van Horn, the tactics were changed. It was decided to go after Dutch Henry first—as the more alert and slippery of the two—and as quietly as possible the silent invaders rode slowly along the creek past Gorman's place up to Henry's.

Day was breaking as the riders, dismounting and leaving their horses on the creek bottom, crept noiselessly, under Stone's guidance, up a wash to the bench on which Henry's cabin stood. Hiding just below a shallow bank at the head of a draw, they lay awaiting developments. Where Stone had posted them they commanded the cabin perfectly. He had lived part of one year with Henry when they two preyed jointly on the range and he knew the ground well.

They had hardly disposed of themselves in this manner and were beginning, in the gray dusk, to distinguish objects with some certainty, when the door of the distant cabin opened and a mongrel collie bounded out followed by a man who left the door ajar. The man, carrying a water pail, set it down, yawned, stretched himself and tucked his shirt slowly inside his trousers. Wild with joy the dog danced, leaped and barked about his master—only to be rewarded by a kick that sent him yelping to a little distance, where turning, crouching with extended paws, whining and frantically wagging his tail, the poor beast tried to beg forgiveness for its half-starved happiness. The man, giving this demonstration no heed, picked up the pail and started for the creek.

His path took him in a direction roughly parallel to the line along which his hidden enemy lay.

"Don't fire at that man," exclaimed Van Horn to his companions under cover of the draw. "That's not Dutch Henry," he whispered the next moment. "Don't fire. I'll take care of him."

The rustler, quite unconscious of his deadly danger, tramped unevenly on. His dog, no longer repulsed, dashed joyously back and forth, scenting the trails of the night and barking wildly at his master by turns. The man was walking hardly three hundred yards from where Stone, rifle in hand, lay, and had reached the footpath leading from the bench to the creek bottom when Stone, half rising, covered him slowly with point-blank sights. In the path ahead, the dog had struck a fresh gopher hole and, still yelping, was pawing madly into it, when a rifle cracked. The man with the pail, swung violently half around by the shock of a spreading bullet, jerked convulsively and the pail flew clattering from his hand. He struggled an instant to keep his footing, then collapsing, fell prone across the path and lay quite still.

Stone, followed by a man nearest him, scrambling down the draw, hurried along the creek bottom, and ran up to reach the path where the murdered man lay. The dog, barking and dashing wildly around his prostrate master, spied the foreman and sprang furiously down the trail at him. Stone, rifle in one hand and revolver in the other, was ready, and, firing from the hip, broke the collie's back. With a howl the stricken brute turned, and, dragging his helpless hindquarters along the ground with incredible swiftness, pawed himself back to the dying man's head and yelping, licked frantically at the hand of his master. Coming up into plain sight, Stone got a good look at the man he had killed: "Stormy Gorman!" he exclaimed, with an oath of surprise. "Who'd 'a' thought," he continued, "that big bum would be up at Dutch Henry's this morning!"

The old prize-fighter was struggling in his last round. His heavy-lidded eyes, swollen with drink and sleep, were closed, and from his mouth, as his head hung to one side, a dark stream ran to a little pool in the dust. Only a stertorous breathing reflected his effort to live and even this was fast failing. Van Horn hurried up the path from the bottom, whither he had followed Stone; anger was all over his face: "Kill that damned dog," he exclaimed, out of breath, to those about him. Two of the three men drew revolvers and shot the collie through the head.

"Damnation!" cried Van Horn in a fury. "Stop your shooting. Couldn't you knock him in the head? Do you want to start up the whole country?" he demanded, as he saw the man who lay at his feet and had taken the brief count for eternity was Gorman. He turned on Stone with rage in his eyes and his voice: "Now," he cried, punctuating his abuse with the fiercest gestures, "you've done it, haven't you!" Anger almost choked him. "You've got Gorman with a brass band and left Dutch Henry in the cabin waiting for us, haven't you? Why," he roared, "didn't you obey orders, let this tank get down to the bottom and knock him on the head into the creek?" A violent recrimination between Stone and Van Horn followed. But the milk was spilt as well as the blood of the stubborn rustler, and there was nothing for it but new dispositions.

Gorman's presence indicated that Henry was at home. If he were at home, he was, no doubt, within the cabin; but just how, after Stone's blunder, to get at him, was a vexing question.

Van Horn started down the foot trail back to

the bottom and around to the first hiding place. Lingering with a companion to look at Gorman in his blood, Stone turned for approval: "See where I hit him?" he grinned. "Poor light, too."

A brief council was held in the draw. Watched for more than an hour, not the slightest sign of life about the lonely cabin could be detected. Various expedients, none of them very novel, were tried to draw Henry's fire should he be within. But these were of no avail. A dozen theories were advanced as to where Henry might or might not be. To every appearance there was not, so far as the enemy could judge, a living man within miles of the spot. The older heads, Pettigrew, Doubleday, Van Horn, even Stone, talked less than the others; but they were by no means convinced that the house was empty.

One of the least patient of the cowboys at length deliberately exposed himself to fire from the sphinx-like cabin. He stood up and walked up and down the edge of the draw. Nothing happened. Emboldened, he started out into the open and toward the cabin. No shot greeted him. A companion, jumping up, hurried after him; a third, a Texas boy, sprang up to join them. For those watching from hiding it was a ticklish moment. Toward the draw there was a considerable growth of mountain blue-stem, none of it very high and gradually shortening nearer the house. The three men were hastening through the grass, separated by intervals of perhaps fifty feet. The foremost got within a hundred yards of the cabin door, which still stood open as Gorman had left it, before Van Horn's fear of an ambush vanished. He himself, not to be too far behind his followers, then rose to join the procession through the blue stem and the crack of a rifle was heard. Van Horn, with a shout of warning, dropped unhurt into the draw. But the last man of the three in the field stumbled as if struck by an ax. Of the two men ahead of him, the hindermost dropped into the grass and crawled snakelike back; the man in front dropped his rifle and started at top speed for safety; from the edge of the draw his companions sent a fusillade of rifle fire at the cabin.

Apparently the diversion had no effect on the marksman within. He fired again; this time at the Texan crawling in the blue stem, and the half-hidden man, almost lifted from the ground by the blow of the bullet, dropped limp. Meantime the first cowboy in his dash for safety was making a record still unequaled in mountain story. He jumped like a broncho and zig-zagged like a darting bird, but faster than either. The efforts of his companions to divert attention from him were constant. Some of them poured bullets at the cabin. Others jumped to their feet, and, yelling, sprang from point to point to expose themselves momentarily and draw the fire of the enemy. This was of no avail. The hidden rifle with deliberate instancy cracked once more. The fleeing cowboy, slammed as if by a club, dashed on, but his right arm hung limp. No snipe ever made half the race for life that he put up in those fleeting seconds; and by his agility he earned then and there the nickname of the bird itself, for before the deadly sights could cover his flight again he threw himself into a slight depression that effectually hid him from the range of the enemy.

A swarm of hornets, roused, could not have been more furious than the company under the lee of the draw. Shooting, shouting, cursing deep and loud, they made continual effort to keep the deadly fire off their fallen companions. They saw the half-open door of the cabin swing now slowly shut and they riddled it with bullets. They splintered the logs about it and, scattering in as wide an arc as they dare, continued to pour a fire into the silent cabin. At intervals they paused to wait for a return. There was no return. All ruses they had ever heard of they tried over again to draw a fire and exhaust the besieged man's ammunition. Nothing moved the lone enemy—if he were, indeed, alone. The day wore into afternoon. By shouting, the assailants learned that two of their three hapless companions lying in the blue stem were still alive—the Snipe very much alive, as his stentorian answers indicated. He called vigorously for water but got none. His refuge was too exposed.

How to get rid of Dutch Henry taxed the wits of the invaders. The whole morning and the early afternoon went to pot-luck firing from the trench along the draw, but although it was often asserted that Henry must long since be dead—having returned none of the shooting that was meant to call his fire—no one manifested the curiosity necessary to prove the assertion by closing in on the cabin. Stone was still sulking over Van Horn's sharp talk of the morning when Van Horn came over to where the foreman had posted himself to cover the cabin door: "We've got to get that guy before dark, Tom, or he'll slip us."

"All right," replied Stone, "get him."

CHAPTER 16

THE GO-DEVIL

"I want a wagon," scowled Van Horn. "There's one down at Gorman's place he won't need any more. There's some baled hay down there, too. Take the men you need, load what hay you can find on the wagon and hustle it up here."

Too stubborn to ask questions, and only starting after many hard words—with which all the ground of the morning quarrel and much more was traversed—Stone took two men and started reluctantly for Gorman's. He spent a long time on his job, but came back as directed with the wagon loaded with hay.

The wagon was not much to view. It looked like the wagon of a man that spent more time in Sleepy Cat saloons than on his ranch. A rack, equally old and dilapidated, had been set on the running gear. The paint had long since blown off the wheels, and one of these, a front wheel, had lost a tire on the rough trip up the creek. But the felloes hung to the spokes and the spokes to the hub.

Van Horn inspected the outfit grimly. With half a dozen men he set quickly to work and under his resourceful ingenuity the wagon and hay were speedily turned into what would now-a-days be termed a tank. Only lack of hay kept him from making a mobile fortress of it. By means of wire he slung along the sides what baled hay he could spare, and with much effort to avoid exposure the armored wagon was dragged over the roughest kind of ground, to the north and west of the cabin. From this direction the ground, fairly smooth, sloped from a ridge fringed by jutting patches of rock, directly toward the cabin itself and eager hands made the final preparations to smoke Henry out. With the load of hay set ablaze and the wagon run down against the cabin the defender was bound to be driven from cover or burnt.

When the bustling, contradicting and confusion finally subsided, the wagon was stealthily pushed over the ridge, the hay fired and the blazing outfit, christened a go-devil, was started with a shout down the slope.

If there existed in the minds of those that talked least a lingering suspicion that Dutch Henry was still alive it was soon strongly justified. Before the wagon had rolled twenty feet the challenge of a rifle-shot from the cabin answered the attack. Everybody dodged quick, but no one was hit and a yell of derision rose from behind the rocks. With ropes, borrowed from the men that carried them, and knotted together, the wagon was kept under partial control and the line, as paid out, served in some measure to guide it. On it went accompanied with shouts and yells. From the threatened cabin came no answering defiance. Henry's case looked bad as the wagon rolled down on him, but his rifle fire, though seemingly wasted, answered unflinchingly.

Stone danced with joy: "He'll be running the gauntlet next clip. He's not hitting anybody. He must be shooting," yelled the excited foreman, "at the blamed wagon."

A steady fire, undismayed, did continue to come from the cabin. Van Horn, who had run to the extreme right of the new sector, and was keeping a close watch on the go-devil, was the first to perceive trouble. "Hell's delight, boys," he cried, taken aback, "he's shooting up the wheels."

The words flew around behind the rocks. The rifle fire was explained. Every eye was turned to the danger point, the wheel without the tire which, as the wagon wobbled, was unluckily exposed to the cabin fire. It could easily be seen where the deliberate marksman was getting in his work. He had knocked one felloe off the rim and was hitting at the spokes. It began to look like a race between the burning wagon and Henry at bay. The hay was a mound of flame and sparks and smoke shot high into the air. A hundred feet more would lodge the fire trap against the rear wall of the cabin. But under the steady pounding of a rifle that seemed never to miss its mark the injured wheel showed fast increasing signs of distress. A second felloe was tracking uncertainly.

As a diversion, Van Horn, active, energetic and covering every part of his little line at once, ordered an incessant fire centered on the threatened cabin. Nothing seemed to check the regular report of the hidden high-powered rifle and the bullets that were splintering the old oak spokes. When the roaring wagon struck a loose stone or rough spot in its trackless path it wobbled and hesitated. Yet, jerked, steadied, halted and started by means of the long cable, it rolled to within twenty yards of its mark. There it pitched a bit, recovered and for another ten yards sailed down a smooth piece of ground. The cowboys were yelling their loudest when a lucky shot from the cabin knocked off a second felloe. A second and third shot smashed rapidly through the spokes of the staggering wheel. A threatening boulder lying to the right of the wagon's course could not be avoided. The men on the line jerked and swore. It was useless. One side of the wheel collapsed, the front axle swung around and the blazing wagon straddled the troublesome boulder like a stranded ship. The men guiding heaved to on the line—it parted; the cabin stood safe.

At once, the rifle fire from the cabin ceased. No taunt, no threat could draw another shot from the silence. Chagrined, eyes flashing, silent in his defeat, Van Horn, contemplating the last of the burning wagon and watching the cabin as a dog, baffled, watches a cat on a fence, was let alone even by the most reckless of his companions; for the failure no one tried to bait him. Nor were he and Doubleday ready to quit. They got ready a circle of fires to block any attempt made to escape the beleaguered place after dark. This proved a difficult undertaking, both because fuel was scarce and because the dead line, drawn by the rifle fire of the wary defender, extended a long way in every direction around his log refuge.

The night, however, was fairly clear and a pretty good moon was due by ten o'clock. The fires were lighted, not without some sharp objection from the cabin, the moment darkness fell. The difficulty then was to keep them replenished and maintain an adequate guard. Dark spots and shadows fell within and across the circle around the cabin. Van Horn ordered a rifle fire directed into these places; it was placed so persistently that when the moon rose, the besiegers felt pretty confident Henry had not escaped. And just before its light had penetrated the narrow valley, the invaders had a cheering surprise when the wounded man, nicknamed "The Snipe," crawled from his hollow between the lines back to his comrades and told them in immoderate terms what he thought of them for leaving him wounded and thirsty under the enemy fire. Volunteers, inspired by his abuse, crawled out to the second man that had fallen in the morning and by really heroic effort got him back into the draw; badly hit, he was given long-needed attention. The first man, shot through the head, the rescuers reported dead.

When midnight came, the men had been fed and the watch well maintained. A steer, interned earlier, had been cut up for the men's supper and Van Horn and Doubleday were seated together before the camp fire near the creek eating some of the reserve chunks of meat when a hurried alarm called them up the draw—the cabin was on fire.

Nothing could have happened to take the besiegers more by surprise. There was hasty questioning but no explanation. Of all the possibilities of the night none could have been so unexpected. But whatever the cause, and theories were broached fast, the cabin was ablaze. Smoke could be seen pouring through the chinks in the roof and little tongues of flame darted out at the rear under the eaves. Though there was not a breath of air stirring, the roof within fifteen minutes was in flames and the cowboys, confident of victory, set up, Indian fashion, their death chant for Dutch Henry.

The old shack made a good fire. The roof collapsed and with the incantations of the cowboys, the stout walls, worm-eaten and bullet-splintered, falling gradually, blazed on.

"The jig's up here, boys," announced Van Horn, as the fire burned down. "The two biggest thieves on the range are accounted for. It's a good job. If I guess right you'll find the Dutchman in the fire. Yankee Robinson's next. He won't put up much of a fight, but the hardest man to get is still ahead of us. This was a boy's job beside rounding up Abe Hawk. He'll never be taken alive, because he knows what's comin' to him.

"There's not a minute to lose now. Stone and I will take two of your men, Barb, and round up Yankee Robinson. From there we'll ride over to Abe's place on the Turkey. About our only chance is to catch him before he's up. If he's got wind of this, we'll have a hell of a chase to get him. Feed the horses, the rest of you eat, and we're off! You can follow us with Pettigrew and the bunch, Doubleday, just as soon as you look the cabin over after daylight." Within half an hour Van Horn and Stone and the two men crossed the creek, rode into the hills and disappeared into the night.

Setting a watch, Doubleday and his men curled up on the ground. When earliest dawn streaked the sky the logs were still smoking, and the cowboys, rifles in hand, walked down to where the cabin had stood.

Everything within the walls had been consumed. Long after daylight, with some of the men asleep, and others waiting for the fire to cool, one of Doubleday's cowboys, poking about the sill log of the rear wall with a stick, gave a shout. What had been taken for a half-burned log was the charred body of a man. The invaders gathered and the body was presently declared by those who knew him well to be that of Dutch Henry. There was nothing more to detain the men that were waiting. The cowboy worst wounded had started with a companion for home. The Snipe insisted on going on with Doubleday.

The horses had been left in good grass a little way down the creek. When they were disturbed it was found that one was missing. A hurried search failed to recover the horse.

While trackers were at work, the Snipe, always alert, found a clue that upset all calculations. It was a small dark red spot soaked into the dust of the creek trail. It was very small, such as might have been made by a single drop of blood; but one such sign was enough to put on inquiry a man versed like the Snipe in mountain craft. Keeping his discovery to himself, he tracked back and forth from his single spot, almost invisible in the dust, until he found a second similar spot. This he marked, and dodging and circling, like a hound on a scent, the Snipe ran his trail from his first tiny spot to the trees near the creek where the horses had been left. Doubling, he patiently tracked the telltale spots up the path that led to the cabin. Then he called to Barb.

Doubleday, much out of temper, was in the saddle waiting to get started. He bawled at the Snipe, and not amiably.

"Keep cool," was the answer; "I'm 'a' comin'. But look here before you start; there was two men in that cabin, Barb."

"What are you givin' us?" blurted out a cowboy. Doubleday stared ferociously. "There was two of 'em, boys," persisted the Snipe.

"You must 'a' seen double when you was runnin'," was the skeptical suggestion of another man. But Doubleday listened.

The Snipe took him from the cabin down to the creek. Then back to the cabin. There he showed him where someone had dug what might have been a hole under the sill log, near the door.

A horse was certainly missing. Then, shells from two different rifles were picked out of the ashes. One size had been fired from a Winchester rifle; the others, much more numerous, belonged to a Marlin.

"Who was it, Barney?" asked Doubleday, breathing heavily. He was so wrought up and so hoarse he could hardly frame the words. But he was already convinced.

The Snipe shook his head. "There's two or three fellows up here shoots a Marlin rifle. If I got one guess on this man that's made his get-away, Barb, I'd say—" The Snipe poked further into the ashes.

"Well, say!" thundered Doubleday.

"I'd say it was Abe Hawk."

CHAPTER 17

Van Horn Trails Hawk

A bomb exploding in the smoking remnants could hardly have caused more consternation among the man hunters than the Snipe's naming of Abe Hawk. But however Doubleday's jaw set at the unwelcome surprise he was not the one to swerve in the face of any personal danger, and those with him were not men to bolt whatever adventure they embarked in. However, it was remarked by the Snipe that those least acquainted with Abe were least disturbed by the news of his almost certain presence in the cabin the day and night before and his escape after the fight.

Common prudence made it necessary to cross the small divide with care and to get word of the unpleasant discovery as soon as possible to Van Horn in order that he and his companions might not be picked off by the wounded man from ambush. The Snipe was assigned to Hawk's trail and two men were sent to the wings to scout for him among the rocks. Bradley rode to warn Van

Horn; but the old man did not sweat his horse in the effort.

The trackers soon made it plain to those behind that the escaping man had ridden a pretty straight course himself, and had picked his way in the night like one thoroughly at home in the hills of the Turkey. And though losing the trail at times, the Snipe had no serious trouble in picking it again from the grass or the rocks.

The country lying north of the forks of the Turkey is rougher than to the south and pretty well covered with pine. On the Northern slope, Hawk's trail led down a long and winding break mile after mile and in the end pointed straight for his shack on the creek.

Moving as nearly as possible in the order in which they had started, the party emerged from the hills half a mile from the creek, and not much farther from Hawk's, when they encountered Bradley and Van Horn with one of his men. Doubleday hoarsely asked for the news.

Van Horn rode up close before he answered, and, though his tone was confident, his manner showed his annoyance at the way things had turned: "Robinson's shack was empty," he said. "Whether he got wind of yesterday I don't know; anyway, he's skipped—there's nothing left on his place."

"What's there to this talk of Barney's about Abe Hawk?" demanded Doubleday.

"From what Bradley says, it looks as if he

might be right," said Van Horn. "The horse Hawk took is eating grass in front of his cabin; we saw him when we got here and waited for Hawk to show himself."

"He didn't do it," interrupted Doubleday hus-kily and baring his teeth as he spoke.

"Stone's watching the place."

"Is Abe there?" demanded Doubleday.

"You tell," responded Van Horn. "He may or may not be. That horse may be a stall. We've got to close in somehow on the shack and find out."

A cowboy clattered up from the creek and pulled his horse to its haunches between Doubleday and Van Horn: "He's just closed the door," declared the cowboy. "The door was open when we got here—wasn't it, Harry?" He pointed his finger at Van Horn in his excited appeal.

Van Horn scowled and waved his head from side to side in irritation: "The door was open, yes; the door is shut, yes." Then he swore at the alarmist: "You blamed monkey," he pointed to the cottonwood. "Don't you see how the wind is blowing? That door has been swinging half an hour. The shack is empty."

But nobody could be found with confidence enough in Van Horn's belief to close in and demonstrate its truth. After a litany of hard words in which everybody took more or less part, Van Horn declared he would demonstrate. Whatever his faults, he was dead game, a formidable antagonist in an encounter. He was risking his life on his belief that either Hawk was disabled, or the cabin was empty. Stripping himself to shirt and trousers, turning his effects over to a cowboy, bare-headed and with only a six-shooter in hand, he shook out his long, brown hair, hooked up his belt and started to crawl up a little wash breaking into the creek not far from the cabin.

There was no point from which he could be seen and his companions, secreted where they could watch, bent their eyes along the course of the wash up which their hidden leader was making his way.

Fortunately for the slippery undertaking, Van Horn, by a little digging as he made his way carefully ahead, was able to crawl to within fifty feet of the door without exposing himself to fire. Reaching the nearest spot he could attain with safety, he called in stentorian tones to the cabin:

"You're surrounded, Abe. You can't get away. If you want to surrender, I'll guarantee your life. Come out unarmed and I'll meet you unarmed. If not, it's what Gorman and Dutch Henry got, for you, Abe."

The cabin gave no answer back. But Van Horn would not be baffled. Knowing it would be suicide to venture closer he patiently sought his answer on the ground he now began to cover on his way back to the creek. And on the ground he found it.

"He's slipped us," Van Horn called out when Doubleday arrived, "but I've got his trail."

"Two hundred and fifty dollars to the man that gets him!" shouted Doubleday, huskily. Some of the boys gave a whoop and began to look around, but they did not scatter much.

Van Horn, losing no time, led Doubleday part way up the break along which he had crawled. Telltale traces of blood at irregular intervals, sometimes imprinted as if by a hand on the flat face of rock that bedded the wash; sometimes smeared on a starving bunch of grass, where it clung desperately to a crevice in the scant soil—all so slight and so well concealed that only the mere chance of Van Horn's crawling up the very break chosen by Hawk for his escape to the creek had revealed it to his pursuers. The tracker took the slender trail, followed the wounded rustler to the creek bottom and thence down the creek to its junction with the North Fork. There they lost the trail in a pool of water, nor could they pick it up again.

A mile below the fork of the Turkey stood Jim Laramie's cabin. The raiders had already entered on his land; his cattle and some of his horses were, in fact, grazing in and about the creek fork. The following of Hawk's trail had been a nerve-racking job. Hawk, his enemies knew, might be waiting at any turn in it and that meant, in all probability, death for someone. In consequence, the pioneering fell chiefly on Van Horn; even Stone showed little stomach for the job. But the trail was completely lost.

"There's a bunch of horses grazing at the fork," reported Van Horn, as Doubleday reached the front, "Laramie's, I guess—anyway, the trail's gone."

A council was held. Doubleday, long-headed and crafty, listened to all that was said. Van Horn finally asked for his opinion.

"I don't know no more than the rest of you; but a blind man can figure a few things out. He's hit, ain't he?" Barb put the question as one not to be gainsaid and found none to say him nay. "He's looking for help, that's more'n likely, ain't it? He's a mile from Jim Laramie's cabin, not more; he's three miles from anybody else's—what?" he exclaimed, as Bill Bradley interrupted to suggest that it was less than two miles over to Ben Simeral's. "All right," shouted Barb, "Hawk's here, ain't he? He's close to Laramie. Laramie's his friend. Where would he go—what?"

Chopping his ideas out as with an ax, Doubleday showed his companions what they should have thought of without being told. "The thing to do," he added, "is to go down to Laramie's cabin and see what we can see—and find out what we can find out."

It was precisely what Bradley had feared would happen, but there was no escape from Doubleday's logic and no help for what others as well as Bradley feared might follow.

CHAPTER 18

HAWK QUARRELS WITH LARAMIE

On the morning the raiders entered the Falling Wall, Laramie had started with Henry Sawdy for the Reservation to appraise some allotted Indian lands. Laramie rode home that night; Sawdy, promising to stop at the ranch on his way down in the morning, stayed overnight at the Fort with Colonel Pearson. Laramie got home late. He was asleep next morning when a door was pushed open and a man walked unceremoniously in on him. To what instinct some mountain men owe their composure when disturbed in their sleep by a friend, as contrasted with the instant defense they offer in like circumstances to an enemy, it would be difficult to say—certainly there is a difference.

Laramie half opened his eyes to realize that Abe Hawk had come into his room and seated himself on the one chair. The sleepy man was not inclined to wake up. "You're early, Abe," was his only greeting. Hawk made no answer.

After a further effort the drowsy man roused himself to the attention that seemed demanded in the case: "Going somewhere?" he mumbled perfunctorily.

"Yes." Hawk's hard tone might have surprised

191

his host for a moment; but if it did, drowsiness overpowered his senses once more and it was some time before he realized that his visitor was sitting silent at his side and that he himself ought to say something. In protest he shifted his comfortable position in bed: "Get your breakfast ready, Abe," he suggested, hospitably, but with his heavy eyes closed.

"I've had breakfast."

"Where you bound for today?"

"On a long trip."

"Which way?"

"Home."

"What do you mean, 'home'?"

"I mean hell, Larrie—the home long waiting for me."

Laramie's eyes batted slowly. Not a half a dozen times in all their long acquaintance had Hawk shortened Laramie's name in speaking to him; and then only when he spoke as he rarely did from a depth always hidden from the men among whom his wasted life had been spent. Roused by something in the utterance of his guest, Laramie looked up.

If the sight was a shock, the mountain man gave no outward sign of it. The lower right side of Hawk's face had been torn away as if by some explosion, and blood, darkened by clay and rude styptics, clotted the long beard that naturally fell in a glossy black. His disordered garments, blood-smeared and hanging loose—his coat sleeve and his shirt torn from his forearm for bandages, his soft hat jammed low over his eyes— for an instant, Laramie hardly recognized him. But the cold black eyes that looked out of the wreck of a man before him pierced so clearly the long shadows of the early light that Laramie had no choice but to realize it was Hawk and even the shock only served to restrain and steady him. He showed but little of his amazement when he sat up and spoke quietly: "What's up, Abe?"

"Night before last I was playing cards with Gorman over at Henry's. After daylight Gorman went out for a bucket of water. We heard a rifle crack. I looked out the window. Stormy was tumbling.

"You know the draw that runs down past his corral? Barb Doubleday, Pettigrew, Van Horn, Stone and a bunch of cowboys and Texas men lay in that draw. It was hell to pay from daylight till dark. The Dutchman got laid out cold right at the start. They tried to rush me. I stopped three of 'em and dug myself in. We went at it hammer and tongs. In the afternoon they put a hole through my whiskers. After awhile they clipped my shoulder. Then I got a bullet through my arm." He held up his left forearm swathed in a mass of soiled and blood-soaked bandages. And he told of Van Horn's go-devil.

"The raid's on," muttered Laramie.

"Soon as it was dark, I began to dig under the sill," Hawk went on. "They began lighting fires. I knew they couldn't keep those going a great while. About ten o'clock I crawled out under the front sill and got to the creek; I never was so gone for water in my life. I set a candle so it would fire the shack when it burned down and sneaked a horse from their bunch and got over to my place." He looked at his arm. "I tried to keep things bound up. Maybe I left a little red behind me. If I did, they'll be after me."

His story haltingly told; his utterance through his torn cheek thick and painful but savagely uncompromising; carrying a physical burden of wounds that would have overwhelmed a lesser man but with a deadly hate showing in his manner, Hawk, from sheer weakness, paused: "I went to my cabin to look for more cartridges," he added slowly, "and not a one was there left on the place." He hesitated again. "I didn't want to come here—"

Laramie sprang to his feet: "Where the hell else would you go?"

Hawk heard unmoved the rough assurance; perhaps his eyes flashed, for Laramie's voice rang strong and true. He already had his hand on Hawk's chair: "Come over here to the light," he said, "till we get some of this dirt off you. You need a bath, Abe. For a clean man you look like—"

Hawk put up his right hand: "I'll do for all the job that's left ahead of me."

"What job's left ahead of you?"

"You've got a rifle like mine, Jim; the Marlin you don't use."

"Well?"

"I come to see if you'd lend it to me again."

"Why not?"

"Got any shells for it?" snapped Hawk.

"I guess so."

"I left the horse at the cabin to stand 'em off awhile. They'll lose a little time there. They'll come down the creek—can't come any other way. I'm going to wait for 'em in the timber."

"What for?"

"I'll finish with Doubleday and Van Horn, anyhow. Maybe I can with Stone."

"And they'll finish with you."

"After I get them three the rest are welcome to what's left of me. I've got to be moving."

"Hold on a minute, Abe." Laramie sat down on the side of his cot, his knees spread apart, his elbows resting on them, and his hands clasped as he leaned forward, head down, to think.

"Them fellows are riding every minute," Hawk reminded him grimly.

"Let's talk this thing over," persisted Laramie.

"I'll pay you for your rifle right now," mumbled Hawk, feeling with his right hand in his trousers pocket for some gold pieces.

"Don't talk monkey stuff, Abe."

"Then don't make a monkey out of *me*," snapped Hawk. "Give me your rifle and let me go!"

"After we've talked it over."

Hawk pulled himself up out of the chair. "You blamed fool," he said brokenly. "Don't you know that bunch will track me to your door and smash us with lead or burn us up in this shack if they get here first? Give me the rifle," he thundered, "or I'll go into the timber with this six-shooter. What do you mean? Are you going to turn yellow on me because I'm a thief?"

Laramie moved neither hand nor foot: "You're an older man than I am, Abe," he replied, without even looking up. "I can take words from you, I'd hate to take from anybody else—you know that; and you know why. You won't talk; all right. Now I'll tell you where you get off; you're not going down to the timber—not a blamed step," he added deliberately. "Finger your six-shooter as much as you like." Laramie waved his hand with his words. "Use it on me if you like. But, by—, Abe—" As his voice changed, he jumped to his feet, adding like lightning, "you're not going to use it on yourself!"

He sprang for Hawk, reaching with his left hand for the gun. In tigerish ferocity the two men came together. Sleepy Cat worthies had sometimes speculated on what might happen if the two men most known and most feared in the Falling Wall country, Hawk and Laramie, should ever quarrel. They met now; but in a quarrel the wildest gossip had not fancied. Reeling, feet slipping, knees and hands locking, eyes staring, no word spoken and breathing hard, the two struggled in the middle of the cooped-up room—Hawk striving to free and kill himself; Laramie determined to wrest the gun from his grasp.

It was an unequal contest. Weakened by loss of blood, Hawk was not long a match for the only man on the range who under other conditions could have stood up before him. Gradually, with the gun in his right hand, Hawk was bent backward, with Laramie's left hand slipping along the barrel closer and closer to the grip. Prolonged by the fear of further injuring the wounded man, the tempestuous effort for mastery ended when Hawk was forced to the bed and Laramie's iron fingers, closing on the gun, wrenched it from him.

Hawk was done out and Laramie without more resistance straightened him out on the bed.

"You're worse hit than you think," panted the conqueror. "I've got a scheme better than yours, if there's time to put it through. Wait till I get a couple of horses."

The clatter of a horse outside cut into his last words. Laramie instantly slipped Hawk's revolver back into his hand, picked up his own gun and holster, strapping it to his waist as he ran, crossed the room, tore up a board in the floor, snatched a pair of rifles from their cache and hastening back to Hawk, his eyes glued all the while to the door, pushed one rifle into Hawk's hand and swung the other to his hip.

Not a word had been spoken. But preparations for a reception had been made complete and eventualities thoroughly considered. Heavy footfalls outside announced the approach of a man. The next moment the door was flung open and the intruder heard Laramie's voice in savage emphasis:

"Pitch up!"

The intruder did not, however, pitch up. It was John Lefever. He stood amazed. "For the love of God," he exclaimed, "what's broke loose?"

"Come in, John," cried Laramie, seizing his arm. "I want your horse a minute. Stay here till I get back—come, Abe, lively!"

"Where you going?" demanded Lefever, staring as he tried to collect his wits.

Laramie hurried Hawk past him: "That'll depend on the shooting, John," was all Laramie hastily said. "Doubleday and Van Horn have got a bunch of Texas men raiding the Falling Wall."

Lefever, gazing stunned at Hawk, talked as if he saw nothing. "I know all about that," he cried. "Man alive, that's what I'm here for. Hold on, can't you?"

"Not now. Stick around till I get back."

Lefever caught his breath in time to fire one more question:

"What about Abe?"

"He's not coming back. Scout around down along the creek, John, so you can see those fellows when they ride in. Hold 'em as long as you can and for God's sake keep 'em out of this cabin—there's blood on everything."

CHAPTER 19

LEFEVER RECEIVES THE RAIDERS

Laramie knew Lefever to be quite equal to the highly particular job he had assigned to him and that John would give his best to it. Hardly thirty minutes later, the raiders rode out of the timber along the creek. Van Horn stopped his pack for a word of warning: "Look to your guns," he said harshly. "You can guess most o' you what you'll be up against, if there's trouble at this joint." Leaving the creek, the party rode out on a rarely used trail that, Stone told them, led to Laramie's cabin. They followed this for some distance, keeping two men ahead as they had done in the early morning. These two men, reaching the bench, which at that point had been cut sharply away by a flood, halted. The main party riding up the hill debouched on level ground at the crest and joined their scouts. Half a mile to their right stood Laramie's cabin. The bench land lying in front of it was as smooth as a table and covered with mountain blue stem. Out of the level ground, a hundred yards from the edge of the bench where Doubleday's party had halted, rose a huge and solitary fragment of rock.

Beside this rock stood a large man facing the intruders; slung over his left forearm he carried a rifle and his right hand he held well out toward them with its open palm raised in the air. The raiders understood the signal; it warned them to advance no farther.

"What's that fat buck doing up in this country?" asked Van Horn, angrily.

"Who is it?" demanded Doubleday.

"John Lefever," returned Van Horn, greatly nettled. "What are you doing here?" he bellowed at the unwelcome sentinel.

John pointed a stubby forefinger at Van Horn and returned a perfectly intelligible retort: "That's not the first question, Harry; that's the second question," he yelled. "What are *you* doing here?"

This was not in all respects a question easy to answer. But Van Horn was resourceful: "We're on our way down the creek, John. Rode up from the bottom to see Jim Laramie a minute."

"Just a friendly call," assented John. "Well, how about sidearms," he shouted, "and how many of you are there?"

Van Horn looked around him: "Why, maybe a

dozen, I reckon, John. You know most everybody here."

"How many of you are there want to see Jim a minute, Harry?" asked Lefever, calm but conveniently close to the rock and quite conscious of the delicacy of his position should shooting begin.

There was some exchange of talk before the question was answered: "Look here, Lefever," roared Doubleday huskily; "what the hell's all this fuss about?"

"Why, it's like this, Barb," returned Lefever, nothing abashed. "When I seen you crossing down there at the forks I thought maybe you'd lost your Bibles in the creek. That's the way you acted. But when I seen you and Harry Van Horn and Tom Stone loading your rifles in the timber, I reckoned you must be comin' up to ask Jim to run for sheriff on the cattle ticket."

Sarcasm could hardly convey more defiance and contempt. The riders realized they had been watched and that deception was useless; Van Horn was furiously angry. "Look here, Lefever," he called out, short and sharp.

"I'm looking right there, Harry," yelled Lefever irreverently. "With a bunch of mugs like that on the horizon I sure wouldn't dare look anywhere else!"

"These boys won't stand any more fooling," roared Doubleday.

"I wouldn't either, Barb, if you'd got me into this scrape as deep as you've got them," was the retort.

Nothing less than violent outbursts of profanity served now. And these proceeding to a climax of strength and rapidity, gradually subsided as such outbursts do and the two sides started to argue all over again.

After much parley and protestations of peace- ful intent, provided they were treated fair, Doubleday and Van Horn were allowed to ride up to the rock, but not to dismount. "Now," suggested Lefever to the two, "talk just plain business."

"Right you have it, John," returned Van Horn briskly. "The rustlers have got to go. We're look- ing for Abe Hawk. Gorman and Dutch Henry are lifting cattle now in the Happy Hunting Grounds. We're going to clean out the rest of 'em. We've tracked Abe here. Without any hard words, we want him."

"Then, boys, you want to ride right on; keep on riding, for he's not here. I don't know anything, but that much I do know," asserted the big fellow positively.

"How do you know?" demanded Doubleday grimly.

"I just walked down here from the cabin; there's no one there. I rode in here this morning from the Reservation, Barb. A buck looking for horses over on the North Fork yesterday saw the fight at

Gorman's—everybody knows about it."

Van Horn showed his teeth: "You're a pretty good artist, John, with your buck looking for horses."

Lefever deprecated the compliment: "You must remember, Harry, I worked seven year for you. Seven year—and then didn't get all was coming to me."

"If you had," returned Van Horn candidly, "your headstone would be covered with moss by this time, John. Where's Laramie?"

Lefever stood with his left hand eagerly extended and appeared as if sensitive at Van Horn's incredulity: "All the same, Harry," he exclaimed, "I can take you to that buck inside two hours' ride and get his story. I've got five twenty-dollar gold pieces in my pocket that says so. I'll put 'em up in Barb Doubleday's hands right now against your five."

"A man couldn't pry you loose from five twenty-dollar gold pieces if you had five thousand in your pocket, John. What are you stalling around for?" demanded Van Horn suspiciously. "Where's Laramie?"

Lefever was frankness itself; almost over-frank in his genuine simplicity. Had it not been for his big, blunt eyes and round, smooth face he might have been suspected of duplicity—but not by the two men now talking to him; they knew beyond a doubt that John was "stringing" them. Unfortunately they could not prevent it. He answered Van Horn's sharp question as innocently as a child.

"That's more than I can say this minute, Harry, where Jim Laramie is; but he's not far, I can tell you that, for the coffee pot was on the stove when I got to the shack a while ago."

"Then what are you holding us up here for?" barked Doubleday with rough words.

"I'm a peace officer, Barb, a deputy marshal." The bursting expression of disgust on his questioners' faces did not ruffle John's candor. "I know what you fellows are up to. I won't have any bloodshed here this morning—that's flat. Laramie gets hot sometimes and this is one of the times for folks to go slow. If you want to talk to Laramie come along up to the shack. But send them longhorns over there down to the creek," he added, as an afterthought and in the bluntly candid tone of appeal that distinguished his persuasiveness.

"Long hell!" spluttered Doubleday.

"Longhorns," persisted Lefever.

Barb growled at the proposal to send the boys down to the creek, and Van Horn objected, but there was no escape from Lefever's stubbornness, except a fight and this was not wanted. Lefever passed his word that Hawk was not in the cabin, but he was adamant on sending the men to the bottoms and his demand was grudgingly acceded to. In point of fact, John reckoned himself on foot with a rifle equal to two men on horseback, even if Van Horn were one. But not being able to take care of a dozen horsemen he was resolved to have no volleying applause from other guns, if the unexpected should happen on the open bench land.

After Doubleday and Van Horn's following had at length filed down to the creek bottom, Lefever walked beside the two horsemen toward the cabin, and, since he would not walk fast and the two refused to ride ahead of him, the pace was deliberate all the way. Nor could Lefever be persuaded even to walk between the two horsemen; he kept them both religiously on his left, his rifle lying carelessly across his forearm as he entertained them with a moderately timed and unfailing flow of Reservation small talk.

But he could not control Van Horn's quick, flashing eyes, and these were busy every moment and every foot of the way with reconnaissance and inference. It did not escape either him or Doubleday that a bunch of horses had been but lately driven over the ground they were crossing, and every trail leading to and from the cabin obliterated; this, however, only assured both that their man was close at hand and strengthened their determination to get him in their own way when they were ready. So intent were they on reading the ground as well as on keeping a sharp eye on the cabin itself, that they had almost reached it before Van Horn, halting, fixed his eyes on the hills to the left—that is, down the creek—and exclaimed sharply: "Who's that?"

Riding in a leisurely fashion down and out of the rough country to the South, a mile away, a man emerging from a rift between two hills could be seen following one of the cattle trails toward the creek.

Lefever, after a minute's study, answered the question blandly: "I'm thinkin' that's Jim Laramie, right now."

He waved his hat at the distant horseman, who also rode with a rifle slung across his pommel and carried his lines high in his right hand. The horseman continued for some moments toward the creek, then looking, seemingly by accident, toward the house he saw the signaling, stopped his pony, paused, and reigning him around, headed at an easy pace for the group before the cabin. It was, as Lefever had said, Laramie.

A few minutes later he trotted his horse across the field and slowed him up in front of Van Horn and Doubleday. His greeting to his visitors was dry; their own was somewhat strained, but Lefever at once took the initiative: "Jim," he said, identifying himself in his bluntly honest way with the interests of the raiders, "we're looking for Abe Hawk."

Laramie's response was merely to the point: "He's not here."

"Has he been here?" demanded Van Horn.

"Yes," answered Laramie. Lefever at intervals

looked virtuously from questioner to questioned.

"How long ago, Jim?" continued Van Horn.

Laramie regarded him steadily: "Several times in the last few weeks."

"Was he here yesterday?" asked Van Horn suddenly.

"I was on the Reservation yesterday."

"Has he been here this morning?"

"Yes."

If Lefever jumped inwardly at this most unexpected admission he suppressed all outward sign of surprise; his wide open eyes did not blink and his close-cut mustache preserved its honesty undefiled. But he wondered what might be coming.

"How long ago?" continued Van Horn.

"Early. What's all this questioning about?" Laramie demanded in turn, looking from Van Horn to Doubleday and to Lefever. "Who wants Hawk?"

"Jim, we're cleaning up the rustlers," said Van Horn. "Things have got so bad it had to be done. We want Hawk. We've got Gorman and Henry. Now, if it's a fair question, is Abe here?"

"He's not."

"Not in your shack?"

"No."

"Are you willing we should search it?"

"Search hell! What do you mean?" asked Laramie curtly. "Isn't my word good as to who's in my shack?"

"Jim!" Lefever held up a peacemaker's hand.

"We thought maybe he might have come in since you rode away."

"Well—" Laramie cooled somewhat, "if it'll do you any good, I'll look inside and see."

Van Horn sarcastically demurred: "Don't take the trouble, don't take the trouble, Jim."

"Still he might be there," urged Lefever, "in the way I say—he might've walked in since you went into the hills—what? No objection to my looking in there, is there, Jim?"

"No man can search my cabin," snapped Laramie. "Have you got a warrant for Abe Hawk?" He threw the question sharply at Lefever.

With Lefever's disclaimer, Doubleday interposed a savage rejoinder: "A rope'll fit Abe's neck better than a warrant."

Laramie eyed the old cattleman unmoved: "And you're here to get me to help you slip the noose, are you?"

"We're here to clean out these cattle thieves," stormed Doubleday.

"There are no cattle thieves here," retorted Laramie undisturbed. "You're wasting the time you'll need on your job. Move on!"

Even Van Horn was taken aback by the rude command; he pulled his horse around: "Look here, Jim; let me talk to you a minute alone."

Laramie, guiding his horse with his heels, followed Van Horn twenty feet away and listened: "Jim, I'm leading this bunch, and whatever

208

troubles you've had with Barb and his friends, now's the time to fix 'em up. They'll give you the best of it. If you've got any line on where Hawk is, say so and it puts you with us; say nothing, and you're against us."

Laramie eyed him without a quiver: "I'm against you, Harry."

Van Horn did not give up. He talked again, and talked hard. It was useless. Doubleday rode over to where Van Horn held Laramie in deadly earnest conference. Van Horn, ready to quit, gladly let the older man take over the case. But Doubleday made no better success. Laramie could not be moved. If coaxed, he was obstinate; if threatened, impatient—contemptuous. Doubleday, when Laramie coldly refused even to answer his questions concerning Hawk, boiled over.

He moved his horse a step and opened his vials of wrath: "Laramie, you've turned down the last chance decent folks on the range'll ever try to hand you—the last chance you'll ever see to pull away from these Falling Wall thieves. Now," he exclaimed, raising his right hand and arm with a bitter imprecation, "we'll show you who's going to run the Sleepy Cat range. I'll drive you out of this country if it takes every cowboy I can hire and every dollar I've got. This country won't hold you and me after today. D'ye hear?" he shouted, almost bending with his huge frame over Laramie and beside himself with rage. Then spurring his horse, he wheeled it around to rejoin Van Horn.

Even then Laramie was too quick for him. Almost in the very instant, he jumped his own pony after the angry man and gaining the head of Doubleday's horse, caught the bridle and jerked the beast almost to its haunches.

It was a ticklish instant. Van Horn, with his hand on his revolver, attempted to spur to Doubleday's assistance. Lefever interposed with a sharp move that put him plumply in front of Van Horn: "Not till them two are through, Harry. We stay right here till them two's done."

The very impudence of Laramie's move had taken Doubleday by surprise and Laramie was hurling angry words at him before Lefever had intervened: "Hold on, Doubleday," Laramie said bluntly, "you can't put your abuse all over me first and then run away with it. You'll hear what I've got to say. I rode this range before you ever saw it; I'll ride this range when you're gone. I was born here, Doubleday; my father lived here before me. The air I breathe, this sky over my head, this ground under my feet, are mine, and I stick here in spite of you and your cattle crooks. If men run off your cattle it's your sheriff's business—you own him. And it's your business to run 'em down—not mine. You come here without a warrant, without a definite complaint, and ask me to turn an old man over to a bunch of lynchers! Not on your life. Not today or any other day."

Doubleday interrupted, but he was forced to listen: "You talk about thieves," Laramie spoke fast and remorselessly, "and you belong to the bunch that's tried to steal every foot of land I own in the Falling Wall. After you and your lawyers and land office tools have stolen thousands of acres from the government, you talk as if you were an angel out of heaven about the men that brand your mavericks. Hell!" The scorn of the expletive drew from the very depths of furious contempt. "I'd rather stand by a thief that calls himself a thief, than a thief that steals under a lawyer. Send your hired men after me; give 'em plenty of ammunition. They'll find me right here, Barb— right here where I live."

CHAPTER 20

The Doctor's Office

When Sawdy rode into Sleepy Cat next morning it was known that he had come from the Reservation and he was besieged for news from the Falling Wall. At Kitchen's, where he put up his horse; on his way up street to his room over McAlpin's pool hall, he was assailed with questions. Pretty accurate reports of the two exciting days in the North country had already trickled into Sleepy Cat. To these, Sawdy listened with stolid attention but he managed to add to them very little. He possessed to a degree the faculty of talking freely, sententiously even, without contributing anything strictly pertinent to a subject. What he conveyed, when he meant to withhold information, was really no more than an air of reserve in which wisdom seemed discreetly restrained. On this present occasion he realized it would be known that he had encountered the raiders the day before at Laramie's—but while admitting this profusely, he minimized all else.

Not until he had bathed, slept, shaved and set himself down near nightfall at Belle Shockley's did he tell any considerable part of his story. But all that prudence would permit he told, or rather, Belle demanded and received at his hands. Where the heart is involved the strongest men are helpless.

"I ran into the bunch on my way down, right at Laramie's cabin," Sawdy said to Belle. "Laramie and Doubleday were having the hottest kind of a row when I rode up. I made sure we'd be shooting in the next couple of minutes. But John Lefever was watching pretty close and holding Van Horn. Barb cooled down when he saw three of us on deck. I told him on the side, the Governor had telephoned Pearson and the Colonel was going to send cavalry down after them and they'd better scatter. It was a bluff, but for a few minutes I had him and Van Horn guessing. They said they'd go home when they got Hawk. Lefever is staying up there for a day or two."

"What did they do after that?" demanded Belle, referring to the men whose names were on everybody's tongues.

"Beat the bushes from Laramie's to the Reservation," answered Sawdy. "Didn't leave a square yard of country unturned from the Falling Wall to the Crazy Woman."

"Will they ever find Hawk?"

"Did you ever find a needle in a haystack?"

"I never looked for one."

"Them fellows are looking for the stack. They can't locate the hay. Slip me that Worcestershire sauce, Belle. Yours truly. No more potatoes. This is a good piece of ham, Belle. I wish to God you'd serve a glass of beer with a man's supper."

"You can get all the supper and all the beer you want at the hotel," flared Belle. "This is no blind pig—"

"It's the only place in Main Street, then, that ain't."

"And it never will be," averred Belle, indignantly.

"Come up to the hotel with me right now," returned Sawdy coldly, "and I'll buy you a bottle of beer. Bet you ten dollars you da'ssent do it— who the devil—" Sawdy almost choked as the two heard a knock at the door—"who the devil is that?" he repeated. The door opened and Jim Laramie walked in.

He sent his hat sailing toward a side table, stepped forward and, catching at a chair on the way, greeted Belle and her guest and sat down before a plate cover opposite Sawdy. He pointed to what remained of Sawdy's supper and, with knife and fork, started in: "There's enough for me right here, Belle," he said.

Sawdy raised his chin: "Not this time, Jim. Not on your life. That's the way you always eat my supper."

"You eat too much, Henry—it will kill you some time," observed Laramie, losing no time in his initiative. He ignored Sawdy's stare and the big man, disgusted, sat dumb: "Don't surrender, Sawdy," counseled Laramie. "Keep going, and excuse me if I seem to begin."

Sawdy paused, his knife and fork firmly in hand, but pointing helplessly into the air: "This is the first square meal I've had for two days," he said, as one whose hopes have been dashed.

"First I've had for ten days," returned Laramie.

"What are they doing up there, Jim?" asked Sawdy peremptorily.

"Killing their horses."

"They won't find him," Sawdy predicted in words inaudible six feet away.

"I hope not."

"How's he holding out?"

"Hard hit, Henry."

"Will he make it?"

"You can't kill a cat."

"Well"—Sawdy resumed his supper, "it's your game, Jim, not mine; but I'd think twice before I'd get that range bunch after me on any man's account."

Laramie's eyes flashed, but he spoke quietly: "I couldn't see Abe killed like a rattlesnake."

"What are you down for?"

"I've got to have a couple of needles, a little catgut and some gauze."

"Where are you going to get them?"

"Going to steal them over at Doc Carpy's."

"Nervy."

"You can do it for me, Henry."

"Me?"

"I'll give you the key to his cabinet."

"Where'd you get that?"

"Met him on my way in. He was going up to Pettigrew's to look after the wounded. The window in the end of the wing opens into the operating room, where the supplies are."

"I'd look fine climbing into a window at two hundred and twenty pounds."

"It's on the ground floor," returned Laramie, unmoved.

"What will the family be doing while I'm burgling?"

"Mrs. Carpy and the girls are in Medicine Bend. The house is empty. When you're through, leave the key in the skull of the skeleton behind the door."

Sawdy stared without much enthusiasm at the

215

little key that Laramie passed to him; then he slipped it without comment into his pocket. The talk went on in low, leisurely tones until the second portion of ham had been served, when both resumed their supper as if nothing had been eaten or said. Afterward, Laramie spent an hour getting together some things he needed at home. He met Sawdy later at Kitchen's barn. Sawdy, with abundance of grumbling at his assignment, had the gauze and the catgut, but he had brought the key back. He could not find the surgeon's needles. There seemed nothing for it but for Laramie to go to the office and make the search himself. He thought of Belle; she would do it for him, he knew, but he felt it would not be right to mix her up in what might prove a still more tragic affair. After brief reflection he started for Carpy's himself.

The doctor's house stood back of Main Street, a block and a half from the barn. Laramie walked half a mile to reach it, choosing unlighted ways for the trip. The night was dark and by crossing a vacant lot he reached the rear of the house unobserved. The office, divided into a consulting room and an operating room, consisted of a one- story wing connecting with the residence— the consulting room adjoining the residence, the operating room occupying the end of the wing. This latter was the room Laramie sought. The window that Sawdy had already burglariously entered, opened easily, and Laramie, standing alone in the dark room, felt in his pocket for a match.

He had been in the office more than once before and knew about where the cabinet containing the surgical instruments stood. A connecting door led from the room he had entered to the office proper. He tried this. It was unlocked and he left it closed. The curtains of the windows were drawn and he took a match from his pocket, lighted it and looked around. The first thing he saw was the articulated skeleton suspended near the door from the ceiling. It would have been a shock had he not seen it before and been familiar with the label fastened to the breastbone reciting that this had once been Flat Nose George, an early day desperado of the high country.

Turning from this relic, Laramie set about his work, disdaining to inspect various gruesome specimens in alcohol ranged along a shelf. Aided by an occasional match which he lighted and shielded in his left hand, he found the cabinet and with his key opened the door. The flame of his match too carefully guarded, flickered in his fingers, failed and went out. He thrust it hastily into one pocket, drew a fresh match from another and was about to scratch it across his leather wristlet when he heard a door open. The next moment he saw, under the door leading from his room to the consulting room, a flash of light.

Awkward as it was to be interrupted, he faced the surprise with such composure as he could muster. Who could it be? he asked himself. The family was accounted for, the house locked. He scratched the match again. As it flared up he looked into the cabinet, found the packet of needles, tore a card of them in two, slipped one piece into a waistcoat pocket and closed the cabinet door. He turned to listen to the office intruder. Laramie hoped that nothing would bring the unwelcome visitor into the operating room, but as he stood awaiting developments the unlocked door was pushed open and a tiny flashlight was thrown into the room in which he stood.

Fortunately Laramie outside the circle of light was left in the dark. The intruder was a woman. He shrank back and she luckily turned her light from him but only to encounter, as she stepped forward, Flat Nose George, no less forbidding now than he had been in life. The woman with the light started back in horror and a sharp little exclamation betrayed her identity; Laramie was at once aware that he was facing Kate Doubleday.

Nothing could have pleased him less. In so small a room it was impossible to escape detection. He could almost hear her breathe and would have reveled in her presence so close, but that the apprehension of frightening her weighed on him like a mountain. Hardly daring to breathe himself he cursed the erratic doctor's skeleton pet—hung, of all places, where every little while he was cutting people open.

The skeleton had already set the girl's nerves on edge. What would happen if she discovered a live man as well as the ghastly remains of a dead one—not to mention alcoholic clippings from other subnormal notables of the mountains? With the flashlight she was evidently searching for something and Laramie surmised it must be the electric light switch: "I think," he suggested in as steady a tone as possible, "you'll find the light button to the right of the door behind you."

He was prepared for a scream or a swoon. Instead, the flashlight was turned directly on him: "Who are you?" came sharply and quickly from behind it.

"I might ask the same question. You can see I'm Jim Laramie. I can guess you're Kate Doubleday."

"I am, and I've come here for dressings for wounded men at Pettigrew's. What are you doing here?" she demanded, peremptorily.

His lips were sealed for more reasons than one. Least of all would it do for him to expose Doctor Carpy's friendliness and embroil him in a feud which Laramie knew he ought to face alone.

Kate held the light excitedly on him. It was an instant before he had his answer in hand: "I've lied to a good many people at different times about different things," he said deliberately. "I've still got my first lie to tell to you, Kate. And I certainly won't tell it tonight. Don't ask me what I'm doing here. Turn on the light by the door, or let me do it, so I can see you. You here alone?"

"No, there are plenty of men outside with me," she exclaimed abruptly.

"I shouldn't have asked that question," he continued in the same tone. "I know you're alone. You say 'men' because you're afraid of me—"

"I'm not the least afraid of you. And don't deceive yourself. There are men here."

"But they are mostly in bottles, Kate—and in pieces. Live men don't ride up to a place like this without making a noise. Flat Nose George is the only man here besides me, outside the alcohol, and I can claim him as well as you can."

"I'm sure you would feel perfectly at home with Flat Nose George," she retorted swiftly.

If the words stung, Laramie kept his temper. "Probably there's a good deal I deserve that you haven't heard about me," he said slowly. "But from the way you talk, you've heard a few things maybe I don't deserve. Nobody's got any right to class me with Flat Nose George or anybody else in Carpy's museum."

"You've classed yourself with him," she exclaimed vehemently. "Defending cattle thieves and harboring them! Everyone knows that!"

"I did talk rough to your father this morning. I was pretty angry. Just the same, don't believe everything you hear about me. At present, it's just us two. What do you want to do, surrender to me?"

"No!" she snapped the word out furiously. "I won't, not if you kill me."

"Suppose I surrender to you? What do you want me to do—stick up my hands? So far, they haven't been up—if I remember right. But I expect I'll have to learn sometime how to surrender."

"I want no surrender, no parley with you. The doctor told me his house was empty and directed me here for the dressings. When I come, I find you. I'll get away at once. Before I go—"

"No, I'll go. But let me turn on the light." He stepped to the door and pressed the button. "I wanted," he continued, as a light flooded the queer room, "to have just one look at you before I go." She stood before him quite unafraid. Her eyes flashed as if she were actually mistress of the situation instead of really helpless in the presence of her father's most resourceful enemy.

Laramie half-smiled at her serenity: "Why don't you go?" she exclaimed.

Still regarding her, he shifted his position a little and replied with entire good-nature: "I only live along, from one sight to another of you. I'm just filling up, like a man at a spring. You don't object to my only looking at you for a minute?"

"I object to being delayed and annoyed," she declared in a blaze. "I've come here for dressings needed for wounded men—"

"Well, so have I, if you must have it."

"I was sent here by Doctor Carpy for things he

wants tonight; you have no more right here helping yourself to his property than you have taking other people's."

"Don't say I take other people's property!" Laramie spoke fiercely. "Don't call me a thief." His words burned with anger. "My hands may not be as white as yours—they're just as clean!"

Stunned as she might well have been at the outburst, Kate stood her ground: "Did Doctor Carpy give you permission to come here tonight?" She shot the words at Laramie without giving him time to breathe.

Laramie checked the flood of anger he had loosed: "I don't need permission from Doctor Carpy to come here night or day. Ask *him* if you want to," he said with scornful disgust. He sank down on the chair at his side in complete resentment of the whole situation and, leaning forward with a hand spread over one knee and one fist clenched on the other, he stared not at Kate's eyes, but at the floor, with only her trim boots in his field of vision. "What's the use?" he exclaimed, drawing the words up seemingly all the way from his own disorderly and alkali-stained foot coverings. "What's the use?" he repeated, in stronger and more savage tones. "I've treated her from the first instant I saw her, and every instant since, as I thought a woman ought to be treated— would like to be treated. Now I get my reward. She calls me a thief—and, my God! I take it. I don't ride out and kill her father who taught her to do it, quick as I can reach him; I just take it!" he exclaimed.

He hesitated a moment. Then he flung a question at her like a thunderbolt: "What do you want here?"

She was frightened. His rage was plain enough; who could tell the lengths to which it might carry him?

She kept her dignity but she answered and without quibbling: "I want some gauze and some cotton and some medicines."

He strode to the cabinet and, concealing the movement as he unlocked it with Carpy's key, he threw open the glass door: "You'd be all night finding the stuff," he said curtly, taking the supplies from various cluttered piles on different shelves. "You say he wants this tonight," he added, when her packet was complete: "How are you going to get it to him?"

"Carry it to him."

"At Pettigrew's? What do you mean? It would take an experienced horseman all night to ride around by Black Creek."

"I'm going over the pass."

He could not conceal his anger: "Does your father know that?"

"He said I might try it."

Laramie flamed again: "A fine father to send a tenderfoot girl on a night ride into a country like that!"

She was defiant: "I can ride anywhere a man can."

"Let me tell you," he faced her and his eyes flashed, "if you try riding 'anywhere' too often, some night your father's daughter will fail to get home!"

Ignoring the door, he stepped to the open window by which he had entered and, springing through it, was gone.

CHAPTER 21

THE HIDING PLACE

Disdaining any further attempt at concealment, Laramie rode angrily over to Kitchen's barn; anyone that wanted a dispute with him just then could have it, and promptly. Kitchen got up his horse and, cutting short the liveryman's attempt to talk, Laramie headed for home.

The sky was studded with a glory of stars. He rode fast, his fever of anger acting as a spur to his anxiety, which was to get back to dress Hawk's wounds.

His thoughts raced with the hoofs of his horse. Nothing could have galled and humiliated him more than to realize how Kate Doubleday regarded him. Plainly she looked on him as no better than one of the ordinary rustlers of the Falling Wall country. This was distressingly clear; yet he knew in his own heart that hers was the only opinion among her people that he cared anything about. Furious waves of resentment alternated with the realization that such an issue was inevitable—how could it be otherwise? She had heard the loose talk of men about her— Stone, alone, to reckon no other, could be depended on to lie freely about him. Van Horn, he was as sure, would not scruple to blacken an enemy; and added to Laramie's discomfiture was the reflection that this man whose attentions to Kate he most dreaded, held her ear against him and could, if need be, poison the wells.

To these could be added, as his implacable enemy, her own father. This last affair had cut off every hope of getting on with the men for whom he had no respect and who for one reason or another hated him as heartily as he hated them.

Under such a load of entanglement lay the thought of Kate. What utter foolishness even to think of her as he let himself think and hope! Clattering along, he told himself nothing could ever come of it but bitterness; and he cast the thought and hope of knowing her better and better until he could make her his own, completely out of his heart.

The only trouble was that neither she, nor the bitterness would stay out. As often as he put them out they came in again. The first few miles of his road were the same that she would soon be riding

225

after him. Again and again he felt anger at the idea of her riding the worst of the Falling Wall trail at night to Pettigrew's. More than once he felt the impulse to wait for her, and even slackened his pace.

But when he did so, there arose before him her picture as she flung the hateful words at him; they came back as keenly as if he heard them again and he could feel his cheeks burning in the cold night air. Self-respect, if nothing else, would prevent his even speaking another word to her that night. His hatred of her father swelled in the thought that he should let her attempt such a ride.

For several miles beyond where he knew Kate must turn for the pass, Laramie rode on toward home; then watching his landmarks carefully he reined his horse directly to the left and headed for the broken country lying between the Turkey and the mountains. At some little distance from the trail, he stopped and sitting immovable in his saddle, listened to ascertain whether he was followed. For almost thirty minutes—and that is a long time—he waited, buried in the silence of the night and without the slightest impatience. He heard in the distance the coyotes and the owls but no horseman passed nor did the sound of hoofs come within hearing. Then reining his pony's head again toward the black heights of the Lodge Pole range he continued his journey.

Soon all semblance of any trail was left behind

and he rode of necessity more slowly. More than once he halted, seemingly to reassure himself as to his bearings for he was pushing his way where few men would care to ride even in daylight. He was feeling across precipitous gashes and along treacherous ledges esteemed by Bighorn but feared by horse and man; and among huge masses of rocky fragments that had crashed from dizzy heights above before finding a resting place. And even then they had been heaved and tumbled about by the fury of mountain storms.

Laramie was, in fact, nearing the place—by the least passable of all approaches—where he had hidden Hawk. Yet he did not hesitate either to stop or to listen or to double on his trail more than once. Maneuvering in this manner for a long time he emerged on a small opening, turned almost squarely about and rode half a mile. Dismounting at this point and lifting his rifle from its scabbard he slung his bag over his shoulder and walked rapidly forward.

The hiding place had been well chosen. On a high plateau of the Falling Wall country, so broken as to forbid all chance travel and to be secure from accidental intrusion—a breeding place for grizzlies and mountain lions—there had once been opened a considerable silver mining camp. Substantial sums had been spent in development and from an old Turkey Creek trail a road had been blasted and dug across the open country divided by the canyon of the Falling Wall river. In its escape from the mountains the river at this point cuts a deep gash through a rock barrier and from this striking formation, known as the canyon of the Falling Wall, the river takes its name.

Where the old mine road crosses the plateau an ambitious bridge, as Laramie once told Kate, had been projected across the river. It was designed to replace a ferry at the bottom of the canyon but with the ruinous decline in the value of silver the mines had been abandoned; a weather-beaten abutment at the top of the south canyon wall alone remained to recall the story. The earth and rock fill behind this abutment had been washed out by storms leaving the framing timbers above it intact, and below these there remained a cave-like space which the slowly decaying supports served to roof.

Laramie on a hunting trip had once discovered this retreat and had at times used it as a shelter when caught over night in its vicinity. During subsequent visits he found an overhang in the rock behind the original fill that made a second smaller chamber and in this he had as a boy cached his mink and rat traps and the discard of his hunting equipment.

To the later people coming into the Falling Wall country with cattle the existence of all this was practically unknown. Nothing visible betrayed the retreat and to men who rarely left the saddle and had little occasion to cross the bad lands, there was slight chance to stumble on it. It was here, a few miles west of his own home, that Laramie had carried Hawk.

Making his way in the darkness toward the dugout, Laramie whistled low and clearly, and planting his feet with care on a foothold of old masonry swung down to where a fissure opening in the rock afforded entrance into the irregular room.

A single word came in a low tone from the darkness: "Jim?"

Laramie, answering, struck a match and, after a little groping, lighted a candle and set it in a niche near where Hawk lay. The rustler was stretched on a rude bunk. The furnishings of the cave-like refuge were the scantiest. Between uprights supporting the old roof, a plank against the wall served as a narrow table; the bunk had been built into the opposite wall out of planking left by the bridge carpenters. For the rest there was little more in the place than the few belongings of a hunter's lodge long deserted. A quilt served for mattress and bedding for Hawk and his sunken eyes above his black beard showed how sorely he needed surgical care. To this, Laramie lost no time in getting. He provided more lights, opened his kit of dressings and with a pail of water went to work.

What would have seemed impossible to a surgeon, Laramie with two hours' crude work accomplished on Hawk's wounds. But in a country where the air is so pure that major operations may be performed in ordinary cabins, cleanliness and care, even though rude, count for more than they possibly could elsewhere. The most difficult part of the task that night lay in getting water up the almost sheer canyon wall from the river three hundred feet below. It would have been a man's job in daylight; add to this black night and the care necessary to leave no traces of getting down and climbing up.

Leaving Hawk when the night was nearly spent, Laramie returned to his horse, retraced his blind way through the bad lands and got to the road some miles above where he had left it. He started for home but left the road below his place and picking a trail through the hills came out half a mile northwest of his cabin. Here he cached his saddle and bridle, turned loose his horse and going forward with the stealth of an Indian he got close enough to his cabin to satisfy himself, after painstaking observation, that his cabin was neither in the hands of the enemy, nor under close-range surveillance. When he reached the house he disposed of his rifle, slipped inside and struck a light. On the stove he found his frying pan face downward and the coffee pot near it with the lid raised. From this he knew that Simeral in his absence had cared for his stock; and being relieved in his mind on this score he laid his revolver at hand and threw himself on the bed to sleep. Day was just breaking.

CHAPTER 22

STONE TRIES HIS HAND

In getting home safely, Laramie had not flattered himself that he was not actually under what in mountain phrase is termed the death watch. In matter of fact, Van Horn and Doubleday had gone home to stay until the excitement should blow over. But they had left Stone and two men charged with intercepting Laramie on his return. The investing lines had not, however, been skilfully drawn and Laramie had slipped through.

He slept undisturbed until the sun was an hour high. Then peering through a corner of the blanket that hung before the window he saw Stone and two companions half a mile from the house, riding slowly as if looking for a trail; particularly, as he readily surmised, for his own trail. As to his horse betraying him, Laramie had no fear, knowing the beast would make straight for the blue stem north of the hills. It was no part of Laramie's plan of defense to begin fighting or to force any situation that favored him—as he believed the present one to do.

Few men that knew his enemies would have agreed with him in this view; they would, indeed, have thought it extremely precarious for Laramie to be caught in any place he could not escape from unseen. But Laramie was temperamentally a gambler with fortune and he put aside the worries that occasionally weighed on his friends. Standing at his one small window—though this was by no means the only peephole in the cabin walls—he watched without undue concern the scouting of the trio, who beyond doubt had been hired to kill him and were only waiting their chance.

After a long inspection of the ground—much of it out of sight of the cabin—broken by frequent colloquies, the three rode from the creek bottom out on the upper field and, halting, surveyed the distant cabin with seeming doubt and suspicion. Two of them reined their horses toward the creek. The third man spurred up the long slope straight for the house.

This put a different aspect on things. Laramie tightened a little as he watched the oncoming rider. If it should prove to be Stone—he hesitated at the thought, deciding on nothing until sure who the man might be. But watching the approach of the unwelcome visitor coldly, Laramie put out his hand for his rifle. He thought of firing a warning shot; but to this he was much averse since it would mean a fight and a siege—neither of which he sought. As the man drew closer it was apparent that it was not Stone and Laramie decided that milder measures might answer. He held his rifle across his arm and waited. But the man, as if conscious of the peril to which he was so coolly exposing himself, galloped rapidly away, rejoined his companions and the trio disappeared.

Laramie at the window watched the departing horsemen. It appeared, from what he had seen, as if the watch had really been set on him. He got out his little bottle of oil and a rag and ramrod to clean his rifle. He made the preparations and sat down to his task in a brown study.

The rifle had not been fired for some time, and it was a very long time since it had been trained on a man. He took it apart slowly, thinking less of what would next appear through the range of the sights than of Kate, as she confronted him the night before in Carpy's office. He realized with a sort of shame that he was trying to forgive her for calling him a thief—which, in point of fact, he argued, she had not actually done. And though she had certainly spoken careless-like, as Bill Bradley might say, she had only credited the tales of his enemies in her own household.

Laramie poked and squinted as he pondered his difficulties. He had refused to give up Hawk to be merely murdered; he could not do less and respect himself. It had made her father more than ever his enemy; still he wanted Kate. Stone would assassinate him at any time for a hundred dollars; Van Horn, now that he was aware Laramie liked Kate, would do it for nothing. Laramie, indeed, realized that if he stood in Van Horn's way with a woman he would not figure any more in Harry's calculations than a last year's birds' nest. And back of all loomed rancorous Barb Doubleday.

How, he asked himself, could a girl like Kate, pick such a bear for a father? All of which troublesome thinking brought him no nearer a solution of his difficulties. He had his life to look out for, Hawk to take care of and a strong-willed girl to bring to his way of thinking.

He reached, at last, the conclusion that the sooner he knew whether he could leave his own place and ride to and from Sleepy Cat without being "potted" from ambush, the sooner he would know what to do next. Persuading himself that the watch would wait for him somewhere down the road, Laramie, making coffee and cooking bacon, breakfasted, made his final preparations for death by shaving himself with a venerable razor, and rifle in hand, got down as directly and briskly as possible to the corral. He got up a horse, rode back into the hills, and recovering his saddle, started for Simeral's. Having spoken with Ben, Laramie made a detour that brought him out on the creek a mile below his usual trail. Thence he rode as contentedly as possible on his way.

The country for a few miles ahead was adapted for ambuscades. The valley was comparatively narrow and afforded more than one vantage point for covering a traveler. It was wholly a matter,

Laramie felt, of bluffing it through. And beyond keeping a brisk pace with his horse, he could do nothing to protect himself. "You're a fool for luck, Jim," he remembered Hawk's saying once to him, "but you'll get it sometime on your fool's luck, just the same."

When old Blackbeard, as he sometimes called Hawk—though no one else ventured to call him that—uttered the warning, it made no impression on Laramie. Now it came back. Not unpleasantly, nor as a dread—only he did recall at this time the words—which was more than he had ever done before. And he reflected that it would be very awkward for Hawk, if their common enemies should get his nurse at this particular time.

While this was running through his mind, he was not sorry to notice ahead of him the dust of the down stage. At that particular stretch of the road it would be less nerve-wearing to ride beside it a way. He overtook the wagon and to his surprise found McAlpin on the box. McAlpin, overjoyed to see him, explained with a grin he was filling in for a sick man. In reality, he had substituted for the northern trip in the hope of seeing some fighting while out and the sight of Laramie was the nearest he had got to it. Laramie, after a long talk, made an appointment to meet him in town in the evening and as they reached the foot of the hill where the road climbed to the Sleepy Cat divide, Laramie feeling he had no further excuse for loitering, put spurs to his horse and took a bridle trail, used as a cut-off, to get into safer country.

He rode this trail unmolested, crossed the divide and coming out of the hills could see, to the south, Sleepy Cat lying below. He made up his mind that his judgment was more nearly right than his apprehension, and rode down the slopes of the Crazy Woman, over the Double-draw bridge and up the south hill in good spirits. He had, in fact, got half-way up the long grade when he heard a rifle shot.

Knocked forward the next instant in his saddle, Laramie drooped over his pommel. As his heels struck the horse's flanks, the beast sprang ahead. The rebound jerked back the rider's head and shoulders. While the horse dashed on, Laramie with as little fuss as possible pulled his rifle from its scabbard, trying all the time to get his balance. A careful observer could have noted that the rifle was drawn but held low in the right hand as if the rider could not bring it up. Yet even a close observer could hardly have detected in his convulsive swaying that the wounded man was closely scanning the sides of the narrow road along which his horse was now flying. At all events, he seemed with failing strength to be losing his seat as he lost control of his horse, and a hundred yards from where he had been struck he toppled helplessly from the saddle into the roadway. The speed at which the horse was going sent the fallen rider rolling along the grade, the sides of which had been torn in spots by summer torrents. Near one of these holes, Laramie had left the saddle, and into it he rolled headlong.

The hole, between four and five feet deep, looked like an irregular well with an overhang on one side and to the bottom of this, Laramie, covered with dust, tumbled. He righted himself and turning under the overhang took breath, put down his rifle, whipped out his revolver, looked toward the top of his well and listened.

Not a sound broke the stillness of the sunny morning. With his right hand, but holding his eyes and ears very much at attention, he drew a handkerchief, wiped the dust from his eyes and face and twisted his head around to investigate the stinging sensation high on his left shoulder, almost at the neck. The rifle bullet had torn his coat collar and shirt and creased the skin. He could feel no blood and soon inventoried the shot as only close. But he was waiting for the man that fired it to appear at the hole to investigate; and with at least this one of his enemies he was in a mood to finish then and there.

Taking off his coat, as his wits continued to work, he spread it over a little hump in front of him so it would catch the eye for an instant and with patient rage crouched back under the overhang. He so placed himself that one could hardly see him without peering into the hole and that might mean any one of several things for the man that ventured it—much depended, in Laramie's mind, on whose face he should see above the rim.

An interminable time passed. The first sound he heard was that of horses toiling up the long grade and the creaking of battered hubs; this he reckoned must be McAlpin with the stage. Where his hat had rolled to, when he tumbled out of the saddle to simulate death, he had no idea. If it lay in the road he might expect a visit from McAlpin. But without stopping, the stage rattled slowly up the grade.

It seemed then as if the distant gunman, after waiting for the stage to pass, would not fail to reconnoiter the hole. Yet he did so fail. The high hours of midday passed with Laramie patiently resting his Colt's up between his knees and studying the yellow rim of the hole and the heavenly blue of the sky. His neck ached from the cramped position, long held, in which he had placed himself; but he moved no more than if he had been set in stone. Neither hunger, which was slight, nor thirst, at times troublesome, disturbed his watch. But it was in vain.

He sat like a spider in its web through the whole day without an incident. A few horsemen passed, an occasional wagon rumbled up and down the hill; but none of the travelers looked in on Laramie. Toward dusk he heard a freighting outfit working laboriously up from the creek. Resolving to give up his watch and go into town with this, he felt his way cautiously out of his hiding place. Without really hoping to recover it, he began to search for his hat and to his surprise found it in another gully near where he had tumbled from his horse. The driver of the freighting outfit wondered at seeing Laramie on foot. He explained that he had been hunting and that his horse had taken a short-cut home.

Stone's companions under instructions had left him and returned to Doubleday's before the shot across the Crazy Woman. Stone himself got back to Doubleday's ranch at about the time that Laramie started for Sleepy Cat in the evening. But Barb Doubleday and Van Horn, he was told, were in town. He followed them and discovered Van Horn in the bar room at the hotel.

"I hear you got him," muttered Van Horn, bending his keen eyes on Stone.

"Who said so?" demanded Stone.

"His horse came into Kitchen's barn this afternoon, all saddled. McAlpin is telling he heard a rifle shot on the Crazy Woman. They're wild down at the barn over it. Did you get him?"

Stone paused over a glass of whisky; his face brightened: "I tumbled him off his horse, if you call that getting him."

Van Horn asked questions impatiently. Stone answered with the indifference of the man that had turned a big trick. But Van Horn insisted on knowing what had become of Laramie.

"He tumbled into a hole," said Stone. "I didn't cross the creek to look for him."

"Why didn't you?" asked Van Horn nervously.

Stone dallied with his glass: "I watched the hole all day. He didn't come out. That was enough, wasn't it?"

"No," snapped Van Horn.

"Well, I'll tell you, Harry; next time you and the old man want a job done, do it yourself. I never liked Laramie: I didn't care for getting too close to the hole he tumbled into. After he was hit, he stuck to his horse a little too long to suit me," said Stone shrewdly.

Van Horn's retort was contemptuous and pointed. He laughed: "Afraid of him, eh?"

Stone regarded him malevolently: "Look here!" he exclaimed harshly, "I'll make you a little proposition. When I get shaved we'll ride over to the Crazy Woman and you c'n look in the hole for yourself."

The uncertainty irritated Van Horn. When Stone, newly plastered, emerged from the barber shop, Van Horn took him with his story to Doubleday whom they found in his room, chewing the stub of a cold cigar and looking over a stock journal. He did not appear amiable, nor did his face change much as the news was cautiously conveyed to him. When Van Horn announced he would ride out with Stone to examine the road hole, Doubleday, whose expression had grown colder and colder, broke in:

"Needn't waste any time on that," he said with a snap of his jaw.

Stone snorted: "Maybe *you* think he wasn't hit."

"Hit!" exclaimed Barb. "Hit!" he repeated, raising a long forefinger with deep-drawn disgust. "He's sittin' in that room across the hall right now——"

"What's he doin'?"

"Playin' poker," muttered the old cattleman grimly, "with Doc Carpy and Harry Tenison."

CHAPTER 23

KATE RIDES

In strict point of fact, Laramie had left the room across the hall and at that particular moment was sitting down for a late supper at Belle Shockley's whither Sawdy and Lefever had dragged him from the hotel. Carpy had come with them.

At the table—after Laramie had told part of his story—the talk, genial to cheerfulness, was largely professional criticism of the shot across the Crazy Woman. The technical disadvantages of shooting uphill, the tendency to over-elevate for such shots, the difficulty of catching the pace and speed of a horse, all supplied judicial observations for

Lefever and Sawdy, while Laramie—so nearly the victim—leaving the topic to these Sleepy Cat gun pundits, conferred with Carpy about the care of gunshot wounds; and protested against Flat Nose George and the Museum of Horrors in the Doctor's office.

"But I want to tell you, boys," remarked the doctor, when the talk turned on the discomfiture of the enemy group, "what Barb asked me tonight— this is on the dead." The doctor looked around to include Belle—who was standing with folded arms, her back against the sideboard and listening to the conversation—in his injunction of secrecy. "He came to me at the hotel. 'Doc,' says Barb, 'I want to ask you a question. There's stories circulating around about Laramie's getting shot this morning, on his way into town. Has Laramie been to you to get fixed up, at all?'

" 'Well, Barb,' I says, 'that's not really a fair question for me to answer—you know that. But since you spoke about it, Jim was in awhile ago—'

" 'Was in, eh?'

" 'For a few minutes—'

" 'Hit?'

" 'That I couldn't say. What he asked for, Barb, was a bottle of Perry Davis' painkiller—said the rheumatiz was getting him to beat the band.' "

Carpy paused: " 'Rheumatiz!' says Barb. He didn't stop to swear—he just bit his old cigar right square in two in the middle, dropped one end on the floor and stamped on it." The Doctor leaned forward and spoke to Laramie: "How's longhorn, Jim?"

Laramie looked troubled: "If it wasn't for dragging you into it, I'd ask you to go out and see him."

"Jim, a doctor's place is where he's needed."

"I left a twenty dollar gold piece in your medicine chest for the stuff I took."

"You go to hell!" The Doctor pulled a handful of money from his pocket and threw a double eagle at Laramie. "There's your gold piece."

"Belle, look at them fellows," exclaimed Sawdy moodily, "pockets loaded. I never had more than twenty dollars at one time in my life. My mother told me to take care of the pennies and the dollars would take care of themselves. The blamed dollars wouldn't do it. I took care of the pennies. I've got 'em yet—that's all I have got. Jim, I'll match you for that gold piece."

"Gamblers never have a cent," commented Belle darkly.

"That gold piece," explained Laramie, "is not my money, Harry. It's Carpy's money and he'll keep it if I have to make him swallow it."

"That's not the question," declared Carpy. "Did you get what you wanted?" Laramie told him he did. "And by the great Jehosaphat," added the doctor, "you bumped into Kate Doubleday!"

"What else did you expect?" retorted Laramie, not pleased at the recollection.

Carpy, throwing back his head, laughed well: "After Kate Doubleday told me she was going for the dressings herself, I says to myself, 'There'll be two people in my house tonight—a man and a woman—I hope to God they don't meet.' "

"Jim," intervened Belle, "you ought to get Abe Hawk to a hospital."

"He's got to get him to one," affirmed Lefever. "I've seen that man," he added emphatically, "I know."

"How's he going to do it," inquired Carpy, "without starting the fight all over again?"

Lefever stuck to his ground: "Get him down to Sleepy Cat in the night," he insisted.

"Can he ride?" asked Sawdy.

"He may have to have help," said Laramie.

"There's a moon right now. They'd pick you off like rabbits," objected Sawdy, "and they've got that whole trail patroled to the Crazy Woman. They're watching this town like cats. You'll have to waste a lot of ammunition to get Abe to a hospital."

"From all I hear," observed Carpy, "if Abe gets any more lead in him you won't need to take him to the hospital. He'll be ready to head straight for the undertaker's."

"We've got to wait either for a late moon or a rainy night; then we'll get busy," suggested Lefever.

"He might die while you're waiting," interposed Carpy.

244

Lefever could not be subdued: "Not as quick as he'd die if Van Horn's bunch caught sight of him on the road," he said sententiously. "We'll get him down and he won't die, either."

"Well, pay for your supper, boys, and let's get away," said Carpy. "I want some sleep."

But for Lefever and Sawdy there was little sleep that night. The echoes of the "fatal" shot—almost fatal, as it proved, to the prestige of the enemy— were being discussed pretty much everywhere in Sleepy Cat and wherever men that night assembled in public places, Sawdy and Lefever swaggered in and out at least once. The pair looked wise, spoke obscurely, looked the crowd, large or small, over critically, played an occasional restrained and brief finger-tattoo on the butts of their bolstered guns and listened condescendingly to everyone that had a theory to advance, a reminiscence to offer, or a propitiating drink to suggest.

Wherever they could induce him to go, they dragged Laramie—at once as an exhibit and a defi; but Laramie objected to the thoroughness with which his companions essayed to cover the terri- tory, and unfeelingly withdrew from the party to go to bed. Sawdy and Company, undismayed by the defection, continued to haunt the high places until the last sympathizer with Van Horn and Company had been challenged and bullied or silenced.

But the differing sympathies on the situation in Sleepy Cat were not to be adjusted in a single night, either by force or persuasion. The whole town took sides and the cattlemen found the most defenders. What might be designated, but with modesty, as "big business" in Sleepy Cat stood stubbornly, despite the violence of their methods, with Van Horn, Doubleday and their friends; the interest of such business lay with the men that bought the most supplies. The banks and the merchants were thus pretty much aligned on one side. The surgeon of the town professed neutrality—at least as regarded operations—for he was needed to administer to both factions. Harry Tenison, as dealer of the big game in town and owner of the big hotel, was of necessity neutral; though men like himself and Carpy were rightly suspected of leaning toward Laramie, if not even as far as toward Abe Hawk. The open sympathizers of the Falling Wall men were among trainmen, liverymen, the clerks, the barbers and bartenders, and those who could be usually counted as "agin the government."

Meantime, the element of mystery in the still unclosed tragedy of the upper country concerned the disappearance of Hawk; and this naturally centered about Laramie. None but he knew to a certainty the fate of the redoubtable old cowboy, so long a range favorite. And whenever Laramie appeared in town, speculation at once revived every feature of the situation, and Kate Doubleday when she came to Sleepy Cat, whether she would or not, could not escape the talk concerning the Falling Wall feud.

Loyalty to her own and the intense partizanship of her nature, combined to urge her to sympathize with the fight of the range owners against the Falling Wall men. But in this attitude, Belle Shockley was a trial to Kate. Belle would not drag in the subject of the fight but she never avoided it; and Kate, even against her inclination, seemed impelled to speak of the subject with Belle. She instinctively felt that Belle's sympathies were with the other side; and felt just as strongly in her impulsiveness, that Belle should be set right about rustlers and their friends—meaning always, by the latter, Jim Laramie. Belle, stubborn but more contained, clung to her own views. Though she rarely talked back, the attempt to assassinate Laramie had intensified everyone's feelings, and for days only a spark on that subject was needed to fire more than one Sleepy Cat powder magazine. One afternoon rain caught Kate in at Belle's and kept her until almost dark from starting for home, and one magazine did explode.

The two women were sitting on the porch watching the shower. McAlpin on his way uptown from the barn, had stopped at Belle's a moment for shelter.

"I'll tell you, Kate," said Belle, after listening as patiently as she could to what Kate had to say about the Falling Wall fight and its consequences, "I like you. I can't help liking you. But the only reason you talk the way you do is because you haven't lived in this country long. You don't know this country—you don't know the people."

McAlpin nodded strongly: "That's so, that's true."

"I, at least, know common honesty, I hope."

"But you don't know anything at all of what you are talking about," insisted Belle, "and if you think I'm ever going to agree with you that it was right for Van Horn and your father and their friends to take a bunch of Texas men up into the Falling Wall and shoot and burn men because they're rustlers, you're very much mistaken. And I can tell you the people of this country won't agree with you either, no matter what some folks in this town may say to tickle your ears."

"Do you mean to say you stand up for thieves, too?" asked Kate, hotly.

McAlpin looked apprehensively out at the clouds. Belle twitched her shoulders: "You needn't be so high and mighty about it," she retorted. "No, I don't. And I don't stand up for burning men alive because they brand mavericks. You talk very fierce—like everybody up your way. But if Abe Hawk or Jim Laramie walked in here this minute, you wouldn't agree to have them shot down. And don't you forget it, Jim Laramie doesn't claim a hoof of anybody's cattle but his own."

Kate would not back down: "Why do they call him king of the rustlers?" she demanded.

"King of the rustlers, nothing," echoed Belle in

disgust. "That's barroom talk. No decent man ever accused him of branding so much as a horse hair that didn't belong to him."

"And his reputation is, he's not very slow when it comes to shooting, either," declared Kate.

McAlpin thought it a time for oil on the waters! "You've got to make allowances," he urged with dignity. "Ten years ago—less'n that, even—they was all pretty quick on the trigger in this country. Jim was a kid 'n' he had to travel with the bunch."

"And he was quicker 'n any of them," interposed Belle, defiantly, "wasn't he, Mac?"

McAlpin was for moderation and better feeling: "Well," he admitted gravely, "full as quick, I guess."

"It seems to me," observed Kate, still resentful, "as if men here are pretty quick yet."

"Oh, no," interposed McAlpin at once; "oh, no, not special now'days. More talk'n there used to be—heap more."

"Bring over my pony, Mr. McAlpin, will you?" asked Kate, very much irritated.

McAlpin looked surprised: "You wouldn't be ridin' home tonight?"

"Yes," replied Kate, sharply, "I would."

As McAlpin started on his way she turned on Belle: "And you mustn't forget, Belle, that vigilantes, no matter whether they do make mistakes or go too far, have built this country up and made it safe to live in."

Belle's face took on a weariness: "Oh, no—not always safe to live in—sometimes safe to make money in. There's nothing I'm so sick of hearing as this vigilante stuff. The vigilante crowd are mostly big thieves—the rustlers, little thieves—that's about all the difference I can see."

"Well, is there any difference between being a rustler, and protecting and being the friend of one?"

Belle's restraint broke: "You'd better set your own house in order before you criticize me or Jim Laramie. He's never yet tried to assassinate anybody."

"Neither has my father, nor the men that raided the Falling Wall."

"Don't you know," demanded Belle, indignantly, "that the men who raided the Falling Wall are the men that tried to murder Laramie?"

"I don't believe it," said Kate, flatly. "Father doesn't believe *any*body tried to murder him."

Belle's wrath bubbled over: "Your father's as deep in it as anybody."

She could have bitten her tongue off the instant she uttered the angry words. But they were out.

Kate sprang to her feet. Even Belle, used to shocks and encounters, was silenced by the look that met her. For a moment the angry girl did not utter a word, but if her eyes were daggers, Belle would have been transfixed. Kate's breast rose sharply and she spoke low and fast: "How dare you accuse my father of such a thing?"

Belle, though cowed, was defiant: "I dare say just what I believe to be true."

"What proof have you?"

"I don't need proof for what everyone knows."

"You say what is absolutely false." Kate's tranquil eyes were aflame; she stood child, indeed, of her old father. Belle had more than once doubted whether Kate *could* be the daughter of such a man—she never doubted it after that scene on the day of the rain. Barb himself would have waited on his daughter's words. "You're glad to listen to the stories of our enemies," she almost panted, "because they're your friends; you're welcome to them. But my father's enemies are my enemies and I know now where to place you."

White with anger as she was herself, Belle, older and more controlled, tried to allay the storm she had raised: "I didn't meant to hurt you, Kate," she protested, "you drove me too far."

"I'm glad I did," returned Kate, wickedly, as she stepped back into the living-room, pinned on her hat and made ready as fast as possible to go. "I know you in your true colors."

"Well, whether I'm right or wrong, you'll find my colors don't fade and don't change."

A boy stood at the gate with Kate's pony.

The two women were again on the porch. Belle looked at the sky. The rain had abated but the mountains were black. "Now, Kate, what are you going to do?"

Kate had walked out and was indignantly throwing the lines over her horse's neck. "I'm going home," she answered, as sharply as the words could be spoken.

Belle crossed the sidewalk to her side: "This is a poor time of day for a long ride. We've quarreled, I know, but don't try a mountain trail a night like this. The rain isn't over yet."

"I'll be home before it starts again," returned Kate, springing into the saddle. "I'm sick of this town and everybody in it."

So saying, she struck her horse with the lines and headed for the mountains.

CHAPTER 24

NIGHT AND A HEADER

For John Lefever the rainy night promised to be a busy one; darkness and the storm would, he felt, give Laramie a chance to get Hawk safely into town; but to do this successfully would call for precaution.

The rain had hardly begun to fall that afternoon—to the discomfiture of Kate and her undoing with Belle—before Lefever began to cheer up in speculating on what might be done. He found Laramie at the hotel and set out to round up Sawdy. The rendezvous was set at Kitchen's barn and half an hour later the three men were shut up in the old harness room back of the office to talk the venture over.

Laramie made no effort to discourage John concerning the project; it had become a pet one with the big fellow; but he did not give the idea strong endorsement. "You're too blamed pessimistic, Jim," growled Lefever.

"No, John," protested Laramie evenly, "I'm only trying to see things as they stand. Don't figure we are going to pull this thing without trouble. Harry Van Horn's got a good guess that Dave is pretty well shot up; and that he's hiding out. He knows a man can't hide out without friends."

"I grant you that," interrupted John. "But if you can get him across the Crazy Woman, Jim, it's a cinch to run him into town."

"Don't figure that every mile of that road isn't watched, for it is. I ride it oftener than you and I see plenty of sign. And Harry knows what a rainy night means just as well as we do. He'll be on the job with his men—that's all I'm saying. Now, go ahead. You want Abe brought in—that's your business. I'm here to bring him in—that's my business. Shoot."

Laramie and Lefever arranged things. Number Seventy-eight, the through fast freight, would be due to leave Sleepy Cat for Medicine Bend at 4:32 in the morning. The crew were friendly. Could Laramie make it with Abe, starting by midnight?

He could. It was impossible to meet Laramie outside town because no one could tell which trail he might have to choose to come in on. But Sawdy and Lefever could look for him out on the plateau at the head of Fort Street. Henry Sawdy, his heavy mustaches sweeping his thick lips, and his bloodshot eyes moving from one to the other of the two faces before him only stared and listened.

"Why don't you say something, Henry?" demanded Lefever, exasperated.

Sawdy turned a reproachful look on his lively partner: "When you're talking, John, there ain't no chance to say anything. When Jim's talking, I don't want to say anything."

Laramie ordered his horse, got into oilskins, and riding out the back way of the stable started for the Falling Wall. The day was spent and the rain had turned soft and misty. He rode fast and with a little watchfulness, exercised before reaching the Crazy Woman, satisfied himself that he had not been followed out of town.

What had actually happened was that he rode north not long after Kate herself started for home. But Laramie followed old trails out of town— even at the price of rounding fences and at times dodging through wire gates for short cuts. Night was upon him when he reached the bluffs of the creek. Between showers the sky had lightened, but the north was overcast, and Laramie knew what to look forward to. When he had got up the long hill, and reached the northern bluffs, it was raining steadily again, and night had spread over mountain and valley.

Abating something of his usual precaution in riding to reach Hawk's hiding place, Laramie went slowly into the bad lands by a route less dangerous than that he usually followed. As the night deepened, the wind rising brought a heavier rain. The trail became increasingly difficult to follow; rough at best, it was now almost impassable. Sheets of water trickled over stretches of rock causing the horse to slip and flounder. In other places rivulets shooting out of crevices cut the loose earth from under the horse's feet. Leg-tired, the horse finally resented being headed into the driving rain and went forward slipping, hesitating and groping like a man on hands and knees.

When Laramie got him to the old bridge, the pony was all in. Laramie found shelter for him under a ledge and rifle in hand clambered along the side of the canyon toward the abutment. Close to the entrance he set his rifle against the rock, listened carefully, as always, felt down at his feet for the few chips of rock he had so placed that they would be disturbed if trodden by an enemy, listened again carefully, and with his revolver cocked in his right hand, and the muzzle lying across his left forearm, Laramie slowly zigzagged his way to the inside. Once there, he stood perfectly still in the darkness and called a greeting to Hawk. He failed to receive the usual gruff answer. This never before had happened, and without trying for a light, Laramie moved slowly and with much caution over to the recess within which Hawk lay. There he could hear the cowboy's labored, but regular breathing as he slept. The storm, waking the water crevices of the mountains into a noisy chorus, had lulled the hunted man into an untroubled sleep.

Laramie shook his oilskins in a heap on the floor, cautiously lighted a candle and set it on the board that served as a table. In spite of his slickers he was wet through. He hung his hat on the end of a broken timber and laid his revolver beside the candle. Bethinking himself, however, of his rifle, he picked up the six-shooter again, stepped outside the entrance, brought in his rifle, wiped it, stood it in a convenient corner and turned toward Hawk.

The candle, burning at moments steadily and at moments flickering, threw its uncertain rays into the recess where the wounded rustler lay. They lighted the sallow pallor of the sleeping man's face, fell across his sunken eyes and drew the black of his long beard out of the gloom below it. Laramie seated himself on a projecting ledge and looked thoughtfully at his charge. He was failing; of that there could be no doubt. Steel-willed and hard-sinewed though he was, the wounds that would long ago have put an ordinary man out of action, were undermining his great vitality and Laramie, in a study, felt it.

Yet such was the younger man's natural stubbornness that left to his own devices he would have fought out the battle against death right where the failing man lay; only the judgment of Lefever and Carpy swayed him in the circumstances.

Believing sleep was the best preparative for the ordeal of the ride to town, Laramie hesitated about waking Hawk—yet the hours were precious, for the trip would be long and slow. Fortunately he had not long to wait before Hawk woke.

Laramie was sitting a few feet away and silently looking at him when Hawk opened his eyes. They wandered from one object to another in the dim candle gloom, until they rested on Laramie's face; there they stopped.

Laramie's features relaxed into as near a smile as he permitted himself on duty: "How you coming, Abe?"

Hawk eyed him steadily: "What are you doing here tonight?"

Laramie answered with a question: "How about trying the gauntlet?"

"That what you want?"

"It's what Lefever and Carpy want."

"They running things?"

"They think you'd get well full as quick at a hospital."

"What do you think?"

"I guess you would."

"Tired taking care of me?"

"Not yet, Abe."

"Raining?"

"Hell bent."

"What's the other noise?"

"Thunder; and the river's up."

The roar of the waters was not new to the ears of the two men who listened, however much it might have disturbed others unused to their tearing fury.

Hawk listened thoughtfully: "Why didn't you pick a wet night?" he asked.

"We had to pick a dark one, Abe."

"Where's the horses?"

"Over at my place—*what's that?*"

The last words broke from Laramie's lips like the crack of a pistol. He sprang to his feet. Hawk's hand shot out for his gun. Only practised ears could have detected under the steady downpour of rain, the deep roar of the canyon and the reverberation of the thunder, the hoof beats of a stumbling horse. The next instant, they heard the horse directly over their heads. Laramie, whipping out his revolver, looked up. As he did so, a deafening crash blotted out the roar of the storm—the roof overhead gave way and amid an avalanche of rock and timbers, a horse plunged headlong into the refuge.

In the narrow quarters so amazingly invaded, darkness added to an instant of frantic confusion. Laramie was knocked flat. In the midst of the fallen timbers, the horse, mad with terror, struggled to get to his feet. A suppressed groan betrayed the rider under him.

Laramie, where he lay, gun in hand, and Hawk, had but one thought: their retreat had been discovered and attacked. It was no part of their defense to reveal their presence by wild shooting. The enemy who had plunged in on top of them was at their mercy, even though unseen. He was caught under the horse, and to clap a revolver to his head and blow the top off was simple; it could be done at any moment. Of much greater import it was, carefully to await his companions when they rode up, above, and pick them off as chance offered. Escape, if the raiding party were properly organized, both men knew was for them impossible—and they knew that Harry Van Horn organized well. The alternative was to sell their lives as dearly as possible.

This was by no means a terrifying conclusion to men inured to affray. And for the moment, at feast, the situation was in their hands, not in the enemies'.

A deluge of wind and rain swept through the broken roof. Laramie, stretching one arm through the debris, felt the shoulder of the rider, flung in the violence of the fall close to him.

259

The prostrate horse renewed his struggles to get to his feet.

Laramie, exposed to the pouring rain, covered with mud, bruised by broken rock still rolling down the open crater, and caught among rotten timbers, struggled to right himself before his enemy should do so. He raised himself by a violent effort to his elbow, freed his pistol arm and reaching over, pushed his cocked revolver into the side of the fallen horseman.

A bolt of lightning shot across the crater, leaving behind it an inky blackness of rain and wind. The sudden onslaught from overhead might well have confused his senses; but he had seen the lightning sweep across a white, drawn face turned toward the angry sky—and in the flash he had caught the features of Kate Doubleday.

Stunned though he was by the revelation, he knew his senses had not tricked him. There was in his memory but one such riding cap as that which shaded her closed eyes; for him, but one such coil of woman's hair as that falling now in disarray on her neck. Completely unnerved, he carefully drew away his revolver, averted the muzzle and spoke angrily through the dark: "Who's here with you?"

There was no answer. He asked the question sternly again, listening keenly the while for sounds of other riders above. Had she discovered the retreat and led to it his enemies? Could it be possible that even they would allow her with them on such an errand and on such a night?

He called her name. The roar of the canyon answered above the storm; there was no sound else. Once more he stretched out his arm. His hand rested on her breast and he was doubly sure his senses had not tricked him. But she might be dying or dead. The fear struck home that she *was* dead. Then her bosom rose in a hardly perceptible respiration.

A storm of emotion swept Laramie. He squirmed under the débris that pinned him and got nearer to her. He listened still for sounds of an enemy, of those who must be with her—where could they be? The delicate breathing under his heavy hand came more regularly. Then a moan of pain checked and, again, released it.

Feeling slowly in the stormy dark for obstructions that might have caught her, Laramie freed one of her feet caught in the stirrup and by pushing and lifting at the shoulder of the horse succeeded after much exertion in freeing her other foot, caught under it. He felt his way back to Kate's head and getting on his feet placed his hands under her shoulders to draw her toward him.

As he did so, a sharp question of fear and confusion was flung at him: "Where am I? Who are you?"

"Who are you?" echoed Laramie, pulling her away from the horse which had begun to struggle

261

again. "Who's here with you?" he demanded. There was no answer.

"Who's here with you?" he repeated sternly. "Tell me the truth."

"I've lost my way. Where am I? Who are you?"

The truth in her manner was plain. Incredible as it seemed that she could have strayed so far, all apprehension of an attack vanished with her questions.

"You're a long way from home," he said, shortly.

She made no reply.

"Your horse took a header. You fainted. I suppose"—he hardly hesitated in his words—"you know who is talking to you?"

In her silence he heard his answer.

CHAPTER 25

A GUEST FOR AN HOUR

"Can you stand on your feet?" he asked.

Supporting her as she made the trial he felt his way from where the horse had plunged through to where he found a partial seat for her. "Are you much hurt?" he asked again.

She could not, if she would, have told in how many places she was broken and bruised. All she was sharply conscious of was a pain in one foot so intense as to deaden all other pain. It was the foot that had been caught under the horse. "I think I'm all right," she murmured, in a constrained tone and, in her manner, briefly. "How did you find me here?" she asked, almost resentfully. "Where am I?"

He knew from her words she had neither headed nor followed any expedition against him but he did not answer her question: "I'll see whether I can get the horse up."

While he worked with the horse—and once during the long, hard effort she heard between thunder claps a sharp expletive—Kate tried to collect in some degree her scattered and reeling senses. What quieted her most was that her long and fear-stricken groping for hours in the storm and darkness seemed done now. Without realizing it she was willingly turning her fears and troubles over to another—and to one who, though she stubbornly refused to regard him as a friend, she well knew was able to shoulder them. She heard the kicking and pawing of the horse, then with new dismay, the low voices of two men; and next in the terrifying darkness, more kicking, more suppressed expletives, more heaving and pulling, and between lightning flashes, quieting words to the horse. The two men had gotten the frightened beast to his feet.

Laramie groped back to Kate. He had to touch her with his hand to be sure he had found her: "I'm taking you at your word," he said, above the confusion of the storm.

"What do you mean?"

"That you're alone and don't know where you are."

"I am alone. I wish I might know where I am."

Both spoke under constraint: "It's more important to know how to get home," he replied, ignoring the request in her words. "Your horse is here for the night—that's pretty certain," he declared, as a sheet of rain swept over the crater. "I've got a horse near by and we'll start for where we can get more horses."

There was nothing Kate could say or do. She already had made up her mind to submit in silence to what Laramie might suggest or impose. One thing only she was resolved on; that whatever happened there should be no appeal on her part.

His first thought was to get her out of the pit by the way she had plunged in. A moment's reflection convinced him that such a precaution was unnecessary. When he asked her to follow him he held her wet gloved hand in his hand. "Look out for your footing till we get to the horse," was his warning. "The way we're going, we should never make but one slip. Take your time," he added, as she stepped cautiously after him out into the drive of wind and rain. "It's only about twenty steps."

In obeying orders she gave him nothing to complain of, but there was little relaxing of the tension between the two. Every step she took on her injured foot was torture, made keener by the uncertain footing. More than once, even despite the dangers of her situation, she thought she must cry out or faint in agony. The twenty steps along the steep face of the canyon, pelted by rain, were like two hundred. Kate made them without a whimper. Thence she followed him slowly between rocky walls guarding the nearly level floor of the widening ledge, till they reached the horse. She stumbled at times with pain; but if it were to kill her she would not speak.

Hawk had followed the two from the abutment. He joined them now. Kate was only aware that a second man had come up and was moving silently near them. Laramie spoke to him—she could not catch what he said—then helped her into the saddle. "I'm going to the house again," he said, "this man will stay with you. I'll be back in a moment."

Little as she liked being left with another, she could not object. The rocky wall saved her partly from the storm and as to the other man she was only vaguely conscious at intervals of a shapeless form outlined beside the horse.

Laramie was gone more than a moment but under Kate's shelter nothing happened. The horse, subdued by storm and weariness, stood like a statue. Uneasy with pain, Kate was very nervous. New sounds were borne on the wind from the darkness; then she heard Laramie's voice; and then a rough question from another voice: "How the hell did you get him out?"

"Walked him out," was the response. Laramie had brought back her own horse. "Get on him," added Laramie, speaking to the other man. "I'll lead my horse—he's sure-footed for her. You know the way down."

Kate made only one effort as the man she knew must be Laramie came to the head of the horse she was on, patted his wet neck and took hold of the bridle. She leaned forward in the saddle: "I'll try again to get home if you'll help me get out of here."

"I'm helping you get out," was the reply. "If you knew where you were, you wouldn't talk yet about trying for home." He stepped closer to the saddle, tested the cinches and spoke to Kate: "It's a hard ride. You can make it by letting the horse strictly alone. I'll lead him but he won't stand two bosses in this kind of a mess, over the only trail that leads from here. How you ever got in, God only knows, and He won't tell—leastways, not tonight. Sit tight. Don't get scared no matter what happens. If the horse should break a leg all we can do is to shoot him and you can try your own horse; but your horse is all in now."

To ride at night a mile in the chilling blackness of a mountain storm is to ride five. To face a buffeting wind and a sweep of heavy rain mile after mile and keep a saddle while a horse pauses, halts, starts and staggers, rights himself, gropes painfully for an uncertain foothold among rocks where a bighorn must pick his way, is to test the endurance even of a man.

Laramie, moving unseen and almost unheard in the inky blackness, piloted the nervous beast with an uncanny instinct, past the dangers on every hand. He guided himself with his feet and by his hands, halting on the edge of crevices and heading them with the horse at his shoulder, feeling his way around slopes of fallen rock and clambering across them when they could not be escaped, holding the lines at their length ahead of the horse and speaking low and reassuringly to urge him on: waiting sometimes for a considerable period for a flash of lightning to give him his bearings anew.

Kate could see in each of these blinding intervals his figure. Each flash outlined it sharply on her retina—always the same—patient, resourceful, silent and unwearied. The man who had been directed to ride her own horse she never caught sight of. When they reached open country and better going her guide did not break the silence. He spoke only when at last he stopped the horse and stood in the darkness close to her knee:

"This brings us to the end of our trail—for awhile. We're in front of my cabin. Of course, it's small. And I've been thinking what I ought to say to you about things as you'll find them here. The man that rode behind us and passed us on your horse is Abe Hawk. You know what they call him over at your place; you know what they call me for taking his part—you know what you called me."

She repressed an exclamation. When she tried to speak, he spoke on, ignoring her. "Never mind," he said, in the same low, even tone that silenced her protest, "I'm not starting any argument but it's time for plain speaking and I'm going to tell you just what has happened tonight, so, for once, anyway, we'll understand each other—I'm going to show my cards."

The chilling sheets of rain that swept their faces did not hasten his utterance: "When you get home and tell your story, your men will know it was Abe Hawk you ran into whether you knew it or not. They'll ask you all about his hiding place and you'll tell them all you know—which won't be much. I don't complain of all that—it's war; and part of the game. All I'll ask you not to say is, that I brought Abe Hawk with you to my cabin. Abe won't be here when they come—it isn't that. We can take care of ourselves. I'm speaking only because I don't want my place burned. It isn't much but I think a good deal of it. Burning it won't help get rid of me. It will only make things in this country worse than they are now—and they're bad enough. I wouldn't have brought you here if there'd been any other place to take you. There wasn't; and for awhile you'll have to make partners with the two men your father and his friends are trying to get killed."

She almost cried out a protest: "How can you say such a thing?"

"Just the plain fact, that's all."

"Is it fair because you are enemies to accuse my father in such a way?"

"Have it as you want it but get my view of it with the one you get over at your place. And if you'll climb down we'll go under cover."

"Now may I say something?"

"No more than fair you should."

She spoke low but fast and distinctly; nor was there any note of fear or apology in her words: "You must put a low estimate on a woman if you would expect her to go home with tales from the camp of an enemy that had put her again on her road. It may be that is the kind of woman you know best—"

Laramie tried to interrupt.

"I've not done," she protested instantly. "You said I might say something: It may be that is the kind of woman you understand best. But I won't be classed with such—not even by you. If you've saved me from great danger it doesn't give you the right to insult me by telling me you expect me to be a tale-bearer. It isn't manly or fair to treat me in that way."

"You mustn't expect too much from a thief."

"You shame yourself, not me, when you use a word I never in my life, not even in anger, ever used of you."

269

"You shame your friends when you call me or think of me as anything else. I'm no match for you—"

"I've not done—"

"I'm no match for you, I know, in fine words—or in any other kind of a game—don't think I don't know that; but by—" he checked himself just in time, "thief or no thief, you've had a square deal from me every turn of the road."

Bitter with anger, he blurted out the words with vehemence. If he looked for a quick retort, none came. Kate for an instant waited: "Should you wish me," she asked, "to look for anything else at your hands?"

"Well, we're not holding up this rain any by talking," he returned gruffly. "Get down and we'll get inside. You can stay here till morning."

"Oh, no!"

"Why not?"

"Just put me on the road for home and let me be going."

"This is my cabin. I told you that."

"I can't *stay* here."

"This is my cabin. I'm responsible for the safety of everyone that steps under my roof."

"I know, but I must go home. They have most likely been searching the trails for me. Father would telephone"—she was desperate for excuses—"to Belle and learn I'd started home—and the storm—"

He did not hesitate to cut her off: "Afraid of me, eh?"

The contempt and resentment in his words stirred her. Without answering she sprang as well as she could in her wet habit from the saddle and faced him, close enough almost to see into his eyes in the darkness. From the fireplace inside a gleam of light, from the blaze that Hawk had started, piercing the tiny window sash shot across her face: "Does this look like it?" she demanded, her eyes seeking his. He was stubborn. "Answer me!" she exclaimed in a tone of a dictator.

"Then why don't you do what I ask you to do instead of giving me a story about Barb Doubleday telephoning?" he demanded. She winced at her mistake in urging an impossible thing. She felt when she made it, Laramie would not credit so wild an assertion. Her father would not take the trouble to telephone to save even a bunch of his steers from a storm, much less his daughter. "But there may be others over there," Laramie added grimly, "that would."

The reference to the man he hated—Van Horn —was too plain to be passed over. "Now," she returned, as if to close—and standing her ground as she spoke, "have you said all the mean things you can think of?"

He evaded her thrust. "The wires are down a night like this, anyway," he objected. "If you'd be as honest with me as I am with you we'd get along without saying mean things."

"I am honest with you. Can't you see that a woman can't always be as open in what she says as a man?"

"What do I know about a woman?"

"But since you make everything hard for me I shall be open with you."

"Come inside then and say it."

"I couldn't be any wetter than I am and if I've got to say this to one man I *won't* say it to two: You ask me to stay all night in your cabin as if I were a small boy—instead of what I am."

"You could take all the shooting irons on the place into your own room with you."

"I shouldn't need to. But what would people say of me when they heard of it? That I had stayed here all night! You know what they can do to a woman's reputation in this country—you know how some evil tongues talk about Belle. I would like to keep at least my reputation out of this bitter war that is going on—can't you, won't you, understand?"

He was silent a moment. "Come in to the fire, then," he said at length, "and we'll see what we can do. You've been on the wrong road all night. There's no need of any secrets now on anybody's part, I guess. But I'd rather turn you over to ten thousand devils than to the man you're going back to tonight."

"Surely," she gasped, "you don't mean my own father?"

"You know the man I mean," was all he answered. Then he threw open the cabin door and stood waiting for her to pass within.

CHAPTER 26

The Crazy Woman Wins

It would have been idle for Laramie to deny to himself, as she stepped without hesitation under his roof, that he loved her; or that he could step in after her and close his door for her and for him —even for an hour—against the storm and the world, without a thrill deeper than he had ever felt.

He leaned his rifle against the cabin wall; a blanket had been hung completely over the window and he let down two heavy bars across the door. Kate, in front of the fire, followed him with her eyes. "Don't mind this," he said, noticing her look. "The place is watched a good deal. I couldn't afford too much of a surprise any time."

While he was searching for a lamp, her eyes ran quickly over the dark interior, lighted fitfully as the driftwood, snapping on the stone hearth, flared at times into a blaze. Kate herself, despite the doubts and fears of her situation, was conscious of a strange feeling in being under Laramie's roof—

at one with him in so far as he could make her feel so. Like a roll of fleeting film, strange pictures flashed across her mind and she could not help thinking more and more about the man and his stubborn isolation.

He had taken off his coat and was trying to light the lamp. She looked narrowly at the face illumined by the spluttering flare of the wick as he stood over it, looking down and adjusting the flame; he seemed, she was thinking—for her at least—so easy to get along with—for everyone else, so hard.

A pounding at the door gave her a start. Hawk was returning from the barn where he had taken the horses. Laramie showed no surprise and walked over to lift the double bar only after he had got the lamp to burn to suit him. She felt startled again when Laramie in the simplest way made the formidable outlaw, who now walked in, known to her. The picture of him as he swung roughly inside from the wild night was unforgettable. Erect and with his piercing eyes hollowed by illness, his impassive features made slender by suffering and framed by the striking beard, Hawk seemed to Kate to confirm in his appearance every fantastic story she had ever heard of him.

Not till after Laramie had urged him and Kate herself had joined in the plea, would he come near her or near to the fire.

"A wet night and a blind trail do pretty well at mixing things up," observed Laramie. "However, we needn't make any further secrets. Abe, here, has got it in his mind to head for a hospital tonight. You," he looked at Kate, "are heading for home. I don't like either scheme very much but I'm an innocent bystander. We'll ride three together till the trails fork. Then," he spoke again to Kate, "we'll put you on a sure trail for the ranch, and the two of us will head into town. It isn't the way I planned, but it's one way out."

"The sooner we get started the better," said Hawk, curtly. The two men discussed for a moment the trip; then Laramie and Hawk left the house for the barn and corral to get up horses. Before leaving, Laramie showed Kate how to drop the bars and cautioned her not to neglect to secure the door. "Some of this bunch Van Horn has got out wouldn't be very agreeable company."

"Surely they wouldn't harm me!"

"It would mean a nasty fight for us when we bring up the horses."

Kate secured the door. Wet and uncomfortable but undismayed by the various turns of her predicament she sat down to study the fire. Her eyes wandered through the gloom to the dark corners of the rough room and over the crude furnishings.

The long, slender snowshoes on the wall, the big beaded moccasins with them, the coiled lariats hung on the pegs in company with old spurs; the bunk in the corner strewn with Indian blankets from the far-off Spanish country, and overflowing with the skin of a grizzly—all brought to mind and reflected an active life. The firelight glinted the bright, bluish barrels of the rifles on the rack, to Kate, almost sinisterly, for some of them must suggest a side of Laramie's life she disliked to dwell on—yet she allowed herself to wonder which rifle he took when he armed not for elk or grizzlies but for men. And then at the side of the fireplace she saw fastened on the rough wall a faded card photograph of a young woman—almost a girl. It was simply framed—Kate wondered whether it might be his mother. Over the crude wooden frame was hung an old rosary, the crucifix depending from the picture. The beads were black and worn by use as if they had slipped many times through girlish fingers.

She had a long time to let her thoughts run. The two men were not soon back and she was beginning to wonder what might have happened, when, standing at the door to listen, she heard noises outside and Laramie's voice. She let him in at once. "You didn't have the door barred," he said, suspiciously.

"Oh, yes, but I heard you speak."

He was alone. "We're ready," he said. "No dry clothes for you, but we can't help it."

She protested she did not mind the wet. Hawk in the saddle was waiting with their horses. Rain was still falling and with the persistent certainty of a mountain storm. Kate, mounting with Laramie's help, got her lines into her hands. "It's pretty dark," he said, standing at her stirrup. "We'll have to ride slow. I go first, Hawk next, then you; if our horses can make the trail yours likely can. I don't think we'll meet anybody, but if we do it's better to know now what to do. If you hear any talk that sounds like trouble, push out of the line as quick as you can and throw yourself flat on the ground. Stay there till you don't hear any more shooting, but hang on to your lines so you don't lose your horse.

"The only other trouble might be your getting lost from us." He spoke slowly as if thinking. "That must depend a good deal on you. Keep as close as you can. Can you whistle?" Kate thought she could. "If you can't make us hear," he continued, "shoot—have you got a pistol?" She had none. He brought her a double action revolver from the cabin and showed her how it worked. "Don't use it unless you have to. It might be heard by more than us."

Kate stuck the revolver under her wet belt. "Why couldn't I ride with you?" she asked.

"There's more danger riding ahead."

"No more for me than for you."

"I wouldn't say that. But if you want to try it, all right. Keep close. Don't be afraid of bumping me—and Hawk can follow us."

There was nothing in the night to encourage heading into it. That men could find their way with every possibility of landmark and sight blotted out and nothing of sound above the downpour except the tumultuous roar of the Turkey which they were following, was to Kate a mystery of mysteries. Even the lightning soon deserted them. Their pace was halted by washouts, obstructed by debris in the trail. In places, the creek running bank-full, backed up over their path.

At times, Laramie halting his companions, rode slowly ahead, sounding out the overflows and choosing the footing. Where streamlets poured over rock outcroppings the horses slipped. Frequently to get his bearings, Laramie felt his way forward by reaching for trees and scraped his knees against them as he pushed his horse close. And in spite of everything to confuse, intimidate and hold them back, they slipped and floundered on their way, until quite suddenly a new roar from out of the impenetrable dark struck their ears.

Laramie halted their party, and the three in silence, listened. "That," said Laramie, after a moment, to Hawk, "sounds like the Crazy Woman."

He went ahead to investigate. He was gone a long time, yet he groped half a mile down the road and made his way back to his companions without a signal. He was on foot. "We're all right," was the report he brought, "it's a little dryer ahead. While I'm down," he said to Kate, "I'll try your cinches. It's a mean night."

"Did you ever see such a night?" she echoed, shuddering.

"Plenty of 'em," returned Laramie. "Once we cross the creek the going will be better."

Of the going between them and the creek, Laramie prudently said nothing. It was the worst of the journey. Two stretches were filled with backwater. Across these they cautiously waded and swam the horses. When they gained high ground adjoining the creek, Kate breathed more freely. There was a halt for reconnaissance. For this, Laramie and Hawk, after placing Kate where she would be safe whether they should come back or not, went forward together.

The splashing and floundering of their horses as the two left her side, was gradually lost in the roar of the night and she was alone in the darkness. They were gone a good while but Kate had enough of confused and conflicting thought to occupy her reflections. After a long interval the report of a Colt's struck her anxious ear. She swallowed in sudden fear to listen more keenly. If there were a fight it would be followed by another report and more. With her heart beating fast she listened, but there was no successor to the single shot and, calming somewhat, she speculated on just what it might mean. Again she waited with such patience as she could until the measured splash of a horse's feet nearing her through the shallow water announced someone's approach. Laramie was back and alone.

Almost anybody in the world would have been

welcome at such a juncture. He called and she answered quickly, but he brought unwelcome news—the little bridge that spanned the creek at this point was out.

"We can't get across, can we?" she exclaimed in disappointment.

"We can swim the creek if you're game for it."

"Could we possibly get across?"

"If I didn't expect to get across I'd sure never try it. It'll be a wet crossing."

"I couldn't be wetter."

"Hawk asked if you could swim."

"I can't."

"I told him I didn't suppose you could."

"Are we all to go together?"

"He's over now. He signaled a minute ago. I told him I'd get you across if he'd get you out. It's close to daybreak. Better take off your coat."

While he strapped her coat to the saddle, she lightened and freed herself as much as possible, disengaged, as he directed, her feet from the stirrups, and they started for the creek. At the point he had chosen for the plunge, he gave her a few admonitions, chiefly to the effect of doing nothing except to cling to her seat in getting into the flood and getting out. Just as her horse poised beside Laramie's a wave of dread swept over her. It was very literally a plunge into the dark. "Are you afraid?" he asked, divining her feeling.

Pride dictated her answer: "No," she said stoutly.

"Though, of course," she added with an attempt at lightness, "I'd prefer to cross on a bridge."

"All in getting used to it, I suppose. I guess I've crossed here a hundred times before there was any bridge. Don't get scared if your head goes under water when your horse jumps in. The bank here is a little high, but it's clean jumping. Say when you're ready."

"I'm ready."

"Go!"

With his hand on her bridle, he spoke loudly and sharply, kicked her horse with one foot and punched his own horse with the other at the same time. The next instant, gripped by an overpowering fear, and breathless, Kate felt herself jerked into the air, then she plunged headlong forward and sank into the boiling flood. Down, down she went, her ears swooning with water, mouth and eyes tight shut, and moving she knew not where or how until her head rose out of the flood and a voice yelled above the tumult: "You're all right! Horse's doing fine. Hang on!"

Then she was conscious of a hand clutching her upper arm, a hand so strong her flesh winced within its grip. And she could feel the powerful strokes of her horse as he panted and swam under her.

Above the terrifying swirl of the waters, carrying in the hardly distinguishable light of the breaking day, a mass of debris that swept about the two riders, the only sound was the hard breathing of the horses and a shout repeated by Laramie, until at last it was answered by Hawk somewhere in the darkness ahead.

Urging the horses to their task, Laramie guided them to where Kate could make out portions of the creek bank. She could realize how fast they were being carried down stream by the wild sweep of the current. Trees flashed past her like phantoms, as if the bank were mad instead of the creek. It seemed impossible she could ever make the bank, now very near, and get up out of the water; only Laramie's hand locked firm now in her horse's mane, his strong voice as he urged the horses or called to Hawk, gave her the slightest hope of coming out alive.

Laramie cried to her to duck as a cottonwood leaning over the water almost tore her cap and hair from her head. The next instant the cottonwood was gone and, looking ahead, she saw a horseman on a slope in the bank, his own horse half submerged. They had reached one of several old fords. Here the two men had purposed to get Kate ashore. But she did not know that this was the last of the ford crossings for a mile—the only shelving bank— nor why Laramie made such superhuman efforts to head her horse toward Hawk, to get to where the horse could ground his feet. Hawk, in an effort to catch Kate's bridle, spurred down to them till his own horse was afloat. Kate's horse struggled desperately, lost headway and was swept below the ford opening. The two men with shouts, curses and entreaties, guiding their own horses, urged the hapless beast to greater effort; it was evident he could not reach the ford.

"The roan can't make it," shouted Hawk. "Crowd him up to the ledge where I can get hold of her."

Hawk, reining his horse hastily about, got him back up the shelving ford, spurred down the bank to where Kate, despite Laramie's efforts, was being driven by the sweep of the water and sprang from his horse. Where Kate's horse struggled at that moment the creek bank rose vertically above the peak of the flood. Deep water gave the horse no chance for a foothold and it swam helplessly. Hawk, running along the ledge, awaited his chance. It came at a moment that Laramie succeeded in crowding the roan to the bank. Hawk saw the opportunity and held his hand out to Kate: "Reach up!" he shouted.

"Give him both hands!" cried Laramie, punching and pushing her horse against the bank. As Kate swept along, her hands upstretched, Hawk caught her wrists and, bracing himself in the slipping earth, dragged her up and out of the saddle. The roan, with Laramie's hand on his bridle, swept on downstream. The clay bank, under the strain of the double load, gave under Hawk's feet. But without releasing Kate's hands he threw himself flat and, matching his dead weight against the chance of being dragged in, caught her with one arm and flung the other backward into the dark. A clump of willow shoots clutched in his sinewy fingers gave him a stay and, putting forth all his strength, he drew Kate slowly up. She scrambled across his prostrate body to safety.

The force of the gnawing current had already undercut the soft clay. The next instant the whole bank began to sink. Hawk shouted to Kate to run. She saw him struggling in the crumbling earth. Crying out in her excitement she stretched her hands toward him. He waved her back. As he did so, a great section of the bank on which he was struggling broke, and in the big, soft splash, Hawk went into the creek.

CHAPTER 27

KATE DEFIES

The instant he saw Kate in Hawk's keeping, Laramie rode down with the flood, looking sharply for a chance to get out the two horses; when finally he did get them ashore he was spent. Leading Kate's horse, he made his way up-creek through the willows to where she should be with Hawk.

Hawk's horse he found browsing in the heavy wet grass at the old ford. Neither Kate nor Hawk were in sight. Laramie walked down to the water's edge where Hawk had pulled her out. Familiar with the meander of the bank below the ford, he saw what had happened. The bank, under-cut, had been swallowed by the flood. Laramie ran down stream and came suddenly on Kate standing alone on a rock jutting out above the torrent.

In the uncertain light of the gray morning he saw her anxious face. She explained what had happened. Laramie showed no alarm. "I guess Abe will handle himself," he said.

"Can't we do anything to help him?"

"I'll put you on your trail, then I'll ride down the creek and look for him. He'll make it if his strength doesn't give out."

Laramie took Kate up the creek and, riding through the hills, brought her, unexpectedly, out on a trail within sight of her father's ranch-house hardly three miles away. He pointed to a break heading from the creek. "You can follow that draw almost to the house," he explained. Then, reining about, he wheeled his horse to take the back trail. "Are you going to run away without giving me a chance to thank you?" she exclaimed, with a feminine touch of surprise.

"There's a gate near the head of the draw where you can get through the wire," he rejoined stubbornly.

"I can't see how I can ever repay you for what you've done tonight," she persisted.

He was coldly uncompromising. "You needn't bother about any pay, if that's what you call it."

Skillfully she drew her horse a step closer to him. "What shall I call it?" she asked innocently, "debt, obligation? I owe you a lot, ever so much to me—my life."

"I've done no more for you than I've done for less than a human being," he returned impatiently.

"I'm sure that's so. But human beings," she added, with a touch of gentle good-nature, "are supposed to have more feeling than cows or steers, you know."

"I never had a cow or a steer call me names," he retorted rudely.

"If you weren't a human being you wouldn't mind being called names; you wouldn't be so angry with me, either."

"I'm not angry," he said resentfully. His very helplessness in her hands pricked her conscience at the moment that it restored her supremacy. His strength might menace others—she at least had nothing to fear from it.

"Do you know," she exclaimed, shaking off for the moment all restraint, "what I'd like to do?"

He looked at her surprised.

"I'd like to ride back this minute with you and help find Abe Hawk. I know I mustn't," she went on as he listened. "But I'd like to," she persisted hurriedly. And then, afraid of herself more than of him, she repressed a quick "good-by" and, without giving him time to answer, galloped away.

She reached the ranch-house without further

difficulty. No one was stirring. She stopped at the corral and turned in her horse and, walking awkwardly on her swollen ankle to the kitchen, built a fire, warmed herself as best she could and went to her room. By the time her father was stirring, Kate, under her coverlets, quite exhausted, was fast asleep.

It was broad day when she woke. Through an open window, she saw sullen gray clouds still rolling down from the northwest, but between them the sun shot out at ragged intervals—the storm had broken. Walking gingerly from her room, on her lame foot, she found the house empty. Her father, Kelly told her, had gone out early, and she sat down to a late breakfast glad to be undisturbed in her thoughts. Her mind was still in a confusion of opinions; some, long-cherished being crowded, so to say, to the wall; others, more than once rejected, growing bolder. It was in this mental condition that her seclusion was invaded by Van Horn.

He swept off his hat with a show of spirits. "Just heard you'd got home." He sat down with her at the table. "Everybody thought you stayed in town last night. Got lost, eh?"

Kate raised her coffee cup non-committally. "For awhile," she murmured between sips.

"What time did you get here?"

"I was so glad to get to bed I never looked at my watch." Again she regarded him, quite innocently, over the rim of her cup. "Did anybody lose any stock?"

He did not abandon his inquisition willingly, but each time he asked a question, Kate parried and asked one in turn. He gave up without having gained any information she meant to withhold.

It was not hard to keep him in good humor; indeed, it was rather too easy. He pushed back his chair, crossed his legs, talked of a strong cattle market for the fall and spoke of Hawk and the hunt he was keeping up for him. "They had a story around—or some of the boys had the idea—that his friends would pick a wet night like last night to take him into town."

"Is he still in the country?"

"Sure he is. Say, Kate," he changed his attitude as lightly as he did his subject—uncrossed his legs, squared himself in his chair and threw his elbows on the table.

She met the new disposition with a tone of prudent reserve: "What is it?"

"When are you going to do something for a lonesome old scout?" he asked bluntly.

With as little concern as possible, she put down her knife and fork, and, with her hands seeking her napkin, looked at him. "What do you mean?" she returned collectedly, "by 'doing something'?"

"Marry me."

"Never."

The passage was disconcertingly quick. Van

Horn, thrown quite aback, remonstrated. His discomfiture was so undisguised that Kate was embarrassed. The next moment he was very angry. "If that's the case," he blurted out, "what's the use o' my sticking around here fighting your battles?"

"You're not fighting my battles."

"Maybe you don't call 'em your father's, either," he exclaimed scornfully.

"They're your own battles," declared Kate. "You know that as well as I do."

"All the same, your father gets the benefit of them," he continued hotly.

"I wish to heaven he had kept out of them."

Van Horn eyed her sharply. His face reflected his sarcasm. "Of course, you needn't worry," he grinned, with implication. "They wouldn't steal your horse even if you do always leave it in Kitchen's barn; the Falling Wall bunch think too much of you for that."

Surprised as she was at this outbreak, Kate kept her head. "There are some of the rustlers I'd trust as far as I would some of the raiders," she rejoined coolly.

"Why don't you say Jim Laramie," he exclaimed harshly.

"Jim Laramie," she returned defiantly, "is not the only one."

"He'll be the 'only one' after our next clean-up in the Falling Wall. And he won't be 'one' if he doesn't change his tune."

Kate's eyes were snapping fire. "Take care that next time the Falling Wall doesn't clean you up," she said bitingly.

He snorted. "I mean it," she exclaimed. "Next time you'll need to look out for yourself."

He bolted from his chair. "That's the first time I ever heard anybody on this ranch take sides with the men that's robbing it—or carry a threat to this ranch-house for rustlers."

"Call it whatever you please, you won't change my opinion of you. But, of course, I'm only a woman and don't know anything."

"I'm thinking you know a whole lot more than you let on," he declared.

"Anyway, I wish you'd leave this ranch out of the rest of it. If you keep on 'cleaning up,' as you call it, you'll go farther and fare worse."

He brought down his fist. "Not until I've cleaned out two more pups, anyway! Now, look here, Kate," he went on, "you may be fooling about this marrying, but you can bet I'm not."

"Well, you can bet *I'm* not," she returned, echoing his pert slang sharply.

"Who's the man?" He flung the question at her point-blank.

If she flushed the least bit it was with anger at his rudeness. "There isn't any man, and there isn't going to be any—so please never talk again about my marrying you or anybody else."

She rose and left the table. He jumped to intercept her and tried to catch her hands. She let him see she was not in the least afraid and as he confronted her, she faced him without a tremor. "Let me pass!" She fairly snapped out the words.

Van Horn, without moving, broke into a boisterous laugh. Kelly walked in just then from the kitchen and Van Horn, losing none of his malevolence, did stand aside.

"All right," he said, "—this time."

CHAPTER 28

A DIFFICULT RESOLVE

For two days Kate burned in feverish reaction from her exposure, wretched in mind and body. Her only effort in that time was to get down to the corral and see that Bradley, acting as barn boy, should do something for her cut and bruised pony.

Her father was still in Medicine Bend, and Van Horn, much to her relief, had disappeared. When she left her bed she spent the morning trying to rehabilitate her riding suit. The task called for all her ingenuity and she was still in the kitchen working on it late in the afternoon when Bradley came in.

He had no sooner sat down by the door to report to Kate at his ease, than Kelly interrupted him with a call for wood. Even after he had filled the box, Kelly warned him he would have to split more next morning to get a supply ahead.

"Easy, Kelly," remonstrated Bradley, in his deeply tremulous voice. "Easy. I can't split no wood t'morrow mornin', not for nobody."

"Why not?"

"Got to go to town."

"What for?"

Bradley declined to answer, but Kelly, persistent, bored into his evasiveness until Kate tired at the discussion: "Tell him what you're going for and be done with it," she said tartly. The reaction of three days had not left her own nerves unaffected; she admitted to herself she was cross.

Bradley, taken aback by this unexpected assault, still tried to temporize. Kate refused to countenance it. When he saw he was in for it, he appealed to her generosity: "It'd be most 's much 's my job's worth if they knew here what I'm goin' to town tomorrow f'r."

"If that's all," said Kate, to reassure the old man, "I'll stand between you and losing your job."

Bradley drew his stubby chin and shabby beard in and threw his voice down into his throat: "D' y' mean that? Then don't say nothin', you and Kelly. Least said, soonest mended. I'm goin' t' town t'morrow t' see the biggest funeral ever pulled off in Sleepy Cat," he announced with bleary dignity.

"What do you mean—whose funeral?" demanded Kate, looking at him suddenly.

"Abe Hawk's. It's goin' t' be t'morrow er next day."

If the old man had meant to stupefy his questioner, he could not better have succeeded. Kate turned deathly white. She bent over the table and busied herself with her ironing. Bradley, pleased with his confidence safely made, talked on. He found a pride in talking to Kate, with Kelly in and out of the room, and launched into unrestrained eulogies of the famed rustler, always the friend of the poor man, once king of the great north range itself.

"It's a pity," murmured Kate, when she felt she must say something, "that he ever went wrong."

Bradley had a point to offer even on that. "It's a pity they ever blacklisted him; that was Stone's get-up. And Stone, when I was sheriff, was the biggest thief in the county an' the county was four times as big then as it is now—that's 'tween you 'n' me."

"Were you ever sheriff, Bill?"

"You won't believe it, but it's so—dash me 'n' dash drunkards one and all."

"I hear, though," returned Kate, only because in her distress of mind she could think of nothing else to say, "that Tom Stone has stopped drinking."

"That man," was Bradley's retort, and he kept his tremulous voice still far down in his throat, "is mean enough to do any d—d thing."

"You used to be sheriff?"

"Yes. And when I was sheriff, Kate, I found out it was better to trust an honest man turned thief than a thief turned honest man."

Kate, listening to his halting maunderings, hardly heeded them. She heard in her troubled ears the rush of mad waters; phantom voices cracked again in pistoled oaths at the horses, the fear of sudden death clutched at her heart, and in the dreadful dark a powerful arm caught her again and drew her, helpless, out of an engulfing flood.

She got out of doors. The sunshine, clear and calm, belied the possibility of a night such as Bradley's words had summoned. "Dead," she kept saying to herself. Laramie had been sure he would get out of the creek. What could it mean?

She went back to the kitchen where Bradley, eating supper, had switched from his long-winded topic. Kate had to question him: "What was the matter with Abe? When did he die?" she asked, as unconcernedly as she could.

There was little satisfaction in Bradley's slow, formal answer: "Some's got it one way and some's got it another, Kate. I can't rightly say what ailded him or when he died 'n' I guess nobody else can, f'r sure. Some says he got shot; some says he was drownded 'a' las' Tuesday night in the Crazy Woman; some says they's been a fight nobody's heard of yit, 't' all. The only man that knows for sure—if he does know—is the man that brought him into Sleepy Cat 'n' if he knows he won't tell."

He held out his big enameled cup. "Kelly, gi' me jus' a squirt o' coffee, will y'?"

Kate, on nettles, waited to hear who had brought Hawk in. Bradley would not volunteer the name. Some deference was due him as the purveyor of the big news, and he meant that anyone curious of detail should do the asking. Kate, realizing this, framed with reluctance the question he was waiting for: "Who brought Abe in?"

Even so, she knew there would be but one answer. Bradley gulped another mouthful of scalding coffee and set down his cup. "Jim Laramie," he answered laconically.

She said to herself that Hawk had never got out of the creek; that he had drowned miserably in the flood. She tortured herself with conjecture as to exactly what had happened. And night brought no relief. Sleepless, she tossed, marveling at how close his death had come home to her. Every scrap of the meager news added to what she already knew—pointed to what she most feared.

She lay propped up on her pillows and looked through the open window out on the glittering stars. Strange constellations passed in brilliant procession before her eyes. And while she lay thus reflecting and revolving in her mind the loneliness and unhappiness of her surroundings, a startling suggestion far removed from these doubts offered itself to her mind. Repelled at first, it came back as if demanding acceptance. And not until after she had promised herself she would consider it, did her thoughts give her any peace. She fell into an uneasy slumber and woke with day barely breaking; but without an instant's delay she dressed and slipped from her room out to the barn.

Forehanded as she had been in getting an early start, Bradley was already stirring. Pail in hand, the old man, standing in front of the feed bin, stared at Kate speechless as she walked in on him.

"Who's sick?" he demanded after a moment.

"Nobody, Bill. I'm going to town with you, that's all."

"With *me?*"

She half laughed at herself and at his surprise. "I mean, I'm for town early. Get up a pony for me—Spider Legs will do."

Born of long-forgotten experience in waiting for women, Bill Bradley, as Kate walked away, put in a caveat: "I'm headin' out jus' soon's I c'n get breakfast."

"I, too, Bill. I'll be across the divide before you are."

Curiosity would not down: "What y' goin' t' town f'r?" he called.

Turning half around, Kate, with a little shrug, paused. She would not be ungracious: "To pick up a few things," she answered unconcernedly.

Bill, not satisfied, felt obliged to desist. "Startin' airly," was his only grumble. Had he known what possibilities for that day had lodged themselves in Kate's mind, he would not have been able to slip Spider Legs' bridle over his ears. But his business being only to get up the horse, he discharged it with shaky fidelity and for himself started with high expectations for town. Had he been given to speculating on the variableness of woman, he might have found a text in Spider Legs' standing for hours after he was made ready. And in the end his mistress unsaddled him and turned him back into the corral.

The truth was, Kate had been seized with cruel fits of doubt and for a long time could not decide whether she ought to go to town or not. But as often as she gave up the idea of going, a heart-strong impulse pleaded against her uneasy restraint. She felt she *must* go.

CHAPTER 29

HORSEHEAD PASS

Bradley had not been able to tell her just when the funeral was set for. But it surged in Kate's heart that after what Abe Hawk had done for her, to let the poor, bullet-torn, neglected body be put into the ground without some effort to pay a tribute of gratitude to the man that had once animated it, would be on her part fearfully cold.

The difficulties of the situation were many. She

feared the anger of her father, and owed his feelings something as well. But every time she decided she ought to stay at home, the pricking at her heart grew keener. In the end, her feelings overrode her restraint. She resolved at least to go to town. The funeral might have already taken place—it would be a relief even to learn more about his death.

Late in the afternoon, she got Spider Legs up again, saddled him and, telling Kelly she might not be back that night, rode away.

It was dark by the time she reached town and leaving her horse with McAlpin she crossed the street from the barn and walked hurriedly around the corner to Belle's. The front door stood open and the red-shaded lamp burned low on the dining-room table.

Tapping on the screen door, Kate, without waiting for Belle to answer, opened it and went in. There was no light in the living-room and the portières were drawn. She walked down the hall to the dining-room, where she laid down her gloves and took off her coat and hat. Smoothing her hair, she knocked on the door of Belle's room, but got no answer. Conjecturing that she had gone out on an errand, Kate sat down in a rocking chair and, taking a newspaper from the table, tried to read.

Her thoughts soon blurred the print. She read on only to think of what had brought her so irresistibly to town and to wonder what she should hear now that she had come.

After some struggle to concentrate, she tossed the paper aside to ask herself why Belle did not return, and, being tense, began without realizing it, to rock softly. Her eyes naturally turned to the familiar lamp. Its somber paper shade threw the light in a circle on the table, leaving the room in the heavy shadows of its figured pattern. Kate became all at once conscious of the utter silence, and impatient for Belle's return, got up and walked through the dark hall toward the front door.

Passing the living-room portières, she pushed open the screen door and stepped out on the porch. There she stood for a moment at the top of the steps looking at the stars. Lights here and there burned in neighboring cottage windows. No wind stirred. The street and the town were as still as the night. After some minutes, Kate descended the steps, opened the gate, leaving it to close with a click behind her, and walked to the corner of Main Street. It looked dark. The stores were closed. From the saloon windows spotty lights shot at intervals across the upper street, but these only made the darkened store fronts blacker and revealed the nakedness and desertion of the street itself. Not a man, much less a woman, could she see anywhere moving.

Either the silence, or the night, or her long wait changed her impatience into a feeling of loneliness. She turned back toward the cottage gate. She had not noticed before how very dark the side street was. Reaching the gate she hesitated, pushed it open and then stopped, conscious of a curious repugnance to entering the house.

Her feeling refused to explain itself. Through the screen she could see the lamp still burning on the dining-room table. Things appeared just as she had left them, yet she did not want to go in. But, dismissing the qualm, she walked up the steps, crossed the narrow porch, opened the screen door and, stepping inside, closed it after her.

This time that she passed the living-room she noticed the portières were partly open. Both times she had passed before, she felt sure, they had been closed.

Kate sat down in the dining-room and looked suspiciously back at the portières. She was already sorry she had come into the house, for the silence and her aloneness added to the conviction fast stealing over her that someone must be in the dark living-room.

Once entertained, the suspicion became insupportable. Her ears were pitched to a painful intensity of listening and her eyes were fastened immovably on the motionless curtains.

She carried a ranchwoman's revolver and, putting her hand on it, she rose, stepped close to the door of Belle's room—into which she could retreat—and, with one hand on the knob, called sharply toward the living-room: "Who's there?"

Not a sound answered her.

"Who is in the living-room?" she demanded again. This time, after a moment's delay, she heard something move in the darkness, then a man's step and Laramie stood out between the portières.

Except for a fatigued look as he rested one hand on the portière and the other on his hip, he appeared quite as she had last seen him. "Are you calling me?" he asked.

"Yes," she responded tartly. "Why didn't you answer?"

"I didn't know who you were speaking to at first. I've been here all the evening. I didn't know you were in town till I saw your hat on the table a few minutes ago."

"Where is Belle?" asked Kate, still on edge.

"She went over to Mrs. Kitchen's."

"When will she be back?"

He seemed to take no offense at her peremptory tone. "She said she wouldn't be gone a great while. But," he added, with his customary deliberation, "all the same, I wouldn't be surprised if she stayed over pretty late—or even all night."

This was not just what Kate wanted to hear. "Why didn't you say something when I first came in?" she asked, her suspicion reflected in her voice.

He did not seem nonplused but answered slowly: "I heard someone come in. I didn't pay much attention, that's about the truth."

"What are you doing in there in the dark?"

He was provokingly deliberate in answering. "You probably haven't heard about Abe Hawk?"

Her manner changed instantly and her voice sank. "Is it true that he is dead?"

"Yes."

"He didn't drown that morning, did he?" she asked eagerly anxious. "You thought he could get out—what happened?"

"He got out of the creek. But he strained his wounds—they opened. I wasn't much of a surgeon. I got him to the hospital—he died there. I had no place to take him then. I wouldn't leave him there alone. Belle said I might bring him here. I'm spending my last night with him."

"You're not trying to spare me, are you?" she asked, unsteadily. "He really *did* get out of the creek?"

"He did get out."

She spoke again brokenly: "He saved my life."

"Well," remarked Laramie, meditating, "he wouldn't ask anything much for that. Do you mind if I smoke?"

"Not a bit."

"I'm kind of nervous tonight," he confessed simply. Then he crossed the room, rested his elbow on the mantelpiece and made ready a cigarette. "I wonder," he said, "if I could ask you a question?"

"What is it?"

"You always act kind of queer with me. Why is

302

it? You've never been the way you were the first day we met. Haven't I always been square with you?"

She hesitated but she answered honestly: "You always have."

"Then why are you so different?"

"I've made that confession once. I was acting a part that day."

"No, I can't figure it in that way. That day you were acting natural. Why can't you be like that again."

"But, Mr. Laramie—"

"No—Jim."

"But—"

"Every time you call me Mr. Laramie I'm looking around for a gentleman. Why can't you be the way you were the first time?"

She realized his eyes were on her, demanding the truth—and his eyes were uncomfortably steady as she had reason to know. "If I spoke I should hurt your feelings," she urged, summoning all her courage. "You know as well as I do that the first time I met you I didn't know who you were."

He did not seem much disconcerted, except that he tossed away the unlighted cigarette. "You don't know now," was his only comment.

"I can't help knowing what is said about you— you and your friends."

He made an impatient gesture. "That gives you no clue to me."

"What are people to believe when such stories are public property?"

"Only what they know to be true."

"How are they to find out what is true?"

"By going straight to the person most concerned in the stories."

"Would you honestly expect a young woman to go to work and investigate all the charges against men she hears in Sleepy Cat?"

"We are talking now about the charges against one man—against me. I want to give you an instance:

"I suppose there's been a good many hard words over your way about my keeping Abe Hawk out of the hands of your people. Because I did shelter him—you know how—they've blackened my name here at Sleepy Cat and down at Medicine Bend. A man doesn't have to approve all another man does, to befriend him when he's down and a bunch of men—not as good as he—set out to finish him. I haven't got any apologies to make to anybody for protecting Abe when he was wounded— and if he wasn't wounded, no man would talk any kind of protection to him. But you've been fed up with stories about it—I know that—so," he added grimly, "I'm going to tell you one story more.

"I grew up in this country when the mining fever was on—everybody plumb crazy in the rush for the Horsehead Camp in the Falling Wall country. One winter five hundred men in tents were hanging around Sleepy Cat waiting for the first thaw, to get up to the camp. That's when I got acquainted with Abe Hawk. Abe was carrying the mails to the mines. He hadn't a red cent in the world. My father had just died; I was a green kid with a pocketful of money. Abe didn't teach me any bad habits—I didn't need any teacher. One night we were sitting next to each other, with Harry Tenison dealing faro.

"I heard Abe was going up over the pass to Horsehead with the Christmas bag. The few miners that got in the fall before had hung up a fat purse for their Christmas mail and Abe needed the money. He was the only man with the crazy nerve to try such a thing. And there were twenty men, with all kinds of money, crowding him to take them along: to beat the bunch in might mean a million dollar strike to any tenderfoot in Sleepy Cat.

"Abe wouldn't hear a word of it, not from anybody—and he could talk back awful rough. He was sure he could make the trip alone. He was the strongest man in the mountains. I never saw the day I could handle Abe Hawk. But the pass in December was not a job for any ordinary mountain man—let alone a bunch of greenhorns. Just the same, I made my play to go with him. He cursed me as hard as he did anybody and turned me down.

"One night, after that, I was at Tenison's again. I was losing money. Hawk was near me. He saw it. I waited for him to come out. I knew he'd be starting soon and I was desperate. I tackled him pretty strong. He swore if I talked again about going with him he'd kill me. Old Bill Bradley ran the livery. My horse was in the same barn with Abe's and Bill promised to tip me off when Abe was ready to start. He waited for a blizzard. When it passed he was ready. But I got ahead of him, out of town, and trailed him—I knew how. Only it snowed again, as if all hell was against me; I had to close up on Abe or lose him, but he never saw me till we got so far I couldn't get back; though he could have dropped me out of the saddle with a bullet, and had the right to do it.

"When I rode up he only looked at me. If I had been as small as I felt, he'd never seen me. He ought to have abused me; but he didn't. He ought to have shot me; but he didn't; or turned me back and that would have been worse than shooting. But if he'd been my own father he couldn't have acted different. He just told me to come along."

Laramie paused. He was speaking under a strain: "I didn't understand it then; but he knew it was too late to quarrel. He knew there was about one chance in a hundred for him to get through; for me, there was about one in a hundred thousand—in fact, he knew I *couldn't* get through, so he didn't abuse me.

"You don't know what the winter snow on the pass is. When it got too bad for us, he put his horse ahead to break the trail, but he let me ride mine as far as I could—he knew what was coming. When my horse quit, he told me to tramp along behind him.

"I guess you know about how long a boy's wind would last ten thousand feet up in the air. I wasn't used to it. I quit."

Laramie drew from his pocket a handkerchief and knotted it nervously in his fingers: "He told me to get up," he went on. "I did my level best a way farther. It was no use. I quit again. He was easy with me. But I couldn't get up and I told him to go on.

"Abe wouldn't go. I couldn't walk another step in that wind and snow to save my soul from perdition. I just couldn't. And when I tell you next what I asked of him, then you'll understand how mean a common tramp like me can be. But I've got past pretty much caring what you think of me—only I want you to know what *I* think, and thought, of Abe Hawk. I did the meanest thing then I ever did in my life—I asked him to let me ride his horse. It was useless. I offered him all the money I had. He refused. He didn't just look at me and move on, the way most men would to save their own skins and leave me to what I deserved. He stopped and explained that if his horse gave out we were done—we could never break a trail to the top without the horse.

"It was blowing. He stripped his horse. The mail went into the snow. I tried again to walk. I didn't get a hundred feet. When I fell down that time he saw it was my finish.

"He stood a minute in front of me, looking all around before he spoke. His horse was breathing pretty heavy; the snow blowing pretty bad. After a while he loosened the quirt from his saddle and looked at me: 'Damn you,' he said, 'you were bound to come. All hell couldn't keep you back, could it? Now it's come in earnest for you. You're goin' over the pass with me. Get up out of that snow.'

"I could hear him, but I couldn't move hand or foot. And I never dreamed what was going to happen till he laid the quirt across my face like a knife.

"All I ever hoped for was to get up so I could live long enough to kill him. He gave me that quirt till I was insane with rage; long afterward he told me my eyes turned green. I cursed him. He asked me whether I'd get up. I knew, if I didn't, I'd have to take more. I dragged myself out of the snow again and pitched and struggled after him—to the top of the pass.

"Then he put me on his pony—we got the wind worse up there. Abe had a little shack a way down the pass, rigged up for storm trouble. But the pony quit before we got to the shack, and when the pony fell down, my hands and feet were no use. Abe carried and dragged and rolled me down into the shack. I was asleep. There was always a fire left laid in the stove. Abe had a hard time to light it. But he got it lighted and when he fell down he laid both hands on the stove—so when they began to burn it would wake him up; if the fire didn't burn he didn't want to wake up. The marks of that fire are on his hands right in that room there now, tonight. He saved my hands and feet. He stayed with me while I was crazy and got me safe to Horsehead.

"Do you suppose I could ever live long enough to turn that man, wounded, over to an enemy? He didn't ask me for any shelter after Van Horn's raid. All he ever asked me for was cartridges—and he got 'em. He'd get anything I had, and all I had, as long as there was a breath left in my body, and he asked within reason. And Abe Hawk wouldn't ask anything more."

Kate rose from her chair: "I've a great deal to learn about people and things in this country," she said slowly. "Not all pleasant things," she added. "I suppose some unpleasant things have to be. Anyway, I'll ride home tonight better satisfied for coming in."

"You going home?" he asked.

She was moving toward the door: "I only hope," she exclaimed, "this fighting is over."

"That doesn't rest in my hands. It's no fun for me. You say you're going to ride home?"

"There's a moon. I shan't get lost again."·

He was loath to let her get away. At the door he

asked if he couldn't ride a way with her. "I'll get Lefever or Sawdy to stay here while I'm gone," he urged.

"No, no."

"It isn't that they don't want to," he explained. "But the boys felt kind of bad and went down to the Mountain House. Why not?"

She regarded him gravely: "One reason is, I'd never get rid of you till I got home."

"I'll cross my heart."

"We might meet somebody. I don't want any more explosions. Let's talk about something else."

He asked to go with her to the barn to get her horse. The simplicity of his urging was hard to resist. "I must tell you something," she said at last. "If you go with me to the barn we should be seen together."

"And you're ashamed of me?"

"I said I must tell you something," she repeated with emphasis. "Will you give me a chance?"

"Go to it."

She looked at him frankly: "I don't always have the easiest time in the world at home. And there is always somebody around a big ranch to bring stories to father about whom I'm seen with. Everybody in town talks—except Belle. I must just do the best I can till things get better."

"Here's hoping that'll be soon."

"Good-by!"

"Safe journey."

CHAPTER 30

THE FUNERAL—AND AFTER

The funeral had been set for the following afternoon, but preparations were going forward all morning. In spite of the brief notice that had got abroad of Hawk's death, men from many directions were riding into town that morning to help bury him. A reaction of sentiment concerning the Falling Wall raid was making itself felt; its brutal ferocity was being more openly criticized and less covertly denounced. Hawk's personal popularity had never suffered among the cowboys and the cowboy following. He had been known far and wide for open-handed generosity and blunt truthfulness—and these were traits to silence or to soften reprobation of his fitful and reckless disregard for the property rights of the big companies. He was a freebooter with most of the virtues and vices of his kind. But the crowd that morning in Sleepy Cat was assembling to pay tribute to the man—however far gone wrong. His virtues they were, no doubt, willing to bury with him; the memory of his vices would serve some of them when they might need a lawless precedent.

Up to the funeral hour the numerous bars of Sleepy Cat were points of interest for the drinking

311

men. In front of these, reminiscences of the dead man held heated sway. Some stories pulled themselves together through the stimulus of deep drinking, others gradually went to pieces under its bewildering effects; but as long as a man could remember that he was talking about Abe Hawk or the Falling Wall, his anecdotes were tolerated.

Nor were all the men that had come to town to say good-by to Abe, lined up at the bars. Because Tenison had insisted that it should, Hawk's body lay during the morning at the Mountain House in the first big sample room opening off the hotel office. All that the red-faced undertaker could do to make it presentable in its surroundings had been done at Harry Tenison's charge. Laramie's protests were ignored: "You're a poor man, Jim," declared Tenison, "and you can't pay any bills now for Abe. He thought more of you than he did of any man in the world. But most of his money he left here with me, upstairs and down. Abe was stiff-necked as hell, whether it was cards or cattle, you know that. And it's only some of his money—not mine—I'm turning back to him. That Dutchman," he added, referring with a contemptuous oath to the unpopular undertaker of Sleepy Cat, "is a robber, anyhow. The only way I'll ever get even with him is that he'll drink most of it up again. I played pinochle with that bar-sinister chap," continued Tenison, referring to the enemy by the short and ugly word, "all one night, and couldn't get ten cents out of him—and he half-drunk at that. What do you know about that?

"Jim," Tenison changed his tone and his rambling talk suddenly ceased, "you've not told me rightly yet about Abe."

Laramie looked up: "Why, Harry," he said quietly, "I told you where I found him that night —he got out of the creek at Pride's Crossing."

Tenison shook his head: "But what I want to know is what went on before he got to Pride's Crossing."

"Well, I started with him that night for town."

"That's what you said before," objected Tenison with an impatient gesture. "What you didn't say is what I want to hear."

"Harry, I won't try to give you a long line of talk. I can't tell it all—and I don't want to try to fool you. There's another name in the story that I don't feel I've got a right to bring in—that's all. Some day you'll hear it."

Neither Lefever nor Sawdy could get any more out of Laramie. He showed the strain of sleeplessness and anxiety. Sawdy kept the crowd away by answering all questions himself—mostly with an air of reserve, backed by intimations calculated to lead a man to believe he was really hearing something, and counter-questions skilfully dropped into the gravity of the occasion. Those who could not be put off by Sawdy were turned over to Lefever, who could hypnotize a man by asking questions, and send him away satisfied, but vacantly speculative as to whether he was crazy or Lefever was.

To Lefever also were referred the men arranging the details of the funeral. Not till two o'clock was the word given for the procession to move from the Mountain House, but for two hours before that, horsemen—peers of any in the world—dashed up and down Main Street before keen-eyed spectators, on business if possible, but always on display.

Stage drivers and barnmen from Calabasas and Thief River mingled with cowboys from the Deep Creek country—for Hawk himself had, years before, driven on the Spanish Sinks line. From the barn at Sleepy Cat these men brought out and drafted the old Wells-Fargo stage coach that Abe had driven on the first trip to the Thief River mines. Six of the best horses in the barn were to pull it in the procession. These horses were driven by the oldest man in service on the Calabasas run, mounted on the near wheel horse with the driver's seat on the box empty and covered with wreaths of flowers. Old-time Indians from the Reservation who had known Hawk when he first went into the Falling Wall country, were down to see him buried; they rode behind the cowboys.

At two o'clock the roundhouse whistle blew a long blast. It was taken up by the engines in the yard and those of an overland train pulling out; and the procession, long and picturesque, moved from the hotel. Laramie, Tenison, Lefever and Sawdy rode abreast, behind the hearse, and as the procession moved down Main Street, the cowboys chanted the songs of the bunkhouse and the campfire, the range and the round-up.

"My God!" exclaimed Carpy when it was all over, "if Sleepy Cat could do that much for a thief, what would it do for an honest man?" With Sawdy and Lefever, the doctor sat at a table in the billiard room of the Mountain House. Tenison and Laramie sat near them.

"Not what they did for Abe," averred John Lefever promptly, "and don't you forget it. But I don't call Abe Hawk a thief—never. Abe was a freebooter born out of time and place. He called himself a thief—he wasn't one. He hadn't the first instincts of one—no secrecy, no dark night stuff, no lying. He never denied a raid if he made one. And never did worse when the big cattlemen protested, than to tell them to go to hell. He had a bunch of old Barb's calves branded along with his own one year: 'Well, you're the coolest rustler in the Falling Wall,' I says to him. 'They're my share of Barb's spring drop,' was all he said. You know he lent Barb all his savings one year—that was when he used to save money, before his wife died. He never got a red cent of it back, never even asked for it. But when he wanted money he'd drive off some of Barb's steers. Yes, Abe stole cattle, I admit; yet I don't call him a thief—not today, anyway," said

John, raising his glass. "Why, if Abe Hawk owed a man a hundred dollars he'd pay him if he had to steal every cow in the Falling Wall to do it. But take a hoof from a poor man!" he went on, freshened, "The poor men all used to run to Abe when Dutch Henry or Stormy Gorman branded their calves. They'd yell fire and murder. And Abe would make the blamed thieves drive their calves back! You know that, Jim." Lefever between breaths threw the appeal for confirmation across at Laramie who sat moodily listening and trying without success to interest himself in a drink that stood untouched before him.

Laramie made no response. "Have it your own way, John," nodded Carpy tolerantly, "have it your own way. But whatever they say against old Barb, the man ain't livin' that can say a word against his girl—not while I'm in hearing. And I'll tell you, you could have knocked me over with a feather when I seen her this afternoon and she bound to ride in that procession behind Abe Hawk."

"What do you mean?" asked Lefever.

"I mean riding to the graveyard," insisted Carpy.

"What are you talking about?" demanded Lefever, to bring out the story. "You never saw it."

"I'll tell you what I saw." Only those who knew Laramie well could have told how keenly he was listening. "I drove down Hill Street," said the doctor, "just after the funeral started, and sat there, quiet, to one side, waiting for it to pass; a doctor's got no business around funerals. Right then, Kate Doubleday pulled up close to me on horseback. She was just from the trail, that was sure; her horse showed the pace and the girl was excited—I seen that when she spoke to me. 'Doctor'—then she hesitated. 'Is that Abe Hawk's funeral?' 'It is,' I says. She looked at it and kept looking at it. The tail-end of the procession was passing Hill Street. I noticed the girl bite her lip; she was as restless as her horse. 'Doctor,' she says, hesitating just the same way the second time, 'do you think people would think it awfully strange if I—rode to the cemetery with them?'

"I never was more dashed in my life. 'Well,' I says, 'I expect they would, Kate.' 'I feel as if I ought to do it,' she says. 'Don't do it for the fun of the thing, Kate. The boys wouldn't like that.' 'Oh,' she says, looking at me mighty hard. 'I've got the best of reasons for doing it.' 'Then,' says I, 'do it, no matter what they think or don't think. That's what Abe Hawk would 'a' done!' 'I'm such a coward,' she says, but I want to tell you there was fire in her words. 'Go ahead,' says I. 'Doctor, will you ride with me?' 'Hell!' says I, 'I never went to a funeral in my life.' 'Will you ride to this one with me? I can't ride alone; all the rest are men.' 'Dog gone it! Come over to the barn,' says I, 'till I get a horse.'

"That's the way it happened.

"When we got to the graveyard we kept back to

317

one side. All the same, she saw the whole thing. But just the minute the boys turned from the grave, away we went down the hill lickety-cut. We took the back streets till we struck the divide road, and she turned for home. When we stopped there, she says: 'Doctor, tell me the truth: Did Abe Hawk drown?' 'No,' I says, 'he didn't drown. I reckon he strained himself. Anyway, one of his wounds opened up. The old man bled to death.'"

Laramie felt no inclination that night to go home. In his depression, he could think only of Kate Doubleday and reflect that the years were passing while he faced the future without an aim, and life without an outlook.

It was not the first time this conviction had forced itself on him. And it was getting harder and harder, he realized, to shake it off. But tonight, talk served in some degree as an anodyne, and he sat with the idlers late. The one bit of news that did stir him in his torpor was that Kate Doubleday had had at least the feeling to appear at the funeral of the man who, though rightly regarded as her father's enemy, had, Laramie knew, let go his own life, without a thought, to save hers.

This was the last reflection on his mind before he went to sleep that night. It was the first when he woke. Late in the morning he was sitting in Belle Shockley's at breakfast when McAlpin walked in.

"Jim," exclaimed the excitable barn boss, "I got a word this morning from the Falling Wall."

Laramie regarded him evenly, but did not speak till McAlpin looked inquiringly toward Belle: "No secrets here, Mac," he said briefly.

"Probably couldn't keep 'em from a woman if you tried," returned McAlpin, grinning. He pointed calmly toward the kitchen: "If we're all alone here—"

"Go ahead," intervened Belle impatiently, "we are."

"Punk Budd brought the stage from the Reservation this morning. Coming down the Turkey he met Van Horn. They had a bunch of Barb's boys with them driving in some cattle."

"Whose cattle?"

"Punk says when he run into 'em they was roundin' up yours."

"Was Punk sober?" asked Laramie.

"He sure was," replied McAlpin.

Belle, with folded arms, stood in the archway immovable as a statue; McAlpin sat in silence; Laramie, continuing his breakfast, looked only at his plate. The silence grew heavy, but two of the three had no reason to break it and the third did not choose to.

Laramie, at length, took up his coffee, and, drinking slowly, finished the cup. Setting this down, he wiped his lips and looked at McAlpin.

"Much obliged, Mac," he said, laying down his napkin.

McAlpin regarded him inquiringly: "What you going to do about it, Jim?" he demanded, when he saw Laramie would say no word.

Laramie pushed back his chair: "What would you do?"

McAlpin spoke seriously: "I'm askin' you."

"I can tell better after I know more about it, Mac."

The barn boss evidently thought Laramie was taking the news too quietly. He was for violent measures but Laramie calmed him. "If they've got any of my cattle, they won't run away," said he, "and they won't blow up. They'll keep, and I'll get them back—every hoof. I'm riding home this morning, anyway, so I'll be over after my horse in a minute."

McAlpin went away somewhat disappointed. Laramie only laughed when he talked it over with Belle: "So long as they don't burn my place, I can stand it," he said, philosophically.

Nevertheless, he felt disturbed at McAlpin's news—not for its substance so much as for what it might note in renewed warfare. Getting his horse, he followed the railroad right of way out of town and struck out upon open country toward the north. He had no intention of taking the direct road home; that had long become dangerous, and he rode along abandoned cattle trails. At times he struck, swiftly and straight, across open country, at times disappeared completely in favoring canyons, and emerging again, headed winding draws up to the divide—any ground that carried him in his general direction was good ground.

He tried always to be thinking just what the other fellow must be thinking as to favorable points to pick a man off—the fellow patiently waiting with a rifle day after day in ambush for him. And not having gone home of late twice by the same route, he meant to keep the other fellow continually guessing. Today, he was somewhat handicapped, in that he was riding in broad daylight instead of in the dawn or in the twilight when the uncertain light made it more difficult with the fine sights of a Winchester or Savage to cover a distant man.

This hazard, however, called only for a little more precaution, which Laramie did not begrudge to the pride of disappointing an enemy. At points in his route where the main road could not well be avoided, he rode faster and with quickened circumspection. The Double-draw bridge he could not avoid without a long and difficult detour. Moreover, there, or beyond, he might expect to intercept the raiding party, and this was his business.

He did, however, approach the Double-draw bridge with an uncertainty and a caution not reflected in the pace which he rode toward it; but his horse was under close control and his rifle carefully in hand.

Despite his misgivings, no enemy was sighted. Only a flight of bank swallows, disturbed by the footfalls of his horse, darted noisily from their nests under the south bridge abutment and scattered twenty ways in the sunshine. Spurring freely, as they flew away, Laramie galloped briskly across the bottoms and up the hill. Skirting the long trail toward home, he rode on without meeting a living soul or hearing the unwelcome singing of a bullet.

In fact, things were too quiet; the silence and the absence of any sort of life as he approached his ranch were a surprise. The few head of cattle and horses he usually met, when riding home along the creek, were nowhere to be seen. Evidently the raid had been made. To survey the whole scene without exposing himself, Laramie rode out of the tangle along the creek bottom and took the first draw that would bring him out among the southern hills. As he emerged from the narrow gorge, his eyes turned in the direction of the house. But where the house should be he saw above the green field, only a black spot with little patches of white smoke drifting lazily up from it into the still sunshine.

CHAPTER 31

AN ENCOUNTER

Kate awoke the morning after Hawk's funeral with a confused sense of having consorted with her father's enemies; and of trying to justify herself for having done what she had felt compelled to do to answer her sense of self-respect.

And all this before anyone had accused her. But being extremely dubious as to how her father would take her conduct, she was not only ill at ease until she should meet him, but glad he had been away. And it was something of a shock to her that morning to find his bedroom door closed; it meant that during the night he had unexpectedly come home.

After her breakfast she walked down to the corral to talk to Bradley about the saddle horses. Not that she had anything to suggest, but because she was nervous. Laramie was intruding more and more into her mind; every time she banished him he returned, frequently bringing someone else with him. Between the perplexities and the men that beset her, Kate was not happy. And when, after a ramble along the creek, she returned to the house, she was not surprised to find that her father, coming from the breakfast table, hardly responded to her greeting. He was much engrossed in cutting off the end of a cigar as he passed her and in walking to the fireplace to find a match.

But the matches were not on the mantelpiece, where they belonged, and this annoyed him. If he said nothing, it did not deceive Kate as to his feelings. She hastened to hand him the matchbox from the table. He took it without saying a word, but he slammed it back to its accustomed place with a silent and ominous emphasis.

She knew it was coming. What surprised her was that she felt no further inclination to shrink from the moment of reckoning she dreaded. Doubleday, his cigar lighted, seated himself in his heavy chair beside the fireplace.

"What kind of a trip had you, father?" Kate, as she asked, made a pretense of arranging the papers and magazines on the table.

There was little promise of amiability in her father's answer: "What d'y' mean," he asked.

"Did you get your notes extended?"

"Yes." His heavy jaw and teeth, after the word, snapped like a steel trap. "Did you go to Abe Hawk's funeral?" He flung the question at her like a hammer.

"Were you told I did?" Kate asked.

"Rode to the graveyard with him, didn't you?"

Kate saw there was no use softening her words: "Father," she said instantly and firmly, "the night I came out from town in the storm I got lost. I got on the wrong side of the creek. My horse gave out; I was dead with the cold."

Her father flung his cigar into the fire: "What's that got to do with it?" he broke in harshly.

"Just wait a moment."

"I don't want any long-winded story."

"I won't tell any."

"I won't listen to you," he shouted. "Answer my question."

Her eyes kindled: "You may call it whatever

you like, but you will listen to my answer in the way I make it. When I'd given up hope of saving my life, and my horse was drifting, he fell into a dugout. And in the dugout were two men—Abe Hawk and Jim Laramie. They thought there was a party of men with me. They seized me. They got ready to fight. I was at their mercy."

"What dugout?" demanded Doubleday. His husky tone seemed to indicate he was cooling a little; the question took her off her guard.

"At the old mine bridge."

A flash of cunning lighted her father's eyes. The curtain fell instantly, but not before Kate had seen. "When they questioned me," she hurried on, "I told them what had happened. They believed me. They rode with me back to the creek. We swam our horses across. Mine couldn't make the bank. Abe Hawk pulled me out and Laramie saved my horse. But the bank caved in with Hawk when he pulled me out of the creek and the next thing I heard, he was dead. I didn't go to his funeral except to ride to the cemetery in the procession. Father, could I do any less?" she demanded, wrought up.

Barb's harsh, red features never looked less uncompromising: "D' you expect me to believe that stuff?" he asked, regarding her coldly. She only eyed him as he eyed her: "D' you expect anybody to believe it?" he continued, to drive in his contempt.

Kate turned white. When she spoke, her words

were measured: "Oh, no," she said quietly. "I don't expect you any more to believe anything I say. Those other men would believe me when they had me at their mercy—when they might have choked or shot me or thrown me into the Falling Wall canyon—they only believed me. But my own father—he couldn't believe me—"

Neither appeal nor reproach moved her father; his mind was fixed. Van Horn had been sarcastic over Kate's escapade; Barb's own men were laughing at him. He interrupted Kate: "Pack up your things," he said ruthlessly.

She faced her father without flinching: "What do you mean?" she asked.

He tossed his head with as little concern as if he were discharging a cowboy: "Don't want you around here any longer," he snapped. "Pack up. Get out."

She looked at him in silence. Perhaps, as she turned defiantly away and walked to her room, she thought of the man that had deserted her mother when she herself was a baby in her mother's arms. At any rate, anger fortified her against the shock. Her preparations were soon made. A trunk held all she wished to take. She asked Bradley to get up her pony. Bradley was hitched up for a trip to Sleepy Cat and, putting her trunk in the wagon, was on the road ahead of Kate. She spent a little time in straightening up her room and shortly afterwards rode down the trail for town.

Absorbed in thoughts tinged with bitterness and anger, she rode toward the creek as if casting things up again and again in her mind, but reaching no conclusion. When her horse struck the Sleepy Cat road he turned into it because he was used to doing so, not because she guided him. In this haphazard way she was jogging on, her eyes fixed on nothing more encouraging than the storm-worn ruts along her way when a shout startled her. Looking up, she saw she was nearing the lower gate of the alfalfa patch and across the road a party of horsemen had stopped Bradley with the wagon. She recognized Harry Van Horn—his smart hat, erect figure and scarlet neckcloth would have identified him before she could distinguish his features; and he always rode the best horse. Stone and three of the Texas men were with him. With the exception of Van Horn, they had dismounted, and with their drooping horses close at hand were stacking their rifles against the gate and yelling at Bradley.

Swinging his hat, Van Horn dashed toward Kate just as she looked up and, whipping out his revolver, pulled his horse to its haunches directly in front of her: "You're held up!" he cried.

The shock on her reverie was sudden and Kate was too confused and frightened to speak.

"You can't get by without giving up your tobacco, girlie," Van Horn ran on in sing-song raillery. "Shell out!" He held out his left hand for the spoil and poised his gun high—a picture of life and dash. "You see what's happening to Bradley." The cowboys, in great feather, were dragging the old man with mock violence from the wagon.

Kate recovered her breath: "What's it all about?" she asked.

Van Horn put away his gun. He was in very good humor as he glanced over at the boys crowding around Bradley: "They want tobacco," he laughed.

"Oh."

"You know what I want."

Kate regarded his expectancy unmoved: "How should I know?" she asked, chilling her question with indifference.

"Because," he exclaimed, sweeping back with a flourish the brim of his hat, "I want you."

She eyed him without a tremor and responded without hesitation: "Well, I can say you will never get me if that's all you want."

He laughed again: "Talk it over with me, Kate; talk it over."

His eyes, always bright and liquid, were a little inflamed. Still laughing, he glanced toward the wagon. The boys were boisterous. Kate could hear Bradley's voice in shrill protest: "What'd I be goin' to town f'r, if I had a bottle?" he was demanding angrily. But, while she looked and listened, Van Horn slipped quickly from his saddle and caught her bridle rein: "Come on," he said, at her horse's head, "let's walk down to the creek, girlie, and talk it all over."

Kate was indignant: "I won't walk anywhere—"

"I'll carry you."

She suppressed an angry word: "I'm on my way to town," she exclaimed. "Let go my bridle!" She struck her horse. The beast jumped ahead. Van Horn, laughing, held on. But the shock jerked him almost from his feet. As he staggered forward, clinging to the rearing animal, the half-muffled report of a revolver was heard. Almost like a thunderbolt, it changed the situation. One of the Texas men had fired in the air, but no one had seen him fire and the other Texans jumped like longhorns. Stone, clapping his hand to his holster, whirled from the wagon wheel. Kate, frightened more than ever, struck her horse again; the bridle was jerked from Van Horn's hand and he turned sharply. Quickest to grasp what he saw as his eye swept the road, he yelled: "Look out, boys! There's Laramie!"

The words were not out of his mouth when Kate caught sight of a man down the road leaping from a horse. As the rider touched the ground he slapped his pony's shoulder and the beast dropped flat. The man, rifle in hand, threw himself behind the prostrate animal and Kate heard his brusque yell to Van Horn and the Texans: "Pitch up!"

It would have been hard to say who was most astonished. Laramie evidently was not expecting an encounter. To dash on horseback into any five men on foot, of the enemy's camp, was the last thing he would be likely to attempt. If he did attempt it, he would never choose Van Horn or Stone to be of the party. The ground about the scene was flat, or only slightly rolling, with the branch road and its old ruts running across it. Caught squarely in the open and without a sagebrush for cover, he had been forced to drop behind his horse for shelter. Lying flat and covering Van Horn and the men with his rifle, he awaited the unpleasant odds against him.

The situation of the five men in front was even worse. Their rifles were stacked against the gate hardly a dozen feet away. But to run a gauntlet of a dozen feet against Laramie's rifle fire was a feat none had stomach for, nor were they ready at a hundred yards to pit revolvers against it. One of them might get him but they knew it would be after some of the others had practically ceased to be interested in the result.

The minds of the Texas men were perfectly clear; their hands shot up like rockets. Stone had taken one big step toward the gate post—he changed his mind, halted and his hands went up at the very instant Laramie changed *his* mind, and did not press the trigger against the burly outline darkening the field of his sights. Van Horn, caught, stood helpless and enraged—humiliated in circumstances he least relished for humiliation. Everybody's hands were up. His one chance, Van Horn realized, was to use his Colt's against the

Winchester behind the prostrate horse—it was not a living chance and no one knew it better than he; his hands moved grudgingly up to his shoulders and he sang out savagely: "What the blazes do you want?"

There was no answer from Laramie. To add to a difficult situation, Kate's horse, nervous from the shouting and catching its mistress's own fright, jumped and bucked till she was halfway down the road toward Laramie before she could check him. To add to her confusion, words came from ahead just loud enough for her to hear: "Pull the blamed brute to one side, will you?" It was Laramie speaking, she knew. "If he gets between me and that bunch," she heard him say, "I'm a goner." She jerked her horse violently out of the road; Laramie had raised his voice and kept right on talking: "Turn your back, Van Horn—you, too, Stone. Shoot up your hands, you Texas—higher!" he called to one of the Texans. And with the words not out of his mouth, he leaped as if on springs to his feet. It seemed as if his rifle covered his enemies all the time, even while he was doing it.

With his head forward, his elbows high and the Winchester laid against his cheek; stepping like a cat, and swiftly and with his eyes fixed on the men ahead, Laramie walked toward the wagon. In doing so he approached Kate, whose horse had subsided. Laramie took no note of her. She only heard his words as he passed: "You'd better get out of this." Approaching his prisoners in such a way they could not reach either the gate or the wagon without crossing his fire, Laramie compelled Bradley, really nothing loath, to disarm the three cowboys in turn and drop their guns into the wagonbox. Stone, sullen, was gingerly approached by Bradley, under strict orders to keep out of reach of his arms. But the old man knew all the tricks of the play being staged, even though he was not able to turn them. And when Stone, cursing, was ordered to lower his right arm and hand his revolver to Bradley at arm's length, the old man's feet were planted at least six feet from the foreman for a jump-away in case Stone tried to clinch him and shoot at Laramie from behind Bradley's cover.

But after he was disarmed, Laramie was not through with Stone. Sullen and obdurate, he was ordered to face away, while Bradley from behind searched his pockets. And the crown of his abasement was reached when Bradley drew from a hip pocket a full flask of whisky. The material advantage of the find was not great, but the tactical advantage was enormous. Behind Stone, Bradley silently but jeeringly held it up as an exhibit for the thirsty Texas men; and to show it was full, uncorked and with gusto sampled it. Stone was ordered back to his horse.

"How long is this joke, Laramie?" sang out Van Horn, his humor oozing. "Can't you frisk a few cowboys in less than all day?"

332

"When I frisk a pair of cut-throats with them, it's different."

"Well, don't waste your valuable time on me. This is your innings—I'll wait for mine."

"Drop your gun to the ground," returned Laramie. "Pick that up, Bill," he added to Bradley as Van Horn threw his revolver contemptuously from its holster. He was searched with the same scrupulous care by old Bradley, his morale greatly strengthened by Stone's flask: "I don't give a d—n whether you get me or not," he retorted at Van Horn, in answer to a low threat from his victim.

Laramie having told Van Horn to mount, turned to the Texas men: "Which one of you boys wants to carry the rifles over to that big cottonwood for me?" he asked, pointing toward the creek.

"I do," responded the nearest man, promptly.

"Don't you do it, Tex," called out Stone.

The Texan eyed his foreman: "Why not?" he demanded. "Ain't I been ridin' this country all day with a man squealin' for a drink as loud as I was, an' had his pocket full of it all the time? I'm through with *my* job."

Laramie broke in without losing the precious moment: "Who set my house on fire, Tex?" he demanded.

The Texan nodded in Stone's direction: "Ask him."

"He'd lie, Tex; I'm askin' you."

The rawboned horseman hesitated: "I'll talk

that over with you when I'm rested," he drawled.

"Go get your Colt's out of the wagon, Tex." Laramie pointed the way. "Pick out the guns of the other two boys and tote them over to that tree with you. The boys'll ride over there after you. Tell Barb I'll give him twenty-four hours to get every hoof, round or split, that belongs to me back to the Falling Wall—failing which I'll be over to talk to him privately. Will you do that, Tex?"

"I sure will."

"These rustlers here," he looked toward Stone and Van Horn, "won't be able to carry messages for awhile. They're ridin' to town with me. Bill," he added, turning to Bradley, "dump their rifles into the wagon and follow on along."

"What's this?" snapped Van Horn with an oath. "Going to town with you! Not on your life."

"You're headed for jail tonight, Harry; that's all. You boys," he spoke to the Texans and gave no heed to the oaths and abuse from Van Horn, "ride down to the cottonwood and get your guns from Tex. There's two good trails from here to town and plenty of room on both. Today I'm riding the Double-draw bridge. If any of you are going to town, take the other trail. Lead off now, you two."

He spoke to Van Horn and Stone, both mounted, and with the two headed for town, and the Texans started up the road, Laramie climbed into his own saddle. Not until then did he look around for Kate. She had disappeared.

CHAPTER 32

A MESSAGE FROM TENISON

Speeding in a panic from what she feared might happen behind her at any moment; soon out of sight of the scene, but with ears pitched for the sound of a shot, and a volley of shots; her head swimming with excitement and her heart beating a roll in her breast, Kate urged her horse down the road.

And Belle's silence, her enigmatic face as she listened later to the story only convinced Kate that her own apprehensions of trouble were well founded. "It's coming," was all she could get Belle to mutter, as Belle hobbled on a lame foot at meal time between the table and the stove, "but nobody can say when or where." Both the women could tell even earlier than this, from McAlpin's intimations, from watching groups of men in the street and from the way in which those who could have no direct interest in the affairs of the Falling Wall country were hurrying to and fro, that Laramie had reached town with his prisoners and was busy getting them jailed.

Kate, stunned by her father's utter coldness in casting her out, did not want to talk about it. She had left home resolved to tell Belle everything, despite the humiliating shame of the recital. But the excitement of the ride and the stir in the town were excuses enough to put off explaining. It was possible that her father might become as ashamed of himself as she was of him—in which event, nothing said would be best.

But when Bradley stopped the ranch wagon before Belle's cottage door with Kate's suitcase and trunk, something was needed to satisfy Belle. Kate's intimation that she should spend a few days in town, and might be called East was somewhat disjointed, but at the moment, enough. Bradley, however, after unloading the trunk and while Belle stood wondering, reappeared at the door with two rifles.

"Lord A'mighty, man!" cried Belle, already stirred, "what're you doing with them rifles?"

Bradley tried to placate his nervous questioner: "I'm just leavin' 'em here, Belle, while I go down 'n' get a load o' feed," he explained with dignity.

"Don't you believe you're leavin' any rifles here, Bill Bradley. This is nobody's arsenal, I want you to know."

"Why, Belle, they belong t' the ranch," remonstrated Bradley.

"What's that got to do with it?" she exclaimed, turning from the door and shutting it vigorously in Bradley's face as he stood discomfited. "I wonder if everybody's going crazy in this country."

On this point Kate entertained convictions that she did not express. She was only glad that

Belle's curiosity, usually robust enough concerning ranch happenings, was now under more engrossing pressure.

Concerning what was setting the town ablaze that day, only confused echoes reached the secluded women; and chiefly through the butcher, between whom and Belle a tacit armistice was soon in effect. Chops were slashed ruthlessly as he revealed details of what was going on, and the patent block shook under the savage blows of the cleaver while the butcher hinted at things more momentous to come. From him, Belle learned that Van Horn and Stone had been held some- where up at Tenison's incommunicado, by Lefever and Sawdy, while Laramie, opposed by the cattlemen's lawyer, was demanding from Justice Druel warrants for his prisoners; and that after they had reluctantly been issued, Sheriff Druel had pigeon-holed them until Tenison, backing Laramie, had told Druel after a big row, he would run him out of town if he didn't take his prisoners to jail.

It was five o'clock when the butcher, instead of sending over the boy, brought the meat for supper himself: "They're locked up," he said in a terse undertone, as he handed his package to Belle. "There was a big bunch up there when they was put in. Some of 'em talked pretty loud about a jail delivery. Laramie stood right there to see they went into their cells and they went."

"Were you there?" demanded Belle.

"I was."

"What did Laramie say?"

"All he said to Druel was: 'If you don't keep 'em locked up, Druel, I take no responsibility for what happens.' I come all the way from the jail with Laramie myself," recited the butcher; "walked right alongside him and Harry Tenison down t' the hotel."

"Well, if you walked so far with him, is he coming here for supper?"

The butcher was taken aback: "How in thunder should I know?" he blurted out.

"There you go, slamming away with your blasphemy again. Couldn't you ask him?"

"Why, yes, Belle, I reckon I could. Maybe I can. Say!" he returned after starting down the steps, to point to the package in her hand, "there's a mess o' sweetbreads in there for you."

"Shucks! I can't use sweetbreads tonight, Heinie."

"Throw 'em away then. A present, ain't they? Nobody in town eats 'em but you."

Kate unfortunately suggested braizing the sweetbreads for Sawdy and Lefever.

"What?" exclaimed Belle. "Men don't eat sweetbreads, don't you know that? You've got to give 'em steak—round steak and the tougher the better—tough as cowhide and fried to tears. They'd be insulted. Lefever and Sawdy won't be here tonight, anyway. They're in Medicine Bend on an Indian case. All I'm wondering is, whether Jim's coming."

But Laramie did not come—greatly to Kate's relief. He spent the night at the hotel and left town early. Next morning when Belle heard the news of the street she was thankful he had gone, for it was said that Van Horn and Stone were out of jail. Barb had been summoned in the night by the lawyers, and next day the prisoners were out on bail.

Laramie had made no secret of his riding north, except that, in the circumstances, he preferred to ride the night trail rather than the day trail. He wanted to look up his cattle and see Simeral and he thought he knew Barb well enough to be sure the stock would be sent back very promptly in as bad condition as possible.

He got to his ranch in good time. There were no signs of life anywhere. Riding about noon over to Simeral's he found his shack empty. But he hunted up food and cooked himself a breakfast.

While he was eating peacefully at Simeral's, Van Horn was with Stone and Doubleday, the three breakfasting in the back room of a Main Street saloon. Just what took place at that breakfast was not figured out for a long time afterward, if it really ever was. But the street heard that Van Horn and Doubleday had had a quarrel at breakfast and that Doubleday in a rage had turned the prisoners over to the sheriff and asked to be released from his bail bond.

No news more exciting could have reached Belle Shockley. She heard the story up street and ran halfway home to tell Kate, who remained in seclusion. Kate herself was not less excited; the news meant so much if it were true, and the butcher confirmed it beyond a doubt. By nightfall everybody knew that Van Horn and Stone were locked up again.

One man in town was not altogether at ease over the day's developments. Tenison spent much time that afternoon in the hotel billiard room, it being the best clearing house for the street gossip.

He tried more than once during the afternoon to get hold of Kitchen or Carpy—neither was in town—and with the day drawing to a close, Tenison's restlessness increased. He was standing late in the evening near a favorite corner at the upper end of the bar and above the billiard tables, when among the crowd drifting in and out of the room he caught sight of Ben Simeral. Tenison lost no time. Without moving, he asked the nearest bartender to take a message to the old rancher. And when Simeral passed through the door leading into the hotel, Tenison was behind him. He followed Simeral into the office and back past the wash room, through the hallway leading to the sample rooms. Opening the door of the first of these, Tenison pressed a light button, and motioning Simeral to enter, followed him into the room, closed the door, locked it, and sat down facing the rancher: "I want to get a message to Jim Laramie, Ben," he began at once. "You know what's been going on here today?"

The old rancher nodded silently.

"Can you ride to the Falling Wall for me right away with a word for Laramie?"

Simeral said nothing, but his heavy eyes closed as he nodded again.

"Laramie's gone home. He thinks Van Horn is in jail. The story is," continued Tenison, "that Van Horn and old Barb quarreled, that they came to blows and that Barb turned Stone and him over to Druel again to lock up." Tenison spoke slowly and impressively: "Tell Laramie," he said, "I copper all that stuff—every bit of it. Tell him to look out. I don't know what them fellows have got in their heads; but it's something. Van Horn won't be in jail long."

"He's out again now."

Tenison eyed his messenger steadily: "What do you mean?"

"I just come from Hinchcliffe's saloon. They've been out an hour."

Hard as the blow struck home, Tenison did not bat a lash: "We may be too late," he said. "It's worth trying. Warn Jim if you can."

"I can."

"There'll be a good horse for you at Kitchen's. Ask McAlpin for it. Tell him I couldn't get hold of a man any quicker. Will Jim sleep at your place tonight?"

Simeral shook his head: "No tellin'."

Tenison rose. Drawing from a trousers pocket a roll of bills, he slipped off several and passed them to Simeral.

"What's this f'r?" asked Simeral, looking at the money as it lay across his hand and then at Tenison.

The gambler regarded him evenly: "You're getting old, Ben."

"Not when it comes to doin' a turn f'r Jim."

Tenison literally swore the money on him. "Ride hard," he said. "An hour may make the difference."

Simeral listened to the injunction but he was putting the money away as slowly and carefully as if he never expected to see money again. This done, he hitched his trousers, shifted his quid, pushed his hat and followed Tenison across the room. He was so slow that Tenison was forced inwardly to smile at his own exasperation: "Never get nervous, do you, Ben?" he asked imperturbably.

"Nervous?"

Tenison, unlocking the street door of the long room, only stood by with his hand outstretched to speed his laggard messenger. The old man stepped out into the night. Tenison, looking after him, shook his head doubtfully. But he was doing what he could and he knew that though the old fellow walked slow, once in a saddle, he could ride fast; and that for Laramie, he would do it.

CHAPTER 33

THE CANYON OF THE FALLING WALL

Laramie, after disposing of his prisoners, had ridden north with less of a hunted feeling experienced every time he mentally inventoried the rocks commanding the trail, the boulders looming ahead of him, and the cottonwoods through which he wound his way along the creek bottoms. And when at length he looked across Turkey creek, he was not surprised to see his cows straying down the hills toward their own range.

Even the bitter sight of the ruins of his cabin bore upon him less now that he had put Van Horn actually in jail for the trick. "You can't keep him there long," Tenison had cynically warned him.

"I've put the mark on him, if he's only there overnight," had been Laramie's reply. "He'll be a long time explaining. And I want you to notice, Harry, with all the fighting they've put me to, they've never got me locked up yet—not for a second. I guess for that," he added, reflecting, "I ought to thank my friends."

Never so much as that day had he realized how every aspect of his situation, as he viewed it, was colored by the thought of Kate Doubleday. If he were determined that despite any intrigue worked

343

against him, he would never be locked up alive on a trumped-up charge, it was chiefly because of the disgrace of such a thing in her eyes. If he avoided opportunities now of finishing with Van Horn, he knew it was chiefly because of her. She would probably never see that finish, but she would hear the story of it from his enemies. Laramie was not at any time thinking merely of being justified in the last resort, nor of the justification of his friends, which would in any case be his. But what would Kate think?

Yet he knew what was ahead of him; he knew what lay at the end of the trail he and Van Horn were traveling. Lawing, as Sleepy Cat contemptuously termed it, was the least of it all and the most futile—yet in thinking of the other, her judgment was what he dreaded. This bore on him and perplexed him. It had, more than all else, put two little vertical furrows between his eyebrows; they were there often of late. Suppression of the feeling that had always and irresistibly drawn him toward her, had only intensified this worry. His pride had suffered at her hands; yet he made excuses for her—he had no high opinion of himself, of his general reputation—and had built dreams on the fanciful imagining that she should, despite everything, some day like him. He wearied his brain in recalling a chance expression of her eyes that could not have been unfriendly; an inflection of her voice that might have carried a hope, if only their paths had been less crossed: and his pride, despite rebuffs, sought her as a moth seeks a flame. It drew him to her and kept him from her, for he lacked for the first time in his life the boldness to stake everything on the turn of a card, and ask Kate to marry him.

Simeral had told him that John Frying Pan saw the cabin burning, and Laramie rode up to his place on the Reservation to talk with him. Failing to find him at home, Laramie left word with his wife and turned south. It was then late. The trail had taken him high up in the mountains and he made up his mind to ride over to the old bridge, stay for the night, pick up the few things he had left there and take them over to Simeral's in the morning.

Night had fallen when riding in easy fashion he reached the rim of the canyon and made his way from foothold to foothold until he came to an open ledge with grass and water for his horse, near the abutment. Leaving him in this spot, Laramie, carrying his rifle, climbed by a zig-zag footpath up a hundred feet to the shelter and rolled himself in a blanket for the night.

He woke at what he believed to be near midnight. The night was cold and he began to think about something to eat. With the aid of a candle he found bacon cached under a crevice in a baking-powder can near his bunk, and found some splinters of wood. These he laid for an early breakfast fire and wrapped himself again in his blanket. He had closed his eyes for another nap when a sound arrested his attention; it was the rumbling of a small piece of rock tumbling into the canyon.

Nothing was more common than for fragments, great and small, of the splintered canyon walls to loosen and start in the silence of the night. As mountain trees withstand the winter winds only to fall in summer calms, so it seemed as if the masses of rock that hung poised on the canyon rim through countless storms, chose the stillest hour of the stillest night to ride like avalanches the headlong slopes, plunge over dizzy cliffs and crash and sprawl in dying thunders from ledge to ledge into the river below. All these noises, big and little, were familiar to Laramie's ears. He could hear them in his sleep without losing the thread of a dream; but the echo of a single footstep would bring him up sitting.

The sound that now caught his attention had a still different effect. Listening, he lay motionless in his blanket with every faculty keyed; had a man at that moment stood before him reading his death warrant, he could not have been more awake. The noise was slight; only a small fragment of rock had fallen and the echoes of its journey were lost almost at once; it was the beginning of the sound that he was thinking of—the noise had not started right. He thought of the four-footed prowlers of the night and as a cause eliminated them one after another. He thought of his horse below—it was not where such a sound could start. But always slow to imagine a mystery when a reason could be assigned, Laramie, lying prone, was brought back every time to his first instinctive inference. Numberless times when tramping the canyon walls, his foot slipping before he recovered his balance had dislodged a bit of loose rock. He knew that sound too well and it was such a sound he had just heard. Behind the sound he suspected there was a man.

He tried long to reason himself out of the conviction. For an hour he lay perfectly still, waiting for some further alarm. There was none and the night was never stiller. Nor was there any haste, even if it should prove the worst, about meeting the situation. He was caught not like a rat in a trap but like a man in a blind canyon, with ample means of defense and none of escape except through a gauntlet. No enemy could molest him where he lay, but he could not lie there indefinitely. And with little ammunition and scarcely any food or water, he had no mind to stand a siege.

If his enemies had actually discovered his retreat and put a watch on him, he must in any event wait for the first peep of daylight. The one chance of escape lay down and not up, and the descent of the canyon was not to be made in complete darkness. A moon would have been a godsend. It would have made things easy, if such a word could be used of the situation; but there was no moon. Acting on his premonition as if it had been an assurance, Laramie, at the end of a long and silent vigil, rolled out of his blanket to save his life if he could. He lighted his breakfast fire and fried his bacon unconcernedly. He could neither be rushed nor potted and if there was a touch of insolent bravado in his seeming carelessness he was well aware that while the appetizing odors of a good breakfast would not tantalize an enemy believing himself master of the situation, it would make him believe he had taken the quarry unawares.

Below, he felt that all was safe—no one without passing him could possibly reach his horse.

By the time the eastern sky warned him of the coming dawn he had crawled to the edge of the abutment to look down and estimate his chances for dropping to the narrow ledge on which it stood footed. Then he crawled noiselessly toward the overhead break through which Kate had plunged. The sky was alive with stars. Worming himself close to the opening, he lay for a time patiently scrutinizing the rocks commanding the abutment from above. One of these long vigils disclosed, he fancied, against the sky the outline of a man's hat.

To satisfy himself if it were one, Laramie picked up a chip of rock and flung it down the canyon wall. The suspicious object moved. Laramie slowly took up his rifle and leaning forward raised it to his shoulder. Against the eastern sky the man's head made a perfect target. It was close range. Laramie covered the hat low. The bullet should penetrate the brim just where it covered the forehead. His finger moved to press the trigger before he thought further. Then he hesitated.

It seemed on reflection like murder, nothing less. He did not know the man, though he was no doubt an enemy who had come either to kill him or to help kill him. And to his natural repugnance to blowing off the top of an unknown man's head even in constructive self-defense, there was the thought of another's view of it. This might, after all, be merely a Texan acting as a lookout. It was even possible, though improbable, that it might be Barb himself. And if the man were not alone less would be gained by killing him.

The rifle came down from Laramie's shoulder as slowly as it had gone up. He made immediate disposition for his escape. Retreating noiselessly from the opening, he found his blanket, cut from it four strips, knotted these into a rope and creeping to the face of the abutment, lowered his rifle, ammunition belt and revolver down to the footing some twenty feet below, where they hung in darkness. For himself there was nothing but to drop after his accoutrements. At one point the horizontal footing ledge below jutted out in a blunt tongue something like six feet; this tongue was where he must land; elsewhere the ledge narrowed to only a foothold for a sober man already on it.

Laramie found an old mackinaw of Hawk's, put it on over his coat, and padding his back under it with the pieces into which he tore a quilt, strapped the mackinaw tight and returned to look over the ledge. He thought he knew precisely where the tongue lay, but wanted a little daylight to dispel any misgiving about letting go at a point where he might drop two hundred feet instead of twenty.

From the abutment the depths of the canyon looked in the half light pretty black, but its recesses hid no terrors of sentiment for Laramie. Fairly serene and stuffed in his baggy mackinaw, he lay for a few minutes flat on his stomach peering over the edge. Far below he could hear the rush of the river. Day was racing toward the mountain tops and diffusing its reflected light into their recesses. The rock tongue below outlined itself faintly in an almost impenetrable gloom. Waiting no longer, Laramie, with a careful hand-hold, let himself down over the face of the abutment and hung for an instant suspended. Loosing one hand he swung sidewise and threw back his head. The fingers of the other hand, straightened by his weight, let go.

Falling like a plummet, one of his heels smashed into the rocky gravel and he struck the ledge on his back. With such instinct as the swift drop left him he threw himself toward the canyon wall when he landed and, shocked though he was, tried to rise.

He could not get a breath, much less move. His mind remained perfectly clear, but the fall left him momentarily paralyzed. His efforts to regain his breath, to make himself breathe, were astonishingly futile, and he lay annoyed at his helplessness. It seemed as if minute after minute passed. Listening, he heard sounds above. Daylight was coming fast and every ray of it meant a slenderer chance of escape.

To his relief, his lungs filled a little. Soon they were doing more. He found he could move. He turned to his side, and, beginning life over again, crawled on hands and knees to where his belt, revolver and rifle hung suspended. He stood up, got out of the mackinaw, adjusted his belt and revolver, and with his rifle resting across his forearm looked around. He was battered and had a stinging ankle, but stood with legs and arms at least usable. Listening, he tiptoed as fast as he could to the narrow footpath leading into the canyon, and turning a corner of the rock wall hastened down to where he had picketed his horse. This trail was not exposed from above. But when he reached his horse and got stiffly into the saddle his problem was less simple.

To get out of the tremendous fissure in which he was trapped from above, Laramie had one trail to follow. This led for a hundred feet in an extremely sharp descent across the face of a nearly vertical canyon wall that flanked the recess where the horse had been left. This first hundred feet of his way down to the river, so steep that it was known as the Ladder, was all that caused Laramie any uneasiness; it was commanded every foot of the way from the abutment above.

Making all possible haste, Laramie headed his horse stealthily for the Ladder. He knew he had lost the most precious juncture of the dawn in lying paralyzed for some unexpected moments after his drop. It was a chance of war and he made no complaint. Indeed, as he reached the beginning of his trail and peered downward he realized that he needed daylight for the perilous ride. To take it slowly would be child's play for him but would leave him an easy target from above. To ride it fast was to invite a header for his horse and himself; one misstep would send the horse and rider bolting into space. How far it was to the river through this space Laramie felt little curiosity in figuring; but it could hardly have been less than two hundred and fifty feet.

There was no time for much thinking; the trail must be ridden and the sooner and faster the better. He struck his horse lightly. The horse jumped, but not very far ahead. Again Laramie used his heels and again the frightened beast sprung as little as he could ahead. A stinging lash was the only reward for his caution. If horses think, Laramie's horse must have imagined himself backed by a madman, and under the goading of his rider, the beast, quivering with fear, peered at the broken rocks below and sprang down among them. Concealment was no longer possible.

Like a man heading into a hailstorm, Laramie crouched to the horse, dropped the reins low on the beast's neck, and, clinging close, made himself as nearly as he could a part of the animal itself. The trail was five to six feet wide, but the descent was almost headlong, and down it the horse, urged by his rider, sprang in dizzy leaps; where the footing was worst Laramie tried to ease his frantic plunges. Stricken with terror, the beast caught his breath in convulsive starts and breathed in grunting snorts. Halting and bucking in jerky recoveries; leaping from foothold to foothold as if every jump were his last, and taking on a momentum far beyond his own or his rider's control, the frightened pony dashed recklessly ahead. It was as if a great weight, bounding on living springs, were heading to bolt at length against the sheer rock wall across the canyon.

Half the distance of the mad flight, and the worst half, was covered when a rifle cracked from the top of the abutment. Laramie felt a violent blow on his shoulder. There was no possible answer; there could be no more speed—no possible defense; the race lay between the rifle sights covering him and the four slender hoofs of the horse under him. Ten yards more were covered and a second rifle shot cracked crisply down the canyon walls. Laramie thought it from a second rifle; the bullet spat the wall above his head into splinters. They were shooting high, he told himself, and only hoped they might keep trying to pick him off the horse and let the horse's legs alone. None knew better than he exactly what was taking place above; the quick alarm, the fast-moving target in the gloomy canyon; the haste to get the feet set, the rifle to the shoulder, the sights lined, the moving target followed, the trigger pressed.

It was a madman's flight. As one or other of the rifles cracked at him, Laramie threw himself back in the saddle. With his hat in his hand, his arm shot straight up, and pointing toward the abutment he yelled a defiant laugh at his enemies. In an instant the hat was knocked from his fingers by a bullet; but the springing legs under him were left untouched. The trick for the rider now was, even should he escape the bullets, to check the flight of the horse before both shot over the foot of the Ladder into the depths. Laramie threw his weight low on the horse's side next the canyon wall and spoke soothingly into his ear as his arms circled the heaving neck.

And on the rim of the precipice, high above, two active men, bending every nerve and muscle to their effort, stood with repeating rifles laid against their cheeks, pumping and firing at the figure plunging into the depths below.

CHAPTER 34

KATE GETS A SHOCK

Late that afternoon a stable boy from Kitchen's barn appeared at Belle's, making inquiries for Doctor Carpy. Kate heard Belle at the door answering and asking questions, but the messenger was not able to answer any questions; his business was to ask only. When Kitchen himself came over a little later there was more talk at the door, this time in low tones that left Kate in ignorance of its purport. But the moment Kitchen went away, Belle, never equal to hiding an emotion, passed with compressed lips and set face through the room in which Kate sat sewing. Kate looked up as Belle walked toward the kitchen and noticed the tense expression—fortunately she asked no questions. After some vigorous moments in the kitchen, evidenced by the sound of a creaking bread-board, sharp blows at the stove lids and an unabashed slamming of the stewpans, Belle passed again through the room carrying a plate covered with a napkin, and evidently going somewhere.

Kate felt compelled to take notice: "Where you bound for, Belle?" she asked.

"Not far. But if I don't get back, don't wait supper," was the only answer. The manner rather than the matter of it puzzled Kate as she bent over her work. But the next moment she was alone and thinking about her own troubles.

Half an hour passed rapidly on her sewing—for Kate's fingers were quick—and Belle returned more perturbed than when she left. She gave Kate hardly a chance to question her.

"Why didn't you eat your supper?" she demanded.

Kate answered unconcernedly: "I wasn't hungry —it isn't late, is it?"

Without answering the question Belle asked another. "Kate," she said, unpinning her hat as she spoke, "how long you going to stay here?"

A less sensitive person than Kate could hardly have mistaken the import of the question. She flushed as she looked up. "Why, surely no longer than you want me, Belle," she answered, as evenly as she could; but her voice showed her surprise. Belle stood before her, a statue of implacability and Kate, in growing astonishment, rose to her feet: "What is it? What has happened?" she asked, then as her wits worked fast: "Doesn't my father wish you to keep me?"

"I'm not thinking about what your father wants. Things are getting too thick here for me." Kate made no effort to interrupt. "I don't say I don't like you, Kate—I've always treated you right, or tried to," continued Belle, laboring under evident excitement. "But it's no use shutting our eyes any longer to facts. You're Barb Doubleday's daughter

356

and Barb Doubleday is making war all the time on my friends and hiring men to assassinate them, and it doesn't seem right to me and it won't to other people, me sheltering Barb Doubleday's daughter with such things going on—"

"But, Belle—"

Belle raised her voice one key higher: "You needn't tell me, I know. Now they're trying to murder Jim Laramie and they've close to done it, this day—"

Belle had received and accepted strict injunctions of secrecy on the next point she disclosed, but her feelings were not to be denied. And she was not prepared for the question that Kate, stung by the accusation, flung at her: "What do you mean?"

"I mean he's lying near here bleeding to death this minute and Doctor Carpy in Medicine Bend."

In tones broken with anger and excitement, Belle told the disconnected story as it had come to her in jerks and nods and oaths from McAlpin at the barn, and in the little she had pulled out of Laramie himself when she took food to him. Then came in terribly heated words the brunt of her anger at Kate. "You knew," she said, pointing her finger at Kate, standing stupefied. "You knew where Jim Laramie hid Hawk. Nobody else did know—not even Lefever or Sawdy knew—I didn't know till you told me. Now, after they've burned his cabin, they set a death watch there at the bridge on Laramie. How did they know there

357

was such a place if you didn't tell 'em?"

Stunned by the fire of Belle's wrath, Kate, breathless, tried to collect her senses. It was only her anger at the final implication that cleared them. But even as her words of indignant denial reached her lips, her utterance was paralyzed by the recollection that unwittingly she *had* told her father of the night she was thrown into Laramie's retreat. Yet even this did not check her resentment.

"Who accuses me of telling them?" she demanded. "Who says I conspired to murder any-one—did Mr. Laramie say so?"

She shot the question at Belle in a furious tone. Her eyes flashed in a way that confounded her accuser.

"I'm asking you how they found out," retorted Belle, but in spite of herself on the defensive.

Kate's face was set and her eyes were on fire. All the anger that a woman could feel centered in her words and manner. "Answer my question before you say another word." She confronted Belle without yielding. "Did Jim Laramie accuse me in any way of anything?"

"Oh, you needn't be so high and mighty," flustered Belle. "I'll answer your question; no. Now you answer mine, will you?"

"How can *I* answer how they found out? I will not say another word until I see Mr. Laramie— where is he?"

"You can't see him—nobody knows he is here—he won't talk to you."

Kate paid no attention to her words: "He'll have to tell me that himself," she returned. "If he is near here—he must be at Kitchen's."

Belle could say nothing to check or swerve her. Taking up her hat and ignoring all warnings, Kate walked straight over to the barn. She found McAlpin at the stable door: "I want you to take a message for me to Mr. Laramie," she said, speaking low and collectedly. "Ask him if he will see Kate Doubleday for just two minutes."

McAlpin, in all his devious career, had never passed through more or quicker stages of astonishment, confusion, poise and evasion than he did in listening to those words. But at pulling his wits together, McAlpin was a wonder. By the time Kate had finished, his innocent question was ready: "Where is he?"

"He is here. I must see him at once."

"But I ain't seen him myself for a week. He's not here. Who told you he's here?"

"Belle," persisted Kate calmly, "told me he *is* here. I must see him. Don't deceive me, McAlpin —do just as I ask you, no more, no less."

"No more, no less, sure," grumbled the Scotchman. "You gives me one kind of orders—the boss gives me another kind. I can't do no more, I can't do no less. I can't do nothin'—I've got a family to support and all this damned rowing going on, a man's job is no safer nowadays in this country than his head!"

But words were not to save him. Kate persisted. She would not be put off. McAlpin, swearing and protesting, could in the end only offer to go see whether he could by any chance find Laramie. After a long trip through the winding alleys of the big barn—for Kate watched the baseball cap and crazy vizor as long as she could follow it—then complete disappearance for a time, McAlpin came back to Kate, immovable at the office door, his face wreathed with a surprised smile.

He spoke, but his eyes were opened wide and his words were delivered in a whisper; mystery hung upon his manner: "Come along," he nodded, indicating the interior. "Only say nothing to nobody. He's hit—there's all there is to it. Here's all I know, but I don't know all: About three hours ago Ben Simeral was riding up the Crazy Woman when he seen a man half dropping off his horse, hat gone, riding head down, slow, with his rifle slung on his arm. Simmie seen who it was—Jim Laramie. He looked at horse 'n' man 'n' says: 'Where the hell you bin?' 'Where the hell 'a' you been,' Laramie says, pretty short. 'Ridin' all over this'—excuse my rough language, Kate—'blamed country, lookin' f'r to tell you Van Horn and Stone's out o' jail!'

"Laramie seen then from the ol' man's horse how he'd been ridin' 'n' softened down a bit.

360

'So I heard, Simmie,' he says. 'Who'd you hear it from?' says Simmie. 'Direct, Simmie,' he says. 'Did they pot y', Jim?' 'Nicked my shoulder, I guess.' 'Where you goin'?' 'To town.' 'Man,' says Simmie, 'you've lost a lot o' blood.' 'Got a little left, Simmie.'

"Then John Fryin' Pan c'm along. Simmie tried to ride to town with Laramie—f'r fear he'd fall off his horse. Laramie wouldn't let neither of 'em do a thing. 'This is my fight,' he says. But Simmie and John Fryin' Pan scouted along behind and Simmie rode in ahead near town to tell me Laramie was comin'. God! He was a sight when he rode into this barn. He tumbled off his horse right there"—McAlpin pointed to a spot where fresh straw had been sprinkled—"just like a dead man. I helped carry him upstairs," he whispered. "I'll take y' to him. But y' bet your life"—the grizzled old man stopped and turned sharply on his companion—"y' bet your life some o' them niggers bit the dust some'eres this morning. This way."

Kate, pacing McAlpin's rapid step breathlessly, hung on his half-muttered words: "He's bleedin' to death," continued McAlpin; "that's the short of it, and that blamed doctor down at Medicine Bend. I don't think much o' that man. Can't none of us stop it. Where's this goin' to end?"

He led her by roundabout passages, up one alley and down another, and at last opened the door of an old harness room, waited for Kate to follow him inside and, closing the door behind her, spoke: "I didn't want you to have to climb a barn ladder," he said, explaining. "There's the stairs." He pointed in the semi-darkness and led her toward the flight along the opposite wall. At the top of this flight light fell from a square opening in the hay-mow.

"Walk up them stairs—I lifted the trap-door f'r ye. He's right up there at the head of the steps. When y' come down, open *this* door at the foot, here. It's a blind door; don't show on the other side. See, it's bolted. It takes you right into the office. We keep it bolted from the inside, so no trouble can't come, see?" He unbolted and opened the door a crack to show her, closed and rebolted it. Then starting her up the stairs, McAlpin jerked the crazy vizor on his forehead into a fashion once more simulating child-like frankness and disappeared by the way he had come.

CHAPTER 35

At Kitchen's Barn

To be so summarily left alone and in such a place was disconcerting. Kate, in the semi-darkness and silence, put her foot on the first tread of the steps and, placing her hand against the wall, looked upward. Not a sound; above her a partial light through a trap-door and a wounded man. She stood completely unnerved. The thought of Laramie wounded, perhaps dying, the man that had rescued her, protected her, in truth saved her life on that fearful night—this man, now lying above her stricken, perhaps murdered, by her own father's friends! How could she face him? Only the thought that he should not lie wounded unto death without knowing at least that *she* was not ungrateful, that *she* had not wittingly betrayed him, gave her strength to start up the narrow steps.

When her head rose above the trap opening the light in the large loft seemed less than it had promised from below. There were no windows, but through a gable door, partly ajar, shot a narrow slit of daylight from the afterglow of the sunset. Kate caught glimpses of a maze of rafters, struts and beams and under them huge piles of loose hay. Reaching the top step she paused, trying to look about in the dim light, when Laramie, close at hand, startled her: "McAlpin told me you wanted to see me," he said. She could distinguish nothing for a moment. But the low words reassured her.

"I'm lying on the hay," he continued, in the same tone. "If you'll open the door a little more you can see better."

Picking her way carefully over to it, Kate pushed the door open somewhat wider and turned toward Laramie.

He lay not far from the stairs. The yellow light

of the evening glow falling on his face reflected a greenish pallor. Kate caught her breath, for it seemed as if she were looking into the face of death until she perceived, as he turned his head, the unusual brightness of his eyes.

In her confusion what she had meant to say fled: "Are you very much hurt?" she faltered.

"Far from it." He spoke slowly. If it cost him an effort none was discernible. "Coming into the barn tonight," he went on, very haltingly, "I had a kind of dizzy spell." He paused again. "I've been eating too much meat lately, anyway. They say— I fell off my horse; leastways I bumped my head. I'll be all right tomorrow."

"Belle told me there had been a fight up at the canyon bridge," Kate stammered, already at a loss to begin.

A sickly yellow smile pointed the silence. "I wouldn't call it exactly a fight," he said, dwelling somewhat on the last word. "Far from it," he repeated, with a touch of grimness. "There was some shooting. And some running." She could see how he paused between sentences. "But if the other fellows ran it must have been after me. I didn't pay much attention to who was behind. I had to make a tolerable steep grade down the Falling Wall Ladder to the river. I was on horseback and didn't have much leisure to pick my trail."

"And they shooting at you from the rim!"

"Well, they must have been shooting at something in my general direction. I guess they hit me once. I didn't mind getting hit myself, but I didn't want them to hit my horse. I was heading for the bottom as fast as the law would allow. If they'd hit the horse, I wouldn't have had much more than one jump from the rim to the river. Can't ask you to sit down," he added, "unless you'll sit here on the hay."

Without the least hesitation Kate placed herself beside him. Without giving her a chance to speak and in the same monotone, he added: "Who told you I was a gambler?"

Less than so blunt and unexpected a question would have sufficed to take her aback. And she was conscious in the fading light of his strangely bright eyes fixed steadily on her. "I don't remember anybody ever did. I—"

"Somebody did. You told Belle once."

"It must have been long ago—"

"Is that the reason you never acted natural with me?"

She flushed with impatience. But if she tried to get away he brought her back to the subject. Cornered, she grew resentful: "I can't tell who told me," she pleaded, after ineffectual sparring. "I've forgotten. Are you a gambler?" she demanded, turning inquisitor herself.

He did not move and it was an instant before he replied: "What do you mean," he asked, "by gambler?"

Kate's tone was hard: "Just what anybody means."

"If you mean a man that makes his living by gambling—or hangs around a gambling house all the time, or plays regularly—then I couldn't fairly and squarely be called a gambler. If you mean a man that plays cards *sometimes,* or *has* once in a while bet on a game in a gambling house, then, I suppose"—he was so evidently squirming that Kate meanly enjoyed his discomfort—"you might call me that. It would all depend on whether the one telling it liked me or didn't like me. I haven't been in Tenison's rooms for months, nor played but one game of poker."

"I despise gambling."

"Why didn't you tell me?"

"Why should I?"

"In one sense everybody's a gambler. Everybody I know of is playing for something. Take your father and me: He's playing for my life; I'm playing for you. He's playing for a small stake; I'm playing for a big one."

She could not protest quick enough: "You talk wildly."

"No," he persisted evenly, "I only look at it just as it is."

"Don't ask me to believe all the cruel things said of my father any more than you want me to believe the things said of you. I am terribly sorry to see you wounded. And now"—her words caught in her throat—"Belle blames me even for that."

"How on earth does she blame you for that?"

Despite her efforts to control herself, Kate, as she approached the unpleasant subject, began to tremble inwardly with the fear that it must after all be as Belle had rudely asserted—that her father *was* behind these efforts against Laramie's life. For nothing had shaken her tottering faith in her father more than the blunt words Laramie himself had just now indifferently spoken.

"If I am in any way to blame, it is innocently," she hurried on. "I will tell you everything; you shall judge. My father was bitterly angry when he learned I had been seen at Abe Hawk's funeral. I told him about my getting lost, about falling into the place at the bridge—how you did everything you could and how Abe Hawk had done all he could. He was so angry he would listen to nothing—" she stopped, collected herself, tried to go on, could not.

"Oh, I hate this country!" she exclaimed. "I hate the people and everything in it! And I'm going away from it—as far as I can get. But I wouldn't go," she said determinedly, "without seeing you and telling you this much."

Laramie spoke quietly but with confidence: "You are not going away from this country."

Kate had picked up a stem of hay and looking down at it was breaking it nervously between her fingers. "You will have to hurry up and get well if I stay," she said abruptly. "I'm beginning to think you are the only friend I have here. And," she added, so quickly as to cut off any words from him, "I've told you everything. I only hope my speak-ing about the hiding place at the bridge when father was angry with me—and only to defend myself—was not the cause of *this*."

She was close beside him. "Can it be," she asked, "that this was how it happened?" He heard her voice break with the question.

"No," he blurted out instantly.

"Oh," she cried, "I'm so thankful!"

Listening to her effort to speak the words, he was not sorry for what he had said. "If you're going to lie," Hawk had once said to him, cynically, "don't stumble, don't beat about the bush—do a job!" The moment Kate told her story, Laramie knew exactly how he had been trapped. But why blame her? "It's the first time I ever lied to her," he thought ruefully to himself. "It's the first time she ever believed me!"

"Does Belle know you quarreled with your father?" he asked, to get away from the subject.

"No," she answered, steadying herself.

"She said you'd been acting sort of queer."

"I can't tell people my troubles."

"Why did you tell me?"

"You might die and blame me."

"Who says I'm going to die?"

"They were afraid you might."

"Well, I don't like to disappoint anybody, but dying is a thing a man is entitled to take his time about."

"Can't I do something till the doctor comes?"

He turned very slowly on his side. Kate made an attempt to examine his shoulder. She was not used to the sight of blood. The clotted and matted clothing awed and sickened her. Even the hay was blood-soaked, but she stuck to her efforts. Supplementing the rude efforts of McAlpin and Kitchen to give him first aid, she cut away, with Laramie's knife, the bullet-torn coat and shirt and tried to get the wound ready for cleansing. "I'm so afraid of doing the wrong thing," she murmured, fearfully.

"I don't care what you do—do something," he said. "Your hands feel awful good."

"I've nothing here to work with."

"All right, we'll go to the drug store and get something." After stubborn efforts he got on his feet and insisted on going down the stairs. Nothing that Kate could say would dissuade him. "I've been here long enough, anyway," was his decision. "I'm feeling better every minute; only awfully thirsty."

Kate steadied him down the dark stairs, fearful he might fall over her as she went ahead. Secrecy of movement seemed to have no significance for him. If his friends were disturbed, Laramie was not. He evidently knew the harness room, for he opened the blind door with hardly any hesitation

369

and stepped into the office. The office was empty but the street door of the stable was open. McAlpin stood in the gang-way talking to some man who evidently caught a glimpse of Laramie, for he said rudely and loud enough for Kate to hear: "Hell, McAlpin! There comes your dead man now!"

Kate recognized the heavy voice of Carpy and shrank back. The doctor, McAlpin behind him dumbly staring, confronted Laramie at the door: "What are you doin' here, Jim?" he demanded.

"What would I be doing anywhere?" retorted Laramie.

"Go back to your den. This man says you're dying."

"Well, I'm not getting much encouragement at it—I've been waiting for you three hours to help things along. I'm done with the hay."

"Looking for a feather bed to die in. Some men are blamed particular." As he spoke Carpy caught his first glimpse of Kate. "Hello! There's the pretty little girl from the great big ranch. No wonder the man's up and coming—what did you send for me for, McAlpin? Where you heading, Jim?"

With his hands on the door jambs, Carpy effectually barred the exit. Knowing his stubborn patient well, he humored him, to the verge of letting him have his own way, but with much raillery denied him the drug store trip. A compromise was effected. Laramie consented to go to Belle's to get something to eat. In this way, refusing help, the obdurate patient was got to walk to the cottage.

"Don't let him fall on y'," McAlpin cautioned Kate, as the two followed close behind. "I helped carry him upstairs. He's a ton o' brick."

But Laramie, either incensed by his condition—the idea of any escort being vastly unpleasant to him—or animated by the stiff hypodermics of profanity that Carpy injected into the talk as they crossed the street, did not even stumble; he held his way unaided, met Belle's amazement unresponsively and, sitting down, called for something to eat.

"How does he do it, Doc?" whispered McAlpin, craning forward from the background.

"Pure, damned nerve," muttered Carpy. "But he does it."

They got him into bed. While the doctor was excavating the channel ripped through his shoulder, Laramie said nothing. When, however, he discovered that Kate was missing, he crustily short-circuited Belle's excuses. Words passed. It became clear that Laramie would start out and search the town if Kate were not produced.

"She wanted to see *me,*" he insisted, doggedly. "Now I want to see *her.*"

Carpy found he must again intervene. He despatched McAlpin as a diplomatic envoy over to his own house whither he had taken Kate as his guest when she peremptorily declined to return to Belle's.

CHAPTER 36

McALPIN AT BAY

However others may have felt that night about Laramie's affairs, one man, McAlpin, was proud of his ride, desperately wounded, all the way to town. Laramie had made a confidant of no one but Kate. His experience in being trapped was not so pleasant that he liked to talk about it and neither McAlpin's shrewd questioning nor Carpy's restrained curiosity was gratified that night.

In the circumstances, McAlpin's fancy had full play; and distrustful of his imagination unaided, he repaired early to the Mountain House bar to stimulate it. Thus it gradually transpired along the bar, either from the stimulant or its reaction or from McAlpin's excitement, that a big fight had taken place that morning in the Falling Wall from which only Laramie had returned alive. It was known that he had come back and inference as to who the dead men might be could center only on his two active enemies, Tom Stone and Harry Van Horn. The pawky barn boss, who possessed perfectly the art of tantalizing innuendo, thus stirred the bar-room pool to the depths.

McAlpin chose the rustler's end of the bar—as Abe Hawk's old stand was called—and held the interest of the room against all comers. As the place filled for the evening, his cap, its vizor more than ordinarily awry, was a conspicuous object and it became a favor on his part to accept the courtesies of the bar at any man's hands.

"I knowed how it had to end," he would repeat when he had rambled again around all aspects of the mysterious encounter. "I knowed if they kept after Jim how it *had* to end. Why, hell, gentlemen," he would aver, planting a hob-nailed barn boot on the foot-rail, while swinging on one elbow from the polished face of the mahogany, "I've *seen* the boy stop a coyote on the go, at 900 yards—what could you expect? No, no, not again. What? Well, go ahead; just a dash o' bitters in mine, Luke. Thank you.

"Well, boys, accordin' to my notion, there's two men never would be missed in this country, anyway, if nobody ever seen 'em again. 'N' if my count is anywhere near right, nobody ever will see 'em again. They chased Laramie one foot too far—just one foot—'n' it looks as if they got what was comin' to 'em. I won't name 'em—they won't bother no more in this country."

He had become so absorbed in his recital that the entrance into the bar-room from the barber shop of a booted and spurred man escaped him. The man, advancing deliberately, heard the last of McAlpin's words. He got fairly close to the unsuspecting barn boss unobserved. A few in

373

the listening circle, noting the approach of the new arrival, stepped back a little—for, of all men that might be expected, after McAlpin's dark intimations, to appear, then and there, alive and aggressive, was Tom Stone.

Freshly barbered, head forward, keen eyes peering from under staring, sandy brows; thumbs stuck in his belt and his face framing a confident leer, Stone sauntering forward, listened to McAlpin. So intent was McAlpin on impressing his hearers that the foreman elbowed his way, before McAlpin saw him, directly to the front.

"So you won't name 'em?" grinned Stone, confronting the startled speaker. McAlpin caught his breath. The wiry Scotchman was not a coward, but he knew the merciless cruelty of Stone. Armed, McAlpin would have been no man to affront his deadly skill; he now faced him unarmed.

Stone, leaving his right hand hooked by the thumb in his belt, rested his left elbow on the bar. The bartender, Luke, just back of him, leaning forward, mopped the bar more slowly and, listening, moved a little farther down the bar until his fingers rested on an electric button underneath connecting with Tenison's office in the hotel.

"Name the two men, McAlpin," said Stone, ominously, "while you're able to talk."

McAlpin exhausted his ingenuity in his efforts to evade his danger, but Stone drew the noose about him tighter and tighter. He played the unlucky man with all the malice of an executioner. He baited him and toyed with him. McAlpin, white, stood his ground. His fighting blood was all there and he broke at length into a torrent of abuse of the man that he realized was bent on murdering him.

Made eloquent by desperation, McAlpin never rose to greater heights of profane candor. It was as if he were making his last will and testament of hatred and contempt for his murderer, and when he had showered on his enemy every epithet stored in a retentive memory he struck his empty glass on the bar and shouted: "Now, you hellcat, shoot!"

It might have been thought Stone would check such a public castigation. He did not. Impervious to abuse, because master of the situation, he seemed to enjoy his victim's fury. "I'm finishing up with your gang around here, McAlpin," he snarled, never losing his grin. "You've run a rustler's barn in Sleepy Cat long enough. I've warned you and I've warned Kitchen. It didn't do no good. Fill up your glass, McAlpin."

"Stone, I'd never fill up a glass with you if I was in hell 'n' you could pull me out."

Stone's grin deepened: "Fill up your glass, McAlpin."

Onlookers, knowing what a refusal would mean, held their breaths. But McAlpin, white and stubborn, with another oath, again refused.

"Fill it, McAlpin," urged a quiet voice behind

the bar. Looking quickly, like a hunted animal, around, McAlpin saw Harry Tenison, white-faced and cold, pushing the bottle in friendly fashion toward him. Every man, save one, watching, hoped he would humor at least that much his expectant murderer. But the barn-boss had reached a state of fear and anger that inflamed every stubborn drop in his blood. He swore he would not fill his glass.

Tenison spoke grimly: "Will you drink it if I fill it, you mule?" he demanded, picking up the bottle and pouring into both glasses in front of him.

In the dead silence McAlpin's brain was in a storm. He collected a few of his wildly flying thoughts. Perhaps he remembered the wife and Loretta and the babies; at all events he stared at the liquor, gulped to see whether he could swallow, and, reaching forward, picked up the glass. Stone lifted his own. The two men, their glasses poised, eyed each other.

Stone barbed a taunt for his victim: "Goin' to drink, air you?" he sneered, wreathing his eyes in leering wrinkles.

"No," said a man, unnoticed until then by any except Tenison and Luke, and speaking as he pushed forward through the crowd to face both Stone and McAlpin. "He's not going to drink."

Stone's glass was half-way up to his lips; he looked across it and saw himself face to face with Jim Laramie. Laramie who, unseen, had heard enough of the quarrel, stood with his coat slung over his right shoulder; one arm he carried in a sling, but as far as this concerned Stone, it was the wrong arm. Daring neither to raise the whisky to his lips nor to set the glass down, lest Laramie, suspecting he meant to draw, should shoot, Stone stood rooted. "McAlpin's not going to drink, Stone," repeated Laramie. "What are you going to do about it?"

The mere sight of Laramie would have been a vastly unpleasant surprise. But to find himself faced by him in fighting trim after what had taken place in the morning was an upset.

"What am *I* going to do about it?" echoed Stone, lifting his eyebrows and grinning anew. "What are *you* going to do about it, Jim?" he demanded. "You and me used to bunk together, didn't we?"

"I bunked with a rattlesnake once. I didn't know it," responded Laramie dryly. "Next morning the rattlesnake didn't know it."

"Jim, I'll drink you just once for old times."

"I wouldn't drink with you, Stone. No man would drink with you if he wasn't afraid of you. And after tonight nobody's going to be afraid of you. You're a thief among thieves, Tom Stone: a bully, a coward, a skulker. You shoot from cover. When Barb made you foreman, you and Van Horn stole his cattle, and Dutch Henry sold 'em for you and divvied with you. Then, for fear Barb would get wise, you and Van Horn got up the raid and killed Dutch Henry, so he couldn't talk.

"Now you're going to quit this stuff. No more thieving, no more man-killing, no bullyragging, no nothing. Tenison will clear this room. Hold your glass right where it is, till the last man gets out. When he gets out set down your glass; you'll have time enough allowed you. After that, draw where you stand. You're not entitled to a chance. God, Stone, I'd *rather* bunk with a rattlesnake than with you. I'd rather kill one than kill a thing like you. Your head ought to be pounded with a rock. You're entitled to nothing. But you can have your chance. Get the boys out of here, Harry."

Not for one instant did he take his eye off Stone's eye, or raise his tone above a speaking voice, and Laramie's voice was naturally low. To catch his syllables, listeners crowded in and craned their necks. Few men withdrew but everyone courteously and sedulously got out of the prospective line of fire.

What it cost Laramie even to stand on his feet and talk, Tenison could most shrewdly estimate. From behind the bar he coldly regarded the wounded man. He knew that Laramie must have escaped Carpy and escaped Belle, to look for the men that had tried that morning to kill him. Having found Stone he meant then and there to fight.

Tenison likewise realized that he was in no condition to do it, and promptly intervened: "Don't look at me, Jim," he said. "But I'm talking. There's no man in Sleepy Cat can clear this room now.

Most of this crowd are your friends. They want to see this hell-hound cleaned up. But you know what it means to some of 'em if two guns cut loose."

Stone saw the gate open. He welcomed a chance to dodge. Eyeing Laramie, he swallowed his drink, set his glass on the bar. With a voice dried and cracked, he cried: "Keep your hands off, Tenison. I'll give Jim Laramie all the fight he wants, here or anywhere."

Tenison was willing to bridge the crisis with abuse. "Shut up, you coyote," he remarked, with complete indifference.

"You'll throw a man down no matter how much of your whisky he drinks, won't you, Tenison?" cried Stone.

Tenison, both hands judicially spread on the bar, seemed to fail to hear. "McAlpin," he said contemptuously, "walk around behind Laramie and lift Stone's gun."

Stone started violently. "Look out, Tenison! I lift my gun when there's men to stand by and see fair play!"

A roar of laughter went up. "I don't lift it for no frame-up," he shouted, turning angrily toward the unsympathetic crowd. "Get out!" cried one voice far enough back to be safe. "Send for Barb," shouted a second. "Page Van Horn," piped a barber, as Stone moved toward the door.

The baited foreman turned only for a parting shot at Laramie: "I'll see *you* later."

"If I was your friend," retorted Laramie, unmoved, "I'd advise you not to. If you ride my trail don't expect anything more from me. And I make this town," he hammered home the point with his right forefinger indicating the floor, "and the Falling Wall range *my* trail."

"Stone ought to have tried it tonight," observed Tenison at the cash register. He was speaking to his bartender long after Stone had disappeared, Laramie had been put to bed again and the billiard hall had been deserted. "He'll never get a chance again at Laramie half shot to pieces."

CHAPTER 37

KATE BURNS THE STEAK

Laramie, held for a week in bed, learned from the Doctor of Belle's outburst at Kate, and, acting through him and with him, arranged peace.

Complaining of a cold, with her other troubles, Belle took to bed when Laramie was moved to the hotel and Kate turned in to nurse her.

"You won't starve while she stays, Belle," declared Carpy, leaving Kate in possession at the cottage, "and while I think of it," he added, turning to Kate, "Laramie says he wants to see you. You call him up on the telephone, will you?"

"What for, doctor?"

"To oblige me, girl. I want to hold that fellow in his room a few days more and keep his arm in a sling. He's no easier to handle than a wildcat."

Kate looked perplexed: "What shall I say to him?"

Carpy stood at the door with his hand on the knob: "Jolly him along—you know how. He says he's coming down here for dinner tonight. Tell him Belle's sick."

Belle listened. The more Kate considered the mandate, the more confusing it seemed. But she rang up the hotel, called for Laramie and heard presently a man's voice in answer.

"Is this Mr. Laramie?" she asked.

"It is not," was the answer.

"Isn't he there?"

"No."

"Can you tell me when he will be in?"

"He won't be in."

She sighed with impatience: "I want to speak to him. And I think this is he speaking. You know very well who I am," she persisted.

"I do."

"And I know very well who you are."

"In that you may be mistaken."

"Surely I'm not mistaken in believing Mr. Laramie a gentleman."

"But you are mistaken in believing any person by that name here."

"There is a person there who loves to persecute me, isn't there?"

"There is not."

"Is there one there that likes to have his own way?"

"No more than you like to have your own way."

"Is there a man named Jim there?"

"Speaking, Kate."

"I've a message from Belle."

"What is the message?"

"She is in bed with a cold and fever and wants you not to come tonight. As soon as she is up she will let you know."

Belle held her peace till Kate left the telephone. "I can't make Doctor Carpy out," she grumbled. "If he didn't want Jim Laramie to come down here what did he ask *you* to call him up for? If he doesn't know any more than that about doctoring," she added, contemptuously, "I'd hate to take his medicine."

She waited for Kate's comment but Kate possessed the great art of saying nothing. "I guess," continued Belle, at length, "it's time to take that pill he left, but I guess I won't take it. What do you think about it?" she asked, referring again to Carpy.

Kate was not to be drawn out: "I found out a long time ago that Doctor Carpy doesn't tell all he knows," she observed dryly. "But I do know he wants Mr. Laramie to stay in his room. He says his shoulder will never heal if he doesn't keep still."

Belle made no response, but when Laramie

knocked at the door in the evening she knew who it was. Kate received him.

Talking in leisurely fashion to her, he walked to the door of Belle's room, looked in, wanted to know whom she had been fighting with and asked if she would get up and get supper for him.

He carried his right arm at his side with the thumb hooked into his belt: "Where's your sling?" demanded Belle, tartly. Laramie pulled it out of his pocket: "I put it on when Carpy comes around," he explained.

"You keep fooling around the streets this way and they'll get you sometime," said Belle, tartly.

He turned the remark: "That idea doesn't seem to worry me as much as it used to. Have I got to cook my own supper?"

This venture after discussion was assumed by Kate. She put on her hat to go across the street to get a steak. Laramie insisted on going with her. She asked him not to.

"Why not?" he asked.

Kate was keyed up with apprehension: "Why take chances all the time?" she asked in turn. "Someone might shoot from the dark."

Belle answered for him: "Nobody in this country would shoot a man when a woman's with him," she said. "Go along."

The butcher stumping in from the back room to wait on them showed no surprise at the two from hostile camps asking for one steak, but he tried so hard to watch the pair and to hear what they were saying that he nearly ruined one quarter of beef before he got what Kate wanted. What he finally cut off and trimmed looked more like a roast than a steak but neither customer seemed disturbed by this.

Laramie paid, over indignant protests, and placing the package in the loop of his left arm, opened the shop door for his companion. He passed out behind her in excellent spirits. The butcher, looking after them, took his surreptitious pipe from his pocket, watched the shop door close, shook his head and ramming the burnt tobacco down hard with the finger that lacked the first joint, stumped back to his lonely stove.

The kitchen was farthest removed from Belle's room. Laramie started the fire with kerosene. When he lighted it there was a flare-back that alarmed Belle in her bed, but she could hear nothing of what was going on in the kitchen. While the supper was being cooked, Laramie stood on the other side of the stove from his enemy's daughter, watching every move. If Kate walked over to the cupboard, his eyes followed her step— she walked with such decision and planted her heels so fast and firm. If she turned from the stove to the table, his eyes devoured her slenderness in amazement that one so delicately proportioned could so crowd everything else out of his head. It seemed as if nothing before had ever been shaped like her ankles—there was so little of them to bear uncomplainingly even so slight a figure—and Kate was by no means diminutive.

As the supper progressed, Laramie watched almost in awe the short-arm jabs she gave the meat on the broiler. The cuffs of her shirtwaist, half back to her elbows, revealed white arms tapering to wrists molded like the ankles, and hands that his eyes fed on as a miser's feed on gold. The blazing coals flushed her cheeks and when she looked up at him to answer some foolish question her own eyes, flushed and softened by the heat, took on an expression that stole all the strength he had left. When she asked him how he liked it, he exclaimed, "Fine," and Kate had to ask him whether he liked the steak well done or rare.

"Any way you like it," he stammered, "but lots of gravy."

As he watched her laugh at his efforts to help her by picking up the hot platter, a sense of his own clumsiness and size and general roughness overcame him. She was too far removed, he told himself, from his kind to make it possible for her ever to like him.

The closer he got to her daintiness and spirit and laughter, the more hopeless his wild dreams seemed. Whenever she asked if the steak were cooked enough, he suggested—to prolong the pleasure of watching her hands—that she give it one more turn. Every moment he saw something new to admire. While she was attending to the meat he could look at her hair and see where the sun had browned her pink throat and neck. As the broiling drew near an end, almost a panic gripped Laramie. The happiest moments of his life had been spent there at the stove. They were slipping away. She was lifting the steak the last time from the fire. He asked her to turn it once more.

"Why, look at it," she exclaimed, "it's burnt up now; hold the platter closer."

It brought him closer in spirit than he had ever been to heaven, to feel her elbow brush against his own, as she deftly landed the smoking steak on the platter while Laramie held it.

A great melancholy overcame him: "What do you want me to do?" he said suddenly.

Kate's eyebrows rose. She looked at him: "Why, set it on the table," she laughed.

"No, I mean what do you want me to do— myself."

She could not wholly misunderstand his look, though little did he realize how she feared it; or what a dread respect she secretly had for the grave eyes so closely bent on her own. She laughed really to gather courage, and it was easy to laugh a little because he *did* look so odd as he stood before her, with the platter in both hands, but terribly in earnest. "Set the platter on the table before you burn yourself," she pleaded.

"You must want me to do something," he

persisted, "get off the earth or stay on it—now, don't you? Say what you want me to do, and, by—" He checked himself. "And I'll do it."

She could restrain him but she could not turn him. He did put the platter on the table without getting any answer but now that his mind was set, it reverted stubbornly to the one subject and when supper was over and they sat opposite each other in the little dining-room talking, she said she knew he had burned his hands. "I wouldn't mind if I had," he remarked frankly. "Almost every time I've talked with you I've held the hot end of a poker; I'm getting to look for it." He drew a deep breath. "You never liked me, did you, Kate?"

"That isn't so."

"You always kind of held off."

"Perhaps I was a little afraid of you."

"You're not afraid of me now—are you—with one arm out of commission? Are you?"

She looked at him in a troubled sort of way: "Why, no—not very," she returned, half laughing.

"You were never half as much afraid of me as I was of you," he murmured.

His eyes across the table were growing very importunate. She could not realize how flushed and soft and tantalizing her own eyes were, framed by the warm color high in her cheeks. She rose with a hurried exclamation and looked dismayed at him, her hands tilted on the table, her brows high and her burning eyes still laughing: "We've left the light on by the stove all this time," she whispered. "Belle will be furious!"

She slipped hurriedly out into the kitchen and turned off the light. Her face was hot. She was thirsty and stepping to the water faucet she picked up a glass. The mountain water tasted so cold and good; in some way it made her think of great peaks and the crisp, clear air of his home far up among them. She had not realized how heated she was. "Do you want a drink?" she called back to the dining room.

He was standing directly behind her. She turned only to stumble against him and before she knew what had happened he was raining kisses on her resisting cheeks. Then his lips found hers and, faint with the moment, she resisted no more.

After a long time she got one hand around his neck and laid the other across his mouth: "Don't make so much noise," she whispered wildly. "Belle will hear us!"

CHAPTER 38

THE UNEXPECTED CALL

The hush that followed the brain storm in the kitchen put Belle, quite unsuspecting, to sleep. Laramie, with a tread creditable to a cat—and a stealth natural to most carnivorous animals—

closed the door without breaking her heavy breathing. The shades, always drawn at nightfall, called for no attention. In the living-room, there was preliminary tiptoeing, and there were futile efforts on Kate's part to cool her rebellious cheeks by applying her open hands to them—when she could get possession of either one to do so. The small couch which served as sofa was drawn out of range of even the protected windows, and the floodgates were opened to the first unrestrained confidences together.

When they could talk of more serious things, Kate could not possibly see how she could marry him; but this, in the circumstances, seemed to cause Laramie no alarm. She admitted she had tried not to like him and confessed how she had failed. "Every time I met you," she murmured, "you seemed to understand me so well—you knew how a woman would like to be treated—that's what I kept thinking about."

"You used to talk and laugh with Van Horn," he complained, jealously. "When I came around, I couldn't drag a smile out of you with a lariat."

"You're getting a smile now that he isn't getting, aren't you?"

"Somehow you never acted natural with me."

"Jim!" It was the word he most wanted to hear, even if the reproach implied the quintessence of stupidity. "Don't you understand, I wasn't afraid of *him,* and I was of you!"

"And I only trying to get a chance to eat out of your hand!"

"How could I tell—after all I used to hear—but that you'd begin by eating out of my hand and finish by eating me?"

He had to be told every word of her troubles at home, but her uneasiness turned to the dangers threatening him. These, she protested, he belittled too much. Ever since he had come in wounded she had been the prey of fears for him. "It's a mystery how you escaped." He had to tell every detail of his flight down the canyon. "By rights," he said in conclusion, "they ought to have got me. No man should have got out of that scrape as well as I did. Van Horn didn't get into action quick enough. And it seemed to me as if Stone himself was a little slow." The way he spoke the things strengthened her confidence. And his arm held her so close!

"I'll tell you, Kate," he added. "You can easy enough hire a fellow to kill a man. But you can't really hire one to hate a man. And if he doesn't really hate him, he won't be as keen on your job as you'd be yourself. These hired men will booze once in awhile—or go to sleep, maybe. It's work for a clear head and takes patience to hide in the rocks day after day and wait for one certain man to ride by so you can shoot him. If you doze off, your man may pass while you snore. And the kind of man you can hire isn't as keen on getting a man as the man himself is on not getting 'got'—

that's where the chance is, sometimes, to pull out better than even."

Because his aim was to reassure, to relieve her anxiety, he did not tell her that all the unfavorable conditions he had named, while never before arrayed against him at one time, were now pretty much all present together. Kate herself, he knew, stood more than ever between him and Van Horn. Stone had been twice publicly disgraced by Laramie at Tenison's—he would never forgive that. He had the patience of the assassin and when hatred swayed him he did not sleep—these were still, Laramie knew in his heart, bridges to be crossed.

But why spoil an hour's happiness with the thought of them now? Laramie drew his hand across his heated forehead as if to clear his eyes and look again down into the face close to his and assure himself he was not really dreaming. "What do I care about them all, Kate," he would say, "now that I've got you? No, now that you've given yourself to me—that's what I'll say—what do I care what they do?"

But she would look up, sudden with apprehension: "But don't you think *I* care? Jim, let's leave this country soon, soon."

Laramie laughed indulgently: "Somebody'll have to leave it pretty soon—that's certain."

A rude knock at the door broke into his words. Kate threw her hands against his breast. She stared at him thunderstruck, and sprang from the sofa like a deer, looking still at him with wide-open eyes and then glancing apprehensively toward the door.

Laramie sat laughing silently at her get-away as he called it, yet he was not undisturbed.

Nothing, in the circumstances, could have been less welcome than any sort of an intrusion. But a knock at the door, almost violent, and coming three times, stirred even Laramie's temper.

The door was not locked. Laramie rose, his fingers resting on the butt of his revolver, and stepping lightly into the dining-room, turned down the lamp. He stood in the shadow and beckoned Kate to him. His face indicated no alarm.

"This may be something, or it may be nothing. You step into the kitchen. I'll go to the door."

She clung to him, really terror-stricken, begging him not to go. As he tried to quiet her fears the heavy knock shook the flimsy door the second time. Kate, declaring she would go, would not be denied. Laramie told her exactly what to do.

She reached the door on tiptoe and stood to the right of it. The key was in the lock. Kate, reaching out one hand, turned the key. With the door thus locked and standing close against the wall she called out to know who was there. Laramie had followed behind her. He stepped to where he could look from behind the window shade out on the porch. He turned to Kate just as an answer came from outside, and signed to her to open. Standing where she was, Kate turned the key swiftly back in the lock and threw the door wide open.

Stooping slightly forward to bring his hat under the opening, and looking carefully about him, her father walked heavily into the room.

Laramie had disappeared. Kate, dumb, stood still. Barb closed the door behind him, walked to the table, put down his hat and turned to Kate. "Well?" he began, snapping the word in his usual manner, his stupefied daughter struggling with her astonishment. "You don't act terrible glad to see me."

Kate caught her breath. "I was so surprised," she stammered.

"What are you staying in town so long for?" demanded Barb. His voice had lost nothing of its husky heaviness.

She answered with a question: "Where else have I to stay, father? I've been waiting for money to get East with and it hasn't come yet."

"What do you want to go East for?"

"I've nowhere else to go."

"Why don't you come home?"

"Because you told me to leave."

He sat slowly down on a chair near the table and with the care of a burdened man.

"Well," he said, "you mustn't take things too quick from me nowadays." She made no answer. "I've had a good deal of money trouble lately," he went on, "everything going against me." He spoke moodily and his huge frame lost in the bulk of his big storm coat overran almost pathetically the slender chair in which he tried to sit. His spirit seemed broken. "I reckon," he added, taking his hat from the table and fingering it slowly, "you'd better come along back."

She was sorry for him. She told him how much she wished he would give up trying to carry his big load, and she urged him to take a small ranch and keep out of debt. He laid his hat down again. He told her he didn't see how he could let it go, but they would talk it over when she got home.

This was the point of his errand that she dreaded to meet and putting it as inoffensively as possible she tried to parry: "I think," she ventured, "now that I've got some clothes ready and got started, I'd better go East for awhile anyway."

"No." His ponderous teeth clicked. "You'd better wait till fall. I might go along. Tonight I'll take you out home. Put on your things and we'll get started."

She did not want to refuse. She knew she could not consent. She knew that Laramie in the shadow, as well as her father in the light, was waiting for her answer: "Father," she said at once, "I can't go tonight."

"Why not?" was the husky demand.

"Belle is sick in bed," pleaded Kate.

"Is that the only reason?"

She saw he was bound to wring more from her. "No," she answered, "it isn't, father."

"What else?"

"I'm afraid—" she hesitated, and then spoke out: "I can't come back—not just as I was, anyway."

"Why not?"

"It's too late, father."

"What do you mean?" he asked.

"When I come back from the East," she spoke slowly but collectedly, "I expect to go into a new home."

"Where?"

"In the Falling Wall."

For a moment he did not speak, only looked at her fixedly: "What I've heard's so, then?" he said, after a pause.

"What have you heard?"

"The story is you're going to marry Jim Laramie."

Kate, in turn, stood silently regarding her father, and as if she knew she must face it out.

"Is that so?" he demanded harshly.

She burst into tears, but through her tears the two men heard her answer: "Yes, father."

Barb picked up his hat without wincing: "I guess that ends things 'tween you and me." He started uncertainly for the door.

"Father!" Kate protested, taking a quick step after him as he passed out. "You don't do him justice. You don't know him."

But slamming the door shut behind him, he cut off her words. If they reached his ears he gave them no heed.

CHAPTER 39

Barb Makes a Surprising Alliance

By a happy chance, on the night of Laramie's great hour, Sawdy and Lefever returned from Medicine Bend. It was late when they arrived—into the early morning hours, in fact, and at the Mountain House the bar was not only closed but securely closed—barricaded against just such marauders. Even the night clerk had gone to bed. But this was less of an embarrassment, for the two adventurers, turning on the lights, took his pass keys from the drawer and, opening the doors of one room after another in the face of a variety of protests, kept on till they found satisfactory quarters that "seemed" unoccupied—quarters in which at least the beds were unoccupied.

The hardy scouts slept late. They breakfasted late, in what Sawdy called the hotel "ornery," and while they were reducing the visible supply of ham and eggs, Tenison walked in on them to ask about complaints made at the office by indignant guests whose privacy had been invaded during the night. Rebuffed on this subject, all knowledge being disclaimed, Tenison was called on for the story of events since the two had been away, and of these Laramie's escape from the canyon came first. Tenison reported further, in confidence, Laramie's success with Kate. Had the news provided every man in the Falling Wall with a brand-new wife, it could not have been more to the humor of Sawdy and Lefever.

Sawdy rose and stretched himself from the waist down to make sure his legs touched the floor: "I've got to have a good cigar on that," he declared. "Take away, Mabel." He nodded courteously to the waitress. "Harry, we had the dustiest trip I ever seen in my life," he added, as with his companions he left the table. "The old Ogallala trail wasn't a marker to it. Why, the dust was a mile deep. My tonsils are plumb full of it yet."

Not everyone in Sleepy Cat was so quick to credit the news that Kate Doubleday was going to marry Jim Laramie. The cattlemen sympathizers looked grumpy, when approached on the subject. They preferred not to talk, but if taunted would retort with an intimating oath: "That show ain't over yet."

"Jim Laramie acts as if it was, anyway," grumbled Belle, when the butcher told her what they were saying. In fact, all of Laramie's intimates were out of patience with him when he announced he was going to rebuild the cabin on his Falling Wall ranch and live there.

"Wait till this cattle fight is over," they would urge.

"It is over," he would retort. And heedless of

397

their protests, he spent his time getting his building materials together.

"What do you want me to do?" he demanded, stirred at length by Belle's remonstrances against going back to the Falling Wall. "I've got to live somewhere. Danger? Why, yes—maybe. But I can't keep dying every day on that account. Here in town a man was run over just the other day by a railroad train."

Kate said little either way. She heard all that Belle could urge and held in her heart all the men said. But when Jim asked her what *she* wanted to do she told him, simply, whatever *he* wanted to do. Then Belle would call her a ninny, and Laramie would kiss her, and Belle in disgust would disappear.

There came one morning the crowning sensation in the suspense of the situation. Barb Doubleday drove into town in the buckboard, headed his team into Kitchen's barn to put up and gave McAlpin a cigar.

An earthquake, where one had never been known, could not have stirred the town more. When McAlpin ran up street to the Mountain House to be first with his news, he was reviled as a vender of stories calculated to start a shooting.

But McAlpin, with a cigar in his mouth—where no cigar, except a free cigar, was ever seen—his face bursting red with import, stuck to his guns. He walked straight to the billiard room bar, and attracted attention by brusquely ordering his own drink. This, it was known, always meant something serious.

When Sawdy saw the commotion about the barn boss, he walked in and after listening began a stern cross-examination.

"Explain?" McAlpin echoed scornfully. "I don't explain. No, he wasn't drinking! Nor he wasn't crazy!" McAlpin took the burning cigar from his mouth. "That's the cigar he give me, right there— and a bum one. Barb never smoked a good one in his life—you know that, Henry? I don't explain—I drink. Hold on!" he exclaimed, as he emptied his glass with a single gulp. He was looking across the street and pointing. "Who's that over there comin' out of the lumber yard with Barb Doubleday right now—blanked if it ain't! It's Jim Laramie, that's who it is."

Doubleday had in fact run into Laramie in the lumber yard. With nothing more than a greeting, he opened his mind: "I want a talk with you, Jim," he said bluntly. "Where's Kate?"

Not even the freedom of the bar fully established could hold McAlpin after he had seen Laramie and Doubleday walk out of the lumber yard and start down Main Street together. McAlpin had the reputation of having missed no important shooting in Sleepy Cat for years. He had been witness in more than one inquest and did not mean to imperil his importance by slacking now. As he hastened out to trail the long-day bitter enemies, he was framing in his mind the preliminary answers for the coroner. He would be compelled to testify, he felt, that the dead man had showed no sign of intoxication or excitement when he drove his team into the barn—for in the circumstances, the barn boss already figured Barb as the inevitable victim.

Thus ruminating, he trailed the unsuspecting pair as far as Belle's. At Belle's without sign of heated argument, they knocked and entered the cottage together. This left McAlpin across the street with nobody but the butcher to talk to, while he listened intently for the first shot.

Lefever was bolder. He followed the two men unceremoniously to Belle's porch and bluffed Belle herself into admitting him to the living room. Laramie had gone into the back part of the house to hunt up Kate; Barb, alone, sat in the rocking chair, chewing an unlighted cigar.

Lefever greeted the big cattleman effusively; Barb's response was cold. He looked Lefever over critically: "What'you doing?" he asked, without warm interest in any possible answer.

"Buying a relinquishment now and again, Barb."

"Railroad man, eh?" muttered Barb, irrelevantly.

"No, no. I've quit that game; I've got a claim up near you. I'm going to try to live the life of a small but dishonest rancher, Barb."

"You ought to do well at that, eh?"

"Why, yes and no. But I'm thinking, if I can't

figure out the game, some of my neighbors can help me catch on—what?"

Barb's retort—if he had one—to Lefever's continued laugh, was cut off by Laramie's entrance with Kate. John saw that he was *de trop*, that it was a family conference, and only extracting from Laramie a promise to see him—about nothing whatever—before leaving town he made what he termed a graceful getaway. Kate and Laramie faced her father. Belle, too, was for going out. Doubleday stopped her: "No secrets, Belle; stay if you want to."

All sat down. Kate was for a chair, but Laramie domineering, made her sit with him on the sofa. Barb spoke first: "This Falling Wall fight is off," he began briefly. "Anyway, I quit on it. I've got to, Jim. The settlers there are in to stay," declared Barb philosophically. "They've got to be reco'nized." The settlers, in this instance, meant Jim Laramie, since practically everyone else had been driven or frightened out. But all understood what was intended; for if the fighting ceased the park would fill up.

"Since yesterday," Doubleday went on, "I've found out something else." He was speaking directly to Laramie. "That man Stone," he exclaimed, "has been robbing me."

The old man paused. No one made any comment. Abe Hawk had long ago told Laramie as much. "He's been misbranding on me—him and that rascally Van Horn have been selling my steers to the railroad camps on the Reservation. I've got the evidence from some Indians that came over yesterday with the hides. Last night," continued the victim coolly, "I fired Stone. He went right over to Van Horn's. I told him that's where he belongs. I'm through with 'em both."

"Why don't you have 'em arrested?" demanded Belle.

"I might, yet," muttered Barb vaguely.

Laramie held his peace; but even Kate realized *that* would never do. "Jim and me has had our differences," added Barb, "but they're ended. If you two get married—"

"There ain't goin' to be any 'if,' Barb," interposed Laramie, "there's just going to be 'married,' and married right off."

"Well, that's for you and the girl to say; but when you say it, you've got to have a house to live in. I met Jim," added her father, speaking now to Kate, "over in the lumber yard this morning. When you get your house up, turn the bill in to me."

Kate's kisses confused and stopped her father. Belle made ready a good dinner. The four ate together. Belle was excited, Kate happy and Laramie content. But for the old man it was somehow hard to fit in. Having had his say, he relapsed into grim silence and taciturn responses. Even his presence would have repressed Belle but for Kate's happy laugh. She looked at her father, talked to him, thought of him, studied him, and throwing off lingering doubts—for she never felt she quite knew her father—enjoyed him, eating as he was in peace with her husband-to-be.

When Laramie's cigars were lighted after the dinner, Barb seemed to feel more at his ease. He told stories of his old railroad days and laughed when Kate and Belle and Laramie laughed. Later, his daughter and his new son-in-law walked up street with him. They went with him on his errands and then to the barn. McAlpin, personally, hitched up the ponies, both in compliment to a new customer and to hear every word that passed in the talk.

"Damme," he muttered to the hostler in the harness room, "y' can't get around old Barb. Look at him. What do I mean? Don't he fight Laramie five years 'n' get licked? Now he turns him into his son-in-law and gets the Falling Wall range any-way—can y' beat it? Coming right along, sir!" he shouted, as Barb in the gangway bellowed for more speed. And with a flutter of activity, real and feigned, McAlpin and his helper fastened the traces.

When ready, the wiry team and the long narrow buckboard looked small for Barb, who cautiously clambered into the seat and gingerly distributed his bulk upon it. Laramie had taken the reins from McAlpin; he passed them to Barb who, as he squared himself so as not to fall off his slender perch, was huskily demanding when Laramie and Kate would be out. At the last minute, Kate insisted on and was given, a good-by kiss. She and Jim promised to go out next day. Barb spoke to the horses. They jumped half-way out of the barn. Kate, with Laramie following, hurried forward to see her father drive away.

The broad back, topped by the powerful shoulders and neck, and the big hat bobbing up and down with the spring of the buckboard, the little team plunging at their bits, and her father heedless of their antics—all this was a familiar sight, but never had it been so pleasing. The setting sun touched with gold the thin cloud of dust that rose from the wheels. It was the close of a beautiful day and it had been next to the happiest in her life, Kate thought, while she stood, watching and thinking. The ponies reaching a turn in the road dashed ahead and her father disappeared.

CHAPTER 40

Bradley Rides Hard

The evening was spent at Belle's. Lefever came in late with congratulations. He told them about his trip and the wonders.

"I'll bet you're glad to get back to Sleepy Cat," objected Belle.

Lefever pointed a serious, almost accusing finger at her: "Thank you for saying it, Belle; and that's never hinting the Panhandle's not a good country—not a bit of it. But, just the same, I'm glad to get back to my own. There's no place like hell, Jim, is there?—especially if you've got friends there—you know that."

"You ought to be ashamed, John Lefever, to say such things," exclaimed Belle, indignantly. But nothing could check Lefever's spirits. His laugh was contagious: "I am, Belle, I am. I want you to feel that I am."

"And you came back across the Sinks?" interposed Laramie.

"We did," responded John, starting all over again, "and I want to tell you the Sinks are picking up. There's a better class of people going in. I was laid up at Thief River—something I ate. I felt pretty bad."

"How do you feel now?" Laramie asked.

"Why, not very good to tell the truth. I had a kind of a sleepy night. You wouldn't believe it, Jim, but there's quite a town at Thief River. And the Sisters here at Sleepy Cat have got a little hospital going. They treated me fine. Everybody, in fact, seemed to take an interest in getting me on my feet. There's an awful nice undertaker there. I forget his name; but he knew Henry de Spain well; said he'd done a good deal of business for Henry, off and on—when he could get the coffins. He sent some flowers over to me at the hospital with his card. I sent back my own card—wrote: 'Not yet.' When we were leaving I went over to thank him and tell him I was sorry I hadn't been able to throw him a job. Even then, I didn't feel I could logically say good-by to an undertaker—I just said '*Au revoir.*' "

The two men afterward joined Sawdy at the Mountain House. In the morning, breakfasting together early, Sawdy and Lefever with Laramie walked in the bright sunshine down to Kitchen's barn to saddle up and ride across the river to look at some horses. Laramie stopped at Belle's to see whether he could get Kate to go over with them; and while Sawdy went on to the barn, Lefever waited at Belle's gate to find out whether Kate was going.

When Laramie came to the door after a few moments to say that Kate would go, Lefever stood outside the gate looking intently into the north.

"Somebody from the Crazy Woman," he observed as Laramie joined him, "must have an urgent call in town this morning."

He was watching what appeared to be little more than a speck on the northern horizon, but even at that distance it was moving fast. Lefever walked over to Kitchen's to order the fourth horse. Rejoining Laramie he found him still at the gate. And when Kate, fresh as the morning, appeared, the two men though talking of indifferent things, had their eyes fixed on a horseman galloping at breakneck speed down the long slope of the northern divide. He was now less than a mile away and the dust thrown from his horse's hoofs rose evenly behind him in the stillness of the sunshine. He must pass the barn to reach town. Kate asked a question.

"It may be one of your father's horses," mused Lefever aloud, "and it rides something like old Bill Bradley."

Still pushing his speed to the limit and cutting in reckless fashion the turns of the open road, the rider drew rapidly nearer. They could see he was hatless and coatless and urging his horse. "It's Bradley," declared Lefever decisively. Laramie said nothing. Kate instinctively drew closer to him. The horseman disappeared at that moment behind the railroad icing plant. The next, he whirled with a sharp clatter of hoofs into Main Street, and, dashing past Carpy's, pulled his foaming horse to its haunches in front of Kitchen's barn.

McAlpin and Sawdy were leading the four saddle ponies to the stable door. The group at Belle's gate could not hear what Bradley shouted; but they saw McAlpin start. Sawdy, too, spoke quick, and pointed, with his words, across the way. Bradley jerked his panting horse around and spurred toward Belle's gate.

The old man, his thin hair flying and his blood-shot eyes bulging, reined up before Laramie with his arm out, to speak. But the ride and the excitement had been too much. His features worked convulsively but he could not utter a word.

"For God's sake, Bill," cried Lefever, catching his arm and jerking him. "What's up?"

Bradley, his eyes glued on Laramie, got back his voice: "It's Barb, Jim!" he shouted wildly. "Tom Stone shot him this morning!"

Kate's sharp cry rang in Laramie's ears. He caught her in his arm. Belle ran out, only adding to the confusion with her scream. Lefever, joined now by Sawdy and McAlpin, who had hurried over, got Bradley off his horse, into a chair on the porch, refreshed him with water and steadied his whisky-wrecked nerves with whisky.

Stone and Van Horn came over from Van Horn's early, Bradley told his hearers brokenly. They asked for Barb and he was down at the creek. Barb had sent Bradley about a mile below the house to repair a small break in the irrigation ditch and had ridden down to show him what he wanted done. After giving instructions, he had started back for the house. Before he got far, Stone and Van Horn met him. Bradley heard voices up the creek but paid no special attention to them, and busied himself with his job. Some minutes later he heard the voices again, loud and angry. As they were close by, Bradley, shovel in hand, walked along the ditch bank to where he could see what was up.

"They'd all got off their horses," continued Bradley, "and was standin' not fur apart. I was close to the willows along the ditch. 'Fore you could say Jack Robinson, Stone and Van Horn snapped out their guns and begun to shoot. The old man was game, boys, but he didn't have no show. He managed to get his gun out, both men a-shootin' at him."

"Both!" echoed Laramie, bitterly. Sawdy swore a withering oath.

"Is my father dead?" cried Kate in agony.

"Not yet," replied Bradley disconcertingly.

"We must get Carpy up there quick. Hunt him up, will you, John?" said Laramie to Lefever.

"Hold on," interposed Bradley. "Carpy's there afore this. I met him drivin' north and he put right out for the ranch."

"Couldn't you do something while they were trying to murder Father?" sobbed Kate, wringing her hands as she appealed to Bradley.

"Why, what could *I* do?" stared Bradley. "*I* didn't have no gun. Kelly and me got the wagon down and picked Barb up 'n' got him to the house. He told me to put out for town and get you and Jim Laramie; he's out of his head, you see."

"Did they see you, Bradley?" interrupted Laramie.

"Never seen me, Jim."

"Did Barb hit either of them?" asked Laramie.

" 'Tain't likely. He only got in one shot. When they seen him wrigglin' on the ground, all doubled up—you know, Jim—they jumped their horses and put across the creek."

For a moment Kate's suppressed sobs broke the silence. Laramie held her in his arm. He promised her he would get her right out to her father as soon as he could take measures for pursuit. When the other men questioned Bradley, Laramie listened. He urged Kate to go inside with Belle, but she begged to stay: "I won't cry, Jim," she pleaded in a whisper. "I must stay. Let me stay."

He placed her in a chair. Belle, schooled in silence during such moments, stood beside her. Laramie placing himself near Kate, half sat on the edge of the porch floor, one foot resting on the ground and the other curled under. Lefever facing him, sat on the end of the porch steps while Sawdy stood with the horses. McAlpin had hurried over to the barn to get Kitchen and telephone Tenison to come down.

"There's two ways they can get out," said Laramie, casting up the situation with his companions. "One is across the Falling Wall and over the Reservation. If they've gone that way they've got a start; but they're easy to trail. The other way would be to strike east or west for the railroad. That's the big gamble—it's the easiest to play and the worst if they lose. They may separate."

"My Godfrey, Jim, don't let 'em get away," exclaimed Belle, fearfully.

"And there's one more angle," remarked Laramie. "They may show up right here and try to bluff it out."

Sawdy shook his head against that idea. Lefever supported him. Laramie did not urge the view.

"Van Horn plays cards different from everybody else," was all he said.

Kitchen drove up and Tenison was in the buggy with him.

What help might be had from the sheriff's office was put in Tenison's hands to manage. The railroad men were warned across the division. Outgoing train crews were notified and the enginemen told what to do, if stopped. Sawdy and Lefever were directed to strike for the Falling Wall and watch the Reservation trails, while Laramie, with Kate, was to ride straight to the ranch and pick up the trail across the creek.

The news of the shooting of Barb Doubleday filled the corners of Main Street with little knots of men eager to hear all that was known and to be first to catch what might come. Women sometimes stopped to listen and men making ready to ride the northern trails supplied clattering in the streets for every moment and added to the tense scene. The chances for the escape of Van Horn and Stone were canvassed among critics and listeners, and with almost as much insight as they had been cast up in the war council at Belle's. The men that might be expected to give battle if they encountered the fugitives were watched for and every time they rode past, the maneuvering and fighting abilities of each were speculated on with surprising accuracy; records were recalled and inferences drawn as to the possibilities now ahead.

The picture of the busy street, constantly renewed and dissolved, changed fast. Lefever and Sawdy, together, were the first to clear for their long ride. Kitchen, strapping on, for the first time in years, a well cared-for Colt's revolver, got fresh ammunition, and throwing himself on a good horse, rode for where he had sworn he would never appear again, the Doubleday ranch—to get the cowboys started at poking out the hiding places along the creek.

McAlpin, with much ado, enlisted every man with any sort of a claim to being a tracker—and this included pretty much every loafer interested in a drink or a fight. He assembled a noisy crew at the barn and despatched them singly with orders to scatter and watch the trail points outlying the town. But birds of this feather were hard to keep scattered. Urged both by prudential and social reasons, they tended continuously to flock together. They kept the barn boss busy by riding back furiously in bunches to report nobody seen, to ask for further orders and to get a drink before reestablishing a patrol.

Knowing the value of every moment in a long chase, and working with all possible haste, Laramie had to throw out his dragnet carefully before he could get away himself. He had told Kate to prepare at Belle's for a hard ride and he would get her to the ranch.

With every minute lingering like an hour, both women, nervously expectant, waited, talked, and watched for Laramie's return.

CHAPTER 41

THE FLIGHT OF THE SWALLOWS

Divide lands north of Sleepy Cat lie high and over their broad spread, trails open fan-like, north, northeast and northwest. Each of the trails penetrates at a negotiable point the broken country running up to the mountains that battle with the northern sky.

The first highways of the country followed the easiest travel lines. Without fences or boundaries, their travelers, to escape washouts or dust, were free to broaden them as they fancied. In this way older ruts were gradually abandoned and new ones formed. And with heavy travel these trails grew into sprawling avenues.

As settlers took up lands and fenced their claims, such pioneer roads were blocked at intervals. To meet this difficulty new trails were made around the gradually increasing obstacles and in the end roads along section lines were laid out, with grading and bridging. But the wagon and cattle trails of the early days, rut-cut, storm-washed, and polished by sun and wind and sand to a shining smoothness, still stretch across country, truncate and deserted. Under their weather-beaten silence lies the story of other days and other men and women.

Along one of the earliest and broadest of these trails running into the north country, Laramie, an hour after Bradley's arrival, was galloping with Kate Doubleday.

But for the shadow of her father's condition there was everything in the ride to make for Kate's happiness. The sweep of the matchless sky, the glory of the sunshine, the wine of the morning air, the eager feet and spreading nostrils of the horses, and at her side—her lover! The trust a woman gives to a man, the security of his protection, the daily growth of her confidence in her choice and her surrender—these could temper, if they could not extinguish, her confused grief.

For Laramie the shadow meant less; sympathy drew him closer to Kate; there was even happiness in knowing that she turned in her distress to him for consolation and guidance.

Timidly, she tried to tell him, as they rode, of some of the better traits of her father, traits that might extenuate his cold, hard brutality—as if to build him up a little in the eyes of one she wished not to think of him too harshly.

"Don't worry over what I'm going to think about him," said Laramie. "If I worried over what a lot of people think about me, where should I be? There's some good in most every man; but it doesn't always get a chance to work."

Kate's anxiety was reflected in her manner. "If only," she exclaimed, "they haven't killed him today."

414

The two had crossed the first divide. Below them lay the Crazy Woman, spanned by the Double-draw bridge.

"His friends were his worst enemies," continued Laramie. "But they've got to get out of this country now. And the worst men are out of the Falling Wall. Still if you don't like it there, we won't live there," he added, sitting half sidewise toward Kate in his saddle to feast his eyes on her freshness and youth.

"I shall like it anywhere you are, Jim," she said, looking at him simply.

The picture was too much for his restraint. He reined eagerly toward her.

With a laugh she shied away, struck her horse and dashed ahead. Laramie spurred after her. But they were on the level creek bottom and riding swiftly. She gave him a long run—more than he had looked for.

He realized, as they raced toward the bridge, that he had for one moment forgotten everything but his complete happiness. He called to Kate to stop. In her zest she spurred the harder. He knew she must not reach the bridge ahead of him. Yet he realized the difficulty he faced; she would not understand; and at every cost he must stop her. Animated by this sudden instinct of danger he crowded his horse, forged abreast the flying girl, caught her bridle, and to her astonishment dragged her horse and his own rudely to their haunches. They were almost at the bridge itself.

"Back up!" he exclaimed. "Back up!"

"Jim!" she cried, "*please* don't throw me!"

"Don't speak—back!!" he said low and sharply. Something in the tone and manner of the command admitted of no parley.

With her horse cavorting, half strangled, as he was jerked and backed, Kate, looking amazed at Laramie, saw in his face a man new to her—a man she never had seen before. Not her question-ing look, nor the frantic struggles of the rearing horses touched him; nothing in the confusion of the sudden moment drew his eye for an instant from the bridge before him and his drawn revolver was already poised in his hand. Kate knew her part without another protest. She tore her horse's mouth cruelly with the curb. Where the danger was, or what, she did not know, but she could obey orders. Her eyes tried to follow Laramie's, bent ahead. The bottoms spread level in every direction. The approach to the little bridge and beyond was as open as the day. Not a living creature was anywhere in sight, nothing with life had anywhere stirred, nothing of sound broke the silence of the morning, except—when Laramie allowed them to stop—the startled breathing of the horses.

"Jim!" exclaimed Kate in awed restraint. "What is it?"

His eyes were riveted straight ahead, but he

answered in a most matter-of-fact tone: "There's somebody under that bridge."

She strained her eyes to see something he must have seen that she could not see. The dazzling sunshine, the dusty road, the rough-built, short wooden bridge before them, were all plain enough. And Kate realized for the first time that Laramie, who had been riding on her right was now on her left and presently that his revolver was sheathed and his rifle, which had hung in its scabbard at the horse's shoulder, was slung across the hollow of his right arm.

"Kate," he said, speaking without looking at her, "will you ride back about a mile and wait for me?"

She turned to him: "What are you going to do, Jim?"

"Smoke that fellow out."

She spoke almost in a whisper: "Is it Van Horn, Jim?"

"I don't believe he'd hide there. It's more like Stone."

"Jim! Stone's a deadly shot!"

Looking into the distance he only replied: "From cover. This may be a long-winded affair, Kate." He added, pausing, "you'd better ride as far as the hills."

She looked at him bravely restrained but with all her love in her eyes: "I don't want to leave you, Jim."

"It's poor business for you to be in," he returned

firmly. "There's no way to make it pleasant."

"Don't drive me away!"

He hesitated again: "You might do this: Ride back fast about eighty rods. Leave the road there, bear to the west and circle around the little knoll you'll see. There's a clump of willows below the west side of that knoll."

"Do you know every clump of willows in this country, Jim?"

He answered unmoved: "I know that one for I've crawled up there more than once to take observations under that bridge myself. Get around behind those willows and you can see the creek bottom all the way to the bridge. I'm going up the creek about five hundred yards. I'll work down. Whoever's under the bridge can't get away except down the creek. If you see a man trying that, just fire two shots—in the air, close together—I'll understand. If you get into any kind of trouble— which you're kind of trying to do—fire two shots a few seconds apart. I won't be far off."

With a plea to him to be careful—behind which all her agony of apprehension was repressed and mastered—Kate wheeled her horse and galloped back.

Laramie, skirting a depression, rode into a break leading to the creek bed. The creek was practically dry; just a thread of water here and there among the rocks marked the course of flood time. Dismounting, Laramie shook himself out of the saddle and laying his rifle across his arm, walked carefully down-stream along the bed of the creek.

He knew if he were seen first, the fight would be over before he got into it; of chances to kill from cover, the criminal he felt sure he was hunting, would need but one. No man from the Falling Wall country was Stone's superior in the craft of hiding; but none was Laramie's equal in the art of surprise; and Laramie meant, for once, to make an antagonist formidable from cover, show in the open.

With this alone in purpose, he stalked with the patience of an Indian from point to point and cover to cover down toward the bridge; crouching, halting and peering; slipping from the shoulder of a rock to the shelter of a boulder; flattening on his stomach to worm his way under a projecting ledge and sliding noiselessly on his back down the face of a water-worn glacis—but drawing closer all the time to the bridge.

He knew every inch of the ground. He knew how well his quarry had concealed himself to render surprise impossible. But Stone's very safety in this respect made his retreat more difficult. A man lying in wait under the Double-draw, staked practically everything on one chance: that the man he sought to kill should cross the bridge. It were then easy to pick him off from behind. But if the intended victim, suspicious, should get unseen into the creek bed, the skulker could hardly avoid a fight.

Three hundred yards above the bridge, the creek walls open in an ellipse, narrowing abruptly where the bridge spans them. This open space has been scoured by floods until the bedrock lies like a polished floor and it was now dry except where the piers of the bridge stood in stagnant pools. Once within this amphitheater whose vertical walls rise twenty to thirty feet, no fighting cover is available.

Behind a rocky point that guarded the upper entrance of the opening, stood Laramie. He was watching the shadow cast by a shrub that sprang, shallow-rooted, from a crevice in the bedrock. For an interminable time he waited, only noting the slow swing of the narrow shadow as the morning sun, flooding the rock-basin, rose in majestic course. Gradually the deflection of the slender indicator, moving like a finger on the rock dial, marked the turn of the sun well past the shoulder of the point at which Laramie must emerge. When that moment came he looked sharply out, sprang from behind the point and ran sidewise into the narrow shadow thrown from the curving wall.

Stone, uneasy and alert, stood under the bridge, his rifle across his arm. The two men saw each other almost at the same instant. For Stone, it was the climax of a hatred long nursed because of a supremacy long challenged. And for him it was an open field with weapons in which his skill was as matchless as Laramie's was held to be, at close quarters, with a Colt's revolver.

Nor had Laramie underestimated the chances of an encounter under such circumstances. He counted only on the slight advantage of a surprise—knowing from disagreeable experiences how a surprise jars the poise; and there persisted in his mind, what he had never until then hinted to another, that Stone, shooting as an assassin from cover and Stone himself facing death, might shoot differently. On these slender hopes he covered Stone, as the ex-rustler jumped his rifle to his check, and cried to him to pitch up.

Stone's answer was a bullet. His shot echoed Laramie's, and as Laramie whipped the hat from his enemy's head, his bullet tore through the right side of Laramie's belt. Bare-headed, and thirsty to close on his antagonist, Stone, jumping from Laramie's second bullet, ran forward, hugging the creek wall, dropped on one knee, fired, and ran in again. Laramie refused to be tempted from the shadow in which he stood, until Stone, rounding the wall again as he came on, firing, threatened to find partial cover should Laramie stand still. It was a contest of deadly fencing, of steady heads and cool wit, a struggle in instant strategy. And if Stone meant to force Laramie into the sunshine, he now succeeded—but at a fearful cost. Laramie jumped not only into the sunshine but into the blinding sun itself, and when Stone ran in again, Laramie tore open his hip with a bullet. It knocked the foreman over as if it had been a mallet. But he was swiftly up and firing persistently almost outlined with bullets Laramie's figure against the rock wall. He splintered the grip of Laramie's revolver in its holster, he cut the sleeve from his wrist, and tore hair from the right side of his head; but he could not stop him. Enraged, and realizing too late how every possibility in the fight had been figured out by his enemy before he stepped into sight, Stone, crippled, yet forced to circle, dropped once more on his knee to smash in a final shot.

He was covered the instant he knelt. A bullet from Laramie's rifle shook him like a leaf. His head, jerking, sunk to his breast. With a super-human effort he rallied. He looked at Laramie—narrowly watching—shook the hair from before his eyes and fumbling at the firing lever tried to elevate his rifle to pump. But he swayed on his bent knee; the rifle slipped from his grasp. He sank to the rock floor, clutching with his big hands at the gravel, while Laramie running to him turned him over, snatched his revolver from its holster and throwing it out of reach, lifted his enemy's head.

When Kate, in an agony of suspense, made her way to the creek bed she found Laramie scooping water up in his hands for Stone. She could not go near the wounded man. Only by word from where she stood, piteously, and by dumb sign, she drew Laramie to her to learn whether *he* was hurt. When he declared he was not, she would not believe him till she had felt his arm where one bullet had cut his sleeve, and where the deadliest had raised a sullen red welt along his temple.

Ben Simeral was first to come along on his way to town, in his wagon. John Frying Pan was with him. With their help, Laramie got Stone up to the bridge and into the wagon to take to town. He had shut his eyes and refused to talk. Kate made Laramie tell her every detail of the fight and breathed anew the terrors of each moment.

"I stole toward the bridge the minute I heard the firing," she confessed, unsteadily. "Oh, yes, I know! I might have been killed. But if you were, I wanted to be. How could you tell, when you stopped me so, Jim, there was a man under the bridge?"

"A bunch of bank swallows nests under that bridge right where Stone was hiding," he said, reflecting. "Those swallows always fly out when I ride up to it. If they don't fly out, I don't cross. Today they didn't fly out."

CHAPTER 42

WARNING

By nightfall Kate had the hope that her father might live. Doctor Carpy, indeed, promised as much, though he confessed to Laramie that he was partly bluffing. It was, he explained, a question of constitution and nerve and he thought Barb had both. For better care he had him brought to town, and within the same hospital walls that sheltered Doubleday, lay Stone, in even more serious condition. The sole promise Carpy would make concerning him was that he would fit him up either for trial, or for his museum—or, as Lefever suggested, for both.

The excitement of the town lay in the pursuit of Van Horn. Laramie during the first uncertain days of her father's condition stayed within Kate's call.

"While Van Horn's loose, Jim," said Tenison one day, "you're the man that's in danger; don't forget that."

"I'd like to forget it," he returned. "But I guess it wouldn't be just exactly safe to. Barb warned me yesterday to look out for a surprise—Van Horn's good at them. Then again he may have left the country—there's no word of him from anybody yet.

"Things up at Barb's ranch have got to have some attention," he continued. "Barb will be laid up a long time; and if I don't see after things the banks will. I'm going to take McAlpin up there tomorrow."

The two men were sitting before a large window in the hotel office. As McAlpin's name was mentioned they saw the man himself stepping sailor-fashion at a lively pace up Main Street. He made for the hotel, burst through the office door and headed straight for Laramie:

"Kitchen's just rode into the barn, Jim, with word from Lefever and Sawdy—they've got track of Van Horn. He come to Pettigrew's ranch yesterday for food and a fresh horse. One of John Frying Pan's boys seen him. Lefever says they've got him located near the head waters of the Crazy Woman. You know that rough country east of Pettigrew's? Lefever says if you'll get right up there and watch the creek, he can't get away. The boys at Pettigrew's say he's got lots of ammunition; Lefever and Sawdy stayed at Pettigrew's last night."

At the barn, Kitchen, who had ridden in from the Doubleday ranch, had few details to add. But the Indian runner that brought the word from Lefever and Sawdy had made it clear to Kitchen the two were depending on Laramie to help them bottle Van Horn up.

Laramie laid the news before Kate at the hospital. He called her from her father's room and they talked at the end of the corridor.

She looked at him wistfully: "I don't want you to go, Jim," she whispered.

Her hands lay on his free arm. "I don't want to go, Kate," he said. "But the boys have sent to me for help—what can I do? He's a hundred times more my enemy than theirs. The only interest they've got in rounding him up is friendship for me and you. Suppose they close with him and get killed?"

Kate could only look up into his eyes: "Suppose you get killed, Jim?"

He hesitated. Then he looked down into her own eyes: "You'd know I did what I ought to do, Kate."

She withdrew herself from his embrace and looked at him: "I know you're going, Jim; only, don't ask me to say 'go.' I couldn't bear to think *I* sent you."

McAlpin had armed himself and was determined, despite Laramie's protests, to ride with him. The plucky boss was saddling the ponies and stood momentarily expecting Laramie at the barn when the telephone rang.

Too occupied with his watch for Laramie to give it any heed, McAlpin let it ring. And the barn men let it ring. It rang, seemingly, more and more sharply until McAlpin, with an impatient exclamation, ordered a hostler to answer. "It's you, McAlpin," bawled the hostler from the office, "and they want you quick."

McAlpin hurried to the instrument and glued his ear to the receiver. Tenison was on the wire. He spoke low and fast: "Is Laramie there?"

"No."

"Where is he?"

"Couldn't tell you, Harry, I'm lookin' for him every minute."

"Drop everything. Find him quick or you'll be too late. Van Horn's in town."

McAlpin gasped and swallowed: "What d' y' mean, Harry?"

"Damnation!" thundered Tenison. "You heard me, didn't you?"

"I did."

"Do as you're told."

CHAPTER 43

The Last Call

The canny Scot knew well what the message meant. With little ostentation and much celerity he hurried up street. Belle, at her, door with Kate, drawn-faced, could only say that Laramie had promised to come there before starting. "Warn him," was McAlpin's excited word. "You know Van Horn, Belle."

Red-faced and heated, McAlpin ambled rapidly in and out of every place where he could imagine Laramie might be. Deathly afraid of running into Van Horn—who bore him, he well knew, no love —but doggedly bent on his errand, McAlpin asked fast questions and spread the rapid-fire news as he traveled. More than once he had word of Laramie, yet nowhere could he, in his exasperation, set eyes on him. How nearly he succeeded in his mission he never knew till he had failed.

Laramie had completed his dispositions and

was free, after a brief round of errands, to start north, when Carpy encountered him in the harness shop next to the drug store. Laramie was in haste. But Carpy insisted he must speak with him and, against protest, took him by way of the back door of the shop over to the back door of the drug store and into the little room behind the prescription case.

The doctor sat down and motioned Laramie, despite his impatience, to a chair: "It won't take long to tell you what I've got to tell you," said Carpy, firmly, "but you'll be a long time forgetting it. And the time you ought to know it is now.

"Jim!" Carpy, facing him four feet away, looked squarely into Laramie's eyes. "I know you pretty well, don't I? All right! I'm going to talk pretty plain. You're going to marry Kate Doubleday. Whatever her father's faults—and they've been a-plenty—they'd best be let lie now. That's what Kate would want, I'm thinkin'—that's what her husband would want—anyway, her children would want it. Barb, after he deserted Kate's mother, went out into the Black Hills. He got into trouble there—a partnership scrape. I don't know how much or how little he was to blame; but his partner got the best of him and Barb shot him.

"The partner's friends had the pull. Barb was sentenced for manslaughter. He broke away the night he was sentenced. He came out into this country, took his own name again, got into railroad

428

building, made money, lost it, and went into cattle.

"Two men here know this story. I'm one; the other is Harry Van Horn. He lived in the Hills when this happened. He wouldn't tell because he wanted Kate.

"Jim, if Van Horn comes in alive, he'll be tried for this job on Barb. He'll plead self-defense and spring the Black Hills story. Van Horn has done his best to kill you and hired Stone to do it. You and Kate ought to know why. It's up to you whether he comes in alive and blackens her father's name to get even with both of you. Now start along, Jim—that's all."

Laramie did not rise.

For himself he cared nothing. But he cared for Kate. And though she had little reason to care for her father, and the tragedy of a record such as his was not a pleasant memory for any daughter; how much more would she suffer if his record were exposed by one whose interest it would be to blacken it?

"I said that was all," continued Carpy; "it ain't quite all, either. Van Horn will swear everything in this Falling Wall raid on old Barb to make feeling against him—it'll be a mess."

Laramie's eyes were fixed on the floor. When he raised them he spoke thoughtfully: "I see what you mean, Doctor. I'll talk plain, too—as you'd want me to, I know. No one can tell till it's over how a man hunt is going to work out. But whatever my feelings are, there's something else I've got to think about. You're leaving it out. No matter what stories have been told about me, my record up to this, is clear. I've never in my life shot down a man except in self-defense. I couldn't begin by doing it now. You know what I've stood from these cattlemen in the last year—"

"Why," demanded Carpy, "did you do it?"

"Why did Kate Doubleday shun me like a man with the smallpox? Because they put it up to her I was a man-killer. When they couldn't make me out a rustler, they made me out a gambler. When they couldn't make me out a thief, they made me out a gunman. I had a fine reputation to live down; and all of it from her own father and his friends—what could you expect a girl to do?

"I won out against the bunch. I couldn't have done it without playing straight. It's too late for me to switch my game now. I'd hate to see more grief heaped on Kate. And Van Horn doesn't deserve any show. But if his hands go up—though I never expect to see Harry Van Horn's hands over his head—I can't do it, Doctor, that's all there is to it—he'll come in alive as far as anything I have to do with it."

Carpy laughed cynically: "Jim," he exclaimed with an affectionate string of abuse, "you're the biggest fool in all creation. It's all right." The doctor opened the door of the little room as Laramie rose. "Go 'long," he said roughly, "but bring back your legs on their own power."

Laramie passed around from behind the prescription case where the clerk was filling an order, and, busily thinking, walked rapidly toward the open front door. A little girl waiting at the rear counter piped at him. "How d' do, Mr. Laramie!" It was Mamie McAlpin. He stopped to pinch her cheek. "I don't know you any more, Mamie. You're getting such a big girl." Passing her, he stepped into the afternoon sunshine that flooded the open doorway.

The threshold of the door was elevated, country-store fashion, six or seven inches above the sidewalk. Laramie glanced up street and down —as he habitually did—and started to step down to the walk. It was only when he looked directly across to the opposite side of the street, lying in the afternoon shadow, that he saw, standing in a narrow open space between two one-story wooden store buildings, a man covering him with a revolver.

At the very instant that Laramie saw him, the man fired. Laramie was stepping down when the bullet struck him. Whirled by the blow, he staggered against the drugstore window. Instinctively he reached for his revolver. It hung at his left hip. But struggling to right himself he found that his left arm refused to obey. When he tried to get his hand to the grip of his revolver he could not, and the man, seeing him helpless, darted from his hiding place out on the sidewalk and throwing his gun into balance, fired again.

It was Van Horn. Before the second shot echoed along the street a dozen men were out. Not one of them could see at that moment a chance for Laramie's life; they only knew he was a man to die hard, and dying—dangerous. In catching him at the moment he was stepping down, Van Horn's bullet, meant for his heart, had smashed the collar bone above it and Laramie's gun arm hung useless.

Realizing his desperate plight, he flung his smashed shoulder toward his enemy. As the second bullet ripped through the loose collar of his shirt, he swung his right arm with incredible dexterity behind him, snatched his revolver from its holster, and started straight across the street at Van Horn.

It looked like certain death. Main Street, irregular, is at that point barely sixty feet wide. Perfectly collected, Van Horn trying to fell his reckless antagonist, fired again. But Laramie with deadly purpose ran straight at him. By the time Van Horn could swing again, Laramie had reached the middle of the street and stood within the coveted shadow that protected Van Horn. In that instant, halting, he whipped his revolver suddenly up in his right hand, covered his enemy and fired a single shot.

Van Horn's head jerked back convulsively. He almost sprang into the air. His arms shot out.

His revolver flew from his hand. He reeled, and falling heavily across the board walk, turned, shuddering, on his face. The bullet striking him between the eyes had killed him instantly.

Twenty men were running up. They left a careful lane between the man now standing motionless in the middle of the street and his prone antagonist. But Laramie knew too well the marks of an agony such as that—the clenching, the loosing of the hands, the last turn, the relaxing quiver. He had seen too many stricken animals die.

Limp and bleeding, overcome with the horror of what he had not been able to avert, he walked back to his starting point and sat down on the edge of the sidewalk. His revolver had been tucked mechanically into the waistband of his trousers. Men swarming into the street crowded about. Carpy, agitated, tore open his bloody shirt.

Laramie put up his right hand: "I'm not damaged much, doctor," he said slowly and looking across the street. "See if you can do anything for *him*."

While he spoke, the tremor of a woman's voice rang in his half-dazed ears—a woman trying to reach him. "Oh! where is he?"

Men at the back of the crowd cried to make way. The half circle before Laramie parted. He sprang to his feet, held out his right arm, and Kate with an inarticulate cry, threw herself sobbing on his breast.

CHAPTER 44

TENISON SERVES BREAKFAST

"I'm telling you, Sawdy," expostulated McAlpin, in the manner of an ultimatum, "I'm a patient man. But you've got to get out of that room."

Sawdy stood a statue of dignity and defiance: "And I'm telling you, Hop Scotch, I'll get out of that room when I get good and ready."

"A big piece of ceiling came down last night," thundered McAlpin.

Belle was listening; these sparks were flying at her gate: "Whatever you do," she interjected contemptuously, "don't get a quarrel going over that room."

McAlpin, inextinguishable, turned to Belle: "Look at this: Henry Sawdy gets into that bathtub. He turns on the water. He goes to sleep. Every few weeks the ceiling falls on my new pool tables. First and last, I've had a ton of mortar on 'em. If there was any pressure, I'd be ruined."

"If there was any pressure," interposed Sawdy, "I wouldn't go to sleep. Do you know how long it takes to fill your blamed tub?"

McAlpin in violent protest, scratched the gravel with his hobnailed shoes: "I'll ask you: Am I responsible for the pressure, or the water company?" Sawdy undisturbed, continued to stroke his heavy mustache. "The water it takes to cover you, Henry," sputtered McAlpin, "would run a locomotive from here to Medicine Bend."

"I have to wait till everybody in town goes to bed before I can get a dew started on the faucet," averred Sawdy. "Sometimes I have to set up all night to take a bath. Look at the unreasonableness of it, Belle," he went on indignantly. "I'm paying this Shylock a dollar and a half a week for my room—and most of the time, no water."

McAlpin ground his teeth: "No water!" was all he could echo, doggedly.

"Do you know what this row is about, Belle?" demanded Sawdy. "He's trying to screw me up to a dollar seventy-five for the room. And everybody on the second floor using my bathtub," continued Sawdy, calmly.

"*Your* bathtub," gasped McAlpin. "Well, if you could get title to it by sleeping in it, it surely would be your tub, Sawdy."

"I don't want your blamed room any longer, anyway," declared Sawdy. "I'm going to get married."

McAlpin started: "Henry, don't make a blamed fool o' yoursel'."

"I said it," retorted Sawdy, waving him away. "Move on."

"I've had no notice," announced McAlpin, raising his hand. "You'll pay me my rent to the first

435

of the year. You rented for the full year, Henry, remember that!" With this indignant warning, McAlpin started for the barn.

Sawdy followed Belle into the house. He threw his hat on the living-room table: "Sit down, Belle," he said recklessly. "I want to talk."

Belle was suspicious. "What about?" she demanded. "You can't room here, I'll tell you that."

"Now hold your horses a minute—just a minute. Sit down. I know when a thing needs sugar, don't I? You know when it needs salt, don't you? Why pay rent in two places? That's what I want to know. Let's hitch up."

"Stop your foolishness."

"My foolishness has got me stopped."

"If you expect to eat supper here tonight, stop your noise."

"Honor bright!" persisted Sawdy, "what do you say?"

Belle took it up with Kate: "With him and John Lefever both nagging at me what can I do?" she demanded, greatly vexed. "I've got to marry a fat man anyway I fix it."

When Lefever learned Belle's choice had fallen on his running mate he was naturally incensed: "I've been jobbed all 'round," he declared at Tenison's. "First, Jim sends me up to the Reservation on a wild-goose chase after his two birds and bags 'em both himself within gunshot of town. Then my own partner beats me home by a day and cops off

Belle. Blast a widower, anyway. He'll beat out an honest man, every time. Anyway, boys, this town is dead. Everything's getting settled up around here. I'm sending my resignation in to Farrell Kennedy today and I'm going to strike out for new country."

"Not till I get married, John," said Laramie, when John repeated the dire threat. "And Kate wants a new foreman up at the ranch. You know her father's turned everything over to her."

"What'll she pay?"

"More than you're worth, John. Don't worry about that!"

Some diplomacy was needed to restore general good feeling, but all was managed. From the men, John got no sympathy. The women were more considerate; and when Kate and Belle threatened there would be no double wedding unless John stood up with the party, he bade them go ahead with the "fixings."

The breakfast at the Mountain House, Harry Tenison's personal compliment to the wedding party, restored John Lefever quite to his bubbling humor. It was a brave company that sat down. And a democratic one, for despite feminine protests it numbered at the different tables pretty much every friend of Laramie's, in the high country, including John Frying Pan—only the blanket men from the Reservation were excluded. Lefever acted as toastmaster.

"Jim," he demanded, addressing Laramie in

genial tones, when everything was moving well, "just what in your eventful career do you most pride yourself on?"

Laramie answered in like humor. "Keeping out of jail," he retorted laconically.

"Been some job, I imagine," suggested Lefever cheerily.

"At times, a man's job."

"But you're not dead yet," persisted Lefever.

"I'm married—that's just as good."

"Why, Jim!" protested his bride with spirit.

"I mean," explained Laramie, looking unabashed at Kate, "I'm looking to you now to keep me out."

The boisterous features of similar Sleepy Cat celebrations were omitted in deference to Kate's feelings and the too recent tragedies: her father still lay in the hospital.

But her guests were agreed that she looked very happy over her new husband. The telltale glow not wholly to be suppressed in her frank eyes; the unmanageable pink that rose even to her temples and played defiantly under her brown hair curling over them; the self-conscious restraint of her voice and the sense of guilt bubbling up, every time she laughed—these were all "sign," plain as print to married men, like McAlpin and Carpy, and grounds for suspicion even to confirmed bachelors like John Lefever and the old priest that came down from the Reservation to perform the ceremony; and in

438

everyone of them the observing read the trails that led to Kate's heart.

Laramie, on the other hand, disgusted those that expected a stern and heroic showing. Towards the close of the breakfast he was laughing deliriously at every remark, and looking dazed when an intelligent question was put at him; Harry Tenison pronounced it disedifying.

But when the young couple swung into their saddles for the wedding trip—their destination, naturally, a secret—criticism ceased. Laramie again looked his part; and those who had heard him pledge his life to cherish and protect Kate, felt sure, as the two melted away into the glow of the sunset, that his word was good.

Center Point Publishing
600 Brooks Road ● PO Box 1
Thorndike ME 04986-0001 USA

(207) 568-3717

US & Canada:
1 800 929-9108
www.centerpointlargeprint.com